D1343779

WOLFSBANE

REBEL ANGELS

BOOK THREE

WOLFSBANE

GILLIAN PHILIP

www.stridentpublishing.co.uk

Published by
Strident Publishing Ltd
22 Strathwhillan Drive
The Orchard, Hairmyres
East Kilbride G75 8GT

Tel: +44 (0)1355 220588
info@stridentpublishing.co.uk
www.stridentpublishing.co.uk

Published by Strident Publishing Limited, 2012
Text © Gillian Philip, 2012
Cover art by LawrenceMann.co.uk

ISBN 978-1-905537-35-8

Typeset in Bembo by
Palimpsest Book Production Limited, Falkirk, Stirlingshire
Printed by Cox & Wyman

The publisher acknowledges support from Creative
Scotland towards the publication of this title

For Lucy and Jamie and for Hayley Nicol,
who approved of the kelpies a long time ago

Acknowledgements

This is another one that wouldn't cooperate. The people who helped me wrestle it into submission through many a tiresome draft included Tanya Wright, Pam Fraser and Derek Allsopp, and I'll love them forever.

Thank you, Steven Allsop, for the Lammyr Sleekshard – you know I adore those monsters.

Lucy Coats is an angel, rebel or otherwise, who fluttered down almost at the last minute and gave me a lot of much-appreciated suggestions, nudges, and slaps. Thank you, foxy lady. *ENORMOUS WINK*

Elizabeth Garrett gave me, yet again, space and time at the unearthly-beautiful Cliff Cottage.

Alison Stroak is a brilliant, lovely, understanding editor who listened to me whine like an unhappy wolf at the most ungodly hours of day and night. She's a sanity-saver.

Lawrence Mann at One Mann Brand is a telepath who is not only enormously talented but knows exactly what my characters look like. And this time he stripped Seth to a t-shirt, bless him.

Keith Charters is the most patient publisher I know, and was willing to put up with my hysterical havering and delays till what had to be the very last minute.

And my good friends on Twitter and Facebook soothed my fevered brow, sent me margaritas through cyberspace, and made me laugh so often, this book probably took even longer than it should have. Bless you, terrible tweeps.

Thank you, all of you.

THE SITHE

(and others)

Kate NicNiven — Queen of the Sithe, by consent.

Seth MacGregor (Murlainn) — Son of Griogair and Lilith; half brother to Conal

Jed Cameron (Cuilean) — Full mortal; half-brother to Rory

Rory MacSeth — Seth's son and Jed's half-brother

Hannah Falconer — A girl from the otherworld

Leonora Shiach — Witch, mother of Conal and bound lover of Griogair

Griogair MacLorcan (Fitheach) — Father of Conal and Seth

Conal MacGregor (Cù Chaorach) — Son of Griogair and Leonora

Stella Shiach (Reultan) — Half-sister to Conal; daughter of Leonora

Aonghas MacSorley — Bound lover of Stella (Reultan)

Finn MacAngus	Daughter to Stella and Aonghas
Eili MacNeil	Lover of Conal
Sionnach MacNeil	Eili's twin brother; Seth's best friend since childhood
Liath & Branndair	Wolf-familiars of Conal and Seth
Nuall MacInnes	Clann Captain of Dunster
Gocaman & Suil	Watchers at the otherworld watergates
Orach, Taghan, Braon, Sorcha, Eorna, Fearna, Carraig, Gruaman, Sulaire (cook), Grian (healer)	Fighters of Seth's clann
Cluaran MacSeumas	A captain of Kate's clann
Nils Laszlo	Full-mortal Captain of Kate's clann
Cuthag, Gealach, Turlach	Fighters of Kate's clann
Sleekshard	A Lammyr
Alasdair Farquhar-Stewart	A blast from the past

Gillian Philip was born in Glasgow but has spent much of her life in Aberdeen, Barbados and a beautiful valley near Dallas (not that one). Before turning to full-time writing, she worked as a barmaid, theatre usherette, record store assistant, radio presenter, typesetter, hotel wrangler, secretary, political assistant, and Celtic-Caribbean singer.

She has been nominated for a Carnegie Medal and a David Gemmell Legend Award, and shortlisted for many awards including the Royal Mail Scottish Book Award. Her favourite genres are fantasy and crime (her novels include Bad Faith, Crossing The Line and The Opposite of Amber), and she has written as one of the Erin Hunters (Survivors) and as Gabriella Poole (Darke Academy).

She lives in the north-east Highlands of Scotland with husband Ian, twins Jamie and Lucy, Cluny the Labrador, Milo the Papillon, Otto the half-Papillon (guess how that happened), Buffy the Slayer Hamster, psycho cats The Ghost and The Darkness, Mapp and Lucia the chickens, and several nervous fish. She is not getting any more pets. No way.

The purple drops shall tinge the moon,
As she wanders through the midnight noon;
And the dawning heaven shall all be red
With blood by guilty angels shed.

Then here's for trouble and here's for smart,
And here's for the pang that seeks the heart;
Here's for madness, and here's for thrall,
And here's for conscience, the worst of all.

James Hogg: A Witch's Chant

In a world the colour of moonstone, anything might lurk. There was light, and plenty of it, but it was the milky whiteness of a blinded eye. He could see nothing. The mist lay low over the mere, silencing everything.

Fir-tops were outlined in softest grey, high up behind him. There were grasses and reeds at his feet. That was all he could see of his surroundings, and he had no plans to move.

Reluctant even to breathe the murk, Turlach stood entirely still. The sheer effort of that and the grating of his nerves made his heart hammer, and he was forced to suck in a harsh breath. It tasted of dank water, of weed-rot and mud. He wanted to spit.

He'd lost his bearings a little, but he knew where he was, that was the important thing. He knew how far the dun was, and his chances of making it there, and if he chose his direction well, and moved silently and fast, he could get there within hours.

Still, it was something of a gamble. He didn't want to choose badly.

They were close behind him, he knew that. There were two of them in pursuit; they were not dear friends of his, and they had brought none along. Nobody else knew. Nobody knew where he was. Or why.

Turlach shivered. The dampness made his throat rasp.

Iolaire had not been caught and dragged back to the queen's fortress; Iolaire had made it to the safety of enemy territory. But those two years ago, Iolaire had been on horseback, and he'd ridden out in weather you could see through, and they hadn't known he wasn't coming back. Anyway, they'd known they could kill him later. They'd lost Iolaire; they'd spawned a renegade, and they hated that. Everyone hated *that*. But with him, with Turlach, it mattered in bigger ways than love and loyalty and pride.

Funny that he hadn't considered going to Kate NicNiven with what he knew: he'd simply left, and as fast as he could. But then even if the queen balked at Cuthag's plan, Turlach knew in his bones the idea would entice her. Gods knew where Cuthag had found the outcast, or why, but Kate had always had a fascination with the man even as she sat in judgement on him, which was often. She'd always regretted the punishments she was forced to impose; had shown a tangible longing to have him back in her fold. The queen might resist Cuthag's pledges and promises, but only for a little while, and only for show. Turlach did not want to be the one to argue.

So the outcast was coming back. As soon as Turlach had come across him in the deepest passageways of the fortress, as soon as he'd overheard the man's bragging talk and Cuthag's laughter, he'd known this was his first and last chance to leave.

He wished he'd been quieter about it, that was all.

Having marked his escape, the two of them wouldn't want to risk him reaching the enemy dun, not with what he had to tell Seth MacGregor. He wouldn't get the leeway Iolaire had got. For Turlach, for his pursuers, there was a deadline.

He rubbed his cold arms. He had to move. If he didn't move soon, they'd smell him anyway, cornered here like a rat.

Cautiously he waded through the water, hating to disturb

its slick surface. The loch-grasses were dense here, and he knew he was edging further from the fringes of the loch, though it barely seemed to deepen. The suck and slosh of the water echoed too loudly.

Throw them off his scent, or throw them off his sounds: he couldn't do both. He hadn't reckoned on the mist, that was all.

A waterbird erupted at his feet with a cry and a clatter. In a mad reflex he snatched at it, stumbled, then stared after its flickering shadow, sweat beading on his forehead. It had vanished into the soupy whiteness, but it must have skim-landed, because water-arrows rippled out of the mist, lapping delicately at his legs. His blood trickled cold in his veins as he watched the ripples subside to stillness. There were other things in the loch, things far worse than noisy waterbirds; worse even than pursuing fighters.

Quite suddenly Turlach knew this had been the most foolish of moves. Stupid to leave himself exposed to danger both from land and from the loch. He waded fast towards the water's ill-defined edge, shoving reeds out of the way. Whatever their brutality, the fighters coming after him were at least human. He'd sooner take his chances with them than wait like a tethered sheep for the creature to come out of the loch.

He skirted the fringe of the water as closely as he could, alert for the slightest disturbance of the surface. But the mist could help as well as hinder him, after all. He was letting the fears of childhood terrify him out of using it to his advantage. That made him angry with himself, and that helped too.

The flank of the fir-tree hill was the best bet. He was happier to cross the marshy ground and get further from the water, and though he didn't want to leave the cover of the mist entirely, it was thinner as he climbed higher and easier to get his bearings. His destination was no more than a few hours beyond the low hill, and for the first time in many miles he began to think he was going to make it. On the solid ground he quickened his steps, stumbling only once as his foot found a concealed runnel of water. Halting, breathing hard, he glanced behind.

At first he thought it was the sun breaking through the heavy blanket of mist: a single spear of light, bright gold and dazzling. He knew in an instant that it was in the wrong position by a half-turn of the earth. No. The sun was behind him, just piercing the mist-line; the light ahead was its reflection on steel.

Turlach broke into a run.

In desperation he cut up towards the high slope, panting with panic and exhaustion, but the sound of hoofbeats was coming from two directions, ahead and behind. Doubling back, he plunged downhill, tripping and crashing headlong into the mire. As he scrambled to his feet, he was slammed back down by a hard blow to the side of his head.

He hauled himself from the mud on all fours, hands sunk in the glaur, unable to stand. And that wasn't exhaustion or the terrain; it was the violent trembling of his treacherous limbs. Sick with shame, he couldn't look up.

'Runaway.' The silky voice had a mocking lilt. 'Run-run-runaway.'

Turlach shut his eyes, sat back on his haunches. Taking gulps of shallow breath, he forced himself to stagger to his feet. If he clenched his fists hard enough, the shaking subsided a little. Just a little. He spat marsh-filth and looked up into the pitiless eyes.

'Any regrets, Turlach?'

Slowly, he shook his head. 'You've played a long game, haven't you?'

Laughter. 'We're Sithe, man! What other kind of game is there?'

'Games that aren't blasphemy, you bastard. I heard what you're going to offer Kate. It isn't right.'

'Right is when we win. Wrong,' and the happy singsong voice was back, 'wrong is when we die in filth and pain, running like a rabbit.'

Did he regret it? He was going to die, he was sure of that. The trouble was, Turlach was old enough to remember this man, and the last time he'd haunted the Sithe lands. He was old enough to remember the brute's reputation. Why else would he have run in the first place? Doubts he might have had in the past, but only this man could have impelled Turlach to leave his own clann. As for the new skill the man brought from his adventures in the other-world, the peace-gift he'd brought to his queen: only such a warping of witchcraft could have persuaded Turlach to try to reach MacGregor, reach and warn him.

And fail.

He twisted his lip; it was as close as he could get to a defiant smile. 'I wouldn't have fought for you anyway.'

'That's a pity.'

A slew of the ice-hard gaze beyond his shoulder, a slight nod, and Turlach felt the slash of a honed blade across his hamstrings. The ground went from beneath him, and he dropped like a shot bird. Shock left him anaesthetised for long seconds, and then the pain kicked in, searing his useless legs. His fingers curled round handfuls of thick mud and he pressed his face against the wet ground to stop himself crying out.

The two of them stood over him, muttering words he couldn't hear for the screaming in his head. A foot nudged his ribcage, the edge of a bloodstained blade tickled his neck.

'Don't, Cuthag.' That musical, contented voice.

No, Cuthag. Do. Please. He could smell his own blood, after all, and the creature's nose was sharper.

'The sun's setting.'

Please.

'It's hungry at this hour.'

Cuthag gave a low laugh, withdrew the blade from Turlach's throat.

Cuthag. Please.

It was only an inner begging. It was nothing he'd let either of them hear. The last thing he could do, at least, was shutter his mind against the pair of them.

'Poor Turlach. It'll smell him. But let's make sure.'

A boot kicked at the blood-soaked glaur around him, sending gouts of it flying, spattering softly onto the mere's surface skin.

'Let's go, shall we?'

Turlach heard them mount their skittish, snorting horses but he didn't listen as they rode away at a perilously hasty gallop. He listened only for the other hoof-falls, the ones he knew were coming.

The white mist was darkening to grey, and the air was colder, thickening. He wouldn't kick, wouldn't struggle and flounder and draw the predator like a crippled fish. He didn't want the escaping killers to hear him scream. *Be still, Turlach.* And besides, in the lifeless twilight, the silence of his mind, a faint hope of survival flickered.

The flickering hope guttered and died at the splash of a

surfacing body, the scrape of a hoof on stone, a questioning whicker. *Oh gods. Don't move. Don't breathe.*

There was nothing to grip but the yielding boggy earth. He trembled, and gritted his teeth, and shut his eyes and tried not to see or hear.

The creature trotted close and straddled his bloody legs, pawing his head with a hoof and tugging experimentally on his hair, its hot tongue licking the skin of his neck. And suddenly, despite himself, Turlach was kicking, squirming, dragging his torso desperately through the clinging mud, clawing towards an escape he knew he'd never reach.

It stopped playing. When it seized him with its teeth, shook him like a rat, and began to feed, the spasms of useless struggle were no longer voluntary at all; and Turlach no longer knew or cared that his screams split the sodden air.

RORY

So all I had to do was tame the kelpie.

Any self-respecting Sithe could master a water horse, or so my father never tired of telling me. If he could do it, anyone could do it. And he was a good bit younger than me when he bonded with his blue roan. And as my late but sainted Uncle Conal (who I don't even remember) once said, *there's nothing like it*. (I may not remember him, but I'm limitlessly familiar with everything he ever said.)

Anyway, truly, I didn't see what the problem was. Neither did my father.

Perhaps that was the problem.

Seth was in one of those high moods of his, happy and hyper-confident. Who ever said kelpies were easy? Not even him, not before today.

Still, maybe it was the weather, but his mood was infectious. The two of us rode out from the dun across a moor gilded with dew and spangled with spider-webs and misty sunlight. The hills in the distance looked too ephemeral to be real, but I knew that as the sun rose higher the day would be diamond-hot. My father hadn't wiped the grin off his face since he dragged me out of bed before dawn. And dawn came *bloody* early at this time of year.

'Language,' he said absently.

I gave him a half-hearted scowl, and blocked my mind. He laughed.

'I hope you're not expecting too much,' I told him.

'Course not.'

Yes, he was. He always did.

The little loch was in its summer mood, innocuous and enticing, looking smaller than it truly was because of the thick growth of reeds and grasses blurring its edges. Seth rode his horse in up to its fetlocks, let the reins fall loose on its neck. He'd left the blue roan behind; no point provoking the kelpie with one of its own kind, he said. The bay gelding he'd brought in its place looked none too happy about being expendable. It tossed its head, pawing the water nervously.

Seth patted its neck, murmuring to it absently as he watched the rippling surface. 'Go on, then, Rory. Get on with it.'

My own horse didn't want to go as close to the water and I didn't blame it. I slid from its back and hooked its reins over a broken stump, then waded into the shallows. The water wasn't even that cold. A moorhen appeared out of the reeds, cocked its red face-shield at me, then vanished without urgency into a clump of bulrushes.

'I don't think it's around,' I said.

'Not yet, it isn't.' There was an edge of impatience in his voice. 'Call it.'

I dropped my block, focused, let my mind sink under the silver glittering skin of the loch. The song in my head was familiar enough; I'd learned straight from my father's brain the way to sing in silence to a water horse, and I'd practised last night in the stillness of the dun till I almost hypnotised myself.

Seth leaned forward on his horse, and I realised he was holding his breath.

The surface trembled, stirred. The marsh birds stopped singing. I knew what to expect, but when the creature's head breached the water I still stumbled back.

It was all muscle, gloss and savagery. Its jaws were open,

ears laid back, its grey mane matted with weed. Loch-water cascaded from its arched neck and its forelock as it twisted its head to stare at me with eyes as black and impenetrable as a shark's.

We looked at each other for an infinite moment, and then it lurched up and forward, squealing and plunging into the shallows, its hooves sending spray exploding upwards. When it was hock-deep, it halted, glaring.

At least my father couldn't interfere. He was too busy swearing at the bay gelding, which was backing and snorting with fear. By the time he'd calmed it, the kelpie was so close to me I could feel its hot jetting breath on my cheek. It pulled back its lips, grazed its teeth along my hair.

I thought my heart was going to stop.

'Keep calling it,' Seth barked. 'Don't let it in your head yet.'

That was easy enough; almost automatic, so long as he would quit distracting me. In fact I doubted I was ever going to get the song out of my brain. Of course, just keeping the kelpie at a mental distance wouldn't stop it killing me. If it felt that way inclined.

I raised a trembling hand to the crest of its neck. Its mane was silk in my fingers; hard to imagine it could lock tight and hold me. Inside my head the song had become a dull constant chant, embedded enough to let me concentrate on the creature, the feel of it. Oh gods, the warmth and power beneath that cloud-white skin. For the first time this wasn't something I was doing for my father; for the first time I really, truly ached for this horse.

I closed my fist round its mane, close to its withers. I shifted my weight to spring.

It jerked aside, violently. Then it screamed and slammed its head into my chest. The breath was knocked out of me and lights exploded behind my eyelids, but I staggered and kept my footing, and rebalanced myself in time to see it lunge, teeth bared.

I threw myself flat onto the sodden ground, felt its hooves hit the water on either side of my head, drenching me as it bolted. I didn't see it plunge back into the loch, but I heard the gigantic splash, and the panicked clatter of waterfowl.

I leaned on my elbows, mired in my father's silence as much as in the muddy water. I did not want to raise my head. Ever.

After an endless wordless time, he blew out a breath.

'Well,' he said. 'I suppose it had just eaten. Luckily.'

There were things my brother had told me about the hideous, perilous otherworld beyond the Veil. Honestly, I sometimes wondered how it would be to live there. I sometimes dreamed of a place where they called social services if your parents sent you to school with the wrong kind of gloves.

I pushed myself up out of the bog and brushed off pond-muck as well as I could. 'Sorry,' I muttered.

'Don't worry,' he said shortly, pulling his horse's head round. 'Obviously untameable.'

'I thought there was no such thing,' I snapped.

'*Obviously* there *is*.'

What he meant was, if his son couldn't tame it, nobody could. And I'd have liked to tame it, to prove him wrong, but I knew I was never going to. And this time, as I hauled myself onto my horse's back, I made sure my block was just perfect; not because I was afraid of Seth knowing I feared failure, but because I didn't want him to know how much his disappointment was going to matter to me.

It's not that I was unduly afraid of kelpies; I was used to

the blue roan, after all. I could ride the blue roan alone, without my father there. Frankly, that pissed him off. I shouldn't have been able to do it, but then there were a lot of things I shouldn't have been able to do. It didn't stop me doing them.

Except that the one thing I really wanted to do, the one thing that would have sent me soaring in my father's estimation, was the one thing I couldn't do. I glared resentfully at the loch and wiped mud off my face.

'Listen,' he said at last, as our horses ambled back towards the dun. 'Forget about it. It doesn't matter. It's not as if it's compulsory.'

'If it wasn't,' I pointed out coldly, 'you wouldn't have said that three times.'

'Jesus, Rory. I won't try and make you feel better, then.'

'I don't need you to make me feel better.' Liar. If I could never be the fighter he was, at least I could have been his equal on a kelpie. Or not, it seemed.

'We're not in a frigging competition. You're my son, not my sparring partner.'

My face burned. 'You weren't meant to hear that. Butt out.'

'So raise a better block.'

I did. 'Just let me come alone next time. It's you that puts me off.'

I didn't look at him for a bit, because he hadn't replied. I didn't want to know how much that last barb had hurt him. Not that he'd think it showed.

'Forget that,' he bit out at last. 'You know fine why you don't get to wander about on your own.'

'I'm fourteen years old. When are you planning to let me grow up?'

'When you start acting it? Hey!'

I'd put my heels to the grey's flanks and I was already way ahead of him by the time he could think about coming after me. As it happened, he didn't. I was heading for the dun and he knew it; and he probably wanted time away from me, just as much as I needed to get away from him. All he did was yell a warning after me.

'You can't tame your own, *doesn't mean you're going near mine.*'

Fine.

Let's see how far he'd go to stop me.

KATE

She wasn't accustomed to anger. Fierce quick flares of it, yes, that were easily assuaged with a flogging or a summary execution or, if she was fond of the offender, a simple grovelling apology; but not this savage gnawing fury that swelled in her belly each day like an unwanted child, immovable and unforgettable. Laszlo, she knew, would have liked to plant a real infant there, in some forlorn hope that it would cement his position, but there was a vanishingly small chance of that, so his insecurity was only a minor irritation, and his constant attentions were still a perfectly pleasant distraction.

Kate trailed a fingertip down his spine, making him stir and moan softly. Sprawled in the tangle of sheets, he woke, turning his head clumsily to face her, and smiled.

'Things to do, people to see,' she sang lightly.

'Not yet.' He reached for her, drawing her back down. For a few seconds she considered giving in, but at last tugged her arm from his grip and swung her legs down off the bed. His eyes followed her hungrily.

'What does bloody Cuthag want anyway?' he grumbled. 'I don't like the man.'

'Liking him isn't necessary. I've never known a fighter so reliable. Now get up.'

Something rebellious flashed in his eyes, but he conquered it, sensibly. Kate gave him a special forgiving smile as he hauled himself out of bed and seized his clothes. Rebellion she didn't mind, so long as it was brief and ultimately regretted. It was the other kind that froze her heart to an icy ball in her chest, that kept her awake and silently raging in the smallest hours of the night.

She was queen by consent. She was chosen, by acclamation of the huge majority of her people. She was loved; and all she ever required was love: love and loyalty. Her best interests matched her people's, however some of them might doubt it. Doubt didn't matter. It was their trust she asked.

Love and loyalty and trust, then. And some couldn't give her even those.

'MacGregor skulks like a stoat in that dun of his. He defies me, he kills my fighters, he spreads lies in all the villages. For all the respect he shows me, he might as well climb on his battlements and present me with his naked arse.'

'I thought he had.'

She slapped him, but not so hard as to seed a lasting resentment. 'He thinks he can go on like this indefinitely, keeping his son from me, denying me my hold on the *Sgath*. I will not tolerate it much longer.'

Laszlo touched his cheek where the red mark of her hand was already fading. 'Go to all-out war and you'll lose more fighters than you can afford. His dun lands are like a bloody ring of steel. His clann have minds like iron walls, you told me so yourself.'

'Most of them.' The soft grey silk, she decided, taking up the dress: lovely as morning, but with a decided suggestion of lethal spiderweb. 'And he draws in more allies every day with that filthy tongue of his. I'd like to cut it out with hot shears.'

He shrugged. 'Say the word and I'll lead an attack anyway.

We'll lose a lot of fighters, but he'll be dead within a month, I promise.'

'I don't want him dead, I want him destroyed. Surely even a full-mortal can understand the difference.'

'Then keep playing the long game,' murmured Laszlo, kissing her neck. 'I thought that was what you liked best. You with all the time in the world.'

Would anyone, ever, now or in her limitless future, understand how it was for her? Did anyone ever stop to appreciate the irony? That she, with *all the time in the world*, should race against time and watch her prize limp ever just ahead of her and out of reach? The one thing she wanted, more than anything, was the thing that tottered feebly towards its own death, and it terrified her that she might never catch it. *Sgath. Sgath, you tattered rotting skin of a Veil. Do not die before I can kill you.* She might not catch it in time, she who was out of time. Out*with* time. Kate wondered if he'd laughed, that creature in the deep, deep dark, as she stood there trembling and made her bargain with a thing that was solid shadow.

Soul-Eater. I've taken as many souls as you, since you took my Name from me. And it's never enough. Did you know that? Of course you did. You knew about the hunger that never dies.

The hunger that never dies.

Like me...

It was worth it. *It was worth it.* Life without the Name that aged and killed it. She could not kill, that was part of the deal; but there would always be those who would do that for her. The strength of her mind was a physical energy, not some feeble linking empathy. And when she dragged the soul and the power from a living man, she felt it always, just for an instant: the spark and fire that burned to nothing, the brief thrill and ecstasy of it. It was enough. Better those fleeting tastes and touches of mortality than to actually end her days, and turn to dust and ashes.

But without the *Sgath,* without the destruction that she must wreak on it to get what she wanted, it had been pointless. How many times had she wished that benighted prophet alive, so she could kill her again? Destroy the Veil, and the NicNiven would have all she desired; let it die or survive, and nothing would be hers.

So much given to you, Soul-Eater, and all for nothing? No.

Laszlo must not see the shudder that quaked through her. Kate turned from him, and snatched up a silver-and-sapphire necklace. She clutched it hard, the elaborate carving biting into her flesh, till her fingers were still once more.

'Time runs short even for me, where the Veil is concerned. There's the long game, and there's the stalemate.' Her equilibrium restored, she locked the silver around her throat. 'Cuthag says he has something that might break the impasse. I'm willing to listen.'

Laszlo was already strapping on his sword; she did not deign to wait for him as she swept out of the room, but she heard him follow on her heels quickly enough. He wouldn't want to be absent, of course, when she spoke with the man waiting for her in her audience room beyond the Great Hall.

Cuthag bent his head in a slight bow as she entered. He could be as oily as his slicked-back black hair, but she liked his deviousness and she liked his unswerving loyalty even better. She did not give him a glance as she walked past him, her footsteps echoing; only when she seated herself in the chair on the high dais did she grace him with a direct stare. The room was deserted except for Cuthag, and that was as it should be in these circumstances. If his idea was something her people would not tolerate, it was best that none of them knew about it.

Laszlo halted at her side; she didn't have to glance at him to know he was glowering. 'Cuthag, my dear one. You often know how to please me. Let's see if you can keep it up.'

There. That was a satisfying one in the eye for Laszlo. Cuthag knew it too; he gave her a grin that exposed all his teeth.

'The proposal's not entirely mine, Kate. I was approached by a... mutual acquaintance. Someone we both once knew.'

'A blast from the past, as they say. How charming.' She smiled. 'And who is this old friend?'

'I used the word *acquaintance* advisedly, Kate.' Cuthag actually laughed, and she raised an eyebrow. 'I hope you'll hear me out.'

She drew herself up in her chair, frowning. 'You've brought him, I take it? Or her?'

'Him. Yes, he's here.' Cuthag looked nervous for the first time as he turned on his heel and looked to the door in the shadows. Silver flame-light flickered on a tall man in a leather coat, bearded and ragged-haired, who took three paces into the room before dropping on one knee.

The silence stretched. One second. Three. Five.

'*You?*' Kate's verdict, when she gave it, was contemptuous. 'Not again. Cuthag, you disappoint me.'

The bearded man didn't rise, but his gaze on hers was so confident it was almost cocky. 'Poor old Cuthag. Give him a chance. And me.'

'I've given you more chances than I care to count, Alasdair.'

Laszlo's intake of breath was audible. 'Is this—'

'Indeed it is.' Kate stared idly at the ceiling. 'Which knee was it last time, Alasdair? I hope you're alternating, or you'll wear one of them out.'

He laughed. 'This time it's different. You'll be glad I came back.'

She sighed and inspected her fingernails. 'Get off the floor, then, and let me hear it.'

'No. I won't rise till I'm forgiven.'

She studied him, surprised. Laszlo was so tense beside her, his whole body was trembling: she could feel it. All the same, he was smart enough not to interrupt. 'How was this exile?'

'Almost enjoyable.' He grinned. 'Who's the pet full-mortal this time?'

Kate glanced at Laszlo, who was just managing to contain his rage. 'He's my Captain, Alasdair. He's what you could have been. In so many ways.'

'Oh well, I've been gone a long time. I think you missed me, really.'

'You'll be missing your most dearly beloved body parts if you don't stop wasting my time.' She gave him her sweetest smile.

'I believe you. It's why I've always loved you. Ah, forgive me!' He held up a hand as she made to snap again. 'It's love based on respect and gratitude. And awe of your astonishing loveliness, obviously.'

Kate yawned. 'And you said you had something useful to tell me.'

'It was a long exile, Kate. I had time and leisure to study and learn. And when I educate myself, it's in the most useful arts. Do you know how many mongrel Sithe and pure-breds live in exile in the otherworld? Certainly enough to fall in with lost causes, and into my hands.'

She made a face. 'Oh, but your methods have always been so crude and uninteresting.'

Cuthag coughed lightly. 'Not this time. There's a... technique. One that Alasdair has developed over years. It would be useful to us against Murlainn. I'd go so far as to say... decisive.'

'One I've never heard of? I'll be fascinated to discover it.' Her tone was acid; if Cuthag was wasting her time, she'd flay his chest for him. Publicly, in the Great Hall. It would be practice for Murlainn, whose clann had so considerately flayed his back already.

~ *I'll not speak it aloud.* The man's eyes, as they slewed to Laszlo, were sheened with contempt. ~ *Some might think it blasphemy; some already told me so, and they're dead now. You may want to explain it to your clann in your own sweet way and time.*

Kate sat back, almost shocked. Laszlo, well aware he was shut out, looked perplexed and angry. Still, she tapped her cheek thoughtfully with her fingers.

'Very well. You've piqued my interest. Tell me.'

* * *

Kate almost felt sorry for Laszlo. To walk out of here would be the ultimate humiliation, so he had to stand there like a fool, deaf to everything Cuthag and Alasdair were saying, deaf to all her own replies. Poor full-mortal. Just as well he made up for that deficiency with his other undeniable qualities. As the two men before her fell silent in her head, she touched his hand gently, and felt his fingers curl into a fist.

'You've a way with people,' she observed of the kneeling man. 'Rather an unpleasant way, but effective.'

'I'm a people person,' he said, his bright smile devoid of apparent irony.

He'd always been able to make her laugh, that was the thing. It was why forgiveness had always come so readily to her, where he was concerned. Murlainn, of course, had made her laugh too; but he was far beyond redemption, and she had the means to punish him now, if this tale was true. Her heart was certainly lighter than it had been in months.

'Get up,' she said.

'Does that mean—'

'Yes. Now get up off your knees.' She rose as he did, and came down the steps to stand close to him, watching his black eyes. 'I'll require proof.'

'Of course. You have prisoners of one family?'

'Several I'd be happy to provide. Laszlo will bring them to me here.' She gave her lover a smile to include him. 'The two MacFarquhars please, Nils, and — let me see — Muillear and her son. Two successes will be enough to convince me.' Kate stood up and paced the length of the dais to a candelabra. She touched a finger thoughtfully to its silver flame. 'Now it's only Rory who needs to play his part.'

'Ha. Murlainn's got that son of his in a stranglehold; it's only a matter of time till the boy wriggles loose. He's already kicking. You know what he can do to the Veil?'

She toyed with a strand of copper hair, watching his eyes follow her fingers. Oh, he was hers, all right. 'Yes. It makes perfect sense, of course, in light of the prophecy. *The Bloodstone will determine the fate of the Veil.*'

21

And *Destroy the Veil, and the NicNiven will have all she desires; let it die or survive, and nothing will be hers.*

No. She must *not* dwell on that. She flung it from her head. 'Murlainn disciplines the boy. He knows all about the Veil; he's always been able to touch it himself. If the boy's been taught anything, it's to keep his hands off the Veil and my hands off him. Well, he's managed the latter so far.'

'A boy will do what a boy can do. He's careful and he's elusive, but he'll slip up one day. You could just wait.'

'I have been waiting,' she snapped. 'He has that damned shield stone of Leonora's; it protects his mind. And if he can rip the Veil at will, it's none too easy to predict where he'll do it.'

'Except that he can't do it close to a dun. The Veil's too tough near fortresses. You know that, I know it, his father knows it. If he wants to use the talents the gods gave him, Rory has to leave his father's protection.' He risked a devilish wink. 'And that he'll do. Willingly.'

'How certain you are.' She gave him a chilled glance in return for the wink.

'I've got good reason. Trust me.' He winked again. *Damn him for his insolence*, she thought, half-admiringly. 'The boy's growing, as boys will. The bait I found? He'll take it. Wouldn't be his father's son if he didn't.'

'All right.' She narrowed her eyes. 'He has to leave the dun. But he can't be so far from it that he can elude us just by slipping through the Veil.'

'He's evaded two patrols that way,' remarked Laszlo. 'Probably more who are scared to admit it. Yes, the boy wanders, and he plays with the Veil, but since he can escape straight through it, he's hard to lay hands on.'

I don't need to hear those excuses again, she thought irritably.

'I'll have him observed,' said Cuthag, watching her face. 'All we have to do is get him in a place where he's beyond Murlainn's sword, but he can't get through the Veil.' He shrugged. 'He's a cocky brat, by all accounts.'

'And in further good news,' said the bearded man, 'Reultan is on her otherworld deathbed.'

That brought Kate up short. She turned on her heel, the hot spark of rage almost hurting her eyes. *Robbed again,* she thought bitterly. 'Good news, did you say? That deathbed should have been made by me.'

The three men watched her in silence. They must know, she realised. They all knew that if they waited for the flare of fury to die, she'd see the potential soon enough; and they were right. Kate laid a hand against a cool pillar, rested her forehead on her hand. Breathing deeply and softly, she let herself smile at last.

'And when Reultan dies,' said Cuthag, 'you know what will happen.'

There was something more than soldierly duty in that slippery voice of his. She knew exactly what hunger had been building in him, and she approved. 'Yes,' she said. She turned to lean against the pillar and study his face, never as impassive as he thought it was.

'You want Murlainn destroyed,' said Alasdair softly. 'Destroyed, not dead.'

That earned him a savage glare from Laszlo. It was so blatant that Kate almost laughed out loud. She couldn't help but twist the blade in Nils's gut.

'You understand so much, Alasdair.'

'You can rip out his heart and leave him breathing,' pointed out Cuthag, 'and punish Reultan in her grave.' He

23

coughed delicately. 'Through her own misbegotten spawn.'

It was almost more than she could bear. Kate clasped her hands over her mouth, eyes brimming with tears of sheer happiness. They were clever enough to stay silent. She liked that. Laszlo started forward, alarmed, but she waved him impatiently back. It was long seconds before she recovered enough to know she wouldn't laugh hysterically.

'I like this plan of yours,' she said when she felt regal again, when she could maintain a straight face, a gimlet eye, and a tone like vinegar. 'I especially like the fact that it seems workable. But I haven't been idle, Alasdair dear. I haven't been waiting for you to ride to my rescue.'

'I never thought you would,' he said humbly.

Oh, he's good. 'I've someone in Murlainn's dun primed to do my bidding: someone he trusts with his life, foolishly enough. I think we can weave two strategies together most effectively.'

'Even better,' said Cuthag.

'And I thank you, my queen.' Alasdair quirked an eyebrow. 'Yet again.'

'Have I ever been able to resist you when you begged?' Kate showed her teeth in a smile. 'All I ask of my captains is loyalty. As for my people, is peace too much to ask?'

'For some of them,' growled Cuthag. 'The rest – the true ones? They'll have it soon enough.'

'I'm indebted to you, Cuthag. Please go with Nils to bring the MacFarquhars. Wait, Alasdair.' She held up a hand till the other two had left the room, till the heavy carved door had swung shut with a final clunk behind them. Then she softened her voice.

'So. Why me and not Murlainn?'

He twisted a strand of dirty beard. 'The otherworld.

There were so many places I fitted in, so many governments that valued me. It's ripe for us, it's panting for us, it'll spread its global legs for us.'

'Such a charming way with words.'

He let that fly over his head. 'MacGregor is as wrong and stupid as his brother was before him. I want the other-world as much as you do. Keep me at your side, and I'll give it to you.'

'An entire world?' This time, his cheek pleased her. 'That's an arrogant promise.'

'You have an arrogant enemy.' He kissed her extended hand. 'You need me.'

She laughed. 'I do believe I've always needed you. Very well.' She tilted her head flirtatiously. 'Bring me a boy, Alasdair. A boy, and a girl, and a world.'

HANNAH

I gazed into the black eyes of a man who'd gambled with the Devil and lost, a man who'd been dead for more than four hundred years, and I thought: *I want to stay with you.*

It was unlikely he'd help me out, since he was nothing but flaking paint on a canvas, but talking to him always helped. We both understood about fates worse than death. Beelzebub had dragged him screaming from his horse down to hell; I'd been dumped by my feckless mother on Aunt Sheena and Groper Marty.

I'd had no intention of going straight back to the house after school. I'd dearly have loved to have no intention of going back, ever, but I had to sleep somewhere, even if a bench in the park with the local jakies often seemed like a more attractive option. Even a whisky-breathing jakey wouldn't massage my arse quite as often as Uncle Marty did.

But I could sleep at the castle instead, if I wanted. I could get a four poster bed with a sixteenth century embroidered coverlet at the castle. One of these nights I'd do exactly that. Well, apart from the four poster bed bit, obviously, because of the security doors and the locks and the burglar alarms. I could easily bunk down in the stables, though. It wasn't as if I'd smell of horse afterwards, since there weren't any.

Castle Cantray wasn't the hangout I'd have foreseen for myself: all pickled history and plaid carpets and pan-piped Celtic music. The one time I'd been dragged there on a school visit I'd nearly expired from boredom, but on my own, I liked it. The atmosphere of the place – once you disregarded the sweating tourists and the tartan – suited me. It was just outside town so it was handy; it cost me nothing, since I knew exactly where to climb over the fence out of view; and nobody ever asked me what I was doing there once I was in. They didn't take a blind bit of notice of me. I carried a notebook, looked studious, and did as I liked. It wasn't even that difficult to swipe a bottle of Budweiser from the café fridge.

I took gulps from one as I listened in to the tour guide, who kept shooting me evil glares as if he knew I hadn't paid but couldn't quite prove it. He needn't have thought I was interested in his turgid lecture; it was just that he was telling his practically-dead bus party about my favourite painting and I never tired of that.

I'm not geekishly keen on mediaeval art, but the man in that painting enchanted me. Old portraits always have a bland psychopathic look, but the Wolf of Kilrevin looked as if he meant it, and his black eyes held a spark, as if he was laughing inwardly at some cruel joke. He fascinated me; more than that, he was my ally, my imaginary friend. I felt at home around him. That probably said more about me than I'd like to hear, but at least it was a bit of cultural self-education.

I wondered what the Wolf would think of his castle museum. I always thought he'd have preferred it pre-renovation, like in the old photo on the interactive display: a heap of sinister stones around a courtyard of shadows, the loch beyond it a dark brooding menace. He'd have liked it in ruins, the way he'd left half the towns of the county. An anarchist, I thought. A rebel. Fun to hang out with.

'If the girl with the red hair could step back from the painting *please?*'

Riled, I blew a slightly beery circle onto the painting's glass, then scrubbed off the mist and the nonexistent dirt with a forefinger. 'Do you mind? It's strawberry blonde.'

Ostentatiously he turned his back on me. 'While the current owner continues to hold Castle Cantray and its lands for his lifetime, he has placed it in trust for the nation and the enjoyment of future generations. His desire is—'

'A knighthood,' I muttered.

'—THAT THE FINE ART COLLECTION be seen by as many people as possible. On the west wall of the library, the massive triptych depicts the expulsion of the rebel angels from Paradise and the creation of Hell and Purgatory, and has been attributed to Hieronymus Bosch, though most experts agree it is a particularly clever fake. Here we see a mortal man taking too much interest in matters that do not concern him, so he is being dragged by one of Lucifer's acolytes into Hell. In two pieces.' He gave me a thin unpleasant smirk. 'To the left of the triptych you see the only surviving portrait of the castle's original owner, the Wolf of Kilrevin.'

Finally. I didn't care how often I heard this story.

'Younger brother of the depraved Bishop of Kilrevin, the Wolf's depredations of the area were legendary, but his evil doings came to an abrupt end on an April night in 1594, when he and his men set out from a night's drinking in a local tavern to return to this castle. They never reached home.' His voice hushed. 'His men, burnt to charcoal, were found next morning by a local farmer. The body of the Wolf was never found, only the skeletal carcass of his horse. Local legend says the Devil himself dragged him screaming down to Hell.'

See, that was what I called a spectacular exit. I liked the

Wolf more and more each time. Still, the guide was far too fond of the sound of his own voice, so I hung back while the party moved on. I should go home soon. Back to the house, I mean. I should grit my teeth and face Marty's wandering eyes and fingers once again.

I should. But I didn't want to.

I fantasised, as I always did, about the painting coming to life. The Wolf striding silently home behind me, sword on his back. Marty opening the door. His eyes and his mouth widening. The sword hacking down and—

One day, I thought: one day I'd be big and ugly and evil enough to get my revenge personally, and not in my head. One day. Not that it helped right now. When I was ten I'd been physically terrified of Marty, but oddly enough, with four more years under my belt, I found him more of a threat. The danger he posed seemed less obvious. Subtler. Nastier.

Two can play at nasty, of course.

True, I shouldn't have tried to tear cousin Lauren's face off with my teeth; but Lauren shouldn't have called my father 'the Dead Drunk, Literally' within a thousand miles of my hearing. Not only was he not a drunk, he wasn't dead, and I knew it with all the desperate intensity of someone who didn't have a clue if that was true, or who he was, or why he'd gone and left me with such a useless un-maternal tramp.

He had his reasons. He did. Bloody hell, *one* of my parents had to have a decent excuse. One day our eyes would meet across a crowded room and I'd *know him*, I was convinced of that. And after I hugged him, and after I slapped his face hard, I'd be asking for a few answers. I shouldn't have confided all this in my diary, but then Lauren shouldn't have broken the padlock with a screwdriver and read it.

The bite marks on Lauren's face were red and savage and magnificent, and I wasn't planning to deny it anyway, so Marty had cornered me in my room on the pretext of giving me a talking-to; it was more than clear – and this is how close he got – that he'd have preferred a seeing-to. I was big, mean and vicious enough now to call his bluff and scare him off, but I knew one day he'd call my bluff right back, and I'd lose my nerve. I didn't want to lose it at a bad moment, like when I was alone with him in the house. Like next Friday.

I scratched the back of my neck, and turned again to look at my friend with the psychopathic eyes. It wasn't that they made me uneasy, however hard they burned into mine. He looked positively understanding. He was more a father figure than the real one.

And that was quite enough soul-searching for today. I shook myself and decided that what I *really* wanted now was to go to the stables.

Funny how much I wanted to get there. So much, I nearly ran.

They'd rebuilt the stone walls and the stalls, they'd put on a timber-and-turf roof and laid some hygienic-looking straw on the old cobbles, and they'd installed a couple of ropey life-size figures in sixteenth-century fancy dress – I suspected old department store dummies – together with an unrealistic carthorse, its mane all plucked and moth-eaten.

I thought: if I do a runner, I could bunk down here. The place wouldn't be too spooky; it wouldn't even be that cold. And it would certainly beat The Paddocks (I ask you – in the middle of suburbia) during Aunt Sheena's forth-coming Girls' Weekend Away, which would inevitably also be Groper Marty's Boy's Night In.

The elderly tourists were trailing into the stables now. There was no getting away from them, or indeed from the imperious little guide, who looked very much as if he was going to ask to see my entry ticket. I sidled behind a fat man chewing a Mars bar, so that even when the guide bounced on his heels, he couldn't catch my eye. He soon forgot about me – it was a talent of mine, making myself unobtrusive – and launched into a long-winded drone about conditions for rural workers in the eighteenth century.

Time to go.

I wriggled through the throng towards the last row of stalls, which I happened to know backed onto the toilets, that led to the café, that was home to the fridge, that held the beers. I nearly jumped out of my skin when I backed into a guy with wild eyes and hair like a bogbrush, until he swayed and I grabbed him and realised he was a dummy. All the same, he unnerved me, and I suddenly needed fresh air. I steadied Bogbrush Man, put my finger solemnly to my lips, and turned towards the toilets.

I halted, amazed.

'Shit,' I couldn't help exclaiming. 'That one's good!'

Silence fell. The guide's jaw opened, then shut, and the tourists stared at me. With grudging admiration, I pointed at the life-size horse in the end stall.

'Now that is clever,' I said. 'That is really clever.'

The guide's face was stiff with contempt. 'I don't know what you...'

'That blue one. Brilliant!'

He finally looked where I was pointing, and screamed.

The horse was blue, sort of, but that could just have been the way its pearly-opal hide caught the light. Not all of it was blue. Its face was black, and so were its mane and tail and powerful feathered legs. It was such a bizarre colour, no wonder I'd thought it was a fake.

Because it was obvious, now, that it wasn't. It took a violent leap forward, the bit digging into its foam-flecked mouth as it fought the blond boy on its back, who was clinging on with an air of desperation. Abruptly the brute screamed like a demon, reared, and shot out of the stall.

I had fifteen-year-old reflexes, so I had enough presence of mind to get out of the way. The formerly catatonic tourists staggered aside, screaming and yelling and shoving each other in a magnificently Darwinian fight for survival. Most of them went sprawling as the horse lunged forward, striking sparks from the cobbles.

I could only gaze at the chaos in admiration as the horse swerved out of control through the stable archway and into the car park. The guide's face was the colour of wet cement, but once he got his voice back he hung onto the door jamb and positively screamed at the boy in fury.

'I remember you! I REMEMBER! YOU'VE GONE TOO FAR NOW! You little–! YOU–! I'll see you PROSECUTED this time, I WILL THIS TIME. You've BITTEN OFF MORE THAN YOU CAN CHEW!'

Yes, I could hear how much he'd bitten off. The car park was a chaos of noise: a ring and clatter of hooves, unearthly howls of rage, the wailing of under-fives and over-seventies. I'll be honest; it thrilled me to bits, like a tiny lightning bolt throwing switches as it travelled down my vertebrae. Wild excitement sang in my blood and I felt a sudden intense longing. Crazy, really. I never got excited about anything. I prided myself on sheer insolent cool. And yet the funny thing was, I *had* to see that horse. Now.

Ignoring the bellowing guide I darted outside, then slid to a halt, staring.

The boy was clinging on for dear life, his heels clamped so hard on the horse's flanks I wasn't surprised it was annoyed. It was just a matter of time before its flailing hooves started doing serious damage to the parked cars, but for now it was thrashing and plunging in the centre of the car park, spinning in a tight circle of fury as it arched its great neck and strained to snap at its rider. The boy's white-knuckled fingers were wound so tightly in the beast's mane there was no way he could let himself be thrown off, or he'd be dragged by the fingers along the tarmac. All the same his yells had an edge of excitement, and a big grin was plastered on his face.

My mouth had hung open too long for dignity, so I clamped it shut. I didn't take my eyes off the horse, though. Now I didn't like the look of it so much. Catching sight of me it paused in its crazed plunging, and greenish light sparked in its blank black eye.

I said, 'Uh-oh.'

It sprang for me, head snaking forward, its bared teeth looking very like a grin. I'd have liked to shut my eyes at this point, but as the monster came at me all I could see, between its ears, was the white alarmed face of the boy. I knew instinctively there was no point shutting my eyes. No point moving. Slaver spattered my skin, and I smelt its hot breath, and I saw its teeth open for my face.

And then someone stepped calmly in front of me. As he held up a hand to catch the horse's muzzle, it skidded to a clattering halt, confused.

'Your master is hunting for you.' Thin and tough, the man wore ripped jeans and a scruffy t-shirt, but he had a soft voice, and his hand was light on the horse's nose. 'Wait for me, *eachuisge*.' He glanced back at me.

I blinked. A sharp-boned face like a fox, wild black hair and a trimmed beard. Vicious curved scars slashed on each cheek. And a strange silver light in his brown eyes that I did not like at all.

At last, unhurried, he looked back at the horse. 'And leave that girl alone. She is not for you.'

The blue horse gave an eloquent snort of disgust. I watched in disbelief as the scarred man grabbed the blond boy's wrist and dragged him roughly off it, sending him crashing to the tarmac. That was bad enough, but I gasped in anger when he gave the boy's ear a hard stinging flick.

'Ow,' said the boy without rancour, sitting up.

'You little git. How many times you going to do this?'

Even in trouble the boy was seriously beautiful, with his penitent grey eyes, his sharp-tipped ears and his elfin face. His sun-bleached hair was unruly, curling down past the nape of his neck, and when he blew a lock of it disconsolately off his brow, it fell straight back into his eyes. He didn't look at the man or the sweating horse, fiddling instead with a circle of silver on his wrist. A little silver charm hung on it, set with a lump of dull green stone.

'Your father will want a word with you, Rory Bhan.'

The boy raised huge spaniel eyes to the man. 'Sionnach, give us a break,' he wheedled.

I barged forward, incredulous. 'This guy isn't even your dad? You could *so* take legal action.'

They stared at me in bewilderment before looking back at each other.

'Stay *there*.' Sionnach pointed at him as the guide came

storming out of the stables towards him. 'So help me, Rory, don't you *move.*'

'Where would I go? Keep your beard on.'

He'd nearly let his stupid pony run me down, but I still felt sorry for him: lonely and glum, slumped unhappily on the tarmac, waiting for Sionnach to calm the tour guide down. Maybe the boy was traumatised by his domestically-violent carer, but it was a funny kind of nervous tic he had: picking at thin air with his fingers, tugging on nothing.

Sionnach was busy, mumbling apologetically to the guide and getting an earful of indignant abuse in return. Sighing, I glanced sympathetically at Rory, still wrapping thin air absently round his fingers. He needed support. He needed a friend, preferably a friend with a lawyer. My eyes were so misted over with fellow-feeling, I thought I imagined it when he scuffed backwards on his bum, winked at me, and vanished.

I started, and blinked in disbelief. He'd tugged aside a curtain and scooted behind it.

Only we were in a car park, in the breezy open air.

And there wasn't a curtain there.

★ ★ ★

I slammed the front door and stood in Aunt Sheena's hall: bare wood and cream sofas and the smell of polish. I had a screaming urge to get right back out of it.

Truly, a *screaming* urge. I had to hang onto the hall table to anchor myself.

Now, it's absolutely a fact that I had no idea why I stayed. Between Sheena, Groper Marty and Lauren of the Bitten Face, it wasn't as if I liked the company. But leaving for good – I refused to call it *running away* – was a decision I wasn't ready to take. Shop doorways were not my preferred sleeping place. And besides, my mother might get it into her head to come back for me, and then how would she know where I was?

Unlikely, but possible.

I was ten when she dropped me off at The Paddocks, and my most abiding memory of that day was her desperation to get back in her boyfriend's car. She'd checked her watch and fiddled with her jacket and sworn she'd be back, even as I curled on the sofa and pretended I wasn't crying. I didn't beg, of course – begging wouldn't have made any difference at all – but the woman could hardly pretend I was glad to see the back of her. She couldn't weep and wail that I'd never liked her, so she had a right to Self-Fulfilment and the Pursuit of Love and the Road Less Travelled.

Well, to hell with her and the boyfriend both; tonight at least I had something more interesting to think about. In fact I was so preoccupied with events at the castle, I had entirely forgotten that Sheena had told me this morning, at about ninety decibels, not to bother coming back.

'Oh, it's you, is it?'

I halted, foot on the bottom stair. Aunt Sheena stood at the door of her granite kitchen in tracky bottoms and a jogging bra, bared shoulders as lean and muscly as her folded arms, glossy caramel hair pulled back in a ponytail. Her hard painted face was bright with distaste, and that expensively buffed aura of hers was not looking good.

'Don't you go *near* my daughter again.'

'Nothing could make me happier.' I smirked.

'I've called the police. They're going to come and talk to you.'

Shit. Had she? I didn't fancy getting taken into care. Turning on the stair, I had the satisfaction of seeing Sheena blanch and take a step back. I hovered menacingly for a few seconds, leering towards her, then laughed in her face.

She flushed angrily. 'Oh, your father made the right decision. I told him so at the time. It was the least I could do. We were *good friends,* you know what I mean?'

'What?' My guts went cold, and my brain swam.

And then my brain righted itself, and I thought: *she's lying.* I don't know how I could be so sure, but I was; the horror evaporated. I grinned. 'Would my father not have you?'

The blood drained out of Sheena's cheeks. 'I beg your pardon?'

'I accept your apology.' The grin stayed put on my face. 'Did he not fancy you? Would he not give you a fu–'

'*Get. Out.'* Sheena could barely speak. 'Before I *hit you.'*

'In your dreams.' My face twisted unpleasantly.

I stalked back out of the front door with an air of world-weariness, refusing to bolt despite the assault on my eardrums. *When your cousin comes tomorrow,* I made out through the incoherent screaming, *when Shania gets back with Darryl, she'll sort you out. She'll know what to do about you, you little REJECT.* Right: in her dreams and all. Older and even fouler than her little sister, Shania still knew better than to mess with me.

'And you can sleep *in the gutter* as far as I'm concerned.' With Sheena's final flourish, the door slammed behind me, and despite my fury I felt a shiver of unease.

At least it was summer.

But it was Scotland. And I hadn't brought my jacket.

My immediate future was something I had to think about, so I started to walk. I'd got as far as the corner when Marty's car turned into his home street. Catching sight of me, he slewed the car up onto the kerb, forcing me to stop.

'Oy! Where you going, Hannah?'

I folded my arms, glared at him.

He swung the car door wide, rose from the driving seat, and grinned amicably at my tits. He shifted his stance.

'In trouble again, love?'

I bit back what I wanted to say. 'She's kicked me out.'

'Ahh.' He slung an arm round my shoulder and I felt his warm murmur in my left ear. 'Sheena's upset about Lauren. I know the kid's annoying but you did overreact there, love.'

I said nothing. Too busy grinding my teeth.

'I'll have a word with her, lovey, but I don't think it'll help. You know Sheena when she makes up her mind.' Drawing back, he twinkled at me like a little star.

'Right.' I hesitated. I wanted to kick him in the bollocks but I needed him, briefly. 'Can you get me my jacket from the house?'

He slid a hand round my waist. 'No need, pet. You're not sleeping outside. Here. Get in the car.'

'What?'

'I'll let you into the office.' He jerked his head in the rough direction of town. 'You can stay there till she calms down. Get in the car.'

I thought furiously. It seemed like a better deal than the gutter. 'Thanks, Mart. I can walk. Give us the keys and I'll let myself in.'

'Don't be daft. We'll get a pizza on the way. I mean, I'll get you a pizza on the way.'

I didn't like the way the strong bulk of him was edging me towards the car. He wasn't fat but he was big and sturdy, and his fingers were tighter on my arm than they'd been a second ago.

'Come on, Hannah love. I'm the only pal you've got right now.'

'Except for him.' I nodded at the nearest lamppost, and when he twitched his head up anxiously I wrenched myself out from under his arm.

He snatched my sleeve, yanking me back. I slapped at him, then kicked wildly, missing his groin by a mile; but he had to swerve. Once again I tore away, and this time I ran.

'Sleep in the gutter for all I fecking care!' His echo of Sheena was all I made out as I skidded and almost fell, pelting round the corner and out of his sight.

★ ★ ★

I couldn't go back there or I'd kill him. Sheena too. I'd kill them all, and that would be bad when the police showed up for our chat. I didn't know what I should do, so I kept walking.

I say I didn't know what I *should* do, but I knew fine what I *wanted* to do. The Screaming Urge was back, and it wasn't all to do with extended-family homicide. I came to a halt at the bus stop and stared up at the timetable. Last bus. Nothing coming back at this hour.

Do it. What's to lose?

I had to practically step in front of the bus to make it stop – you'd think my criminal record was common knowledge, the way drivers ignore me – but at the last moment he braked and let me on. He did give me a very funny look as I got off at the Cantray stop. I couldn't blame him; this was ridiculous. I had no idea what I was thinking. I couldn't get into the main castle, couldn't even get a comforting glimpse of my painted psycho. The sky was that heavy pewter colour that isn't far off night, and though the loch shone silver it only made the clouds seem darker. The light would go off it any minute now. Any minute. It had already slid from the castle walls, leaving them bleaker than winter.

It still seemed like a better option than The Paddocks.

Yes. Even the empty coldness, and the mournful quietness when the bus disappeared: even that was better than The Paddocks, and its locks, and its sterile comforts, and its central heating. And Marty. Yes.

It was better here, despite the whispering summer trees, and the lonely cry of a curlew, and the slow lap of the steely water at the loch fringes. And the rustle of grasses. And the long looming shadow of the castle.

And the crunch of a footstep RIGHT AT MY BACK.

I shrieked and stumbled as I turned.

'Oh, there you are. Finally.'

I glared at the blond boy, who stood there smiling inanely, until my thumping heart calmed down. '"Finally"?'

'I had a feeling you'd be back.' He blew a lock of pale hair out of his eye.

I shook my head in disgust and strode away towards the castle fence.

'Where you going, Red?' He jogged to keep up.

'Strawberry blonde.' I gave him a weary look. 'Aren't you in trouble? Shouldn't you be getting home?'

'I'll put that off as long as I can, thanks. Where are you going?'

'I suggest you just go and get it over with.'

'Ha. You haven't met my dad.'

'Indeed, and I'd rather I didn't. Your dad sounds like he ought to be locked up.'

He gave a snarky giggle. 'I'd like to see anybody try.'

'Get your mother to do it.'

'She's dead. Ages ago and I don't remember her, so don't start apologising.'

'Okay.' I turned with an air of finality towards the castle fence. 'Mine's dead to me and all.'

'Really?' Sympathy started to dawn on his face.

'No. Not *really*. She ran off with a session musician. Apparently she owed it to herself to find herself, but I expect she's still looking. She wasn't that bright.'

'I see.' He caught up and walked peaceably at my side. I looked at him askance.

'Can I, uh. *Help* you with something?'

He stopped, nonplussed. 'Well. No. Not really.' Awkwardly he slewed his eyes aside, then he brightened. 'I'm bored.'

'And I'm not your frigging Xbox. Stop following me.'

He didn't go away. The sky was duller, its layer of cloud sheened with dying sunlight, and I wanted to break into the café for a beer and an uncooked panini before I found a quiet place to sleep. Also, I felt like I wanted to curl up and have a decent cry about various aspects of my life, and I wasn't going to do that in front of the village idiot.

'Don't mind me,' he said.

I came to a halt and turned on my heel. 'Listen, where do you stay? Because you should be getting back.'

'So should you.'

'I'm staying here,' I said.

'You're not,' he said, and I didn't like the confidence in his voice. Actually, quite suddenly, I didn't like *him*. I didn't like his happy smile or his charm or the way his messy hair flopped over his glittering silver eye.

I took a step back. And funnily enough so did he. His hand clutched the air, tore at nothing, and I was so busy watching that, and fearing for his sanity and my life, I didn't see his other hand move.

I didn't see him lunge for me, because he moved faster than anything I could hope to see. I only felt him seize my wrist and yank me, and I screamed and fell with his arms locked round me, and we hit the cold ground together and the world went dark.

* * *

'JESUS,' I screamed. 'What did you do THAT FOR?'

When the world and my vision cleared, I was sitting on top of the blond boy, which made it easy enough to pummel his ribcage with clenched fists. Not since I bit Lauren's face had I wanted to hurt someone as much, as physically, as I wanted to hurt him then. Clenched fists, in fact, weren't cutting it; I began to tear at his eyes with my nails. 'What do you *want*? Why did you *DO THAT*?'

He batted me away, shutting his eyes tight, snatching for my hands.

'Because you WOULDN'T HAVE COME, you *silly cow*.'

'I'm not GOING ANYWHERE.'

'You already HAVE.'

In an instant he was limp and unresisting beneath me, blinking up and biting his lip with a sweet uncertainty that looked well-practised.

I had a horrible feeling, then. I couldn't go on hitting him when obviously I didn't have to. 'What?'

Once again he moved so fast, I didn't know what happened. Only that I was the one on the ground, I was the one winded by a knee in the solar plexus, I was the one staring in breathless astonishment at a grey sky as the boy Rory frowned and chewed one fingernail. His other hand gripped my throat in a very un-amateurish way.

'Ucch,' I rasped.

'Look,' he said. 'Just look.'

I rolled my head to the right, as far as his grip allowed. It must have been tighter than it felt, because my vision was distorted, obscuring my view of the castle. The air seemed torn, like I was seeing double, and I started to panic.

'Don't kill me,' I squeaked.

'Don't be such an idiot.' He rolled off me and stood up, dusting himself down.

Staggering up, rubbing my throat, I backed away from him. 'I'm going now. Don't follow me.'

He smiled. 'Where you gonnae go?'

My breath hurt high up in my throat. I swallowed and made myself breathe more deeply; then, trying to keep one eye on him, I turned a full, slow circle. I wasn't seeing double any more, but I wasn't seeing anything familiar either.

I'd been right. The castle looked a lot better as a forbidding ruin, and I wondered who could have imagined interactive keyboards and overspill car parking in this context. The chain link fencing was gone, and so were the signs. The loch at my feet was a black menacing stillness. I could have been in another place entirely. The illusion was perfect.

'How did you do that?' I whispered.

Rory chewed his lip. 'I'm not supposed to, of course.

But what's the point of being able to do something if you never get to do it?'

I was sure we'd done that one in Ethics, and I believe the moral dodginess of stage hypnosis had actually come up. Sadly I couldn't remember the upshot of the discussion, since I'd bunked off the second period for a fag.

He grinned. 'I *knew* I was going to get on with you.'

I gave him a sidelong suspicious look and sat down heavily on the nearest rock. I decided I wouldn't indulge him by asking.

'Impressed?' he prodded. 'Bet you don't know anybody else who can tear the Veil. What's your name, Red?'

'Hannah Falconer,' I snapped. 'Call me Red again and I'll rip out your throat. Now. Shut up and let me think.' I thought for all of two seconds. 'Click your fingers.'

'What?'

'I have to get home. Click your fingers. Isn't that how it works?'

'No. How what works?'

'Hypnosis.'

'It's not hyp – it's not that.' He blinked. 'Don't be mad.'

'Don't piss me about or I'll tear your pretty head off.' I thought hard and wished I had a cigarette. I glanced over my shoulder and saw the shimmer in the air, and the fleeting glimpses of car park beyond it. I moved my head. The car park disappeared. And reappeared.

'I'm sorry,' he said. 'I thought you'd be okay with this. And I do know the safe places.'

I moved my head again, and shifted my mind sideways while I was at it. I wondered what had been in that beer. 'The safe. Places. There are places that aren't?'

'Well. There's a war on, after all.'

My eyes darted to the derelict castle, the deserted moor, the louring sky and the black forbidding loch. Rory and I might be the only human beings in a hundred miles, except for the sliver of car park that was starting to blur and fade. As I watched, it vanished altogether, and that was when I remembered the curtain that never was, the curtain he'd drawn back and shuffled behind. The one I'd explained to the enraged Sionnach when he returned looking for Rory; Sionnach, who had called me inventive names but who had never once accused me of lying. Who had, with what I had considered outrageous gullibility, believed every word I told him.

I felt sick. Invisible curtains, homicidal horses, a landscape from a hundred years ago. The beer had finally got to me; either that, or this was for real.

Yet when I tried to be surprised I found I couldn't; it was like I'd always known about this, somewhere in the back of my mind, and I'd just forgotten.

'So,' said Rory, and blew his hair out of his eyes. 'Want to come home with me?'

* * *

The only reason I went with him – or rather, after him, since he strode off as if I had no choice, which of course I didn't, since I had no idea how to get back to The Paddocks – was pity.

'What's your dad going to do?' I asked him as we stumbled down a heathery slope. Well, I stumbled.

'Nothing. He'll probably leave it to my brother.'

'What, he'll get your brother to leather your arse?'

'Nah, that would be preferable. I'll get an earful. All my mother's sacrifices, how disappointed he is in me, that sort of thing. And Dad getting shot saving my backside, that's his favourite bit.'

'Well, I don't think it's... *what?*' I don't think I'd ever done a proper double take before.

'Unless Dad's *really* mad about the horse. Which he will be. Sorry about that, by the way.'

I shrugged. 'It was only a horse.'

'It's my father's horse. Nearly killed you. I really am sorry.'

'God. Sometimes I think a father would be just too complicated.'

'Well, yours can't have been that complicated if he just buggered off.'

I stopped dead. 'What?'

He turned, a flush creeping across his cheekbones. 'Sorry.'

It all made instant, blinding, nauseating sense. 'Did Lauren put you up to this? *Did she?*' I clenched fists and teeth.

'No!' He squinted hard, eyes boring into mine. 'I – is she your cousin?'

'You little *shit*.' I flew at him, and he caught my wrists just before they tore into his face. He danced backwards, ducking my headbutt.

'I don't know Lauren!' he yelled, wrestling me to the ground. 'What's wrong with you?'

I was flat on my back again, humiliated and in pain, a heather root digging into my kidneys. Rory knelt on my chest, pinning my arms above my head. I was going to kill him. *Kill him.*

'Don't. Do that.' He was out of breath. ''S my father's job.'

'What?'

'Killing me.' He hissed a breath through his teeth. 'Shit, you're strong. Your back, it's sore. I'm sorry. I'll let you get up if you don't kill me.'

Even as he said it, a fierce twinge went through my body from that sharp hard root. I flinched and twisted.

'Stop wriggling, you're hurting yourself. *Ow*.'

The root stopped hurting just as he cried out.

I froze. A tide of panic was rising in my throat and I thought I might vomit. I wasn't myself any more. I mean I literally wasn't. I could feel my fingers clamped round my wrists, and my ribcage pinned beneath my knee, except that it wasn't my knee, and it wasn't my ribcage or my fingers or my wrists, and just then the root dug into my back again but it was *only half as sore*—

I screamed.

His weight was off me and he scrabbled backwards, his face a vision of guilt.

'What is it? I'm sorry. What?'

I could hardly breathe. 'My head. You're in my *head*.'

He didn't argue, didn't deny it, didn't even laugh. He just got unsteadily to his feet, ran his hands through his unruly hair and shrugged.

'I'm really sorry,' he said. 'I thought you—'

'What?'

'I thought you wouldn't mind.'

The breath felt as if it would never entirely return to my lungs. At last I barked, 'That's NOT EXACTLY THE POINT.'

He swore miserably. 'Oh shit. Oh shit, you can't do it, can you? I'm sorry.'

'Stop saying you're sorry. Sit down. Let me think. If I can do that in private?' I glared at him. 'Sit down and shut up.'

He did, very sharply. He tugged at a handful of rough grass and ripped it loose.

'So how did you...' I felt like slapping him, but I was afraid to now. 'How...'

'I dunno.' Rory dug a stone out of the peat and tossed it into the loch. 'How do you breathe?'

'I breathe because I'm supposed to. Because it's *natural*.'

He gave me an odd look. 'But so's – oh, never mind.'

'Don't do it again. Just *don't*.'

'You sound like my brother. You'll like him.'

'I doubt that. I don't think I'll be meeting him. Take me home. Take me home *right now*.'

'Aw, don't be like that. I'll–'

I never got to find out what he'd do. Something slammed into the ground between us and stuck there quivering, singing faintly with its own vibration, the late light shimmering off satiny steel. Rory leaped to his feet with a yell, and I fell backwards into a peat pool.

I didn't want to open my eyes but I was too terrified not to. I creased them open a slit. Against the bright sky I saw the belly of a horse; there was a silver sword-tip at my own stomach, all ready to open it up. Rory's anxious eyes pleaded as he reached for me, and was prodded away by the blade.

'Sionnach, you've hurt her. Let me–'

'Nice try. As if I'd take my eyes off you again.'

'Sionn–'

'Pick her up. This time, you little arse, you're going straight to your father.'

* * *

As it happened, Sionnach hadn't hurt me, though I thought for about twenty seconds I was going to die of fright. I was shaking when Rory was finally allowed to pull me to my feet and out from under the horse, and I was sodden and mud-stained, and as the wind rose and bit through my thin wet clothes, I hated Rory more than I hated anyone in the world, even Sionnach. *Even Marty.*

And that lasted as long as it took him to say, 'Sionnach, let her ride, at least.'

The man with the scarred face glanced down at me with disdain, but he reached down a hand. I ignored it, so he grabbed my arm and yanked me off my feet. I felt the world turn over, and then I was dumped, straddled, in front of him on his horse, so hard it brought brief tears to my eyes.

'Feck,' I exclaimed through gritted teeth. 'Don't take it out on *me*.'

The man said nothing, and even Rory, walking at the horse's side, could only shoot me a dumb glance of sympathy.

I didn't like having Sionnach at my back, and a sword at his. He might think he could thump Rory with impunity, but he needn't try it on with me. I hated his unsmiling face and his surly silence; I hated *him*. I was furious with Rory for getting me into this in the first place; and I did not want to go wherever it was we were going. Over and over I wished myself back at The Paddocks, with nothing to fear but Groper Marty's fingers and Sheena's tongue.

Funny that despite the cold and the wet and the terror, I wasn't persuading myself.

'Hannah,' muttered Rory, tugging at my leg. 'There, look.'

I tore my gaze from the horse's mane and made myself look in the direction of his nod. I sucked in a breath of surprise. I don't know what I'd been expecting, but it wasn't this compact walled town. It rambled over a craggy head-land as if it had grown there all by itself, the stone walls following every swell and dip of the land. Silver bays glit-tered to the north and south, and the western walls rose from a cliff that fell sheer to the sea below. It was hard to tell where the building ended and the land began.

Below the landward side ragged sheep and stocky black cattle cropped the grass under a summer sun, but a good part of the grazing land had been taken over by what looked like a twenty-five-a-side football match. One woman put her foot on the ball to pause the game while the players watched us in silence.

'Oh, yes,' Sionnach growled, 'You're in disgrace, Rory Bhan.'

The guard at the gate – despite his ordinary jeans and torn jumper I don't know what else you'd call him, with his sword on his back and his lethal stare – signalled us through with a jerk of his head. Inside the walls, when I stopped staring nervously backwards at him, the first thing I noticed was the depressing absence of mobile phone masts. The only sign of civilisation was a cluster of wind turbines circling in the sea breeze. *Oh God.*

Sionnach nudged the horse into a trot to climb a winding unpaved alley, its hooves ringing on bare stone, so when it came to a dead halt I was flung forward, and barely caught myself from sliding humiliatingly down its neck. Rory didn't look at me. He was staring at something, with an odd mixture of dread, defiance and adoration.

In front of a central hall, a stream was channelled through a courtyard, pooling in a stone basin at the centre. A man was stooped over it with his back to us, stripped to the waist and scooping water over his face. I was glad he couldn't see me because I couldn't take my eyes off his back. I'd never seen anything like it.

There was a tattoo on his left shoulder, intricately beautiful knotwork tapering to a point on his bicep, but it was distorted by hideous scars that covered his whole back. He looked like the scratching post of a giant cat but at least those ugly gouges looked old and healed. The two puckered holes between his shoulder blades were vicious and raw, as if they might split open any second and bleed him dry. I swear I could almost see blood and nerves and shattered veins moving beneath the thin chafed skin. They looked like raw pain made into flesh, so they did.

'I find it beyond incredible,' said the man, 'that you would do this again.'

Propped against the horse's shoulder, Rory swallowed hard. 'Dad...'

'Please don't say you're sorry. You lie like that, I don't know if I could stop myself hitting you.' Rory's father stood up straight, easing his shoulders. Reaching for the shirt beside him he pulled it over his head, raked long fingers through his black hair, and turned.

The bones of his face were as sharp as knives, his eyes in their shadowy sockets grey like Rory's, though that was as close as they came to a family resemblance. These ones weren't warm or friendly, they were hard and dark and silver-lit. He wasn't very tall, he was spare and lightly-built, but he was all rangy muscle. And he couldn't be as young as he looked, not with a son Rory's age. I could see where Rory got his looks, but not his personality, or the kind light in his eyes.

Now that I couldn't see the man's scarred back, I had

space to notice the black dog that lay close to his feet in the shadow by the wall, a huge maned thing. Its yellow eyes were fixed on me and I didn't like the look in them any more than I liked the look in its owner's. Rory's father leaned back on the low wall of the reservoir and folded his arms across his chest.

'I, uh... I couldn't leave without Hannah.' Rory shot me a pleading look. 'She was in, uh... trouble. I promised I'd–'

'This close.' A muscle moved in his father's throat as he held up finger and thumb. 'You and a slap.'

They watched each other for about a century and a half, the whole place eerily silent, till the man unfolded his arms and beckoned Rory.

Rory approached to well within slapping distance. His eyes were on his father's, big and round and grey, but the spaniel look he used on Sionnach wasn't there. Clearly he didn't think it even worth trying on this one.

I held my breath and shut one eye, expecting the thump of a fist on flesh, but all the man did was take Rory's head gently in one hand, pulling him into a fierce embrace. Pressing his cheek to Rory's wind-tousled hair, he took a breath that sounded equal parts anger, fear and pure relief.

The father's eyes opened once and looked at me, expressionless, then he closed them again as if he couldn't bear the intrusion of another human being. Blowing out a sigh, I shifted from foot to foot. It was an awkward moment and I was glad when the man kissed Rory's head and pushed him roughly away.

'And who's she?'

Rory's whole face had brightened, as if the humiliation of his return and the stares of his neighbours had never happened. He said – or I thought he said – '*She* is right!'

His father scowled. 'What?'

'Seriously. Dad, look at her eyes. Really look. She's one of us!'

The man stepped closer to me, staring so hard into my eyes my own vision blurred. 'So she is. Halfbreed, I'm thinking.' He sounded less than impressed. 'What am I supposed to do with her, Rory? You going to bring back every mongrel runt you find?'

I gasped, balling my fists. 'Who you calling a runt?'

'Runt my arse,' said Rory proudly, earning a light clip on the ear. 'She's Hannah. This is my dad, Hannah.'

'Hello, Rory's dad,' I said. 'You know smacking's child abuse?'

'My name's Seth, if you want to use it.'

'I'll think about it.' Perhaps, on balance, I wouldn't risk the smacking remark again. Just as I decided that, a grin lit his face, then was gone.

'I'm sorry my son nearly killed you.'

'It was only a fuc…' One look at his face stopped me short, and I sighed. 'It was only a *horse.*'

'It was my horse. Rory, go and see Jed, he's worried about you. I'll take the girl home.' Seth began to turn, then hesitated. He frowned at me.

I wanted to run; it was just that I couldn't. A vision of Marty flashed through my brain and froze me with humiliating terror. I think I shut my eyes.

When I opened them again Rory's father was standing close enough to touch me, but he didn't. His eyebrows drew together in puzzlement and his teeth bit into his lower lip.

'That man,' he said. 'He's not your father.'

I shook my head violently. 'Stop that. Get out.' I jumped back, and that's when I spotted the woman behind him.

She'd approached in silence and now she stood there watching me, her arms folded. Short-cropped dark red hair, golden brown eyes, the most extraordinarily beautiful face I'd ever seen. Seth must have seen my eyes widen, because he glanced over his shoulder. Then back at me. He shook his head as if dismissing a thought.

'Why don't you stay?' he said.

I breathed hard. 'What?'

'You won't find him anywhere else. Probably.'

Tears sprang to my eyes and I blinked furiously, gritting my teeth. 'I'm not looking,' I hissed.

'Yes, you are. He's from here, you know that?'

'Stop it! That's my business! It's my — father!'

He shrugged. 'Sorry. It's like looking in a lit window. Sometimes we can't help it.'

'Doesn't anybody believe in *privacy*?' I almost shrieked.

'I said I'm sorry. But aren't you curious about your father? I know I am.'

'Yeah? I thought I was a *mongrel runt*?'

He hooted a laugh, and then his voice dropped so low only I could have heard it. 'We won't hurt you.' The 'we' was stressed, just enough; then his voice was normal again, volume, tone and all. 'Oh, and *he* wants you to stay the summer.' Seth jerked a thumb at his son.

'He does?' I gave Rory a shocked sidelong glance. He'd brightened so much he almost seemed taller. His face was all hopeful innocence as he raised his eyebrows at me.

Seth had known exactly what to say. That disturbed me a lot more than it encouraged me. The wild prospect of finding my father wasn't one I could just ignore. He knew that. Bastard.

The thing was that I considered the rival attractions.

Vodka hidden in Sprite bottles in the park; drinking it with girls I barely liked and boys I loathed. Shoplifting for fun, taking bets on who'd get the next visit from the community support officer. Trying, without looking too uncool, to avoid the drugs that managed to make me simultaneously hyper and bored. Endless sniping from Sheena; gladiatorial bitching contests with my cousins; Marty's leering eyes and pawing fingers. Oh, and a whole summer's taunting from Lauren, just because I so desperately wanted my father, I'd been stupid enough to put it in writing.

Would they even report me missing? Even if they did, nobody would look that hard.

I took a surreptitious look round the stone courtyard. Those were stables on the south side, and I'd been passed by at least six perfectly normal horses that hadn't tried to eat me. I liked riding; I'd been not bad at it when I was eight, brilliant when I was nine.

To the right was a large sand arena where a woman in a black t-shirt, her long blonde hair woven into a thick braid, was galloping a horse past a line of butts and firing arrows with scary consistency. Out on the machair the anarchic football match was back in progress, and I felt like I could belt right down there and join in, and would be perfectly welcome if I did. The sun was high and warm, and there were two beaches close by, white sands laced around clear turquoise water. I didn't want to go back the The Paddocks. Ever.

And Rory was the hottest thing I'd seen *all year.*

'Here's the deal.' Seth grinned at me. 'You, Ginger, can keep your hands to yourself. And I'll smooth things over with your aunt.'

'It's strawberry blonde,' I said. 'Yes please.'

RORY

I knew the dream wasn't real. Never was, not these days. I was aware even in sleep that I wasn't a small child any more, but not being real isn't the same as not being true. Watching my father crawl on the stone floor of our shared room, moonlight dancing on his twisted back muscles, I was quizzical; and even my unformed baby brain was needled with pity as well as fear. But there was nothing I could do. Never was.

Seth hadn't seen me, didn't know I was awake. He curled on the rug like a wounded animal, clawing at his shoulder blades. When each spasm passed, he hugged his legs, sobbing soundlessly. Everything was done silently. I think it wasn't just pride; I think he didn't want to wake me. He didn't know I was always awake.

Towards the end of the dream – because I always dreamed of that one particular night – he raised his head and blinked and he saw me. The pain ebbed and he drew breath; he uncoiled and clambered onto all fours; and his eyes met mine.

His ribs still heaving, he couldn't speak. He must've thought it was my first time seeing it, and the horror in his eyes was worse than all the grim agony that went before.

'Rory,' he gasped. 'Gods, boy, I'm only fooling.' The rictus smile belied it all. 'Rory. It's a *game*.'

I was three years old. Three.

'Ah, Rory. Oh, lad.' The smile grew more real, and more

regretful, as he regained his sanity and the world. 'You're going to need a room of your own.'

* * *

I could never sleep after that dream, or rather that recalled memory. I hadn't for a second assumed the torment had stopped once he'd banished me from my small cot in his room. I'd taken it for granted that it went on happening; just without me there to see it. And often I thought that it wasn't a dream at all, but Seth himself, in real time, out of control and bleeding into me.

I tried not to feel guilty, because they told me often enough it hadn't been my fault. Seth was shot in the back because he'd betrayed his own brother, and if he'd had to rescue me, it was because he'd handed me over to the enemy queen in the first place. He had no-one to blame but himself; and the clann had had every right to flog him for what he did; and perhaps there was a reason he'd never been competently healed of his wounds.

That didn't mean I couldn't rage at them all, safe in the privacy of my own head. I loved my clann; that didn't mean I thought they could do no wrong. All I could do, on the nights when the dream visited me, was stumble out of bed and walk the stone passageways till I felt tiredness creep up the nape of my neck again. I didn't – couldn't – resent Seth for the disturbed nights, and there was no point being permanently furious with the clann; and anyway, the dun was so still and so peaceful in the small hours. No running feet, no raucous laughter or angry shouts or clipped commands. So late, there wasn't even music. It was always a good time to think.

Tonight I wondered if I should knock on Hannah's door. Maybe she was lying awake herself, wondering what she'd got herself into. I knew she believed the evidence of her senses – she was smart enough for that – but she was willing to use only five of them.

I uncurled my fist just as it touched the smooth oak of her door, and placed my palm softly against it. No. Asleep or awake, it was no time to disturb her. My father, entirely free of scruples where full-mortals were concerned, had taken Eili with him across the Veil and paid a visit to Hannah's aunt and uncle. In minutes the couple who were in loco parentis understood that Hannah should spend her summer not at The Paddocks, in the off-license and in the Sheriff Court, but with distant relatives in an unknown place doing God-knew-what with her time.

I believe he forgot to mention the war.

Hannah had agreed to it all, of course, and with some enthusiasm, but that didn't mean she wasn't thinking it over. About the fact they'd let her go so easily, that they really couldn't have cared less.

Tactlessly, Eili had laughed when she and Seth returned and told their story. There were none so malleable, she told me waspishly, as those who wished to believe. And Sheena, at least, had wished very much to be rid of Hannah. Why, it took barely a tweak of the brainwaves. The reassuring presence of a scrubbed-up and responsible-looking female had been wholly unnecessary, she muttered as she strode back to her forge, ostentatiously messing up her hair with her fingers. She'd clearly resented Seth robbing her precious time just to provide me with a companion.

It was the kind of thing that gave our race an evil name, Sionnach reminded us all: seducing full-mortals across the

Veil and keeping them there for our pleasure and distraction. It wasn't ever *quite* like that but it did give us a bad reputation.

Except that Hannah wasn't a full-mortal. And there was no-one my age in the dun. And growing up a half-breed runt in a clann proud of its bloodlines, you sometimes want to meet someone of your own kind.

I wasn't a runt any more. You can't afford to be a runt when you're allegedly the mythical Bloodstone and the saviour of your race. Or even when you *aren't* – because there's no such thing according to your rationalist father – but you still have to live up to a legend you never earned or believed. Because it isn't only your own clann who believe it; it's the enemy clanns, too, and their powerful queen, and they'd do anything or kill anyone to get their hands on you. As a reason for one's existence it's a lot to live up to, particularly when your own father dismisses it as the superstitious ravings of an ancient madwoman.

It was also why the mother I never knew had died at the hands of a Lammyr, and my uncle Conal had been murdered defending me, and my whole clann spent their years fighting and dying and killing for me. And that was why I'd grown up a virtual prisoner in what would one day – faery queens permitting – be my own dun.

I could hardly be blamed for wanting some fun. I'd have to wait, though, for their memories of my latest escape to dull. When I slipped down the stairs and out through the main door, Sorcha stepped lightly in front of me.

'No, you don't, Rory Bhan.' Her sheathed dagger tickled my chest playfully. 'Seth—'

'Says I'm not allowed out of the dun.' I rolled my eyes. 'That's why I'm not going, then.'

'I've heard that one before,' drawled Sorcha's fellow-guard, a sturdy sod called Eorna who'd once taught my own father to fight.

'Yeah, well. This time I mean it.'

Sorcha narrowed her eyes and leaned closer to me, the leather-and-silver scabbard digging painfully into my ribs. I pushed it crossly aside.

'So help me, you wee bastard. You take one step past the courtyard boundary, and I'll be thrashing your arse before you can take a second one.'

I knew she meant it. As far as Sorcha was concerned, I might still be three years old. I grinned. 'I won't, Sorcha. Promise.'

She grinned back and withdrew the sheathed dagger, slapping my backside with it by way of farewell. 'In that case, bugger off and let us gossip in peace.'

I didn't dare head even vaguely towards the eastern court-yard and the gate beyond, and besides, I'd told Sorcha the truth: the sole point of my small-hours expedition was to visit the stables. I wouldn't be daring to hijack Seth's horse again – well, not for a few weeks – but I felt that if I could only look into its eyes, study the winding course of its unfathomable mind, I might find some keystone clue to its whole species. If I could once tame that kelpie at the little loch in the pass between the hills, my father might finally call me an adult. He might begin to respect me. He might even trust me to leave the dun walls for longer than five minutes at a time, I thought bitterly. If I could only tame the kelpie; and to do that, maybe I needed to understand Seth's.

Unfortunately, on this occasion, he'd beaten me to it. It must have been another sleepless night. I didn't speak to let Seth know I was there; instead I blocked my mind and edged silently back into the shadows.

If there was a creature he could trust with his lonely nights and his racked conscience, it should have been me. Instead he slumped lazily against the partition of the blue roan's stall, barefoot and bare-chested, his eyes shadowed with insomnia but glittering deep down with the moment's happiness. Branndair stood above him, licking his face and neck like a mother wolf quieting a pup, and Seth laughed hoarsely, grabbing the wolf's black-maned shoulders and hauling him down for a hug.

Branndair gave a huge sigh and rolled over in my father's arms. The one arm Seth could still move went round the wolf to rub his belly, and Branndair squirmed with delight. All the while the blue roan shifted lazily above them both, a great protecting beast. Seth closed his eyes as Branndair whimpered happily and wriggled more comfortably against him.

I ached to go and sit beside them, to snuggle beneath my father's free arm and feel it go round me instead of the wolf, but it was out of the question. He'd wake, and the grey eyes would freeze, and that guarded shutter would come down across his face and his mind. I'd disappoint myself, and I'd ruin his easy happiness, and this was such a contrast to the Seth of the daytime I found it was enough just to watch him.

* * *

Just as well I gave myself time to watch in peace. The next day when I got to the arena, fuzzy and yawning from my disturbed night, he and Eili were already hard at duelling practice, silent and intense. His face, when he caught sight of me and raised a hand to stop her, was its normal friendly self. Friendly and stern and proud and paternal and affectionate and entirely a mask; joy and agony were smoothed from his features and absorbed into daytime efficiency. The man, in other words, was obliterated by my father and my Captain.

He leaned on the fence and grinned at me, making a broad gesture of invitation. 'Come and get a thrashing. You deserve one.'

'Sure,' I said. 'Let me wake up first.'

Eili snorted with amused disdain. Which was all very well for a woman who could probably kill in her sleep. 'I'll train him today if you like, Murlainn.'

My father shot me a knowing look. 'How awake are you planning to be, Rory?'

My heart sank, not so much at the thought of Eili's pitiless discipline as the prospect of two fun-free hours. The woman did not believe in either breaks or banter. 'Couldn't Sionnach—'

'Ask him yourself,' said Eili.

She always knew where her twin was, and right now he was jumping down from the fence behind her. He nodded to me; had no need to greet Eili; and drew my father quietly aside. Their conversation was conducted entirely in their heads, and I didn't recognise the combination of emotions that crossed Seth's face. You ask me, he didn't know himself if it was grief, relief or happiness.

'What is it?' I asked, unbearably curious.

Seth still didn't know what he should be feeling, and it showed. He turned with a small helpless shrug, glanced at Eili and then at me.

'Stella's dead,' he said.

I knew the name. My aunt, Uncle Conal's sister. She and my father had never got along; and I'd never met the woman. It was Eili who tensed, suddenly the focus of attention though she never moved or spoke. Something emanated out of her, that was all, and only her brother could have identified it, and he said nothing either.

'Reultan,' she said at last. 'Her name was Reultan.'

And then Eili slung her sword into the sand, and walked away.

SETH

This is how it is, I tell him, when he'll listen.

The world nothing but mist and monochrome, because the day hasn't had time to give it any colour. Rain that's barely enough to wet your skin, yet you feel it down to your bones. A lonely wind off the sea, cold and grey as its mother sky. The smell of – what? The beginning of morning?

It's life in your nostrils, is all: the tang of cold life, mournful and lovely because it might be your last scent of it. It's lying there between earth and sky, knowing that when you raise your head and spring that you're independent of either, mortal and fragile and visible. It's fear and it's hate and it's love, and you can barely tell which is which. But the one thing you can identify is the longing to live through it, and that's the one thing you can't dwell on, because that way lie cowardice and betrayal, and I should know, I should recognise those.

It's the moment before it starts, when the wind sings in off the sea, and there isn't a third dimension to the world, and all the air smells of is indistinguishable *life,* and you can't afford to be scared to lose it.

And to go there, and not run away, you've got to believe you're right, you've got to believe in something and someone, even if it's only the wolf on your right or the friend pissing himself on your left, even if it's only a memory or a thought or a ghost. I can't really explain it. There's no explaining it till you're there.

That's what I tell my son.

But he doesn't listen.

★ ★ ★

The friend on my left on this occasion was Orach, and she'd never been known to piss herself. Other people had, when they saw her coming down on them with a bared blade.

~ *How's the back, Murlainn?*

~ *Fine.*

~ *Uh-huh. It's always fine in a fight.*

~ *Focus,* I snapped. I knew she wasn't accusing me of malingering at other times, but this was hardly the moment for the argument.

~ *Yes, Captain.* She couldn't keep the sarcasm out of her thoughts, and I shot her an evil look.

Dunster was a shabby but compact village on the very rim of the world; at least that was how it felt, and I thought that was probably what had attracted the Lammyr. They'd enjoy the bleakness, and the desolation of the marsh, and I imagined they'd thoroughly approve of the achingly cold wind that swept in with the tide. They liked their home comforts, it was true, but they also had a fondness for a nice bit of atmosphere.

They'd installed themselves in a cluster of old fishermen's huts and set about their business, which doubled as entertainment. I hadn't heard about the killings for months after they began; that was a typical trick. Sowing arguments, feeding resentments, freshening old hostilities until the villagers did their work for them.

From where I crouched below the edge of the sandbank, I could make out the lolling figure at the drowning-stake.

The tide was out now, and the sea was reduced to thin salty runnels that made a glistening jigsaw of the marsh, but it was all too easy to imagine those trickles swelling and rising around you with agonising slowness, and the struggle to keep your face raised above the encroaching water, and the inevitable horrible inundation. The man at the stake shouldn't have slit his captain's throat, of course, but then the captain should never have inflicted the drowning fate on the man's sister, and all on the heels of a savage woman-to-woman argument and a miscarried baby. That was Lammyr-influence for you.

One day, if I could be bothered, I'd trace it back to the original deed: a silent strangling in an alleyway, maybe, or an unexplained poisoning on the back of a too-obvious grudge. It hardly mattered now. It was one of the younger villagers who'd rounded up a delegation to come to me, though Dunster lay just outwith the dun lands and was not officially under my protection. I was angry with their elders for letting it get so far, for sitting on their fat pride and their dignity too long, but that was how it worked. They wouldn't have known the Lammyr were even around, not to start with. Never try to sort out a Lammyr nest yourself; not without a good detachment of fighters and a better assortment of blades.

~ *Poor bastard.* Orach nodded at the sagging cadaver on the marsh below. Her voice in my head recalled me to the moment.

~ *Poor bastards, the lot of them,* I told her briskly. ~ *Shall we get on with it?*

~ *I wondered when you were going to say that.*

There was not the usual over-familiar grin on her face, and she watched me strangely, but I'd farted about for long enough. I gestured half of my detachment round to the back of the hut-cluster and sent two men up with Branndair into the raggedy birks: just as well, since the first Lammyr came from there.

It gave a shriek that could have been a laugh, grabbed a branch with a bony hand and let the rotten limb snap and carry it down onto Braon. She, anticipating it well, sprawled and rolled, and the man who'd followed it down from the trees swept his blade across its scrawny back, severing the spine. By now the others were tumbling from doors and broken windows, but we'd taken them well enough by surprise. They were fast, but we had the space we needed.

There were four of them besides the first, and I'd made allowance for more. That didn't mean it wasn't a fair fight. As I hacked and dodged and flew, I felt always in the back of my skull my reluctant admiration for them. So efficient, so fast, as scruple-free as sharks but smarter. The translucent thinness of them sometimes made it hard to know where your blade had passed, and that was what deluded me: thinking I'd gutted the leader when all I'd done was flesh-wound it. The pallid blood spurted and I somersaulted back out of its way, but it played dead with conviction. When I was stupid enough to turn my back on what I'd thought lifeless, it took Orach to leap to my defence and pin it back to the earth with her sword.

As I caught my breath and my balance it blinked ruefully up at me, patting Orach's blade. 'Spoilsport.' Colourless blood sprayed from its grinning lips.

'What is it with you lot, Sleekshard?' I glanced out at the drowned man in the bay, then up towards the village. 'Haven't you got enough to do at home?' So far as I knew the Lammyr still roamed the queen's lands at will, since her pact with them four centuries ago. I'd always assumed there was plenty to entertain them there.

'Singing for our supper gets dull. And Kate has other pets.'

'What's that supposed to mean?'

'Oh, work it out. I'm off.' Sleekshard rolled its eyes dramatically back in its head, the death-grin already stretching its yellow skin. Irritated, I snapped my fingers, and Orach withdrew her blade, then plunged it belatedly into its shrivelled heart.

'They're never content,' she observed.

'No, but they're happy.' Carraig leaned his hands on his knees, gasping for breath as he rubbed Branndair's neck appreciatively. The wolf had saved his throat, for about the fifth time. 'Are we done?'

It took me a while to be certain of five deaths, but at last we could get down to cleaning our blades in the burn that trickled seawards. I sheathed mine, satisfied. 'Thanks, Orach.'

'You're so welcome.' There was that edge in her voice again, and I cast her a puzzled glance. I'd have asked her, I'd have soothed whatever lay between us and apologised for my forgotten crime, but she turned away as I opened my mouth, nodded to another fighter, and the two of them went out together to retrieve the drowned corpse.

'Women,' I grumbled under my breath.

Sionnach sized me up with his cool eyes, and a couple of the others exchanged amused glances.

But nobody actually laughed.

* * *

The thing with Lammyr is that you know it has to be done, you know it's right. You know the bargain you make with them, and the nature of both sides; everyone's motives are clear. Human beings: now, they're more of a pain in the neck.

I was still riled and distracted by Orach's behaviour when we returned to the village, and I wasn't in the mood for its new captain's attitude. He seemed sulky more than grateful, and he fed and watered us with a bad grace, as if he was looking after his annoying neighbour's strayed sheep. There were plain wooden tables with benches outside the inn; he entertained us there, supposedly to bask in the warmth of the sun, but we knew he wanted shot of us as soon as possible and he didn't want us ensconced inside some cosy building.

'I daresay it was good of you to come,' he said snarkily, when the man who brought the beers had turned away, 'but I'm still not sure who requested it. Dunster isn't your protectorate, Murlainn.'

'Somebody has to protect you,' said Braon mildly, 'since you're clearly incapable of doing it yourselves.'

I liked that woman. I'd liked her since she was nine years old, and a hostage to Calman Ruadh, and I'd rescued her from the noose, but not before she'd rescued me, too, from my youthful over-confidence. I flashed her a grin, she returned it flirtatiously, and Orach followed our exchange, frowning slightly.

Gods, what had everyone got against me lately? Aggravated, I turned back to the village captain. 'Were you going to ignore them till they'd wiped out the lot of you?'

'We handle our problems carefully.'

'You don't handle Lammyr *carefully*,' I said.

'You take the greatest damn care with your queen,' he spat.

'That'll be why she isn't mine,' I began, but as the captain's eyes widened at the blatant treason, a younger Sithe inter-rupted, clearly disturbed by the tone of the discussion.

'It was me, Nuall,' he confessed sheepishly. 'I called Murlainn. It had all gone far enough.'

His captain glared at him. 'I'm your chief and I deal with these things my way. Do you think Kate's going to like it that we called on someone else's justice? Have you any idea how much diplomacy it will take to pacify her? If she'll be pacified.'

'You go on sacrificing your people to diplomacy,' I said, 'and you'll find yourself in my protectorate whether you want it or not.'

That wasn't something I had a right to do, and he opened his mouth to remonstrate, but Sionnach intervened.

'What Murlainn means,' he said, 'is that we should put an offer to your village. See how they answer.'

Heavy silence blanketed the group. Sionnach actually talking must have unnerved the captain, because he back-tracked swiftly, averting his sullen gaze.

'It's not that we aren't grateful,' he muttered at last. 'Lusadair's right, it had gone too far. I thank you for your action, and for your offer. But I decline it.'

'Good call, Nuall.'

The impeccably-blocking newcomer, flanked by two more fighters, hitched himself onto the neighbouring table and rested his booted feet on its bench. He took his time smiling around us all, though his companions wore baleful expressions.

'Dunster has a certain minor strategic importance. Kate values that, and your neutrality. Don't piss it away.'

'Buy you a beer, Cuthag?' asked Braon brightly. 'It's the least I can do before I gut you.'

'In your fevered dreams, Shorty.'

I winced, and Fearna sucked in a breath through his teeth,

but Orach laid her hand on Braon's shoulder. ~ *Let's all be grown ups, shall we?*

'You want to pick a fight, you take it out of Dunster,' said Nuall darkly.

'That's fair enough,' I said mildly, 'but nobody wants a fight right now. Do they, Cuthag?'

'I'm glad to hear it,' said the pompous little shit. 'It's not the time or the place, and Murlainn knows it, even if his pack dogs don't.'

I heard Braon's intake of breath, and this time I put a hand on her arm, feeling the muscles twitch. 'You may not want a scrap but if you're going to insult my fighters, you should stop fingering your pommel.' I gave him a sweet smile. 'Anyway, you'll go blind.'

Braon sniggered as Cuthag snatched his fingers from his knife hilt, glaring at me. 'I don't have to pick a fight with rebels. Ask around, Murlainn. MacSween's clann don't want any part of your treason either.'

His lieutenant chipped in. 'You're on your own, Murlainn. You'll be on your knees to Kate before the year's out.'

'That's two separate statements.' I felt the smile thinning on my face, and I stood up. There was no point trading insults with Cuthag and his sidekicks.

Cuthag took it for an admission of defeat; I could tell by his grin. 'The Bloodstone is Kate's by sovereign right. Let me know when you want to hand him over, Murlainn.'

'Oh, I'll be in touch long before then.' I could feel my temper fraying, and Braon was on the point of killing him. I felt warm breath on my hand and glanced down to see Branndair lick it, then grin up at me. When a wolf had to remind me not to lash out, it was definitely time to leave.

I abandoned my beer half-drunk and let my fighters follow me away from the tables where Cuthag was installing himself. The village captain Nuall followed me.

'I'm not trying to offend you, Murlainn.' He matched his pace to mine with difficulty. 'Dunster isn't just strategic, it's vulnerable.'

Orach knew I wasn't going to engage him in conversation while he made excuses. 'Your vulnerability isn't anything to do with your geographical position,' she remarked.

He shot her a glare. 'But Cuthag was right. You haven't got enough support to defy Kate.'

'Support's irrelevant,' I said. 'She wants the Veil destroyed. I'll fight her to my last breath. Or hers.'

'And take half the clanns in the west with you?' he exploded. 'Don't follow your brother to certain death. He's lost and so is your cause.'

Admirable, that willingness to throw Conal's death in my face. I came to a halt, turned and stared into his eyes, but he had more nerve than I gave him credit for.

'I told you, Murlainn, I don't want to quarrel with you. There are plenty who agree with you, plenty who dread the Veil dying, but Kate has the power and Kate will have her way. Why cling to a doomed life?'

'It's life I'm clinging to, Nuall, doomed or not. You won't hang onto it yourself if she kills the *Sgath*.'

'That's a matter for debate. She promises us protection, and she says she'll keep the full-mortals under control.'

'Aye, right.' I smirked. 'Because they're *so* easy to control, and *notoriously* fond of us.'

An apologetic shrug. 'You can't force our support.'

'But Kate can.'

He inclined his head. 'Maybe that's so. That's the way of

it, Murlainn. Of course you won't let her take your son, but she isn't threatening to take mine. I'm sorry.'

'I understand,' I gritted. 'Believe it or not.'

His voice lost its fierce courage, as if he was suddenly afraid of being overheard. 'And I do thank you for dealing with the Lammyr,' he muttered. 'You're right. We couldn't do it ourselves or we'd rouse Kate against us. We're grateful to you.'

When I walked on, he didn't follow, and I felt a disproportionate tide of relief. I didn't want to continue that argument. My sense of righteousness was easily shaken. He was right: Conal was dead, and no doubt with him any chance we'd ever had of defying Kate. I wished I could believe in our eventual victory. Still, I had to try harder. There was no common ground. Kate wanted Rory, the Bloodstone; she couldn't have him. Even if I lost all faith in Conal's beliefs – even in the unlikely event my clann did too – there was no getting past the fact of Rory.

We'd left the horses in a shallow rocky bowl between the two low hills to the south of Dunster, untethered by anything but our wills. The blue roan might have defied me if he'd felt like it, but he'd clearly chosen proud contempt over disobedience. He hated being left out of a fight.

I mounted him, and turned his head towards the dun. The others fell in at my back, silent. Orach's mind brushed mine, sympathetic but a little reserved, and my mood blackened. So now successful raids saw us sent packing from rescued villages with our tails between our legs. Five dead Lammyr, and an end to their spree of sly killings, left small sense of triumph.

Kate was getting better. And I'd have loved to know where she was getting her freshly-minted confidence.

JED

'Ah, boy.' Gocaman's voice quietened. 'There are humans who touch a Lammyr's desiccated heart. They fall in something like love. Skinshanks had a protégé, and he tired of him, and that is all.'

Jed knew fine there was something wrong with the scenario. The infant Rory had vanished. The horse he rode was a ghostly skeletal nag, and though Gocaman was at his back, he could feel no heartbeat. Nor was Gocaman's touch warm and reassuring; where his fingers touched Jed's bare arm they were cold and clammy, and Jed was filled with so dark a foreboding, he didn't dare look round.

All the same he had to, because he always did. It was the only way he knew out of the wretched dream after so many times. Often he'd waited longer to do it, in the hope of finding that the dream led somewhere else, somewhere better, that he could evade the moment of turning. But that wasn't a hope he held on to any more, not even in his sleep.

'Why, Jed. So nervous! Don't be afraid. I won't hurt you, after all. I like you!'

Jed took a deep sobbing breath, starting to cry so humiliatingly as he always did. Then, as he always did, he turned.

It was Gocaman's dirty rag of cloth wrapped round its head, Gocaman's leather hat tipped rakishly over its eyes, but it wasn't Gocaman's head. It was the head of Skinshanks, smiling at him, the head he'd last seen tied by the hair to Seth's horse. And because that was all, that was it done with for one more night, it was almost with relief that Jed let himself scream.

74

'Jed. Jed.' Iolaire's hand was on his shoulder.

He sat bolt upright, leaning his elbows on his knees and rubbing his hands across his cropped head. The casement window was wide open, but it was too hot in here. He could feel sweat on his scalp, and the back of his neck was wet with it.

'Jed. Rory is here. He's in the dun. It's okay.' Iolaire's voice was low and soothing.

'It wasn't Rory.'

'Skinshanks, then. Again?'

Jed nodded. Shoving the blankets off his body he went to the pitcher of water by the door, gasping as he upended it over his head. The water wasn't tepid at all, it was bitingly cold. It shouldn't be that way on such a hot night. He turned to the white wolf sprawled by the unlit fire, her head raised and her amber eyes fixed on him. Then he frowned at Iolaire, who was tugging the blanket back around his nakedness. 'Is it cold?'

'It ain't warm.' Iolaire shook his head. 'Get dry and come back to bed, Jed. You'll catch your death.'

Jed scraped his fingernails across his scalp again, shivering as his wet skin at last felt the cool air. Better. 'I won't catch my death. Not till *he* does.'

Iolaire lay back grinning, arms behind his head. 'I take it you want to go hunting again.'

'Again.'

'Ten years, Jed. Ten years you've been hunting him, since you learnt to wield a sword and since you grew enough years on you to do it. Skinshanks has been dead for thirteen. Do you think you'll ever get Laszlo now? Do you think the dreams will stop if you do?'

Jed blinked. But why had he learnt to wield a sword, if

not for that? The man Laszlo had slaughtered was, if not his father, then the man who should have been his father, and Laszlo had killed him with trickery. He'd trapped Conal through the people he loved. He'd killed him through Eili and Finn and *Jed,* and that was what Jed couldn't forgive. He didn't see why he should.

Jed scrubbed at his head with a thin towel, digging his fingers into his skull. Sometimes he thought if he scraped hard enough, he could dig the dreams right out.

'I don't care about the dreams,' he lied. 'I'll kill him anyway. If I get twice the dreams, if he haunts me for a hundred years, I'll kill him anyway.' And that part was true.

Iolaire flung back the blanket. 'All right. You want me to freeze to death too?'

Grinning in defeat, Jed lay down at his side but propped himself up on one elbow as he pulled the blanket back around them both. 'It's pleasantly cool, you big girl.' He stared down into Iolaire's laughing eyes. 'Will you come with me anyway?'

'Always. You know that.'

'Iolaire.' He placed his hand on the man's ribcage to feel his heartbeat. 'Do I... do you think I...'

'Could turn into a cold psychopathic killer without the love of a good man? Oh, absolutely.' Iolaire winked solemnly.

'Don't joke.'

'Jed.' Iolaire laid his own hand over his and linked their fingers. 'So Skinshanks liked you. Skinshanks is *dead*. Who knows what goes on in a Lammyr's head? Maybe just a notion to torment you for years with a throwaway remark.'

'No.'

'Yes. Maybe. Meanwhile I like you too, and look at it this way: I'm alive and I'm not a Lammyr.' Iolaire laid his other hand against Jed's cheek, and Jed leaned his head into it, closing his eyes.

'It's not just the Lammyr,' he mumbled wretchedly. 'The Selkyr wanted me. One of the ones that took Leonora Shiach. I used to think I'd misunderstood, that it wasn't me at all, that it was going for Conal because he was wearing his death on him by then like a coat. But I know in my heart it wasn't. It wanted me, Iolaire.'

'Hush.' Iolaire drew down his head and kissed him. 'It's the middle of the night. Things look worse than they are. Dreams hang heavy. If a Selkyr wanted either of us it'd be me. I'm the renegade, I'm the one with the price on my head, so don't you go getting ideas above your station.'

Jed laughed. 'Is that supposed to make me feel better?'

'We'll hunt tomorrow and that's what'll make you feel better. Who knows? We might even track him down. Now for once, will you let me give you sleep?'

'No. Not even you.' Jed lay down as Iolaire's arm closed round his shoulder. 'And don't sneak it to me thinking I won't notice. I'll know.'

'I wouldn't dare.' There was laughter in Iolaire's throat.

Jed closed his eyes, lulled by the echoing beat of his lover's heart through his ribs. He knew the dream wouldn't come again, not tonight, but he thought sleep wouldn't either. He was wrong. It was Iolaire who lay wakeful and motionless, staring at the play of reflected sea-light on the wooden rafters and listening to the little dream-grunts of the white wolf, unwilling to move, unwilling to risk waking Jed.

Sleep was one thing, dreams another. Iolaire lifted a hand and rested it gently, so gently on the back of Jed's neck.

Deviousness and treachery came easier to him than they once had. And one small breach of trust might be forgiveable. His fingertip tingled where it touched the very base of Jed's skull.

Anyway, who said memories couldn't spark unbidden?

★ ★ ★

Nearly two years. So much less distant than Skinshanks, he'd have thought fate might be kind enough to let him dream that every night, instead of the Lammyr. All the same, even in his sleep Jed felt a disembodied kind of shock at the sudden chill and pleasure of the recall.

A light breeze, and a bright summer day, clear to the horizon. Seth had taken the stone steps two at a time to join Fearna on the battlement, the pair of them staring out at the rider, still distant but riding ever closer across the machair.

'He's blocking, Fearna.'

'Aye, but I know his handsome face fine. It's Iolaire MacEarchar.'

Seth slanted his eyes at Jed, five yards away, but Jed could only look away, fix his stare at the man on horseback. He had not felt this panicked terror since he was seventeen and facing his first Lammyr. Seth must know what had stirred inside him the day they brawled with a detachment of Kate's at Kinlaggan. A proper, weaponless slugfest on neutral territory, alcohol-fuelled and cathartic and bloody; and in the midst of it, two rival fighters slumped across each other beneath upturned tables, forgotten, exhausted, and grinning, and finally laughing so hard the fight had flagged and ended before they even staggered back to their feet.

Seth must know it. He'd been in his head often enough, before Jed banished him.

'Send out a guard, Fearna.' Seth's voice broke into Jed's thoughts now. 'Disarm him and bring him in.'

Iolaire's horse ambled at an easy walk, watched by every man and woman on the parapet. Two of Seth's fighters rode out of the gate of the dun, and Iolaire stretched his arms out wide as they drew their horses abreast of him.

Calmly Iolaire reached for the buckle of his sword belt and unfastened it, passing it to the man on his right. He did the same with his dirk, and his hunting knife, then clasped his wrists in front of him to let the woman on his left bind his hands. Only when the three were riding back abreast, only when every other eye in the dun was on them; only then did Jed let himself steal another glance at Seth. This time it was Seth who wouldn't meet his eyes.

Seth reached the courtyard as the guards rode in with the newcomer, and the murmuring crowd drew back to let them pass. Jed was five paces behind Seth, loath to follow, unable to stop himself.

One of the guards dismounted and went to help Iolaire off his horse, but he shrugged her off and swung his leg over his horse's neck, stumbling only slightly as he jumped to the ground. He straightened as Seth approached him.

'What do you want, Iolaire?'

The young man's beautiful eyes burned. The pain in them was like a writhing snake, and its coils might as well have been around Jed's throat.

'I'm your bondsman, Murlainn,' said Iolaire flatly, 'that, or kill me. Up to you.'

Seth wrinkled his nose, then glanced at Sionnach, who raised his eyebrows slightly.

'Iolaire,' he said, and stepped close to him. 'Permit me.'

Iolaire's lip curled, but he didn't flinch as Seth gripped his head. Neither of them closed their eyes. They stared at each other silently for long seconds, and no-one in the courtyard breathed or moved.

Seth took a harsh breath and pulled away, then turned to the man who held Iolaire's weapons. 'Give me his dagger.'

The man held it out, eyeing Iolaire apprehensively.

Seth unsheathed the blade with a sound like ripping silk. Lifting Iolaire's bound hands, he slit the cords and stepped back.

'Give him back his sword, Fearna,' he said. 'Welcome, Iolaire. I'm happy you came to me.' Then he turned and walked away, and he only glanced once at Jed, hanging back on the edge of the crowd, weak with sick relief.

★ ★ ★

Jed shut his eyes, then opened them again. Cowardice wasn't alien to him, but it didn't fit well with his self-image. Before he could change his mind again, he knocked on the door.

'What is it?' The voice was empty.

Forcing stillness into his hands, Jed pushed open the door and stepped inside. Iolaire stood in front of the little bunk, his naked sword in one hand and a whetstone in the other. His hard face softened as he looked at Jed.

'Hello, Cuilean,' he said, and sheathed the blade.

Jed turned slowly, studying the room. Not so long ago it had been a weapons store, only converted recently to a place for sentries to rest and grab an hour's uneasy sleep.

It was so cramped it looked overcrowded by the small hard bed and the rough shelf beside it. And here beneath the gate it was so cold Jed could feel it seeping into his bones already.

Anger and embarrassment constricted his throat. 'This isn't what Murlainn intended.'

'This is fine for me.'

'I'm going to report this,' said Jed. 'Who assigned you this room? They'll be lucky if he doesn't have them flogged.'

'Hey, Cuilean, it's *fine*.' Iolaire tilted his head and watched him. 'Thanks for minding. Really. But the man was in a hurry. And I seem to remember killing a friend of his. Don't get him in trouble for my sake, because it is *fine*.' He smiled wryly. 'Besides, I heard Murlainn banned floggings and burned the post.'

'That's true.' Jed looked at the floor, then back up at him. 'I'm ashamed. You rode a long way. I'll sleep here; I'll show you to my room. You can have it tonight and I'll have a word with Seth in the morning. Quietly. Honest.' He smiled.

'I wouldn't hear of it, Cuilean. But thanks.'

'You don't understand. I'll sleep here; you sleep in my room. If you don't agree, I'll sleep in the courtyard.' He couldn't quite meet Iolaire's sea-coloured eyes. 'And bay at the moon all night outside your door.'

Iolaire was silent for such a long time that eventually Jed had to look at him, and then his expression was unreadable. There was gentleness in it, though.

'You're kind, Cuilean.'

'I'm not, believe me.' Jed gave him a thin smile.

'All right. I agree, then. On one condition: you don't sleep here either. You sleep in your own room too.'

Jed swallowed. 'Fine,' he said. 'I'll take the floor.'

'No,' said Iolaire. He stepped forward, and took Jed's hand, and kissed him.

Jed drew back, though his fingers stayed laced in the man's dark hair. 'Iolaire. Why are you here?'

'Your captain knows. No-one else. I'll tell you. But not now.' Iolaire kissed the corner of his mouth again, but Jed drew back.

'I'm nobody's rebound,' he said softly.

'Indeed you're not.' Iolaire stepped back to pull his jumper over his head, then his t-shirt. He was lean and brown and beautiful. 'That was my old life, Jed, and it is behind me. My new life is you. Understand? I didn't come here first and foremost to be Murlainn's bondsman. I came to be yours.'

Jed raised his eyes to his, the terror of the minutes on the battlement still lingering. 'If he'd killed you?'

Iolaire looked away. 'That would have been fine too. Now, Cuilean.' He turned to him again and gave him a smile of breathtaking beauty and longing. 'This room is lacking warmth. Let's give it some before we leave it forever.'

★ ★ ★

As the rippling silver sea-light faded, and the dawn sun painted the rafters gold, and the white wolf stretched and yawned, Iolaire lay and gazed at the roof, while Jed slept, and did not dream of Lammyr.

HANNAH

'That horse isn't even shod.' I flung another armful of dead wood onto the pile in the courtyard, wondering which of my many newly discovered muscles was going to hurt tomorrow. I was knackered. And I wouldn't have gone anywhere near those massive hooves if Rory's father hadn't had a firm grip of one of them, howking out a stone with a knife.

Seth glanced up with his teeth clenched, but I had the annoying notion they were clenched against a smile. 'Tell you what,' he said, shaking a lock of black hair out of his eye. 'You give me any more cheek and I'll get you to shoe him.'

I curled my lip. 'It's your horse.'

'Yeah. That he is.'

'You're that possessive. I reckon you care more about that horse than you do about—'

'Don't finish that sentence.' His eyes glinted silver. 'It's not possessiveness. You want to ride him, go ahead, and don't blame me when you're dead.' He dropped the roan's hoof and it blew affectionately at his neck. 'And don't go thinking you know more about my son than I do.'

He was a snappy swine, but I liked him. I studied his face as I plaited my hair into a single twist. 'You make Rory nervous, y'know.'

Seth leaned back against the roan's flank, looking nonplussed. 'I make him nervous?'

'Yup.' Coming to the end of my braid, I folded my arms.

Seth was watching me very intently and I thought, as I often had over the last days, that I did not like his eyes. Well, it wasn't so much dislike as sharp discomfort. Sometimes it chilled my spine to look at him but sometimes, if I caught him off guard – which was not often and never for long – I could have watched his eyes indefinitely. After all he had beautiful eyes, grey and crystal-clear and so deep-set that the silver light in them shone out of shadow with fierce intensity. But the open laughter of Rory's eyes wasn't there. Seth's were haunted eyes, and the ghosts weren't friendly. They haunted me too: I saw those eyes in my dreams. Maybe I'd murdered Seth in a past life. More likely he'd murdered me.

'He's a bit on his own, that's all,' said Seth.

I remembered in the nick of time that we were talking about Rory. 'Yeah? So why can't you let him lead a normal life?'

'Don't get me started.'

'Aw, you could give him a bit more freedom. Lighten up, you big Nazi.'

It was supposed to be a joke, but his eyes chilled. 'Thing is, I care where Rory is and what he does. You go where you like and do what you like,' said Seth viciously, 'because nobody gives a damn.'

His venom was so unexpected it was like a punch in the stomach. He'd bitten his lip and sworn at himself before I caught my breath.

'You mean Rory has a father,' I spat. 'Even if it's a shit-for-morals control freak, at least he's got one.'

'Forgive me, Hannah. I...'

'No.'

'All right. I'm sorry anyway.' He folded his knife into its

bone handle with a snap. 'You're something else, you are.'

'Yeah. Like I'm not used to insults.'

'That wasn't an insult.' Half-closing his eyes he eased his shoulder blades and pressed them against the horse's shoulder. Rumbling in its throat, it turned its head to blow into his hair. 'Listen, Hannah, Rory's special. That's not sentiment from his doting father. He has responsibilities to a lot of people and I have a responsibility to keep him safe. There are people who would dearly like to get their hands on him.'

Starting with me, I thought, and Seth laughed aloud.

I gave him a dark glare. 'Cut that out. I mean it. You stay out of my head.'

'I'm not in it. You shouldn't think so loud.' He shrugged. 'Anyway, Rory didn't choose this life, but it found him anyway. He has to thole it for the foreseeable future, and if you want to be his friend, so do you.'

I bristled. 'Is that a threat?'

'It is.' He gave me a gorgeous smile. 'Absolutely.'

I couldn't think of an adequate answer. There wasn't another adult on earth who would dare talk to me like that.

'Listen,' he said more gently. 'Do you want me to deal with your uncle?'

Speechless, I forced my jaw shut. I didn't have to be a telepath to know exactly what he meant. If he'd been joking, I'd have said it was a tempting offer.

When I'd got my composure back, I shook my head violently. 'No. Um, no thanks.'

'I mean, tell me to mind my own business if you like.'

I shook my head again, too dumbfounded to tell him any such thing.

'Only I know what he is, you know.'

'Yeah. Uh-huh. Me too.' I managed a gorgeous smile back. 'But no thanks.'

'Let me know if you change your mind.'

'I can handle him. Really. I appreciate it, honest.' Then I laughed, couldn't help it. 'You're something else too.'

'I'll take that not to be an insult either.' Grinning, he slewed his gaze over my shoulder. 'Rory. Your brother awake yet?'

Rory came silently to my side. 'Nah. Iolaire won't let me near him. That's three days in a row he's been asleep till ten.'

'Good. You would be too if you had his nights. Now listen.' Seth gave him a look that could slice bricks. 'You can go out of the dun, but you take Branndair and Liath with you. It's that or an escort of six guards. And I don't want you near that castle up at the Cailleach's Loch.' Seth shook his head. 'That's a bad habit you've got, sneaking round that place.'

'It's a *ruin*, Dad.'

'It's a ruin *now*. I knew the man it belonged to. It's an evil place.'

'You should see it now. On the other side, I mean. Honest to God, it needs a bit of evil to set off the tartan.'

'I've seen it.' Seth bit back a smile. 'No, it's still evil. If you know where to look.'

'You're thinking of some place else, anyway,' I put in. 'That castle's been unoccupied for hundreds of years. The last owner's horribly dead.'

'I'm not thinking of any place else. I'm sure he is deliciously, horribly and entertainingly dead, but I'd be happier if I'd seen his body.'

'Ghoul.'

'Takes one to know one. Now get this, Rory. I'm going to the watergate at Loch Sgillinn and I won't be more than a few hours. You'd better be here when I get back, okay?'

'Yeah?' I winked. 'What if he's not?'

Seth winked back. 'There'll be a full-scale war and many casualties.' He slipped a bridle onto the roan's head and buckled the throatlash, then gripped its withers and hauled himself onto its bare back. 'I might be bringing somebody back. *Try* and be civilised, will you?' He leaned down to rumple Rory's hair, like he was five or something.

I half-closed one eye. That was the paternal expression I liked least on Seth, the one that made me most uncomfortable. Perhaps it was sheer jealousy, because there had never been anyone to look at me like that; or maybe it was just that it didn't look natural, like it was too recently learned to fit his hard face.

Beneath the weight of the sheathed sword on his back Seth stretched his shoulders as a stablehand led out a garron. Seth took its lead rein, then spoke to his horse and rode out of the dun with the pony behind him.

I gave Rory a sidelong glance, and a wicked smirk.

'And now,' I said, 'let's misbehave.'

FINN

When I broke the surface, and my lungs filled with the right air for the first time in thirteen years, it tasted different instantly. I wanted to laugh. I wanted to hoot. All I could do was stagger forward, undignified, into shallow water. With the weight of my backpack dragging me sideways, I only narrowly saved myself from floundering back for a proper soaking.

Behind me, there was a guttural mortified shriek as Faramach breached the water's skin and vanished into the dull dazzle of sunlight. I pulled a limp strand of weed from my hair and flicked it back into the loch. Watergates: always such a dignified way to travel. And of course, it was at exactly that moment I realised I wasn't alone.

Seth's impulsive smile disappeared as fast as mine. He rode forward from the bank till the blue roan was up to its hocks in the water, then left the reins loose on its neck and folded his arms. The breeze that feathered the gull-wing loch lifted the black hair on his neck and stirred the roan's mane; smelling the distant sea, it snuffed and blew and pawed the water. Beyond them, on the bank, a thickset garron browsed the heather.

I hooked my thumbs into my backpack straps, wriggling my shoulders.

'Glad that still works,' I said, to the roan rather than to Seth. 'Be embarrassing if they had to drag the loch for me.'

Seth didn't smile. 'You've been a while.'

'Longer than I meant to, big cousin.' I looked at the sky. 'Where's Faramach gone?'

'That bird always hated watergates. He'll be back when his dignity is, more's the pity.' He stared at me without a hint of a welcoming smile.

I pushed a wisp of hair out of my eyes. 'Seth. What did I do this time?'

'Nothing.' He bit his lip. 'Nothing, Finn. I'm only selfish. It's kind of hard to change.'

'Don't, then.' I let myself smile at him again as he rode a circle round me.

He didn't look any different. I'd seen him now and again over the years, the last time a year ago, and he never looked any different. He still wore his hair long, and strands of it still fell forward into his clear grey eyes. His face was just as sharp and beautiful as it always had been. He looked as he had when I'd left him on the beach more than a decade ago with a toddler on his shoulders. Thirteen years: that was nothing for him. Nothing.

For me it was forever, that was all.

I found I couldn't speak; not that there was nothing I wanted to say. There was so much of it, it was a logjam in my head. A year it was since I'd said goodbye to him last, since my gaunt and frightened mother had gripped my arm at the door of Tornashee as if afraid he'd steal me away there and then. His eyes meeting hers over my shoulder, his understanding with her complete, their deal unbroken. He'd walked away down the drive with his pack slung over his shoulder, and he hadn't looked back. And I hadn't run to him, I hadn't shouted after him, because if I'd done that he'd have turned back for me, I know he would. And my deal with her was intact, too. Back then it was.

I licked my lips, still trying to say something that mattered, but none of it would come. Instead I grabbed up the bulky extra pack at my feet and lugged it with me as I waded forward onto the beach, dumping it in the sand.

'We don't ever get to travel light, do we? I hope that's everything you wanted.'

He looked at the pack as if he didn't much care, and he didn't check the contents. 'Thanks.'

Frowning, I slipped my own backpack from my shoulders with a grunt of relief, then sat down in the sand and tilted my face to the watery sun. I heard the dull echo of hooves on wet stones in shallow water, then the soft thud of Seth dismounting. Opening one eye, I watched him sit down beside me, his stare focused on the loch and the low rolling hills beyond it.

'I'm sorry about your mother,' he said.

I shrugged. 'She was brave. You've no idea.'

'Yes I do. I knew her a long time. She was always brave.'

'I didn't know. She was so scared, but she was so brave. Seth.' I bit my lip. 'I spent my entire adolescence despising her and when I found out I loved her it was too late.'

'Finn. We all spend our adolescence despising our parents. It's in the job description.'

I chucked a stone at the loch. 'We're not supposed to get that disease, are we? But once it got its claws into her, it wouldn't let go. Why?'

He gave the roan a sharp whistle through his teeth, and it jerked its head round resentfully, striking the water hard with a hoof. It was doing nothing wrong that I could see.

'You look bloody exhausted,' he told me at last.

I didn't want his pity; it made my throat hurt. 'You try

reminding a bunch of full-mortal doctors that they even have a patient.'

He looked at me at last and what I saw in his eyes wasn't pity at all. 'I'm glad it's over.'

It should have been cruel but it wasn't. 'I am too. Seth. Answer me.'

He rubbed his hands over his face. 'I don't know, Finn. I don't know why.'

Round my neck hung a crude claw pendant, a child's practice piece. The stone from its setting had been removed long ago. I rolled it in my fingers and ran a sharp talon point under my thumbnail.

I muttered, 'Was it because she broke her oath?'

'Your fault, you mean?' He gave me one of his old glares. 'Course not. You know what I think, Finn. Oaths, curses: put it out of your head. People believe in superstition and shit, they shouldn't swear oaths. Not if there's a chance they won't keep them.'

'She meant to keep it.' I fumbled for another stone and skimmed it clumsily; it sank as soon as it hit the surface. 'But she came for me anyway, all those years ago. So how could I leave her?'

With an edge of resentment he said, 'If she'd come through, we could have helped her.'

'No, you couldn't.'

'Not that way, no. To her end, I mean. Eili would have done that for her.'

'She would never have come through. Never. What would have been the point? The greatest surrender of her life, and right at the end of it? She wouldn't even contemplate going to the Selkyr.'

'No. Your mother was too damn brave and too damn

proud. And when you feel guilty, Finn, try and remember that keeping you away from here was what kept her hanging on.'

'You are a bastard.' *He's the person he always was; get over it.* 'I couldn't give her my word, so the least I could do was stay till it was over. She had a good death. They don't let you suffer.'

Seth said, 'Nor do we.'

'Seth. Please.' I didn't want to cry.

'Sorry. Told you I was selfish.' Reaching for my hand, he interlinked our fingers. 'It gets better, Finn. At first you don't think it will, you don't even want it to, but it does, like any wound. Then you know you've betrayed them, but it happens anyway. It might leave a dirty great scar but it scabs over, it heals. That's how life works. It's the way it goes on.'

'I've betrayed her just coming here.' He was right: the guilt was a racking thing, all the more so because it had never crossed my mind to respect Stella's wishes. I had waited only for my mother's death before doing what Stella had so desperately wanted me not to do.

Seth was watching me, I could feel it, but he sounded surprisingly kind. 'You've no obligation to the dead, Finn. Our lives would never be our own.'

'Speaking of which. Eili's wound? Has that healed?'

Seth was silent for a long moment. 'Eili's grief is all poisoned with rage. That's my fault. That doesn't heal so well.' He shut his eyes, smiling. 'She'll kill me, of course.'

'She'll have to get through me,' I said.

He raised his eyebrows, amused. 'Who'd have thought it?' Tightening his fingers around my hand, he lifted it to study the puckered white weals on my palm. 'She'd have mended that properly, if you'd asked.'

'I didn't want her to. It doesn't hurt. Does yours?'

'Sometimes. If Eili's in a very bad mood.' His laugh was a little forced.

'It hurts all the time, doesn't it?' I frowned, suspicion scratching at my gut.

'Well. Why did you keep your scars?'

'That's different. I told you, they don't hurt.'

'You kept them to remind you. Eili keeps mine alive to remind me.' He squeezed my fingers. 'It's because of you and Jed it's only the crossbow scars. I get sick when I think how it would be if she'd had access to the... to...'

He still found it hard to say it, I realised. 'The whipping scars,' I finished for him.

'They healed by themselves. You did right to keep the healers away. Especially *her*.' He tried to release me, but I tightened my fingers on his. I was not going to let him withdraw and shrink into himself in that maddening way of his.

'You never explained that one,' I said lightly, touching a deep crude scar on his palm.

'Jings, Dorsal, this is like *Jaws*.' He laughed, and I smiled, pleased I'd pulled him back from his dark place. 'That's nothing sinister.' Mildly embarrassed, he mumbled, 'Blood brother cut.'

'*Murlainn!* How teenage!' I examined it, still not letting him pull away. It was no mere nick. It had once been a savage slash, and it ran from the lowest joint of his little finger to the base of his thumb. 'Were you after a complete blood transfusion?' I flicked it disapprovingly with a fingertip. 'I hope the other guy looks this bad.'

Seth grinned. 'Oh, he does.'

'So who? Why didn't you tell me before?'

'I never told you 'cause you wouldn't believe it.' He pulled me to my feet.

'Okay, be mysterious.' I nodded at the blue roan. 'What kind of mood is he in?'

'Doesn't matter. You're not riding him.' Seth lifted the pack of hardware supplies and tied it onto the garron's saddle, making it sag to the side and earning a reproving glare from the pony.

'You're strapping me onto the pack horse or what?'

He jiggled his eyebrows. 'Don't put ideas in my head.'

'Okay, pal, I'll walk. And the whisky I brought you, I'll drink it myself.'

'Ha! Still a little madam. I wish your Uncle Conal could hear you. You're not walking, Dorsal, and I'll be deprived of the sight of you slung across a pack horse. I've got something for you.' He untied a fabric bundle from the garron's saddle, then unrolled it with care, and when he turned he was dangling a bridle from his fingers. It was black leather, but the cheekpiece and noseband were chased with delicate silverwork.

I stared at it, unable to swallow. 'That was lost.'

'Yes.' He ran a finger across the inlay. 'That was my intention, but it washed up in the dunes after a storm last month.'

I took it, fingertips trembling. 'What am I supposed to do with it?'

'Call him, that's all. You know how, if you don't think about it too hard.' Mounting the roan he swung its head towards the north and west, and the garron fell in behind.

'Yeah?' I shouted. 'And what if he kills me when he gets here?'

'You have his bridle. He wants you.' Seth gave me a grin over his shoulder. 'Call him. I dare you.'

And so – that being the one challenge I couldn't resist – I called him.

* * *

I'm sure the clann were happier to see Conal's horse back than they were to see me, but that was fair enough. We hadn't exactly parted on good terms all those years ago. They held as much against me as I did against them.

The horse seemed to know my feelings. It stood very calmly, making no trouble, accepting the stares and the exclamations of the clann, its head hooked fondly over my shoulder. I saw flashes of its memory, still vivid from the calling of it. Dark cold water, drifting green weed. Blood and prey. Careless silent freedom. And from long before that, visions of fighting and running on the moor: blue sky, bird-song and cirrus. Another mind and body in absolute sync with its own; the weight of a human that was no weight at all; the sharp keen awareness of another self. The vicious triumph and the awful pain of battle. And death, and loss, and a corpse; and freedom again, sadder and lonelier this time.

I touched its muzzle, and knew that it Saw just as much of me. The oddest sensation, but not an unwelcome one.

'It's unusual,' Seth had said, unwilling as ever to express any overt shock or awe. 'Hard enough to get these brutes to submit once.'

Submission was hardly the issue. But I knew he knew that.

If the fires of resentment towards me still burned too fiercely in any of the clann, the horse had at least silenced them for now. For that I was outrageously grateful. Only one of them outstared me, eyes frigid and hostile.

'So you're Finn, are you? I don't remember you at *all*.'

Well, I recognised Rory, even after all these years; I recognised him from his father's eyes and his cocky beauty. He had got himself an acolyte, a hard-faced redheaded girl with the apparently permanent sneer of a teenager with a grudge. She stood at his side like some kind of bodyguard, her expression mirroring all the contempt in his. Rory's eyes had transfixed me since I rode into the dun at his father's side. Or rather, if he'd taken his sullen stare off me it was only to glare at the black horse. There was more to this, I thought, than jealousy of my friendship with Seth.

'Yes,' I said. 'Hi, Rory.'

Folding his arms, he nodded at the horse. It eyed him back.

He said, 'Do you just whistle, and they come?'

I didn't miss the way he raised his voice so Seth would catch the barb in it. Seth didn't miss it either, but he ignored the boy, and went on brushing the roan's hind-quarters.

God, but Rory reminded me of his father: Seth the way he used to be, Seth at his worst. Really, who did the little tosser think he was, when I'd wiped his backside and dried his tears, and risked my life to rescue him, and abased myself before Eili to save the hide of his wretched father?

'I suppose you fancied my brother.'

'I suppose I did.' I was hanging onto my temper by my fingernails. 'Then.'

'I suppose Jed was too young to know any better.'

I'd opened my mouth to tear a strip off him when Rory's head was knocked forward by a casual flick of someone's hand. 'Cheeky wee toerag. Hello, Finn.'

I think my mouth fell open a little with my helpless

smile. Thirteen years had made no difference to Seth but for Jed it had been another whole lifetime. He still shaved his hair to soft brown stubble and his eyes were still dark, deep-set and framed by the longest lashes imaginable, but the juvenile delinquent look was gone. Skinniness had turned to hard leanness, furtiveness into watchful ease, and the wary insecurity into confidence. He was a man, I real-ised. He went and turned into a man when I wasn't looking. And those years meant so much more to Jed than they did to the rest of us.

He looked content. He wasn't happy, not mindlessly happy, but he just reeked of contentment and belonging. For a moment I was even more blindingly envious of him than I'd been all those years ago, leaving him to the life that was rightfully mine. Then the resentment was gone like some half-seen landscape into the past, and I gave him a huge grin.

'Jed.' I let him grab me and lift me up, squeezing me till I thought my ribcage would rupture. 'Jed, you look so *different!'*

'Look who's talking.' Jed gave my cheek a smacking kiss and set me back down, and that was when I caught sight of the scar on his palm. It was only a fleeting glimpse, but I couldn't miss it: so crude and deep, a vicious white wound that ran all the way from his little finger to the base of his thumb.

Seth was watching my thoughts, so I gave him a small piece of my mind.

~ *What have you done to each other?*

'I'm sorry,' said Jed, still determinedly unaware of anything passing between minds. 'I haven't been avoiding you. I was asleep. Iolaire refused to wake me up, on the grounds that I won't let him put me to sleep in the first place.' He scowled at the dark-haired man behind him.

'Hey Iolaire, meet Finn,' interrupted Rory. 'Don't worry. This is the one who put him off women for life.'

'You.' Jed took him by the scruff of the neck, then booted him gently in the backside. 'Get lost. Take your father's horse and finish the grooming.'

'Take Finn's while you're at it.' Seth threw the brush to Rory. 'Don't look so nervous, Hannah. If my horse bites anyone it'll be my son, and that's no bad thing.'

Despite the girl's scowl, her fear of the blue roan was almost tangible. It was oh, so tempting to make her trip over her own feet as she turned to follow Rory, but perhaps I'd grown out of those destructive urges at last. I tried a more genuine smile, but Hannah had turned her back already and she didn't see it.

'Sorry,' said Seth, shaking his head. 'Rory's showing off. It's the girl. There's nobody his own age here and he's far too impressed.'

'She's not from here?' I was startled.

He laughed. 'Rory picked her up in the otherworld. Mother's a runaway, the father's a Sithe. Either he's dead or he's back over here and living in *blissful* ignorance.'

'Or he walked out.' Jed's tone had an edge like a blade. 'It's not like you have to be full-mortal to walk out on your offspring.'

'Well,' shrugged Seth after a brief silence. 'I asked for that.'

I didn't know what to say, so I kept my mouth shut. God, but they had years of history between them, years I wasn't party to. Acutely once more I felt the loss of the time, but there was no point resenting my dead mother, and no point blaming Seth. I'd put myself in exile through my hatred for the clann. It might have taken me years to admit it, but Seth had been right to send me away.

But oh, I was glad to be back.

'Give it a rest, you two.' The man called Iolaire rolled his eyes.

'Anyway, shut it. You're embarrassing Finn.' Seth nodded at me but he spoke to Jed.

'No you're not,' I said.

They both ignored me. 'Let's take her riding. See if she still falls off when she trots.'

'Still wh–? You *cheeky* bastards, I'll run you both into the ground.'

'Aye aye, that definitely sounds like her.' Jed nodded solemnly at Seth. 'You brought the right one. Grown into her looks, hasn't she?'

'Told you she had.' But the laughter had gone out of Seth's voice a little, and he looked at me oddly.

Iolaire winked at me. 'So, Fionnuala. Nice to be back with the grown-ups?'

I realised I knew him. It was a familiar name, and his face was definitely one I remembered: fine-boned and gypsy-handsome, his eyes warm with laughter, his hair mahogany brown. His earlobe was pierced by a small gold ring that was not removable. I could see the tiny flaw in the gold where it had been soldered into an unbroken ring, and besides, I'd seen it before.

'I know you,' I said, and smiled.

Jed preened. 'Yes. That Iolaire. Unsurprisingly, he couldn't stay away from me.'

Iolaire dug him in the ribs. 'What he means is, he was so clearly lost without me, I took pity.'

'You defected from Kate?' I was nervously impressed. I glanced around for the lover I remembered from Kate's caverns. 'And what about Gealach?'

'What about her?' Iolaire shrugged blithely. 'Listen, I need to see to my horse; she's threatening lame. See you later, Finn?' He turned on his heel.

'Wait. I'll come.' Jed shot me a reassuring wink as he went after his lover.

I knew when Seth dropped a casual arm round my shoulders that my faux pas was a bad one. 'Oh, no. I'm sorry.'

'Don't be,' said Seth. 'He's not offended, he's still hurting.' His fingers tightened on my arm, then hung loose again. 'Laszlo took Gealach.'

'Oh. Poor Iolaire. But he doesn't seem, uh–'

'Well, these things happen, and they weren't bound. Iolaire might still have had her, if his pride could take the sharing. But Laszlo's couldn't. He finds it hard enough not being the only one for Kate.'

'Yes.' And Seth should know. 'I see.'

'You don't. Gealach was carrying Iolaire's child.'

'His *child?*' It took my breath away. 'And she went to Laszlo?'

'I doubt she had a choice. The rumour is, Kate spell-bound her. Kind of a gift. Laszlo was getting over-possessive, and Kate needed a second lover for him.' His voice was scathing, but I knew that was as much for himself as anyone. 'For her busy periods, y'know?'

'The–' I swallowed. 'What happened about the–'

'The inconvenient child? Kate charmed it right out of Gealach's womb.'

I felt the blood drain out of my face. Across the years I

heard Leonie tell me: *There aren't many children, Finn.* 'I don't believe it.'

'Don't you?' asked Seth. He put his long fingers against my face and tipped it up so that he could look at my eyes.

I felt him right inside my mind, but surprisingly I didn't resent it, and I didn't fight it. It was like standing back, holding wide the door, letting him look because he'd asked nicely. ~ *All right,* I told him silently. ~ *I've got nothing to hide. You?*

Seth was gone from my head, biting his lip as he half-smiled. 'You do believe it.'

'Yeah. It was only a figure of speech, y'know.'

But I did know what it was to be in thrall to Kate NicNiven. We each knew that the other knew. And one day, I thought, eyeing Seth, I'll find out if you still are.

~ *Thirteen years, woman.* He smiled at me sadly. ~ *Don't we trust each other yet?*

I tried to smile back. I disliked Kate slinking into my life and my mind the moment I came home. High sunlight blazed on the dun, bleaching the flagstones; the scent of the machair was in the air and my skin was warm with summer, but her name inside my head felt as if a shard of dirty ice was lodged there.

Seth was watching me, thoughtful and sad.

'I know,' was all he said.

SETH

'You want to maybe give everybody a *break*?'

I nearly choked on my water bottle. Orach stood over me, blocking out the blazing sun. She upended her own bottle over her sweat-drenched head, shutting her eyes and opening her mouth in bliss. When she'd caught a whole mouthful, she spat it into the sand of the practice yard, then gave me a Look.

I exploded. 'You people don't like training any more? Would you like a day on the damn beach?' I glared across at the bodies sprawled in the sand. They did look knackered, now that she mentioned it, and the teenager I'd screamed at was still in silent tears, whetting her sword blade with a grim intensity. Christ, was that Eorna with his comforting arm round her shoulders? Was he getting soft in his old age or what? I stared back at Orach. 'Would you quit it with the Looks? What have I *done*?'

'It's what you haven't done, you stupid man,' she muttered.

'What did you say?'

'It's what you haven't done, you stupid man, *Captain*.'

I had to make a conscious effort to shut my own jaw. Orach rolled her eyes, blew out a sigh, and sat down against the fence beside me.

'She's back, isn't she? I thought that's what you wanted.'

'Orach, don't do this now—'

'Oh I could *slap* you!'

'Go ahead if it gets it over with!' I gestured angrily at my cheek.

'I wish it was that simple!'

After that we both glowered into the middle distance for a bit. The recovering fighters, I couldn't help noticing, were studiously not looking at us. One of them staggered to his feet, limped to the water trough and plunged his head right in.

'You idiot.' Orach sighed and let her head flop against my shoulder. 'I understand, y'know.'

'I know you do,' I muttered. 'So you know it isn't... It isn't. What you said. That simple.'

'Gods' sake, don't let that stupid soothsayer ruin everything.'

'Why change the habit of a lifetime?' I rested my cheek against her head and closed my eyes. I remembered her weeping the night of my sentence; the only one in the hall who was. I remembered her trying to get into my head, and I remembered shoving her away. Better not do that again. It only made her mad.

'You saved my frigging sanity,' I told her. 'Not to mention my soul.'

'Oh, shut it. You were never mine, Murlainn, and you never pretended to be, and I never imagined you were.'

'I'm sorry about that,' I said. 'You've no idea how much. And you know fine I lo—'

'Don't. Don't even think of saying it.'

'It's not a lie, Orach.'

'I know it isn't. But if you say it out loud I really will slap you.' Awkwardly she sat up straight, and we stared at the fighters again in silence. They were starting to get to their feet once more. Even the kid whose tears hadn't dried yet on her face.

'Take the rest of the day off,' I barked savagely.

None of them waited for me to change my mind; they were out of that arena before I'd taken my next breath. Only one of them looked remotely regretful, and that was the green-eyed woman with the choppy brown hair. She slung her knife belt over her shoulder, and trudged off disappointed.

'You're all heart.' There was laughter in Orach's voice, I was glad to hear.

'Taghan's keen.'

'Taghan's a strange one.'

'Taghan's without a brother, thanks to me.' I'd killed Feorag the day my own brother died. 'Gods know, she's the only person Eili talks to, apart from Sionnach, and he doesn't exactly talk much. What?'

'Nothing.' She chewed her lip and watched the spot where Taghan had disappeared. 'She's loyal, I guess.'

'If she wasn't, she'd have been out of here and into Kate's arms long ago. She's all right. She's got principles.' I sighed and stretched, almost too comfortable to move, but I clambered to my feet. 'I'd better get on with some work.'

'I'll say, after the way you've treated everyone else.' Grinning, she punched my arm gently. 'Murlainn? Do something about it. Anything. Yes?'

'Yes, miss.' I tugged my forelock, and she left me with a deliberately flirtatious wink. Tease.

Soon as she was gone, my mood blackened all over again. *Do something about it.* Easier said.

'She's nothing to do with you,' I said aloud.

On the other side of the fence, Branndair raised his head and yawned quizzically.

'Finn's nothing to do with you,' I told him, and myself. He did that thing canines do in lieu of raising an eyebrow, stretched languidly, then squirmed under the fence. As my fingers ruffled into his neck fur, he got up on his hind legs and planted his paws on my chest.

I gazed into his yellow eyes as I scratched his furry throat. 'You wouldn't take any shit from soothsayers,' I said. 'Why do I?'

He tilted his head and grinned, licking my nose.

It hadn't taken Kate to tell me the whole prophecy, as she'd once promised; Leonora and Stella had been happy to ram it into my ears for years before my queen got the chance. *Griogair's bastard. Leonora's grandchild.*

And why couldn't the soothsayer stick to what she was asked? Why did she need to veer so wildly off-message? The Bloodstone prophecy had caused trouble enough for a hundred malevolent old sibyls.

Splinter-heart, winter-heart, lover-killer. He'll drink the blood of his mother and he'll kill the ones dearest to him.

Well, come on. I'd managed those already, the latter several times over. If that wasn't enough to satisfy a witch, I don't know what was.

Splinter-heart. Lover-killer.

Like I said. What's new?

Griogair's bastard will be the death of his lover's grandchild.

Ah, that part. No wonder Stella had done everything she could to keep us apart. No wonder Leonie used to look at me with death in her eyes. It almost made me want to court the girl in future years just to spite them, except that they were *right*. And I cooperated, truly. I did my part. I stayed away, not least because we found one another mutually repellent.

And then she only went and grew up. She grew up and either her nose wasn't too big for her face any more, or I didn't care. Either her eyes were no longer fish-pale and eerie, or I didn't care. She looked something like her mother, but I didn't even care about that, and besides there were moments and looks and turns of her head when I could see her father. The jawline that was softer than Stella's, the laughter-marks around her eyes. The parts untouched by frost.

I kissed Branndair's muzzle and shoved him down; shocked out of his ecstasy of neck-scratching, he shook himself and trotted with me as I headed for the Great Hall.

I was at the foot of the steps to the hall when I felt it, and hesitated: the feather-touch of something on the back of my hand. Reflexively I flexed my fingers and clasped it tight, then let it go.

Like water, or fog; I never knew which. And here in the dun it was like thick soupy water, or a fog of cotton wool: dense and tenacious. I caressed it once more with the back of my hand; so familiar, so strange. *Sgath*. Touching it was the one thing – the only thing – I could do that my brother never could. I felt guilty just for that, just for the frisson of satisfaction it still gave me.

I wasn't the one Finn loved anyway. The one she loved was dead and gone. Keeping that in mind would keep me sane. Keeping that in mind would keep my resolve as unyielding as the Veil in my fist.

Two guards were watching me, a nervous look on them. I let the Veil slip between my fingers and walked on up the steps and past them. Witchcraft, or at least it came close. I didn't blame them for being antsy when they noticed me touch the Veil. Funny that Rory didn't bother them. I'd worried about that – gods, I'd worried, but there had been no need. They loved the little fiend, and they viewed his Veil-antics as no worse than some party trick.

I couldn't help grinning to myself, remembering the first time. That three-year-old imp with a giggle I wanted to bottle and keep forever: Eili nagged us till she was hoarse about not turning his bedtime into a game. With me, Jed and Sionnach doing the parenting, she might as well have saved her breath. The boy could crawl under tables as fast as a snake, and he learned his blocking very young, so we lost him in the tumult of the Great Hall more than once. His scowl when the three of us finally cornered him was always a sight to scare a Lammyr, but it was nothing to the looks on our faces the day his scowl turned into a fat smirk, and he rolled over backwards, and vanished.

That time, when the tables around us fell silent and Eorna stood up and swore, and the hubbub raced around the whole room till every fighter in the place was on their feet shouting and pointing; that time it was easy enough, when the freezing shock faded, to reach through after him: to clutch him from a dark and windswept ruin on a deserted knoll of west coast granite, and bring him back to his own world.

Trouble was, when Rory saw the reaction he got, he only wanted to do it again. And again. And the wilier he got, the harder bedtimes became, and the more colourful Eili's language grew.

Those were the times I missed Conal. Those times and all the others, obviously, but I know he'd have sorted the little toerag. There were a lot of things he'd have sorted, but there was no point thinking that way. I told myself that again when I found Finn in the kitchens chatting up Sulaire.

And good luck to her on *that* front, I thought as she laughed her filthy laugh at one of his jokes. But it didn't stop the sharp stab of annoyance in my gut.

I laid my sword down on one of the tables with a clatter, which got their attention, but I couldn't do much other than scowl at their nervously expectant faces.

You grew up a good few centuries before she did. Physically speaking.

It isn't even you she ever liked.

She's nothing to do with you, Seth. My daughter is nothing to do with you!

'If you've got nothing better to do than eat, Dorsal,' I heard some bastard of a dun Captain say through my mouth, 'you can get your backside out there for some training.'

JED

'This ain't getting any hunting done.' Iolaire stood up in the river, water flowing fast around his waist, and grinned. 'The water's lovely. Get that fine arse of yours back in here.'

Jed gave him a lazy smile back, but he stayed where he was, naked on the bank, running a whetstone down his blade. 'Like you said. It ain't getting any hunting done.'

Iolaire made a face, but he grabbed an overhanging alder branch and hauled himself dripping from the water. 'I hate to say it, but I'm liking this part better.'

'Pacifist.'

'Obsessive.' Iolaire slumped down in the soft grass and kissed Jed's knee.

'Flirt. Give it up, it won't work.' Jed ran a finger down the honed edge of his sword, examining the reflected light.

'Slave driver.' Iolaire wriggled into his jeans. 'Sometimes I'd like to know what really happens in that head of yours.'

Jed sheathed the blade. 'You know what goes on in my head. You of all people don't have to bloody be there.'

Iolaire knuckled his skull hard enough to make him wince. 'You sensitive wee thing. I knew what I was letting myself in for, remember? Move, then, I'm way ahead of you. Get your kit on.'

Yes, he remembered. He'd dreamed it, unexpectedly, not so long ago. It still sent the echo of a chill into his spine: Seth deciding whether to take Iolaire in, or take his head.

'Ah, he made the right decision in the end.' Iolaire winked.

'You'd better not be—'

'As if. I can read you like a picturebook anyway.' Iolaire pulled his damp t-shirt down over his torso. His expression was martyred. 'And you don't want to laze around any more, so poor me has to trail after you like a lovesick puppy.'

'A lovesick, homicidal puppy.' Jed laughed as he stood up, yanking on his own jeans. 'And you say you don't read my mind. Head for Brokentor? There was a rumour he was—'

'Jed.' Iolaire's head came up.

Jed turned and crouched in one movement. 'Where?'

'Beyond the weir. Four of them.' Iolaire worked his blade loose in its scabbard. He indicated the high wooded slope to the right, then slipped soundlessly up through the birks while Jed backed towards the water's edge.

He could hear the enemy fighters now; they weren't making any effort to suppress their racket. Rough voices, the snap and crunch of dead branches, a brief savage laugh. Jed slid down the bank and into the river, and waded upstream in the shade of tangled alders till he saw movement in the glade ahead. He halted, watching, the flow of the water fast and cold against his legs. He curled one hand round a branch, his toes into the soft silt of the riverbed.

The boy who was shoved hard down the slope could be no more than thirteen. His wrists were bound behind him and he couldn't avoid the thick rhododendron roots seething out of the ground like serpents; his foot caught and he went rolling and tumbling into the hollow, his captors hard behind him. One jumped lightly down and placed a foot on his spine, then kicked him over so he was lying on his back staring up. The combination of terror and bolshie fury in the boy's eyes gave Jed a shiver of recognition.

'I said I won't do it again,' the boy gritted, spitting blood.

'Damn right you won't.' The leader laughed. 'It's not that I haven't got a sense of humour. But jokes are tiresome after the first time. Get him on his feet.'

The two other fighters grabbed the boy by the arms. 'In the river?' asked one.

'In the river. And I don't want to see him come out of it.'

'No!' screamed the boy.

'Go on, give us a smile.' The leader stretched his own lips wide in a grin as he pressed a dirk to the boy's chest and forced him back towards the bank. 'You were laughing your pretty head off half an hour ago.'

They were heading straight towards him. *Whoa, shit.* Jed took a swift breath and ducked right under the water, finding an alder root with his fingers to anchor himself.

The water churned as legs plunged into the water close enough for him to touch; then the boy was there too, his scream turning to bubbles of air as powerful hands held his head under. The boy clamped his mouth shut, his eyeballs white and panicked, and very suddenly they were staring straight into Jed's. If it was possible, they widened.

Jed gave the boy a grin, and dived down under him. The nearest legs were just asking to be seized; he locked an arm round one of them and yanked its owner down.

The yelp of shock was audible even underwater, and then the man was flailing at him, his open mouth sending up a gush of bubbles. There was no point giving him time to recover, so Jed seized him by the throat and thrust his blade up under his breastbone.

The water went pink around him as the man's struggles grew feebler. Jed thrust him away and erupted from the water. The boy was already up and fighting, frantically, as Jed lunged for his second captor, who was staggering back clumsily in the deeper water. There was no way of watching for the leader, but he didn't have to. Iolaire stood behind the man on the riverbank, an arm round his neck, the tip of a bright blade thrust through his chest.

'Hurry up, eh?'

The surviving fighter slammed a fist into the side of the boy's head, knocking him flying into the water with his hands still bound, and drew his blade. Not fast enough, since Jed was already barrelling into him with the head butt that had served him for years before his Sithe life. The man went down with a grunt and a colossal splash, and Jed dropped his sword to concentrate on holding him down. When the fight, and the breath, went out of him, Jed kicked away and lunged for the surface, sucking in air. The boy crawled from the river a few feet downstream.

Iolaire had dropped the leader's limp body, and watched Jed patiently as he staggered up the bank. Jed glowered.

'If you wore a watch you'd be tapping it. Don't help or anything.'

'You were doing fine. I'd only have got in the way.'

'There is that.'

Iolaire blew him a kiss, then shot out an arm to grab the boy as he made a dash for freedom. 'And where do you think you're going?'

The boy twisted in his grip, his feet skidding and sliding on churned mud. 'Out of here. Let go!'

'No. Say thank you, you ingrate.'

'Thanks. Now let me *go*.'

'Go where?' Iolaire gave him a hard tug that almost sent him sprawling, and nodded at the two floating corpses and the land-bound one. 'These guys will have mates out looking for you in a couple of hours. And I meant, say thank you to my friend. He's the one who stopped you getting drowned.'

The look the boy sent Jed curdled his blood. There was fear in it, but there was revulsion too. He was edging as far away as Iolaire's grip would allow.

'Don't let him near me.'

'*What*?' Iolaire let go of his arm to clutch his throat instead. The boy's face turned purplish red, but the hateful glower stayed on his face.

'I know him. He's cursed!' Scratching at Iolaire's fingers, the boy rasped in air, his voice a hoarse crackle. 'Everybody knows it. He's *Lammyr-turned*.'

Iolaire dropped him, and the boy collapsed onto the grass like a sack of stones, retching and gasping. Silent, Jed watched him.

Iolaire flicked a worried gaze at Jed. 'Don't listen to him.'

Jed spat and turned away, wading back into the water to retrieve his weapon. He shoved one of the dead fighters out of his way; the man bobbed and turned in the eddying current. How very little that bothered him, Jed thought; and the water was colder than it had been.

'So where are you going to go?' Iolaire eyed the boy with contempt. 'You can't go back to your home right now.'

'Dunno,' he croaked.

Iolaire shut his eyes and sighed. 'You'll have to come with us, then. For now.'

'I can't.' He glanced sullenly at Jed.

'Die, then.' Jed shrugged as he cleaned his blade.

'Wait.' Iolaire turned and climbed up the slope through the ragged birks, halting and staring out when he reached the ridge. After a few long moments, Jed heard the snap and rustle of horses in the undergrowth.

The patrol was five strong, its leader a woman with a choppy shock of brown hair, moss-green eyes and a belt of throwing knives across her hip. She reined in her grey horse and stared down at them, then nodded at Iolaire.

'Taghan,' he said. 'Can you take this one back to the dun?'

'Must I?' She cocked her head and studied the boy's face. 'What's his name and why's he our responsibility?'

Jed jerked his thumb in the direction of the river, and the two bodies drifting idly downstream. 'Our responsibility? Them,' he said. 'No idea what the brat's name is.'

Lightly Iolaire kicked the boy, who grunted, 'Fuaran. It's Fuaran.'

'Ah, Cuilean.' Taghan shook her head at Jed. 'Causing trouble again?'

'I didn't cause it,' snapped Jed, and instantly regretted rising to her bait. Taghan smirked.

'So the lad doesn't trust you to take him anywhere in one piece? That seems to be a problem with you, Cuilean.' Taghan turned to one of the fighters behind her. 'Gruaman, get the boy. I suppose we're accustomed to taking in refugees. This one won't be any riskier than the last.' Her gaze slewed back to Iolaire, and this time she didn't smile.

When Gruaman had pulled the boy onto the horse behind him, and he and the rest of the patrol had vanished back through the trees, Jed whistled a low note to summon his horse. It crashed through the bracken, halted to snort fondly at his scalp, and Jed rubbed its nose. The dun stallion was uncomplicated, and it trusted Jed. He liked that.

'I don't like that woman,' he said at last.

'Taghan?' Iolaire shook his head. 'It's her manner, that's all. And she still hasn't got over Feorag. Can you blame her?'

'If she was so fond of her brother, she should have gone

over to Kate with him,' said Jed bitterly. 'She wants to fight alongside Seth, she can bloody well stop having a go at the rest of us every time there's an incident.'

'She doesn't like the war.' Iolaire shrugged. 'Doesn't mean she isn't loyal to Seth, or to Conal before him. She stayed with Conal when Feorag defected. Just like I stayed with Kate.'

'That's kind of my point. Minds can change.'

'Hers hasn't. Which means she's truer than I am, doesn't it?'

Jed gave him a sharp look. 'Don't say stuff like that.'

'I'm only saying you don't have to worry. Taghan doesn't like Kate, hates what she stands for, doesn't want the Veil destroyed. So? She doesn't have to like a renegade like me, and she doesn't have to like being at war with old friends. She certainly doesn't have to be happy Seth killed her brother.'

'Like he had a choice.'

'Not the point. Oh, for gods' sake don't let's argue about it.'

'I'm not arguing.' Jed couldn't suppress his smile. 'You are.'

Iolaire gave him a slow grin. 'If Kate's people are out looking for their missing patrol, things could get messy. We should head back.'

'Or it could be a really good time to go looking for *him*…'

'I couldn't agree more.' Iolaire swung up onto his horse. 'But Seth wants us back at the dun anyway. Something about a kelpie.'

Jed rolled his eyes. 'God. Not again. If Rory fails he'll be in a bitch of a mood for days.'

'Seth?'

'Rory. No, both of them.'

'Don't worry. I think Seth's given up on the creature. He probably wants it off his lands.'

'Fair enough.' Jed cocked an eyebrow. 'And once that's done, we'll be out beyond the perimeter with nothing better to do...'

'Than look for Laszlo. Who might very well be out hunting himself.' Iolaire winked.

Jed put his heels to the mare, urging her up through the grass-clogged hollow. 'There are times, gorgeous, when I like how you read my mind.'

'Without even having to be in it. Damn, but I'm talented.' Ducking the low branches, Iolaire goaded his horse past the mare. On the rim of the hollow he broke into a gallop across the open moor. Jed swore and gave chase, but his heart wasn't entirely in the race.

If I let him in my head, he can tell me if it's true. That I'm Lammyr-turned.

Iolaire always said it wasn't true. Iolaire said he'd take more joy in killing if it was.

Well, Jed thought, he might not take joy from death, but it didn't exactly break his heart.

If I let him in my head, he might discover he's wrong.

Jed tried to imagine Iolaire recoiling, horror and disgust in his eyes. He couldn't imagine it, but maybe that was only because he couldn't bear to.

Sod this. He snarled a command at the dun horse and it responded, hooves flying. Iolaire glanced back over his shoulder, his laughing eyes still glowing with the embers of spent lust.

Sleeping dogs, thought Jed. *Let them lie.*

FINN

When I was younger, when Seth had sent me home, when I was missing Jed and raging at my exile and the unfairness of it all, I used to do a lot of gardening. Not so much with a trowel and a little fork; my mother use to call it extreme gardening. You know: hacking down trees, ripping out roots, brutalising rhododendrons. It's therapeutic. I knew that was what Seth was up to now. Extreme ground clearance.

The sun was high and the sea beyond the dunes was calm, and the gentlest of breezes sighed through the fields, bringing a scent of coconut from the whin: the whin, I might add, that Seth was slashing and burning like an enthusiastic orc.

It amused me that he wore thick gloves for the job; he armoured himself for the fields, but not for a fight. There was sweat on his neck; his hair and t-shirt were wet with it, and he hacked at the twisted gorse roots as if this was somehow personal. I shouldn't have made the mistake, of course, of thinking that just because he had his back to me, he couldn't see me shirking.

'Try again,' he barked. 'And *don't snap your wrist.*'

Sighing, I stalked over to the pile of logs where he'd crayoned a crude figure with crossed eyes, a sticking-out tongue and a spiky beard. Only one of my throwing knives had hit the mark and stuck; the rest lay scattered uselessly on the grass. The day was too hot for this, I thought as I trudged back to my ten-foot mark and tried again. I'd rather be swimming. With my horse.

'Wouldn't we all.' He hauled out a stubborn branch that promptly sprang back and caught him a whack on his bare arm. Cursing, he threw it onto the smouldering heap, ignited the lot into explosive flame with a jet of petrol, and turned to me, rubbing a streak of blood from his bicep. 'Gods' sake, woman, don't you *listen*? You're releasing too late. You might get his big toe off, if you're lucky. Here.' Pulling off his gloves he stood behind me, clasping my wrist and lifting my arm in tandem with his. In slow motion he moved it down, stopping on the arc. '*There*.'

'You are a bossy bastard. I've only been doing this for half an hour.' I shook him off.

'So you're lucky Laszlo didn't arrive fifteen minutes ago with his army. Keep going. *Lighter grip,* Dorsal.'

The knives were lovely, as well they might be, since Eili had made them. Practical enough, forged out of single pieces of steel with leather bound round their weighty handles, but beautiful too, with the curved detail and the inlay on each blade. Particularly beautiful was the one that left my hand just at that moment, slamming into the log right between the cartoon figure's crossed eyes. It hung there, shimmering and vibrating, as I turned to Seth with a satisfied smirk.

He shut one eye, looking faintly annoyed. 'Fine, smart-arse. Ten feet further back. You'll give it more power if you use your middle finger.'

I used my middle finger.

'Funny. Get on with it.' He turned back and grabbed a gnarled knot of whin, clearly forgetting he'd taken off his gloves. '*Ow.*'

'Oh you big girl. Let me see.'

'Any excuse, slacker.' But he sat down on the ground

and held out his hand for me to see, his eyes big and doleful.

'It's a big one.' I rubbed my thumb lightly across the splinter, making him wince. A couple of tries with my fingernails proved futile, so I drew a knife and poked at his hand with the tip.

'Why can't you carry a sewing kit like a normal girl? *Ow*.'

I sighed. 'Why can't you act as tough as you do in company?'

He gave me a grin, one of those ones that were half shy, half insolent. 'Because we can be big girls together?'

I should have been rougher on him, but the truth was I hated to hurt him. The knife's tip was needle sharp anyway, so it wasn't so difficult to prise the black splinter loose from the fleshy base of his thumb. He was perfectly still now, though his hand trembled ever so slightly.

All right, he wasn't *that* soft. I frowned, glancing up at him.

He'd been watching me, I knew it, but he looked quickly down at his hand, just as I flicked the splinter free. It was a sizeable thorn with a thick root, and I felt a little sorrier for him. Impulsively I kissed the welling blood, then let go of his hand like a hot coal.

'Jeez, woman, 'tis only a scratch. I mean it *really* 'tis only a scratch this time.'

'Yeah, yeah.' I stood up quickly. 'What did the whin ever do to you anyway? Not to mention those lovely rhododendrons.'

'You give them an inch, they infest the whole grazing. Gods know where the rhoddies even came from. Like everything else, I guess. Over from the otherworld and turning into a pest.'

'Well, *ouch*. Come on, what's really got into you?'

He grinned. 'Did you pry into your mother's life this much?'

I sighed. 'I consider myself reprimanded, Captain.'

'That's better. And since you're in a penitent mood, we'll go and get a couple of swords.'

My heart plummeted. 'I'll never be any good with a sword, Seth. Let me stick with the knives. I'll practise more, I promise.'

He grabbed the back of my head so fast I couldn't even dodge. Then he pulled me in close so he could growl at me.

'This is not a game, Finn! If you can't protect yourself, I'll send you home again.'

I wanted to slap him away and I didn't. I wanted to storm off and I wanted to stay right there. I gritted my teeth and waited for him to feel like an idiot, which he shortly did.

He let go of me very abruptly and turned away. 'Armoury, Dorsal.'

I was shivering as I trudged after him, and my stomach was churning. This was going to be a lot harder than I'd thought.

I'd always known he was stubborn, though. I was too. I tried to remember what happens when an irresistible force meets an immovable object, but I'd paid little or no attention in that physics class. No doubt I'd been sulking that day, again. Who wouldn't like a second try at their teenage years? So long as you could go back with an adult awareness of your future or lack of it, it would be *fine*.

'Sorry,' he muttered, falling back to walk alongside me. 'Didn't mean to snap. I only want you to know what you're getting into.'

'I know, don't you fret.' I stuck my hands in my pockets so that I wouldn't reach out and touch him.

'And I'm not going to make you spar today. I just want

you to have a sword with you. We've got a job to do outside the dun. Not that Rory's going to like it.' He gave a sigh that melted into a deep frown as he watched a patrol ride in through the dun gates. 'Taghan's in early.'

I wrinkled my nose. 'Is she the one that's so pally with Eili?'

'As much as Eili ever has pals, yes. And the gods know Eili needs a social life, for my sake if not her own. Taghan's all right, considering I killed her brother.'

I remembered. I remembered hiding my eyes in Seth's back when his sword cut down. I remembered blood on an indigo shirt. Feorag had been Seth's friend, once, but on that day we'd thought we could be in time to save Conal. We hadn't; but still Feorag had died.

I didn't take my hands out of my pockets, but I felt Seth's fingers touch my bare arm, very briefly. Then he was bounding up the dun steps like a man without a care beyond whin-clearance.

The dun was alive with mid-morning noise. Shouts, bellows of laughter, hoofbeats in the sand of the arena, the *thwip* and *thup* of arrows from the range. The barking of dogs, the distant bellow of cattle; and the echoing ring and hiss of white-hot metal from the forge.

Taghan was there, leaning a shoulder on the doorway, her face already beaded with sweat from the blasting heat. She said something to Eili within; then, when she got a reply, she laughed. As I passed, I saw that she was watching me. Her expression was cool and unreadable, but when Eili spoke again, she grinned. Not the nicest grin I'd ever seen.

I caught Seth up in the armoury. In the dim coolness he ran his fingers along the racks of swords.

'Eili's on good form,' I remarked.

'Eili is always on good form.' Seth grimaced. 'She is not always in a good mood. Just you wait till it's her time of the year. Me, I can wait indefinitely.' He winced.

I frowned, but said, 'Oh, yes. Once a year for Sithe girls. That was a nice surprise.'

'I bet. Not that I'd know.' He gave me a droll look. 'You'll be singing a different tune when you get broody.'

'Broody!' I laughed.

'Uh-huh.' He stopped, a light of shock in his eyes as if the idea had just occurred to him.

'Oh, give me a century or two, why don't you?' I slapped his arm a little too hard. 'I've all the time in the world. Anyway, my name's still mud around here.'

'Don't you believe it. There's guys in the dun would have you tomorrow.'

'Away. Me with the fish-eyes.'

He folded his arms. 'You're gorgeous, you silly tart. You look like your mother.'

I blushed, which made me feel even stupider, but Seth turned abruptly away. 'Sorry. I didn't mean to get personal. Let me know if you get any hassle. Unwanted – hassle.' He picked up a few swords, balancing each one on his fingers.

I took the light blade he passed me, unsheathing it. 'That feels right, I suppose.'

'I thought it would.' He gave me that strange sideways look again.

'What?'

'Nothing.'

He was anxious about Rory, I decided. I wondered what the job was that Rory wasn't going to like, and I wondered why, in that case, he had to be part of it. I couldn't help suspecting that their relationship had gone sharply downhill since I'd arrived, but maybe it hadn't been great to begin with. Rory was fourteen years old; of course he was raging at the bars of his beautiful prison.

'I can't help it,' Seth muttered. 'Risk: it's just a word. When you're that age you think it's the most fun in the world. I know I did. And then it's your own child, and...' He seized another blade, but I knew it wasn't because he liked it better than the others. 'And you're old and scared and you know how fragile life is. I used to tell myself that, when I went over to Kate. She had a point, didn't she? A place beyond this world; unity against the full-mortals instead of war among ourselves. Security on our own terms.'

'She was lying, Seth.' I risked touching his forearm with a finger, and felt a small shiver run across his skin. 'It would have been death for us. It still would. You believe that now.'

'Yes.' He rubbed his temples, then put the sword back and pressed the heels of his hands into his eye sockets.

'Oh, Seth. Kate spell-bound you.'

He raked his hands through his hair and fixed me with cold and bloodshot eyes. 'That's an excellent excuse, Finn. I'll remember it.'

I examined the stone floor. 'I didn't say it was an excuse.'

'I wasn't spell-bound, Finn. Kate seduced me, and I let her. I was eaten up with bitterness and lust, that's the truth. I was a pathetic lennanshee with no self-control, but it was something a lot cruder than love.' He linked his fingers with mine. 'You were sixteen years old. I was four hundred and something and I should have known better.'

'Stop making excuses for me. You're only doing it to make yourself feel worse.'

'And you have to give your consent, if she wants to take your soul. And we both did.'

'She didn't get our souls.' I hated to remember how close we'd come, the pair of us. 'Seth, you thought you were doing the right thing. That makes a difference.'

'Does it?' His jaw was rigid again. 'Made no difference to Conal.'

I turned away on the pretext of looking at the swords. Sometimes Seth was my best friend; sometimes, like now, it felt as if we lived at opposite ends of parallel universes. For sixteen years we'd despised one another, before I discovered who I was and who he was. Maybe that was how we were meant to be. Maybe we'd screwed it up by understanding each other. How odd, I thought with a stab of regret, and how sad.

Scrabbling for a neutral topic, I blurted, 'How's Orach, by the way?'

'Grand. Fine. Better than she's been for four hundred years, probably. She dumped me.'

She. Dumped. You? Not knowing which word to stress, I ended up stressing them all. I could hardly get my jaw shut. 'Sorry.'

'S'okay. It's not like I was committing.'

'Um.' I still couldn't contain my shock. 'You'd think she'd have twigged that a couple of centuries ago, if it was a problem.'

'Yeah. Well.'

Maybe that accounted for his volatile mood, but I didn't feel inclined to press on with the subject. 'Tell me about Hannah, then. Isn't someone missing her?'

Seth scowled at a blunt blade, flicking it with a fingertip. 'The mother's gone to find herself: not expected back any time soon. The parentis-in-loco couldn't give a toss.'

'For God's sake, Seth. There's a war on.'

'Officially. Nothing's happened in all this time, Finn. '

'And speaking of the time—'

'Don't,' he snapped, and I raised an eyebrow in slight surprise. 'It's fine. The balance is *fine*. Gocaman's on the other side, and he's keeping an eye on it for me. If there's any sign of a slip he'll let me know. Look, this stalemate could go on for centuries, and we deny Rory an awful lot in the meantime. I couldn't deny him a friend.'

'Would you let him walk into someone else's *war*?'

He chose not to answer that, leading me back into the sunlight where our horses stood waiting. 'Anyway, Hannah's mad keen to find her father. *Obsessed*. Don't think she'd have stayed otherwise, even for Rory.' He tugged the bridle's headstrap over the roan's ears.

'And what have you done about finding him?' I asked darkly. 'You just wanted a distraction for Rory.'

'Probably.' He blew out a sigh. 'Ach, she's a hellion, but I like her.'

'Of course you do.' I hoisted myself onto the black. 'She's very like you.'

Seth stopped with his fingers tangled in the roan's mane. 'She's a feral wee slapper with an alcopop habit!'

'And a father fixation.' I bit my lip, too late.

He took a breath, ice forming in his eyes. 'Piss off, Finn. You go too far.'

'Fine.' Urging the black forward, I didn't look back at him; I was too angry to apologise. So Rory was under house arrest; but Hannah could be taken from whatever family she had and dragged across the Veil? Besides, I couldn't begin to explain it, but something felt wrong. A thin menace hung over the dun, tingling in my spine.

Or maybe I was just too used to being on my own, a

solitary animal who was jealous of the pack and their strange historic bonds. I'd never understood the clann; Seth had as good as told me so when he exiled me.

Eili, now: there was a woman I'd rather have avoided for the rest of my days, yet without Eili there would be no Sionnach. And Sionnach I'd miss like a piece of my heart. When he trotted his horse alongside mine, the day was suddenly calmer and cooler – in a good way – and he didn't even open his mouth. He just smiled and winked, and I grinned back, and I knew for certain that at least one of the clann was glad to have me back.

His sister was waiting there on her grey horse with Jed and Iolaire. Eili's direct smile at me, as she handed Seth a tangled bridle, was not like Sionnach's.

'Whose is that?' I asked, genuinely curious.

'My kelpie's,' said Rory, giving me a hateful look. He kicked his horse's flanks and headed for the dun gate. 'As I've failed to master it, my father will no longer have it near his lands.'

'It's a killer,' said Seth curtly. 'Well, that's their nature. But you don't keep a masterless killer in your back yard.'

'And naturally my father will have no problem getting it to do what *he* wants.'

Seth took an exasperated breath, but Jed interrupted. 'It needs to go back to the sea and stay there, Rory. It's only a question of... um...'

'Leading a horse to water,' suggested Iolaire with a grin.

'And making it drink,' said Jed, and laughed. 'Well, we all like a challenge.'

'Well. Pay attention, Cuilean, and watch your back.' Seth rubbed the green-stained bridle between his fingers. 'Forget about Laszlo for forty minutes.'

'Don't worry your pretty head, Murlainn. I could kill him in my sleep. I do it all the time.'

There were a lot of things I could have said to that, but none of them sounded right in my head. Of course in thirteen years he'd learned to kill. He'd be dead by now if he hadn't.

I licked my lips. 'Be careful, Jed?'

Jed smiled at me. God, I thought with a wry smile back, he could still make my heart flip. 'Like a kelpie, Finn. He needs dealing with.'

He scared me. Turning the black's head, I rode out of the gate and let the horse pick his way down the rough stone steps onto the grassland. This was what I'd come for, second only to the people I loved: the world where I belonged, and it was beautiful. Summer had brought a rash of colour to the green sweep of grazing between the dun and the sea, a multitude of wildflowers, and the backdrop of the sky was a clear deep blue that made my eyes sting. I heard hoofbeats, felt Seth at my side, but just for a moment I didn't want to look at him.

'I'm sorry,' he growled finally. 'Okay?'

'Okay!' Damn it, but I liked and knew him too well not to forgive. 'Me too. Sorry.'

I used to be just this soft with Conal, I thought wryly. They could both wrap me round their little faery fingers.

'Yeah, you are soft.' With a grin he reached to squeeze my hand. 'Just find your ruthless streak, Dorsal. Before you really need it.'

HANNAH

My people skills, I'd realised, were better when I wasn't in the vicinity of Aunt Sheena. I got along just fine with all the Sithe. Except for Sionnach, of course, so surly and violent; and Finn, who I detested out of loyalty to Rory; oh, and I'd noticed that Seth didn't smile at me so much any more. He watched me like you might watch a sleepy snake: as if he was wondering when to risk stamping on me.

But mostly, I liked them. And the weather had warmed to a hot and cloudless summer, and Rory and I had two white-sand beaches and a crystal sea to ourselves. We had an irresponsible amount of freedom, so there was little besides work to kick against. For me and Rory, it was half boot camp, half anarchy.

More than anything – except Rory, obviously – I liked the horses. The first one they'd given me, Jed's semi-retired bay mare, had been sweet but staid. My new chestnut gelding was a bit of an equine delinquent, so he suited me just fine. He needed a decent run, though, not this lazy meander they called a hunt.

I nudged Rory and he grinned; as he did so often, he was thinking the same as me. Jed and Iolaire had drifted to the left, quite a bit distant and engaged in some private project of their own, and the white dog was staying close to Jed. Seth was ahead with his dog, Finn riding at his flank, and the twins were a good bit further back. They were all far too busy gossiping to notice us ride quietly away from the group.

'Gallop?' I whispered hopefully.

'Sh. Don't draw their attention,' hissed Rory as he veered subtly right. 'I know a short cut here. I'm not letting him get to my horse first. And it *is* my horse.'

'Too right.' Checking behind, I could tell none of the others were watching us, and they were out of sight among the trees surprisingly quickly. As soon as it seemed safe to give the chestnut his head, he was only too willing to break into a smooth trot.

I glanced back as we slowed to a walk again. 'I thought the dogs might follow, but we're okay.'

'I've told you, they're not dogs.'

'They are dogs,' I said wearily. 'They look a bit like wolves, but they're dogs.'

'How could they be dogs? They're out of the same litter and they're four hundred years old. Have you ever heard of a four hundred year old dog?'

I gave him a long sarcastic look. 'Are you seeing the flaw in your logic at all?'

'Ach, shut up.'

So bite my head off, Rory. If it *helps*.

The trees thinned around us and very suddenly there weren't any, apart from a few half-drowned stumps. The horses' hooves sank and sucked in boggy ground, and the brilliant line of the loch ahead of us was dazzling. It was all very pretty, but there was a smell in the air: a dank murky water-smell with a hint of dead things.

'Not planning to swim the horses, are we?'

'Hardly.' He gave a short laugh. Much more slowly he let his horse pace forward, its flanks shivering with tremors. Again I glanced over my shoulder the way we'd come.

'They're way behind,' he said dismissively.

'Cool,' I said, suddenly uneasy. 'Maybe we should wait for them.'

'Let's not.'

Tiny waves lapped at the loch shore, flickering with sunlight. Further out nothing stirred, not a fish or a bird. A crescent of soft sand was better footing for the horses, so we rode along that towards a lonely copse of pines. Not that I didn't appreciate the summer sun, but the shade beneath them was a relief. I stripped off my sweatshirt and tied it round my waist, enjoying the tiny goosebumps that rose on my arms.

Rory turned in his saddle, but whatever he was going to say died on his lips. He frowned, then paled, and lifted his wrist. The silver bracelet flashed a band of light across his eyes, but it was the dangling stone he was staring at.

'Ow,' he said, and clutched his forehead. Then his eyes focused beyond me, and widened.

I rolled my own eyes. 'You're not gonnae make me look. I wasn't born—'

'Shut up!' His voice was a scared rasp. '*Hannah!*'

The jeers dried on my tongue. If he was taking the piss he was doing it way too convincingly. I really, really didn't want to turn to see what he was gaping at, but if I didn't it would be my back that was turned, and that was even more intolerable. Setting my teeth, giving him one savage look to warn him what would happen if he was winding me up, I turned.

The horse on the shore was a pretty colour: white-ish but mottled like a cold sky. Its feathered hooves straddled something on the ground that might once have been a deer or a calf, and its head was lowered as if to protect its prey. But its eyes held me: black, blank and psychopathic. The

green spark in them was ancient and evil like some phos-
phorescent fish: one of those prehistoric creatures that never
ought to see the light.

I stared at it, transfixed. It didn't have the crazed look of
Seth's blue roan, but its upper lip was pulled back from
grinning yellowed teeth. It had canines, abnormally big
and pointed ones, and it whickered invitingly.

So anyway, I thought. Why not?

The chestnut gelding trembled beneath me, rooted to
the ground with terror, but I stared into the empty eyes
of the cloudy-white horse and I suddenly wasn't afraid. I
wanted to touch that horse. I wanted to stroke its powerful
neck, gentle it, tame it. I wanted to *ride* it. I shifted my
weight in the saddle and began to dismount.

Softly a shape rode between me and the white horse. As
Seth reined to a halt I froze, my feet hanging free of the
stirrups and one leg half-over the chestnut's haunches.

What was I *doing?*

My blood was ice-water. Very, very cautiously, I eased
myself back into the saddle and, cringing, found my stirrups.

The windless copse was silent; not even a breath of bird-
song. I'd only just noticed that. I was aware that Finn was
there too, and the twins a bit further behind, but I couldn't
look, not even at Rory. All my attention was locked on
the white horse, my nerves ragged with the fear that it
might dodge Seth and lunge for me.

Gripping the stained bridle, Seth slid off the blue roan
as it shook its neck and whickered. The white horse blew
an amiable response, but its expression was sly and wily as
it angled its head back towards Seth, and the soft skin of
its muzzle was dyed red. Seth dangled the green bridle on
his extended fingertips.

'Come to me, *eachuisge*,' he said. 'I don't care how many you've drowned. I don't care how many you've killed. That's your way.' Seth's voice was low and crooning, and the white ears flickered towards him. 'But come to me. Go back where you came from. Don't you miss the sea?' He gave it a savage grin much like its own. 'Go back to your lair and think your dark thoughts.'

It whickered and flicked its tail. The two of them gazed at each other.

'You are old, so old, *eachuisge*,' Seth lilted. 'Grow older. Go back to your lair and live. Better than being hunted. No-one here wants to master you, not any more.'

The horse took an idle pace forward, tilting its head towards the bridle.

Then it happened, though I didn't know what *it* was: at first I thought it was something Seth was doing on purpose. His back arched violently, as if someone had thrust in an invisible knife.

Stumbling forward, he fell onto his knees. Instantly the white horse jerked its head up, alert. I could read the change in its expression; anyone could. It wasn't seeing Seth. It certainly wasn't seeing a potential rider. All it saw was weakness.

And I think it saw lunch.

As it came at Seth, his blue roan screamed threateningly and went back on its hindquarters, but the white horse took no notice. The bloodstained muzzle snaked towards Seth's throat and I thought he'd duck and roll away, but he seemed paralysed.

Branndair sprang but the white horse lashed out a hoof, catching his skull and knocking him flying into the heather. Rory jumped from his horse, grabbed a rock and flung it;

I slid off the chestnut and fumbled for a stone of my own. The white horse's eyes swivelled maliciously our way.

My fingers closed on a big rock; I was about to throw it at the horse when Seth jerked his head round towards us. I reeled back at a ringing blow inside my head, and Rory staggered too.

Whatever Seth had done to us, it was his last effort. When the white horse turned back to him I knew nothing could stop its yellow teeth closing on his throat. Horror wormed in my blood and bones: I didn't want to see him die. Trying to scramble upright, I scrabbled for another stone but my flesh was mush, as if the horse had already chewed it. Seth was going to die.

The horrible stillness was split by a clear violent scream, and Finn's black horse sprang forward and thundered in like a truck. It slammed into the white horse's head, banging it aside so that the vicious yellow teeth snapped on the air. There was a clattering echo: Finn's barbaric yell, the collision of horseflesh, the clash of thwarted jaws. Then there was only silence.

'Christ,' whispered Seth.

There was no flinging Finn away, like he'd done to us. She was too close, and even I could see that if Seth hurt her he'd only leave her vulnerable. Her black horse straddled him, side by side with the blue roan, both glaring at the white one, while Finn fumbled over her shoulder for the hilt of her new sword.

She couldn't get a grip on it. Now that her rage was gone she looked herself again, shocked and scared and *completely* incompetent.

The white horse drew back its lips, threads and gobbets of bloody flesh streaking its teeth. It reared over Finn, then plunged, and she gave a sob of terror that sounded to me a lot like *Seth*.

A whisper, and a soft thunk, and the white horse flung up its head on its twisted neck.

Eyes rolling, it staggered back on its hind legs, then collapsed. Its flailing muzzle and teeth grazed Finn's face and shoulder and the black's flank.

Dying, it sighed a rattling sigh and sank down onto its forelegs, a shining bolt standing out from its chest. Its gaze, regretful, caught Seth's. Then its savage head sank to the ground and the green light in its eye went dead.

'Ach.' The curse of disgust came from Sionnach, who dropped his crossbow as if it had burned his fingers. Ignoring everybody else he went straight to Finn, catching her as she lowered herself trembling from the black. With his bare hand he wiped the horse's foamy pink sputum off her face.

Seth grabbed the black's mane to haul himself to his feet, but he was almost knocked straight back to the ground by Rory, half-supporting and half-shaking him.

'Dad. Bloody hell, *Dad.*'

Seth righted himself with an arm round Rory, but his cold eyes were fixed on Eili.

There were soft hoofbeats on the undergrowth, and then Jed was flinging himself off his horse, Iolaire right behind him. 'Seth. Seth, I'm sorry. We saw something and followed it. I'm so sorry.'

'Not your fault.' Seth smiled thinly, eyes still locked on Eili.

'Tsk.' Eili shook her head solemnly at Jed. 'That'll teach you to chase phantasms, Cuilean. They may not even exist. Except in your somewhat fevered... *imagination.*'

Jed glared at her, his jaw grinding.

'Bitch,' said Iolaire softly.

'Names, names.' Eili turned her grey's head and rode away.

The eyes of the white horse were open and empty, its forelegs splayed, muzzle on the ground. I felt suddenly sorry for the creature, dead because they'd messed up. Its half-eaten buck lay in the blaeberry scrub beneath the pines, and curiosity drew me closer. I took a step, and another, then stifled my own scream.

A hand fell on my shoulder and I stepped automatically back towards human protection. Jed pulled me back into his arms and turned my face firmly aside. I could feel his racing heartbeat, and his fingers tight on my jaw.

'Iolaire,' he said. 'It's not a buck.'

Stepping past, Iolaire took a shocked breath. 'I know him. He's one of Kate's.'

'If you don't mind me asking,' said Jed dryly, 'how do you know?'

'Scar.' Iolaire pointed to a dismembered thigh. 'Distinctive. I was there when he got it.' Crouching by the remains, he touched a swollen hand gently. 'And he'd lost this finger long ago. Poor Turlach.'

'I think I'm going to throw up now,' I said faintly.

'Go ahead.' Jed released me, squeezing my shoulder. 'Nobody's looking.'

Leaning on a pine trunk and retching with as much dignity as I could manage, I decided I liked him.

'What do you want to do?' Jed asked Iolaire.

'Burn him.' Seth was behind us. 'What's left of him. I can't be responsible for him. Burn him with the kelpie.' The blue roan's reins were in his left hand, the other arm around Rory's shoulder. Across the roan's withers lay the senseless black dog.

135

Rory's voice was icy. 'Why didn't Eili stay for Branndair?'

Seth's fingers tightened on his arm. 'She wasn't thinking, a gràidh.' But I saw the look he exchanged with Jed, the sour tightening of Jed's mouth. They were hiding something from Rory, I knew it.

That wasn't all they were hiding, thank God. Their bodies blocked my view of what lay in the undergrowth. I thought: it could have been just an animal. Maybe. If you thought of it like pictures in a book, if you broke it down into its constituent parts − no, bad thought − if you thought only of a toe, or a hank of hair, or a finger that was missing anyway, you could think of it quite dispassionately.

'What about my friend here?' Iolaire nudged the corpse gently with his foot. 'Not taking a walk in the woods, was he?'

'There's another thing.' Sionnach crouched to pick up his crossbow.

'What?'

'There.' He nodded, turning the weapon in his hands. 'Another.'

'Shit,' whispered Seth.

The dove-grey filly was adorable. Well. She was adorable till she sleepily raised her head from the long grass, blinked her lashes, tossed her silky mane and bared her teeth in a hungry, hating snarl.

There were scraps of flesh in her teeth. Scrambling to her long legs, she gave a screaming desperate whinny at the corpse of the white horse. When she got no response she half-reared, then spun on her hindlegs and fled.

In silence we watched her spring for the water and dive.

Sionnach spat. 'No wonder it wasn't for mastering.'

Seth rubbed a hand across his face. 'Stupid, stupid, stupid *bastard*.'

'Not,' Finn quoted him acidly, 'your fault.'

'I should have guessed. At least it was weaned; it'd had a go at Turlach. Rory, don't even think about it.'

Rory was gazing hungrily at the disturbed water where the filly had submerged. At Seth's words he turned, and the horse-lust turned to high and angry concern.

'Anybody want to tell me what's going on?'

'I froze,' growled Seth. 'It happens.'

'Oh, treat me like a three-year-old, why don't you? It was your back. You went into a spasm. It was your *bloody back*.'

'Fine. It was my back. Leave it.'

'Like you have? Gods' sake, Dad. Why won't you let Eili fix it?'

Jed eyed Seth. Seth avoided looking at Sionnach. Iolaire looked at his fingernails.

It was Finn who fascinated me, because she wasn't avoiding anybody. The woman's fists were clenched and she was shaking, but it wasn't nerves. Finn wasn't scared, I realised: she was furious.

'Dad, let Eili see it. Please. For me.'

'If it would do any good, Rory, I'd do anything for you. But it won't. Trust me on this one.'

Rory looked hopelessly at the rest of them. Nobody was taking him on, least of all the silently simmering Finn. In the awkward silence he turned, spat, and seized his horse's reins. Flinging himself onto its back, he kicked its flanks and drove it into an insanely fast gallop, back in the direction of the dun.

There was nothing I hated more than a family domestic;

it reminded me too strongly of my own home life. I stumbled up through the sandy scrub and unhooked my chestnut's reins from the stump; his flanks were still shivering, but he was quieter now, and his nose snuffled at my pockets in search of a mint.

'You okay?' asked Jed behind me.

'Dandy. What's wrong with Seth's back?'

'Crossbow scars.' Jed was fully into the clann tradition of never meeting my eyes. 'He got shot years ago and the wounds never mended properly. They're infected.'

'Do I look like I came up the Clyde on a banana boat?' I scowled. 'He got shot twelve years ago. If they'd been infected all that time he'd be dead by now.'

Irritatingly, Jed didn't take any offence; he just made a laughing sound in his throat. 'Blood poisoning doesn't happen to Sithe.'

'In that case, he's imagining it. He needs therapy, not a doctor.'

Jed sighed, and his voice when he deigned to answer me was icy cool. 'Every night, those wounds wake Seth. Since my brother was a baby. So Rory's always known the world's a place full of pain, and he doesn't remember a time when he thought otherwise.' He tilted his head thoughtfully. 'Not that Seth screams. He never screams. I suppose he's used to it.'

I swallowed. 'How do you know? I thought you and Iolaire were the item.'

He smiled, uncurled his fist. There was a deep brutal scar across his palm, a ridged line of white. 'I don't let anybody near my mind, so we did this instead. Blood brothers. I know when Seth's in pain because I feel it.' Turning his hand, he examined it thoughtfully, clenching and unclenching the fingers. 'There were nights I thought his spine was going to burst out of his back.'

There was bile in my throat, but I was determined not to be sick again. Jed glanced at me, seeming to remember suddenly that I was there.

'You coming, then?' He mounted his dun horse.

I shook my head as I stroked the chestnut's neck. 'This one's all wound up and so am I. We'll both walk.'

Jed didn't tell me not to be silly, he didn't remind me there were monsters in the mere, he didn't say that of course he wouldn't let me stay out on my own. All he said was, 'Walk fast, then. Liath'll stay with you.'

And then he rode away at an easy amble to where Iolaire waited for him, and they disappeared into the trees.

I twisted and tightened the reins between my fingers. The white dog sat there patiently, tongue lolling, pinning me with her big yellow eyes. I could tell I wouldn't be giving her the slip any time soon.

'Come on then, Lassie.'

She cast me a withering glare, but she rose to her feet, stretched and padded languidly along the shore without a backwards glance.

'Oy! You're supposed to be babysitting me, remember? The dun's that way.' I pointed off to the left.

Now that the dog was ignoring me, I was all too aware that I didn't want to make my own way home after all, but all the others were out of sight and I didn't want the dog to vanish too. I tugged on the chestnut's reins and with some reluctance he followed me, head low and ears back. Partly out of spite and partly because I didn't want to lose sight of Liath, I yanked him into a half-hearted trot.

When we caught up with Liath, I swear she looked smug.

The chestnut settled into a truculent plod and I wiped sweat from my forehead. Some way behind us, a column of oily black smoke curled lazily into the sky. I averted my eyes, swallowing.

'So where are we going, Lassie?' I asked the dog. 'Is Rory trapped in the old mineshaft?'

This time she ignored me altogether, which made me feel like an idiot. I was much more reluctant now to let her out of my sight, and she seemed to know it. If Jed's intention had been to put the wind up me, he'd done a good job. My skin prickled, and I had to stop to pull my jumper back on. I rubbed my arms briskly.

'This had better be a shortcut.' I felt I had to keep talking. If I didn't say anything, the silence was horrible. Liath's whole posture had changed; she was low to the ground, tail stiff, as she slunk into the pinewood. Where the pines thinned, where the heather and the scrub petered out and the ground fell away into a crumbling sandy cliff about ten feet high, she stopped altogether and lay on her belly, ears back and hackles high. But she didn't as much as growl at the moving horse shape I could see across the glade and through the trees. She pricked her ears at me with a curious sort of perplexed trust.

Cold horror loosened my guts as I stared past her. It hadn't occurred to me there might be more than one fully-grown horse-monster in the woods. In my mind's eye I saw clearly what I'd seen in the blaeberry scrub: not something out of a school anatomy lesson, not a dead animal: something that used to be a man. I clamped my lips together. Just as well there was nothing left in my stomach.

And then I heard the voices.

Carefully I looped the chestnut's reins over a sturdy

looking branch, close enough to Lassie to discourage the horse from making a run for it. 'Don't pick right now to *move*,' I hissed at it.

We'd left the mere behind, I realised as I crouched and crept closer, but below me was a rough beach and a smaller loch, the sand and stones criss-crossed with the tangled roots of pines. Between the straight trunks the little loch glinted calm and silver in the summer sun. It was a very beautiful place, but you could have cut the atmosphere with whatever knife had carved those holes in Sionnach's face.

Right now they stood out very white against his skin. He ignored the brown-haired woman who sat on a rock, carving something into a chunk of wood with the blade of her knife. All his fury seemed to be focused on his twin sister.

'Oh, Sionnach.' Eili, adjusting the buckle on her horse's bridle, gave a low laugh. 'I wouldn't have let him be killed. Don't fret.'

'In what way was it up to you?'

Eili shrugged. 'I knew Finn was close enough. I knew she'd save him. And if she hadn't, you or I would have.'

'You made me kill a kelpie!'

'I know, and I'm sorry. That wasn't what I intended.'

Midges were settling on my hairline but I was scared to scratch at them. I was scared to move.

'What was your intention?' asked her brother. 'To kill Seth?'

Shit. I clapped a hand over my mouth to stop myself gasping, but Eili glanced up in my direction anyway, frowning slightly.

She turned back to Sionnach and said, 'I never meant to kill him. Not now, not yet. And as it turned out,' she smiled, 'I didn't.'

The silence dragged. I couldn't breathe. Sionnach said: 'What about Finn?'

'Ah. But for Rory, she's his closest kin. By love, if not by blood. And she's never liked me.' Eili's smile was cold. 'After all, I'd never harm the Bloodstone. I can't hurt that turncoat bastard through *Rory*.'

I wished I hadn't come. I wished I'd abandoned the bloody dog. I wished I could be anywhere but here. Risking a glance over my shoulder, I bared my teeth at Lassie, who'd slunk a little closer. But still she lay there watching me inquisitively, her tongue hanging out.

'And you?' Sionnach's lip curled as he looked at the other woman at last. Taghan, that was her name, I remembered. Taghan, the grumpy one.

The brown-haired woman set down her knife and leaned back on her rock. 'I've no intention of killing Seth. Anyway,' she grinned, 'your sister's claimed him from me.'

'Of course I did.' Eili smiled at her. 'I don't see how you could have stayed in the dun otherwise, Taghan. Someone had to take the revenge from you.'

'See, personally speaking, Sionnach, I don't want Seth dead,' Taghan soothed. 'He's my Captain. But why should he have *her*, when I don't have Feorag? You must see the natural justice. Fair's fair.'

Sionnach spat. He stared at his sword and then back up at his twin. 'Sometimes,' he said, 'sometimes I wish I'd gone to help Conal that day he died.'

For a moment I thought he'd plunged the sword into Eili's belly; that's how stricken she looked.

'I told you to, didn't I?' she said. Her voice was brittle, like the thinnest of thin ice. You could touch it and it would break, and Eili would shatter into a million pieces.

'It's what I wanted. You should have. He was your Captain and it was your duty. If I could have gone to him myself, if I could have been any use to him with my last breath, with the last of my blood running out of me, I would.' Her face was tight with unbearable distress. 'I wish I had.'

'It was him or you. They'd have cut your throat!' Sionnach grabbed her arm, as if he wanted to shake her till her bones rattled. '*Eili*. I held your hand before we were born. I touched your face before we drew a breath, before we saw the light of day. And now you're a stranger to me. How is that right, Eili? You're turning into someone else.'

'I am always and only ever myself.' Eili put her fingertips to his chin, lifting it. 'But I can't always be the same. Sionnach, please. You're the only love I have left.'

He gritted his teeth. 'Seth paid for what he did. Conal wanted you to absolve him, in his last minute on earth he told you that. But you chose Seth's penalty and he paid it.' He took a breath. 'And all these years later? You're still making him pay.'

'You wanted him to pay! You were with me,' she said. 'For a long time.'

'It has been a long time,' Sionnach said gently. 'Too long, Eili. You've given him pain every night of his life since Conal died, isn't that enough? If you healed him for that purpose, it's witchcraft and you know it. It's yourself you're destroying.'

'Oh, no. No it isn't.' She stepped back, head high, eyes cold. 'I always wanted it to take a long time. Why did I make his sword the best in the dun? Why do I always ride at his back to protect him? I want him to last as long as it takes for me to be the one. I want him to live till I kill him.' Her voice dropped to a serpentine whisper. 'And I want him to know it.'

Sionnach stared at her for one moment longer. Then he barged past, shoving her aside. When Eili regained her footing, she was trembling, but she took a breath and smiled at Taghan as the crash of the undergrowth faded with the hoofbeats of Sionnach's horse.

'Don't listen to your brother,' said Taghan, picking up her knife. 'It's your decision. Seth's yours to kill when you want it.'

'I know, But I won't risk the clann, not while we're at war with Kate.' Eili mounted her grey and took the reins. 'Finn, though? I've no compunctions about getting rid of her. You're right, it's only fair.'

For an instant my belly was full of ice, because she glanced in my rough direction once more, a funny smile playing on her lips.

But she can't have seen me, because she put her heels to the grey's sides. 'Now, Taghan, shall we be getting back? I'm expecting visitors.'

★ ★ ★

I couldn't move, physically couldn't. I was terrified that if I stood up she and Taghan would still be there, even after their own horses' hoofbeats had faded. I just lay there in the gritty sand, shivering and trying not to shiver. It was taking up all my energy. I had a sick, tilting feeling in my head and stomach, like being abruptly disconnected from my old life, like I had no chance of seeing and living it again.

So Eili did heal Seth's back; she'd healed it just fine. She did it for a reason, that was all, and now everything made such a horrible unnatural sense. No, unnatural was the wrong word. I thought of the horse, and the corpse in the scrub. And Seth's body buckling, and the yellow eyes of Branndair as he made his suicidal leap at the kelpie's throat, and the insane delighted smile on Eili's lips. The sense it made was all too natural, preternatural: red in tooth and claw.

Tooth and claw. Just as I thought that, I felt hot breath on my cheek, then the rasp of a bossy tongue. I opened my eyes to stare into brilliant yellow ones, and Liath nudged me hard in the face. Then once more in the belly.

That finally got me moving. I stumbled to my feet.

I watched her tail lash. I watched her grin and pant.

I said dully, 'You're a wolf.'

The grin stretched wider. The wolf called Liath turned, and shook herself, and padded back to the chestnut horse.

FINN

'Don't you ever *dare* save my life again,' said Seth.

Cross-legged on the woven rug, I glared at him over the inert form of Branndair. His jaw was clenched but he wouldn't look at me, his hand gentle on the wolf's head. Branndair's eyes were almost closed, but between the lids a glazed amber light glowed. Seth stroked his coarse black fur obsessively with his thumb.

'I could say, don't take it personally,' I said bitterly. 'Like you once said to me. Or we could both grow up and you could just say: "Thanks, Finn."'

'If I thanked you for it you would do it again. Because there will be a next time.' Seth spoke through his teeth. 'We're not responsible for each other. All right? I wouldn't do it for you, so don't put me under some stupid obligation.'

'Yeah. You always said you were a bad liar, which is a very convincing lie, 'cause you're actually a very good liar. Aren't you?'

'It's, uh…' His brow furrowed as he worked it out. 'I… oh, Finn. That's not true. Or fair.'

'It's both,' I told him frostily. 'What's this really about?'

'Your hot little head, that's what.' His sneer came back with his composure. 'Don't get involved in things you know nothing about, *Finny*. I'm responsible for my own life.'

'You're not, though, are you? Eili is. Do you like having your life in Eili's hands?'

'It's not a question of liking. My life is in Eili's hands. It

146

just is.' Seth splayed his fingers across his face. 'I don't want yours to be. Ever again.'

'And I don't want to watch you die. I lost my grandmother and Conal and I lost my mother too, you selfish prick, and I won't lose you!'

Seth ground his fists into his eye sockets and exhaled. 'Finn.'

'I *will not*.' Leaning forward, I rubbed Branndair's thick neck fur so that I wouldn't have to look at Seth.

'Eili will kill you,' he said.

'I'd like to see her try.'

'Finn!' he barked. 'Grow up while you have the option! She'll kill you before she kills me, and she'll do it just for the fun of my reaction. Don't give her the excuse.' He raked his fingers manically through his hair. 'It was *you* she tried to kill today, don't you get that?'

'Of course I get it. But Eili is not going to kill me, and she's not going to kill you either, because I'm not going to let her. What does she want? Does she think it'll bring Conal back?'

Seth laid his fingers against the wolf's throat to feel the pulse of his blood. 'We're upsetting him,' he murmured. 'Finn, all she wants is my death.'

'She can't have it,' I said calmly.

'Stop it, Finn! The trouble is, you want a piece of me too. There is not enough of me to go round, understand?' His fingers tangled with mine in Branndair's fur, but the look he gave me was cold and intense. 'I've told you before. I'm not my brother and I'm not a replacement.'

Yanking my hand away, I slapped his face hard. Then I stood up, and walked out.

★ ★ ★

Behind me in the dun, someone was plucking a mandolin and someone else scraping on a fiddle. I heard muffled laughter, the start of a song, the snort and stamp of disturbed horses. I put my hands over my ears and stared out at the long sweep of machair that ended in the dunes and the metallic gleam of the sea. The land was silvered under starlight like pixie dust, the Milky Way a broad glittering brushstroke across the night.

The guard kept his twenty metres' distance. His mind had touched mine when I came up here ~ *you okay?* – but since then he hadn't bothered. He'd left me alone since his tentative question had glanced off the dour darkness in my brain.

I was not in the mood to confide.

As I sat on the rampart, a ragged shape blacked out the stars and flapped down. Faramach's claws bit into my knee, but I was used to him and I didn't wince. Stretching his wings, craning his head, he let me rub the spiky feathers at his throat.

'Got over your pique, did you? Anyway, crow, I'm glad you're back.'

Faramach cackled and flapped up to stalk along the rampart wall.

It was unsettling, the way that raven knew my mind. I couldn't make his out at all; it was too alien... Well, didn't *that* remind me of someone. I almost managed to laugh: Seth would be horrified to think he had anything in common with Faramach.

Leonie used to be able to link her mind with the raven but I couldn't. That didn't seem to bother Faramach: it probably gave him the superior look he couldn't wipe off his beady face, and he liked me anyway. Hesitantly I bent my mind to his, but there was nothing. Only his eyes, watching me and shielding whatever thoughts ravens thought.

'You're always around, aren't you? You're always going to be. Till I'm dead, or you are.' I gave him a fond look. 'I love you, you bad-tempered sod.'

Yet again I was reminded of someone. Spooky. The raven croaked fondly, and I smiled back. Faramach probably knew my mind better than I knew it myself. He probably knew most things better than I did. Leaning my arms on my knees, I watched him.

'You know, don't you? If you felt like it you could tell me.' I blinked. 'Is *he* still around? Dust on the wind. Ghost in the dun. Just a bit of tattered thought. Oh, Faramach, *anything.*'

The raven tilted his head at me, but he was giving nothing away.

'Because I miss him,' I said, and I heard the break in my own voice.

Faramach lifted his head so that his throat feathers rippled in the breeze. 'Hah. Cù Chaorach.'

'Yes.' I hadn't missed Conal this much for years. No point missing him, though. He wasn't here and he never would be again. I rubbed one eye with the heel of my hand.

The mandolin started up again, fast and furious, and a hammering guitar joined it. Somebody sang a song I recognised, something with a hard modern beat and an alien tinge of bodhran and fiddle. More laughter. Behind me there was a footstep on the stones. My heart flipped, my throat dried, but before I could react, Seth sat down at my side and gazed out at the starlit machair.

'Heh!' rasped Faramach. 'Murlainn!'

'Hey, Faramach.' Seth started a little. 'He does still speak, does he? I haven't heard that bird talk since Leonie died.'

'He talks all the time to me,' I said. 'Sometimes I think he knows what he's saying.'

'Of course he does,' said Seth. 'He's a raven, not a parrot. Want to slap me again?'

'Yeah.' My lips twitched. 'But I can't be bothered.'

'I'm always getting slapped. Do you think it's my person- ality?' He gave me a sidelong grin. 'You bring out the worst in me. Always have.'

My composure back, I managed to be cool. 'How's Branndair?'

'Asleep. Properly asleep. He'll be okay.'

'Good. I'm glad,' I said. 'He has a big piece of you too, doesn't he?'

'Yeah.' Seth offered me his hip flask, then took a swig himself. 'Trouble is, Rory gets the biggest piece and then...'

'Oh, yes. Fatherhood.' Meeting Faramach's black marble eyes, I thought I saw the raven grin. 'Converts are always the biggest fanatics.'

Seth was silent for a long moment. 'All right. That's twice.' His voice was glacial. 'Once more and I'll slap you right back.'

I bent my face to my knees, hugging them. 'Sorry,' I mumbled.

'Guess I bring out the worst in you too,' he said. 'Maybe we should avoid each other.'

I leaned my chin on my hand and stared at him. 'Stop that.'

'Ah. Okay.' He looked uncertain. 'Stop what?'

'Shoving me away. It's just rude.'

'Well, it's just that...' He raked his fingers into his hair. 'Finn, I...'

'I used to live for your visits.' I had to take a deep breath so my voice wouldn't catch on my words. 'The best times I ever had, because I could talk to you. You were my best friend. I counted the days, and not because I was expecting a miracle. Not because I thought your dead sainted *brother* might turn up instead.'

He stared fixedly at the stone battlement. 'Yeah, but that's not what I...'

'You know me better than anybody on the planet.' I had to hiss it through clenched teeth. 'You have the run of my mind and you know it, but you won't give me yours back.'

His head was in his hands and he wouldn't look at me. 'Finn.'

'I'm not looking for Conal, you great tube.' The silence that fell was a very uneasy one. I nibbled my thumbnail and stared back out at the machair. 'Except I'd like to know where he is,' I mumbled.

Seth shrugged. 'You know as well as I do. He isn't anywhere but Brokentor.'

'All right, don't make me feel any better,' I snapped. 'I'm only going to say this once, ever, you ice-hearted tosser. I loved Conal just like you did. Like a brother, like a father. I miss him as much as you do and I always will, but it wasn't him I looked for when I came through that loch.'

'I see.' Running his tongue over his teeth, he stared out at the night. 'And did you see who you... um... did you see who you were looking for?'

I glared at him. Was he thick as well as a jerk? *'Yes.'*

Seth swore obscenely and shut his eyes.

'Thanks for that. I won't mention it again, then,' I said. 'Is this awkward for you? Do you want me to go home?'

'Hell, that isn't what I meant, Finn. I'm sorry I swore.'

He drew his hand down his face, then stretched it out to take mine. 'You are home. Don't go.' Hesitating, he mumbled: 'Please don't go.'

My throat dried again. I'd have liked another gulp at his hip flask. 'You've never said *please* to me in your life.'

'Well, I'm saying it now. Please stay.' His fingers worked awkwardly into mine.

He'd held my hand before, plenty of times. But now it was different, different altogether. I couldn't say anything, so I concentrated on the warmth of blood pulsing through the veins in his palm.

'If we – listen, Finn,' he said quietly, 'Eili will go spare. Are you ready for that?'

I wriggled round to face him, watching his profile because he still wouldn't look at me. 'Not afraid of her, are you?'

He slewed his eyes sideways and grinned. 'Yes.'

I laughed. 'Me too.'

He laced his free hand into my hair, holding my head still so that he could watch my eyes. Edging a little closer, I slipped an arm round his back to touch the puckered crossbow scars through his t-shirt. He didn't flinch.

He shut one eye, touched a forefinger to my lower lip. 'Hang on a tick. This is going to feel a bit funny, Finn.'

He leaned forward and kissed me. He kissed me for rather longer than I'd expected. Since my head was now spinning in the sky, my heart snowboarding crazily ahead of it along the Milky Way, I was gratified to hear the tormented little squeak of shock in Seth's throat. Not just me, then, I thought smugly.

When he drew back, there was comical astonishment in his eyes. He gulped hard. 'Not that funny, though.'

'Not funny at all.' I shivered, and smiled at him stupidly.

'Finn, I'm four hundred and thirty.' His brow furrowed as he visibly counted. 'Or thereabouts.'

'Yeah, but you might as well be thirty. You look younger than me, you swine.'

He swallowed a grin. 'You should see the picture in my attic.'

'Anyway,' I said silkily, 'It's not like you ever acted your age. You've always just been my sort-of cousin. My vile, snarky, foul-tempered–'

'All right!' he broke in. 'Finn, I'm young, and I'll go on being young, because there's no full-mortal blood in me, but I've had a lot more time than you, and it's going to run out. Even a Sithe life doesn't last forever.' He gave an uneasy laugh. 'Finn, if this is just a casual thing that's fine. Believe me, I'm thrilled, I…'

To shut him up I leaned over and kissed him again, but this time I felt his mind brush against mine, a sort of tentative question. He'd come over all rational. Dammit.

'I see,' he said, slowly. 'It's like that? Oh, hell's teeth, Finn. So deep?'

'You see.' Faramach laughed harshly.

'Shut up, bird. If your old mistress is anywhere at all, she'll be throwing the celestial crockery by now.' He drew his hand down his face.

'Nah,' said the raven. 'Liked you.'

'Really? She'd a funny way of showing it.'

'Seth.' I took a breath. I was set on what and who I wanted – had been for years – but I could wait. I didn't much want to be someone else's rebound. 'How upset are you? Y'know. About Orach?'

153

He leaned his jaw on his hand and watched me with some amusement.

'Finn,' he said wryly, 'Orach saw you coming. That's why she dumped me.'

'Oh.'

'She had her pride, see?'

'Of course.' I gave him a level threatening stare. 'Me too.'

He smiled, saying nothing for a while. Then he kissed me again, and drew away with tangible reluctance.

'My brother would have my head on a stake,' he murmured. 'Or possibly not my head.'

'You told me our lives were our own. All those dead people, they had their lives. Now I want mine.'

He gave me a humourless smirk. 'My life isn't my own. It's Eili's.'

'We'll see about that.' What was he supposed to do to atone for Conal? Beyond what he'd done already, that was: beyond accepting and forgiving the brutal vengeance of his own clann.

He studied my face. 'Oh, Finn. They had to do it. It wasn't so bad. Really.'

'Yes. It was.'

'All right.' He touched the corner of my mouth with a finger. 'But it let you forgive me.'

'I'd already forgiven you. I forgave you the moment I saw you ride in from Brokentor. He was my bloody uncle, so why couldn't they?' I gritted my teeth. 'You didn't make a sound.'

'Er, you're not supposed to know what happened,' he pointed out darkly. 'You and Jed were sent out of the hall.'

'We sneaked back in.' It wasn't so hard, confessing all these years after the event. If he was mad at me now, too bad. 'I couldn't imagine how much it hurt you. I wanted to kill them. But you knew what they'd do and you came back anyway. They might have killed you, but you came back.'

'I got back my place in the dun. I got back my clann. That was all I cared about.' The light behind his eyes was elusive as mercury. 'Before, anyway. In theory. It was kind of easier to think that way before I felt it for real. Afterwards? Truthfully? I hated them the way you did, till it stopped hurting.'

I twisted my lip. 'You never let on.'

'I didn't want you to know. You were angry enough already. When the time came to leave Conal and Torc – what was left of them – to leave them and come back to the dun... I kept telling myself nothing could be worse than Brokentor. Nothing could be worse than what I'd brought on myself. The clann couldn't hurt me any more. But you know what?' With a jerky laugh he buried his face in his hands. 'They did. They so did.'

Tentatively I touched the back of his hands, and when he didn't pull away I put my arms around his shoulders and pressed my wet face to his neck.

After a bit, he turned to me. 'You shouldn't have watched.'

'You shouldn't have ordered me about.'

'Enough already!' He got to his feet and pulled me up. 'I don't want to talk about it. Listen, Finn. The only good thing about being the age I am...'

'Is all that wisdom that comes with the years.' I gave him a wicked wink.

'Ha ha.' He skewed an eyebrow. 'The good thing is, I won't outlive my half-breed son. He won't live anything like as long as me, but I won't live to see him die. You're no half-breed, you're all Sithe. Even if I live through civil war and Eili's hate, even if I manage all that, you'll live a long time without me. You'll *have to*. It's why we can't bind, it's...'

'Seth. *Can't* isn't part of it. We will, or we won't.'

He gave a groan of exasperation. 'Know how you just called me a selfish prick? Well, I am, but like it or not, one day you *will* lose me. You'll have to watch me die, Finn.'

I stared at the muscle that jerked below his eye. 'Thanks for your honesty,' I said. 'Though if you like, you could just lie to me.'

'I can lie. All right, I'm a good liar. And a hypocrite. A liar, a hypocrite, a traitor and, um... a fratricide. Oh, Finny, your taste in men stinks.' The corner of his mouth tugged back. 'I won't lie to you about this, though. I don't actually like to lie.'

'Yes, you've always preferred to have the tact of a brick.'

'*Listen*. I'm not going to get old. *Ever*.' He took a breath. 'Finn. I'm just going to die.'

'Like Leonie. Yes, yes.'

'For men it's even quicker.' He shrugged, staring at Faramach. 'I'd love to get old, I'd love a bit of time to get used to not being here, but it isn't going to happen: one day I'll just die, with almost no warning. Can you get your head round that? Because I barely can, after four centuries.' Turning, he pressed his forehead to mine. 'It doesn't matter how much I love you, Finn. I'm just going to leave you and I won't have any say in it.'

'So.' I glanced away, hiding my involuntary smile, because he'd slipped in the only three words I wanted to hear, and he wasn't even aware of it. 'Better that than leave me now.'

'After I'm dead, Finn...'

I put a hand against his cheek and gazed into his eyes. *'Intolerable pain or insanity or my own death.'*

'Oh gods.' He looked tormented. 'Listen to me. Listen. It's survivable. Your grandmother, she survived it. You'd have to promise me. *Promise. Me.* That you'd bear it. I can't be responsible for your death. *I can't.*'

'I know what binding is, Murlainn,' I said. 'She explained it to me. I do know.'

'I should not do this,' he said. Then he narrowed his eyes, as if he'd just taken in what I said. 'Who explained it? Leonie?'

'No. Never mind.'

'Finn,' he said, 'this thing you want?'

'M-hm.'

'Death really is all that breaks it. Not even then, if you believe the superstitious ones. You can't change your mind, do you understand? There's no going back. It's for life.'

'You're my life,' I told him.

He closed his eyes briefly. His fingers tightened around mine. 'You're sure, then.'

'You know I am. You have the run of my mind.' I watched his face. 'And you looked.'

His eyelight cleared. I felt him inside my mind like a physical presence, like the finest pain imaginable, and the loveliest.

'Finn,' he sighed, and put the palm of his hand lightly against my cheek. As he held me there, I felt my own eyelight intensify. I blinked against it but it didn't stop burning; it went on till it hurt. My jaw tightened, my breath caught in my throat, and I was briefly afraid my eyes would explode.

And then they did.

His eyelight ignited at the same moment mine did, and the force crackled between us. It was only an instant. His fingers trembled against my skin and I heard him gasp, then he had his breath back, and the dazzling light faded along with the pain.

'Listen to me, Finn MacAngus. From tonight you are mine, and I am yours, till one of us dies or we both do. If we are apart and you take a lover, tell me. I will do the same for you. It will not come between us and when it's over we will belong to one another as we always did. We have the right to See each other's minds before anyone else alive. I'll protect your life with mine and you'll do the same for me. I will never say any of this to you again, and you'll never have to say it to me.' The glint in his eye dulled, and he whispered: 'And Finn: I will not leave you until I don't have a choice. Do you understand?'

'Yes. And don't ask me again if I'm sure.'

'Too late. We're bound, love of my heart.' He laughed unsteadily, then exhaled through his teeth. 'Now come with me. And leave that bloody bird where it is.'

HANNAH

'What are you doing here?' Sionnach's lip curled as he flung open the door.

The air between us had its very own wind chill factor. He held a chisel in his hand and he was turning it as if he'd like to make a walnut inlay in my face. Oh, Sionnach understood me, and I understood him.

Behind him there was an intake of breath, then Eili stepped forward. 'Sionnach, it's all right. I've been expecting her. Come in, Hannah.'

I edged warily round Sionnach, then blew him a kiss. Sionnach neither turned away nor blushed. He oozed all the welcome of a Saltcoats winter.

'Oh-kay,' I said under my breath.

'Hannah.' Eili spoke my name on an icy exhalation. 'Sionnach, love. Leave us.'

To be honest I was afraid to look back at him, so I waited till the door closed and I sensed he'd gone. Eili I was not afraid of. I glowered at her.

'Why have you come?' asked Eili. She poured herself a tumbler of neat whisky, then lifted it to her lips. Brandishing the bottle, she said: 'Do you?'

About to shake my head, I hesitated and gave her a brief nod. It felt like a challenge. Sure enough Eili poured me a glass, straight-faced, but I had the distinct sense she was laughing at me.

I scowled round the room. It was sparsely furnished, but it was all Eili and it made me shiver. The stone walls were bare of pictures, the wood floor gleamed. A wrist-slitting song played softly, its sleeve laid neatly aside, and the rest of Eili's CDs were stacked in perfect order beside it, instead of spilling haphazardly over the shelf like everybody else's. A pale beechwood desk held a neat pile of papers anchored by a sword-hilt paperweight, a stack of leatherbound books and a row of silver-framed photographs with their backs to me.

Parasites. The Sithe didn't object to technology, it seemed; they just couldn't be bothered making it themselves.

Eili was wearing that unsettling smirk of hers. 'We can always get what we need from you, Hannah, can't we? Within reason. Guns don't work, but crossbows do. We like the modern kind. Sionnach is very good with them. So was Cù Chaorach. He used to say...' She stopped, a muscle working in her throat.

I eyed her. 'Was that your boyfriend? Seth's brother? I thought his name was...'

'Conal,' said Eili. 'Conal.'

It hadn't occurred to me to feel sorry for the glacial bitch, but the grief on her face was intolerable. I looked away.

'Cù Chaorach. It was his Sithe name. His true name.' Recovering, Eili laughed. 'Funny how much importance we attach to names, when something is just what it is. You can call Seth *Murlainn* – a falcon – or you can call him Bloody Traitor. You can call Rory *Bloodstone*, or you can call him whatever Sithe name is eventually found in him. What they are is what they always were. You can call me Bitch, as Iolaire did today, or Witch, as some do. I am neither Bitch nor Witch. I am only Eili, who loved the man I loved. That's all I am. I am always the same.'

'Not to hear your brother tell it.' All the blood must

have drained from my face, because I felt as if I was floating: and not in a good way. This wasn't going as I'd planned it, because the woman was stark staring bonkers, and for the first time I appreciated Sionnach. I'd have liked him back now, all right. At least he was sane, at least he could control his sister. That smile Eili wore was not a bit sane, but I returned it anyway.

'We take what we want from you and leave the rest. If we want your life, we go to your world and live it. Some don't ever come back, like Finn's poor mother, but she was mad with grief by that time. Most of us know when we're well off. We don't take more than we need from your world, any more than we do from our own. Don't you think that's a fine principle? Ah, yes, you do.'

Eili was right there in my mind, and I hated it, hated it, but I wasn't about to argue. Quarrelling with Eili, I decided, wouldn't be like quarrelling with Rory or even Seth. I tried to keep my frantic thoughts on a leash.

'Are you afraid of me, Hannah? Don't be, I'm only trying to explain. Would I give up riding wild? Would I give up the right to fight and kill for my love, give all that up for a bit of technology?'

'See, you're scaring me now,' I said. 'One minute you make sense, and then you say something else and it's like your brain's on the blink and your mind's taken some weird diversion and you scare me.'

'I don't like it on your side.' Eli turned her glass, the crystal sending glints across her skin. 'It's corrupting. Just look at you.'

She was smiling again and I wished she'd stop. 'What are you doing to Rory's father?' I blurted.

'Nothing he doesn't deserve.'

'Look.' I slammed down the glass. Its base cracked, but it was empty anyway. 'Rory's alone except for you lot and all you do is hurt him. *Especially you.* You hurt his father and you hurt him. He loves his father. I mean, God knows why, but he does, and you're to *stop it.* Whatever it is you're doing. Stop it, or I'll...'

Eili threw back her head and laughed. 'Oh, this is more fun than I even thought it'd be. Or what? What will you do?'

I gulped convulsively. 'I'll throw up.'

'Through there.' Eili jerked a thumb. 'Balcony.'

I made a dash for it, banging my elbow hard on the window frame as I stumbled. Just made it. One glass of whisky, I thought in abject humiliation. A big glass, certainly. And it was rough stuff, an awful lot rougher than the vodka I bought by the quarter bottle to mix with Sprite and drink in the park with my gang. But still.

Then I remembered what else today had made me gag, and the image was so awful I retched again.

When I slumped against the balustrade Eili sat down beside me, rubbing my back. 'That took guts. Pity you threw them right up.' There was laughter in her voice.

I was groggy, my vision was blurred, but I felt sober. I hauled myself up, rubbing my temples, and stumbled back to the main room.

'Seth has lived ever such a long time, Hannah. Did Rory tell you? He looks in his twenties, doesn't he? But if you knew how long he's really lived, you might think it's been quite long enough.'

Rory had told me; I just hadn't believed it. I believed it now, all right, coming from this insane woman. 'How? How do you live so long?'

'*We,* Hannah. You're one of us. With your mother's blood you won't live as long as Seth or me, but you'll live a long time. I'll have to warn you of the pitfalls.'

'Pitfalls.' I didn't like her choice of word, in view of the height of that balcony, and I dearly hoped I was going to live longer than tonight.

'Our cells work better than full-mortal cells. They don't decay the same way, they don't multiply out of control. Wonderful immune systems, DNA that doesn't mutate.' She sighed happily. 'We don't get to grow old, though. It's how we've evolved. Reproduction is so ageing. Maybe the full mortals got fertility in exchange for being so pathetically short-lived.'

My lips parted, because I could breathe better that way. I was very, very afraid of Eili now, and at that point I was convinced I was going to die. It was the easy, fond way Eili talked about short lives and sudden death. It was the silver light in her eye and the way it gleamed.

'I'm so glad you came tonight.'

I tucked a strand of sweaty hair behind my ear, once again more furious than afraid. 'Took an instant dislike to me, didn't you?'

'Yes.' Turning her glass, Eili smiled oddly.

'Why?' Whatever it was, she was milking it. 'And why did you help me stay here, if you don't even like me?'

'Because of your father.'

I felt myself sway, like the breath had been sucked out of me. 'What do you know about my father?'

'What wouldn't I?'

I gritted my teeth. 'You're only trying to hurt me.'

'Yes, I am. Though I suppose it isn't your fault.' Eili studied me closely, the horrible smile finally gone, and I felt a trickle of true fear. 'Wouldn't I recognise his face?'

'Don't you dare! Don't!'

Eili turned to the beechwood desk and picked up one of the photographs, holding it out. I fisted my hands at my sides. I didn't want to take it from her.

'Conal had a digital camera. It was a craze of his for a while.' She touched the photograph fondly. 'I kept some of the prints. See? It's the eyes, of course.' She held it up hard to my face.

Seth's eyes, Seth's eyes, and I knew in an instant why I'd found them so troubling. These weren't Seth's eyes at all, but... they were. Eili forced the picture into my hands, closed my frozen fingers round the frame. It trembled in my grip. The fair-haired man in the picture was turning, caught off guard, a sword and a whetstone in his hands. I was scared to look but I had to. I had to study every curve and plane and texture of the angular face that smiled a little shyly at the lens.

'Oh, I knew your face,' said Eili. She was turning every single photograph to face me. 'The face of my own lover.'

It wasn't how I'd imagined it would be, our eyes meeting. Still, I'd always known I'd recognise him straight away. Gazing at his beautiful grey eyes I began to cry, and Eili watched me without pity.

'Now,' said Eili calmly, holding out another picture. 'Look at this one.'

This one was very different. The same man – the man with spiky dark blond hair and high beautiful cheekbones and Seth's eyes – was slouched on a sofa, a baby clinging like a tiny ape on his chest. The baby was three or four months old, an unattractive little thing with a tangle of coarse black hair. It was fast asleep and the man's left hand rested on its back, holding it protectively against him. His right hand held a crime paperback, but he wasn't reading. He had caught sight of the camera and his slanted gaze was cool and slightly resentful, as if photography was an unwelcome intrusion.

Eili's forefinger jabbed at the black-haired baby. 'That's Finn.'

'*Finn.*' It came out on a shocked breath. Violent jealousy made my head throb.

'Yes,' said Eili thoughtfully. 'It's not my favourite picture either, but I kept it. Perhaps just to remind me there was something else he loved, besides me.'

But at least he did love you, I thought, as fury chilled my veins. At least he *knew you*. Conal MacGregor. *Conal.* I mouthed his name silently, practicing the consonants on my tongue, then wiped my eyes with my sleeve.

'He's dead, isn't he?'

'Yes.' Eili smiled properly at last, and took my hand. 'And now I'm going to tell you how it happened. And all about the man who killed him.'

FINN

It was still dark when I woke, so I knew I hadn't slept long. I lay still, sleepily content, blinking at the stone fireplace. So familiar, that fireplace and these walls: funny how the room had looked so different when we closed the door tonight and smiled sheepishly at one another. It's yours now, he'd said: yours as well as mine. Like my mind and my body and my heart. Those too.

A tremor lingered on my skin, a warm aching memory of his touch. I reached behind me for the body that had curled against mine as I fell asleep, but even as I did, I registered his absence. Tensing, I reached out with my mind, and breathed again. He was near. He was in the room. It was fine.

I sensed this was how it would be from now on, that I would grow familiar with the deep night. Though the fire was unlit the air was suffocatingly warm, even with the windows open, but the moon shadows were still and cold. I raised my head.

The brilliant moonlight cast Seth's shadow across the timber floor, across the woven rugs that were leached of all their colours. He stood motionless by the central window, his shoulder propped against the bevelled stone, arms folded as he stared out into the moonlit night.

I curled up, tugging linen sheets around me. 'Seth?'

'Go back to sleep.' He spoke through a clenched jaw.

For a moment I found it impossible to speak. 'Not without you,' I said at last.

'Jed is awake too.' His voice was distant and dispassionate as he stared out at the silver landscape. It was nothing like the voice that had whispered to me, had cried out my name in the earlier darkness, and it made me shiver. 'Finn, go back to sleep. One day you'll have demons of your own, and then you'll be glad of what sleep you got before.'

I slipped hesitantly off the bed and went to him. Seth glanced at me, then gave a mirthless laugh before rolling his head round to press his forehead to the cold stone. 'Finn, are you never going to take good advice?'

'You're not my Captain in this room.'

He shook his head; then his face darkened and he pressed his forehead against the stone again. I reached out, but though I'd stroked my fingertips across the scars not long before, had wrapped my arms around his shoulders and pulled him fiercely against me, now he flinched away from even the threat of my touch.

'Please,' he said. 'Leave me alone.'

Anger tightened the muscles around my lungs so that I could hardly breathe. I laced my fingers into his hair to turn his face to me, then took it in my hands. There were tears at the corner of his eyes, and I wiped them away with my thumbs. He'd done that for me once, a very long time ago, and the memory was sudden and piercing. 'It's like this? Every night?'

He gave a dry laugh and pressed his forehead to mine. Its heat was intense but I made myself stay still. 'More or less. It's a long time since she last made me cry. She knows, Finn. Didn't I tell you she'd go spare?'

I pulled back a little, examining his body. His arms and chest were hacked about with the superficial scars of four hundred years. There were layers of them, some fainter, some more recent. If you bothered to count them, you could probably date him like a tree. The line of his obliques was distorted by a deep ugly dent below his ribcage that hadn't been there thirteen years ago. I raised my hand to push the black hair away from his ear to see again what I'd seen earlier, the straight clean line of the top of his ear where a centimetre of it had been sliced off, and the long corresponding scar on the side of his scalp. He didn't flick me away as I thought he might, only folded his arms and studied my eyes.

'I bet it takes a lot to make you cry,' I said.

He smiled. Then his pupils dilated and his lips parted in shock. He flung the palm of his hand up against my forehead and shoved me away. 'Get out. Get out! Don't be stupid.'

Too late. Recoiling, I yelped once like a scalded dog before my breath stopped in my lungs. When I breathed again it was through clenched teeth. It wasn't my pain but I could feel the echo of it even now between my shoulder blades.

I swore on a high breath.

'You numpty.' He cupped my head in one hand and drew my face into the hollow of his shoulder. I could taste his skin against my gritted teeth, could feel the sting of pity in my heart turning to a wintry rage.

'If it wasn't for Rory,' he said, almost to himself, 'I'd have met her long ago. I'd put an end to it one way or the other, but there's Rory. And now there's you and I've made you a promise.' His thumb stroked the back of my head idly. 'I can't take the gamble.'

The casual touch of his thumb against my scalp at last

began to calm me down, loosening my rage-clenched jaw. 'I'll kill her for you.'

He pushed me away. 'You will not. *Will not*. If I ever have to kill her it'll be on my hands, no-one else's.' His fingers tightened in my hair. 'When my brother needed an end made to him Eili had to do it, because I was up to my neck in shame. His blood is on my hands, Finn. I won't have his lover's too. Not unless it runs off my own blade.'

I'd never heard that dead note in his voice. 'I hate her,' I whispered.

Seth pulled me back against him. 'Don't do that.' His voice gentled. 'She's loyal to Conal, and she spared him a terrible death. Of course it warped her.'

'That was *a long time ago*. I'm grateful to her, okay?' I hissed. 'But Conal wouldn't want her kind of loyalty. She's warped all right. She's a hater.'

'So don't turn into one yourself. Then she would have beaten you. And me.'

Hesitantly I kissed his lower lip. He let me, his breathing quickening with happiness and lust. 'And there's another thing anyway. You're not good enough, Dorsal Finn.' His teeth flashed. 'She'd slice you like a ham.'

I bit his lip hard, making him wince. 'I'm not good enough *yet*.'

'Yet,' he agreed with a wary grin, touching a thumb to his lip. 'Anything you say. I've taken enough of a hammering for one night.' Thoughtfully he said, 'She's finished for now.'

'So come back to bed.' I took his hand. 'Only, Seth? There's a bloody great *wolf* in it.'

'Aw, Finn.' He gave me a spaniel look. 'He isn't well. And he's only at the foot of it.'

'Two words, Seth. No. Fecking. Way.'

'That's three. Just a few nights, Finn. I promise. Then he's back on the hearth rug.'

'If he isn't, the raven gets to roost on the headboard.'

'Oh, gods.' He looked heavenwards. 'What have I let myself in for?'

The first grey fingers of dawn were silvering the window ledge an hour later before I was sure Seth was deeply asleep, enough for me to risk a glance at Branndair. The wolf's yellow eye was open, looking right at me.

Cautiously I craned my head over Seth's arm to get a better look. There was crystal clarity in that eyeball. Not much sign of a concussion now. I opened my mind to the wolf.

In a pig's ear you're not well, I told him.

His eye sparking gold, Branndair raised his head, his jaws opening in a knowing grin. I knew when I was beaten, so I grinned back.

HANNAH

'I don't suppose it occurred to you to ask me,' said Rory. Perched on the top rail of the paddock fence, he was rubbing oil into a bridle like he wanted to erode the leather altogether.

'No,' said Seth. Stripped to the waist in the summer sun, he hammered on a fencepost as I stared at his tattoo. Conal had one the same, Eili said. Only Conal's was presumably not distorted by a traitor's flogging.

Nobody else was working on the fence. Three men and a woman were hacking pretend lumps out of each other, sword-practising in a roped-off section of the courtyard; Sulaire the cook was butchering a deer carcass in the open air, cheerfully drenched in blood to his elbows. Branndair was darting between his cast-off scraps and three kids who had nothing better to do than rub his tummy and pretend to run away.

I got the feeling the rest of the clann were delicately avoiding Seth and Finn and Rory.

As for me, Seth hadn't met my eyes since breakfast. He was avoiding me, the treacherous miserable coward. But I watched his every move, almost every second: mending fences in the sun when he ought to be dead. And my father should be cantering that black horse round the arena. My father, not the black-haired bitch who'd stolen Rory's.

What right does she have to your father's horse?

Taghan had said that; Taghan, with her quiet smile and her green eyes that saw everything. Eili had brought her

171

to me, had leaned back silent on the balcony wall, knowing she herself had said all she needed to say.

What right did she have to your father's love? Taghan had asked me, turning her dagger in her fingers. The picture of Conal and the baby Finn lay between us, so that my own father stared resentfully at me. *Finn MacAngus is the girl Conal was fathering when he should have been a father to you. And how did she repay him?*

By getting him killed. I'd heard the whole story by then.

Taghan inclined her head, lips quirking. *Seth was the true betrayer, but Finn left Cù Chaorach even before he did. She abandoned the man who brought her up, and all for the empty flattery of Kate NicNiven.*

I had my first twinge of doubt then. *I thought she was captured? I thought they took her?*

And she stayed of her own free will. Seduced by Kate, and for a few sweet words. My brother went to Kate out of belief and honour, centuries before Finn was born. And when the fickle bitch changed her mind at last, she sent Seth to kill him. My big brother, Hannah. Finn didn't turn her coat in time to save Cù Chaorach — Taghan gave Eili a lingering look — *but Seth was in plenty of time to kill Feorag.*

Taghan's voice was so low and calm that when Eili finally spoke I nearly jumped out of my skin.

There are some who say Seth has paid for what he did to your father, Hannah. There are some. But no-one believes Finn has paid.

I glanced from one woman to the other, alarmed.

Come, now. When Eili tried to be soothing, it was like the madness burned through her like a visible thing. Her eyes were embers. *We don't want her dead. We want her gone. And so do you.*

172

Taghan laid down her dagger then, right on top of the photograph, and clasped her hands.

I never knew my brother as I should have done. I was so young when he went over to Kate. I never agreed with what he did, but I knew why he did it. I'd have liked the chance to talk to him. She touched her fingers to her temple. *Instead I felt him die.*

Eili came round behind me, laid her hands on my shoulders, bent her lips to my ear. *Why should Seth have Finn, Hannah? When Taghan never had Feorag, and you never had your father?*

Why indeed. *You won't hurt her?*

We'll send her away, that's all. We'll send her away so she can never come back. Just make sure she comes to us. Eili glanced at Taghan, who was sliding her polished blades one after the other into her belt. *Get Finn away from Seth, and bring her. I know the best place. The only place. That's all you have to do, Hannah. We'll take care of the rest.*

I shook my head. *Finn won't just come. Why would she come with me?*

There's only one way to make sure she does. Taghan smiled up at me. *She's bound to Seth. She has responsibilities to him, and to his. Do it.*

It's not as if we'll hurt her, said Eili.

Did I honestly believe them? Maybe not completely, but I believed them enough. Perhaps I didn't want Finn dead, but I certainly didn't want her happy.

And she looked far too happy now, here, despite the atmosphere. There was a shine in her eyes that was not a bit like the insane glow of Eili's, and the looks she cast Seth made me want to throw up.

'I see, Father. You didn't think you should ask me if you were planning to bind.' Fiercely Rory rubbed the bridle's cheekpiece. 'So did you think you might tell me, then?'

'I'm telling you now,' said Seth.

The black horse shook its arched neck as it cantered past, massive hooves sending up duststorms. Rory shot Finn a hateful glare, but too late to connect, so he turned it on Seth instead. 'Don't you think it's my business who you sleep with?'

'No.' Seth wrenched out a length of rotten wood and took a splinter out of his finger with his teeth. 'No, Rory, I really don't.'

Rory examined the bridle's browband, picking at a loose piece of stitching. 'Funny how things change. You never used to let them come between us. You never stayed the night with any of them. I used to wake you up at dawn, remember? I used to crawl in beside you. You were always there. You were always in your own bed.' He raised his voice. 'Even when I knew fine you *hadn't started out there.*'

He'd turned up the volume as Finn rode by once more. She didn't react, except to shoot him a look of understanding. I hated her even more.

Seth slammed a mallet into the new fencepost, then shoved his hair out of his eyes with a forearm. 'I'm not letting anybody come between us now, Rory. Nobody's trying.' He gave me a direct stare and said through his teeth: 'Well. Finn isn't.'

'Right. Now that's out in the open, anything else you haven't told me?'

'Nothing you need to know.' Seth sucked his bleeding finger. At last he glanced my way, and I stared levelly back.

He seemed thoughtful, but he didn't try to read my mind. Too much on his, I thought contemptuously, and just the one thing as well.

Beside Seth, at the gap in the broken fence, the black horse halted, snorting and pawing the sand, and Finn slipped off its back. I couldn't look at her. If I did I might scream, *That's not your horse, you thieving bitch*. Finn was scowling at me, but I was blocking my mind the way Eili had taught me. It wasn't hard; it came easily and naturally, and Seth in particular was easy to block. I knew why that was. He didn't want to look, didn't want to know.

'You know, Rory,' said Seth, 'if you're at a loose end there's plenty needs doing around here. There's ditches need clearing down in the lower fields.'

Rory bit his lip hard enough to hurt. 'I'm your son.'

'What does that mean? You're too good to clear ditches? Because you're not.'

'No,' Rory spat. 'It means your love life's your business, but I'd have liked to know before *Eili.*'

For a long time no-one spoke. *Explain that to him*, I thought with an inward grin.

Getting his breath back, Seth rubbed his temples. 'Eili only knew because she...'

'Because she what? Go on.'

'Because she pried,' Finn interrupted.

'Pried, did she?' Rory's sneer gave him a distinct look of his father. 'How devious. How underhand. How very *Finn MacAngus.*'

Seth hissed through his teeth. 'Watch that mouth, sunshine. You're not too big for a skelping.'

'I think you'll find I am.'

'Then you can get your arse to the armoury and find yourself a practice sword. This arena, five minutes.'

'Gladly, since it's your answer to everything.' Rory

kicked a stone viciously, sending it spinning past his father's ear. Seth didn't dodge, only bared his teeth as Rory turned and slouched towards the armoury.

I smirked; Seth glowered at me. Finn said, 'That went well.'

'If I could give him a spell in somebody else's army, he'd be out of here.' Seth rubbed his face.

'The trouble is,' said Finn, 'he's right.'

'Oh, not you too.'

'I'll talk to him.' She sounded as if it would kill her. I could dream.

'Don't let him give you a hard time.' Seth seized her hand and kissed it brusquely.

I had no intention of leaving Rory to a tongue-lashing from his father's live-in slapper. Ignoring Seth's growl of warning, I ran after them, but my dignity took a bit of a knock when I almost fell over Finn, who had come to a dead halt in the stone alley.

'I realise you two are joined at the hip,' murmured Finn, 'but I want to talk to Rory.'

'I doubt he'll want to talk to you. He hates you.' I liked the effect that had on her face, so I followed it up. 'What's it like?'

'What's what like?'

'Shagging a traitor.'

I was delighted to hear Finn's breath catch in her throat. I was not quite so delighted when her lips thinned and the hand at her side balled into a fist. I hadn't thought much of Finn. I certainly hadn't been afraid of her. Not till now, not till I saw the crackling silver spark in her eye. I slewed my gaze away, but that was even worse, since my eyes lit on her knife-belt.

'Don't look so nervous,' breathed Finn. 'You're a child.'

'You wish. If I was eight, you might scare me.' I didn't even convince myself.

'You scare *me*, you little gossip-swamp. You've got one side of a story in your head. That's dangerous.' The way she leaned in, all conspiratorial, was alarming. 'Eili's had a chat?'

'She's told me about Seth. What kind of a man he is.'

'You have no idea.' Finn's lips thinned. 'Let me state the obvious for you. If it sounds too bad to be true, *sweetie,* then it probably ain't true. Go figure.'

'Seth killed Eili's lover.' I was seething at Finn's sarcastic pity, but I didn't want to provoke her too far. I hadn't seen her in a mood like this.

'No. No.' Finn rubbed her temple with her knuckles. 'Seth didn't kill Conal, none of us did. Clever planning killed him. And his own temper, and loving Jed and me too much to leave us to our own stupid devices. The woman who ordered him dead, and the man who gutted him. Kate NicNiven and Nils Laszlo killed him. Nobody else.' She grinned fiercely, and I saw tears in her eyes. 'What would you care?'

I licked very dry lips. 'I...'

'I do care, you see. I knew him, you didn't. I loved him like a father. I loved him like a brother. I loved him like *Seth loved him.* Conal wouldn't want your pious indigna-tion,' she spat. 'And I think he would like our Eili to get a life.'

A fist of ice closed round my heart. In that moment I hated Finn like I hated Seth. *More.* Oh, I'd like to see her gone, all right; and Eili was wrong. I'd like to see Finn dead.

I took three steps back from her, turned on my heel, and walked away; I wasn't going to waste any more hate on amateur bitch-fests. I was better than that.

So was Eili.

FINN

I shut my eyes. A lump of self-loathing rose in my throat. Hannah had no right to hate Seth on Conal's behalf; that was true, but I'd gone too far and I knew it. And Rory was still in the armoury, waiting to have a go at me, and I'd been dreading it even before that scene with Hannah.

What did I know about children? What did I know about teenagers? I didn't even know the ones I grew up with. I *didn't* grow up with them. I stayed on my own, antisocial. I spent all my emotional energy mourning Conal and my grandmother, and missing Jed and Seth. I grew up with Faramach, with horses, with the constant hungry longing to be back where I belonged.

If I didn't watch myself, I'd turn into a misanthropic grouch like Seth. Conal would turn in his… in his… No, he didn't have a grave. His gathered bones in a hillside hollow, that was all, and teethmarks on the bones…

I shut my eyes, still unable to face what had become of him, tradition or no tradition. I never had come to terms with the images that haunted my imagination. Maybe I should have stayed on Brokentor with Seth all those years ago, endured the awful weeks of Conal's death-ceremony.

Or maybe I wasn't cut out to be Sithe at all. Perhaps my mother had succeeded in severing me from them. Trouble was, I couldn't go back to my mother's preferred world, even if I wanted to. I didn't have a choice any more. I'd made my choice, and the point where my two paths had diverged was already in the past, irretrievable. I'd chosen a Sithe life, and maybe a Sithe death, but most importantly I'd chosen Seth. And now I was stuck with him.

I smiled.

In the armoury Rory was testing the string on a longbow, one eye shut as he drew it back taut. It was aimed right at me; I was glad it wasn't loaded. 'Um, Rory,' I said.

He lowered the bow. 'Well, if it isn't half the new double act.'

'That's your father and me,' I said. 'Alone and Palely Loitering.'

He sighed out his contempt. 'The unfunny half.'

'I'm sorry,' I said.

'You're not.'

'No. Course not.' I shrugged. 'That isn't what I meant. I'm only sorry you're upset.'

'Too right. I'm not to be upset under any circumstances. I'm for keeping in the dark, so they can feed me shit.' Grabbing a sword, he yanked it so carelessly out of its sheath he almost cut himself.

My gut felt cold. 'In the dark? How?'

'Am I the only one in the dun who didn't know?' He turned the blade and ran his fingertip lightly over the edge. 'Did people snigger at me, or did they shake their heads and suck their teeth? You know, when I was little and smitten with her?' His voice was conversational but it sent icy sensations up my spine.

'Who – why would they do that?'

'I always knew Eili didn't like me much, but I was crazy about her.' Rory had drawn a thin line of blood on his fingertip, and he sucked it thoughtfully. He looked exactly like Seth, emotionless, as if it didn't hurt at all. 'I thought it was just the way she was. And now it turns out she hates me, and she hates my father enough to hurt him every night for the whole of my life.'

It was like a hard jab in the belly. Gossip might be rife in the dun, but the business between Eili and Seth had been unspoken and unSeen for more than a decade. Whether they approved or whether they didn't, not one of the clann would have told Rory; I knew that as well as I knew anything about them. Who in God's name would have been malevolent enough to tell him? For a long moment I was breathless and speechless.

'Rory...'

'Do they think my father's stupid or do they think he's a masochist? I mean, why does he keep her with him? Just to pull the wool over my eyes?' His eyes burned. 'Or does he like it?'

'Oh, you are your father's son.' I was suddenly angry with him and with Seth too. 'All that passion, and you so like to pretend you're dead inside. What is it with you two?'

'What makes you think it's your business?' Rory chewed his knuckle hard. 'Oh, yeah, I forgot. You're his bound lover and I have to put up with you and your stupid questions for the rest of his life.'

I took the sword from his unresisting fingers and sheathed it. I would have liked to touch his shoulder but I didn't dare. 'You think I like Eili being around him? I didn't know about it either, Rory. If we'd known it would have made things worse.' I rubbed my temples. 'Look, when she's with him, at least she's in his Sight. Eili saved his life, Rory. At least she didn't leave him to die. I was there, and believe me, she wanted to.'

'She saved his life at a price.'

'But your father's loyal to her because of Conal.'

'Then he's a fool,' spat Rory.

I slapped him before I had time to stop myself. It was only a light stinging slap on his cheek but when he looked back at me his eyes burned bright and silver, sheened with tears.

I swallowed hard. 'Don't you dare. Don't you dare call your father a fool!'

Rory ground his knuckles into his scalp. 'They keep me shut up in here and they can't even tell me the truth.'

'Yeah. They lied to me when I was your age. It's wrong and stupid and it only leads to trouble. But keeping you in the dun, that's to keep you safe. You know Conal died trying to protect you. Your father nearly did too.'

'It was my father handed me over to the other side,' Rory said savagely. 'He was a traitor, and don't you dare hit me again. You think I don't know that story? He abandoned me before I was born and when he got me back, he gave me to Kate NicNiven.' His voice faded as he finished his sentence, as if it was the first time he'd said it aloud and it had done for him.

'Your father thought he was doing the right thing. He was wrong but he didn't mean to *do* wrong.' I dug my nails into my palms. 'And he's paid for it!'

'Yes, and he won't be finished paying till he's dead!' shouted Rory.

'She could have demanded his execution after Conal died, but for your sake she didn't–'

'My sake? I don't think so. She had her project. You never had to see it, did you?' The hate in his eyes made me flinch. *'Want to See it, Finn?'*

He flung his hand to my forehead, and I wasn't fast

enough to stop him. As he shoved his memory into my mind I felt his pain etching itself into my own face. He did it with an easy, casual skill, the memory sharp as a honed blade.

Seth on all fours. His mouth open in a voiceless scream, his back impossibly twisted, the puncture marks glowing so red and angry they might be on fire. Propping himself up on his hands as the pain faded, only to stare straight into his son's eyes. His three-year-old son, wide awake and watching him.

The horror in his face, and then the rictus grin. 'It's a game, Rory! Ha!'

Carefully Rory studied my eyes, each in turn, visibly enjoying my reaction. 'He moved me out of his room after that. Only misjudged it by a couple of years. I'd been watching for so long, since I began to have a memory. And let me tell you, Finn: I *never* mistook it for a game.'

He laughed out loud. And then his rage was gone. Just like that, with nothing to replace it. He was empty of everything, and I knew it, because our link was still there, tenuous and fraying. I snapped it.

'You listen to me, Rory. Of course he kept it from you,' I hissed. 'Don't hold it against him. Not this, and not what he did when you were a baby. *Please*, and I don't care if I'm begging. If he lost you it would kill him.'

'Gods' sake, I don't hold it against him. He won't lose me because, inconvenient as it is, *I love him*.' Rory raked his fingers across his scalp. 'But you think I can live up to those holes in his back? You think I can pay for Conal with my freedom? I'll go mad. I can't be a symbol any more. I can't be the Bloodstone, Finn. *I'm too damn tired*.'

He staggered up straight and lunged at me. Expecting

violence, I flinched, but when he fell against me his head slammed into my chest. Reflexively I held him, shocked, wondering what became of a toddler who watched his father tortured. My gorge rose, realising the echo of pain I'd felt last night was a shadow of what Eili had inflicted when her grief was fresh and young, and her victim unhardened. I sat against the wall and Rory slid down with me.

'I don't want a bloody sword. I don't want to fight him because he thinks it'll make me feel better, and I don't want to learn how to slice my own father's head off. I'm Sithe and this *isn't how its meant to be*.'

I shuddered. 'It's not about taking lives. It's about keeping your own.'

'Comes to the same thing. I wonder what my mum would have thought? I wish I remembered her. I wish I remembered Conal.'

'I wish you did too,' I said, rubbing the bridge of my nose. 'Conal adored you. You were crazy about him.'

'He wouldn't have let Eili hurt my father. I wish he hadn't died. I wish nobody had.' He shook his head at the hopelessness of wishes. 'What's wrong with us?'

'It's no better on the other side, honestly. It isn't. People die, Laochan. Trouble is, you wish you hadn't found out about Eili.'

'It's changed everyth...' He went still in my arms. 'Did you just find my name?'

'What?' I pulled my arm away, panic rising. 'Did I? No, I don't have the right, Rory.'

'It isn't a question of the right.' He stared at me.

'Look. Ignore it. I don't even know what happened.' I scrambled to my feet. 'It'll be okay, Rory. I'll protect your father somehow. I don't know how. He won't let me hurt her.'

Rory laughed scornfully. 'As if.'

'Yeah, don't say it. He already told me she'd slice me like a ham.'

'She would, too. She's amazing with a sword.' There was reluctant hero-worship in his voice.

Indignant, I folded my arms. 'So will I be, too. One of these days.'

'About Dad.' He hesitated and picked at a cobweb on the wall. 'I'm glad it's you.'

I gave him a stupid stunned smile, not unlike the one I'd given his father when he kissed me. 'Thanks.'

'Um, Finn. Don't for Christ's sake tell my father I'm such a bleeding-heart pacifist.'

'Um, Rory. I have a feeling he knows.'

'Gods.' He put his face in his hands, then sat back, blowing out a sigh. 'And another thing. I'm not going to be this nice to you when there's witnesses.'

'Okay. I won't take it personally. I was fourteen once myself, you know.'

'So was my father, believe it or not,' said Rory. 'Though he may be lying. He was probably born forty.'

'On the contrary.' I rolled my eyes. 'He's never stopped being twelve.'

'Thank *you*,' said Seth. He was propped against the door frame, silhouetted against the white sunlight of the courtyard, and neither of us could make out the expression on his face.

'You'd better have only just got there,' said Rory.

'Of course. I'm a lot of things but not an eavesdropper.' He came inside and winked at me, then looked at his son. His eyes widened in surprise. 'You have your name.'

'Yeah.' Rory gave him a slow grin.

I bit hard on my thumb. 'It isn't. Not really.'

'Yes it is.' Seth took Rory's head in his hand and kissed the top of it. 'Laochan.'

'I'm really sorry. It just came out.' I shut my eyes tight and chewed my knuckle.

'Well, that's what happens.' Seth touched my face and brushed my eyes open. 'For gods' sake. I like it.' He put an arm around Rory's shoulders. 'Have you forgiven us, then? Let's go find Jed.'

I watched them go, and after five minutes I heard their horses riding out. I knew Jed and Iolaire were outside the dun, and it was up to Seth to decide if it was safe to take Rory out on his own. At least they were out of the way now. A tremor went down my spine. Confrontations with Rory were one thing, but for my next trick...

Outside the armoury the sun was almost too warm. Hannah was preoccupied for now, cantering the chestnut round the arena in a figure of eight. I turned my face to the intense blue sky and cast around with my mind. Eili wasn't hiding, and I headed for her rooms.

At the top of the stone stairs, turning into the corridor, I almost collided with Sionnach.

'Finn,' he said, and his scarred face lit with a smile. 'What's up?'

Slickly I raised a block in my mind, and the smile left his face. 'I want to see Eili.'

'Eili?' He frowned. 'Finn, listen to me. Please don't fight my sister. Please.'

'I don't want to fight. I want to talk to her, Sionnach. Just talk.' I took a breath. 'Alone.'

He gripped my wrist. 'Finn, I like you. And if she harms you Seth will double my scars, if he doesn't kill me.'

'Don't be so melodramatic. He won't do either, even if she does, which she won't.' I glowered at his hand, and he let me go with a sigh.

'I'm glad you and Seth are together,' he said.

'Yeah?' I looked at him uncertainly.

'Oh, yeah. He's been lovesick for years. ' Sionnach rolled his eyes fondly. 'After that last time he went over to see you? He looked like someone had hit him with a brick.'

'He... really? Did he?' I tried to remember what had been different. For him, anyway. Nothing had been different for me. God, the man took forever to take a hint.

'I suppose you didn't know what he felt.' Sionnach shrugged. '*He* certainly didn't. Just those of us who had to thole his moods.'

'Oh. I'm sorry.' I felt stunned. 'No, I didn't know. You wouldn't, from the way...'

'The way he goes on. Quite. Eili hoped you wouldn't love him back. Anything to hurt him,' said Sionnach unhappily. 'But you do love him back, and I'm glad, even if that's disloyal.'

I kicked at a loose floorboard. 'Sionnach, you wouldn't know disloyalty if it came up and hit you with a stick. I don't know how you manage it, really I don't. You give new meaning to the word *conflicted*.'

He picked at traces of wood glue on his thumb. 'I'm glad you didn't waste time. He needs you. It's right you're together.'

'Not what your sister thinks,' I said dryly.

'My sister is very unhappy. You know this, Finn.'

'Seth's not over the moon about her.' I bit my lip. 'Sionnach. Do you hate him too?'

He tilted his head to rest it against the bare stone wall, and shut his eyes. 'Seth is my friend and my Captain. I would follow him to the end of the world and die for him there, and he knows it. I love him as I loved his brother.' When he opened his eyes there was torment in them. 'But damn him for what he did. Conal might have died anyway, we all know that. Very likely he would. Kate was too clever for us. But if Eili hadn't had to make an end of him, she might have endured it and stayed the same. It was Seth's work she did.'

'It was her choice,' I said dully. 'Seth would have done it if she'd let him.'

'Yes.' Pushing himself away from the wall Sionnach grabbed my head and shook it gently. His eyes were raw with unshed tears. 'But if he hadn't betrayed us all, there'd have been no question of Eili doing his job. It's between them,' he said. 'Believe me, I've tried, but there's nothing more I can say to her. I once had to choose between her and Conal, and I will *never* make that kind of choice again. No-one will ever make me, do you understand? Not my sister and not Seth and not you either. I will not intercede any more, Finn.'

'That is choosing her, Sionnach.'

'Well.' He dropped his hand and walked past me, but glanced back. 'I'm conflicted.'

His footfalls faded down the stone stairs. I stood for a moment, my stomach churning, then took a breath and called Eili. The reply in my mind was immediate, glad and challenging. The heavy oak door swung open, and Eili made a sweeping gesture of invitation.

'Do my brother a favour,' smiled Eili as she closed the door. 'Don't waste his time asking him to betray me.'

'No-one's asking such a thing,' I said. 'But you know that.'

Opera music was playing, the aria making my heart ache though I didn't understand the words. Eili watched me closely. 'Listen, Finn. Do you know what he's saying? He dies in despair.' She closed her eyes. 'When he's never loved life so much.'

I was riveted horribly for a moment. Shaking myself, I turned to the beechwood desk. Without even turning them, I knew what was in those photograph frames.

The air in here felt so oppressive it was malign, but the window was open and the corners of Eili's papers lifted in a feeble breeze. They were anchored to the desk by a black broken sword hilt, a few jutting shards of blunt steel all that was left of its blade. There had once been silver inlay but it was tarnished to the colour of the rest of the hilt. As I touched it with my fingertips, a sensation shivered up my arm. I frowned. There was a stone archway to the left; beyond it I could see one corner of Eili's bed, the linen white and smooth, the corner folded with military precision. There was something else folded on it. I walked to the archway and stared.

It lay flat, the sleeves crossed immaculately, but it hadn't been laundered in more than a decade. Once the shirt had been slate blue, but it was faded to light denim and discoloured by black ancient stains that covered more than half of it. Even from the doorway I could smell him on it, a faint sad presence. I knew what the clinging weight of the air was: it was grief, heavy and pervasive and throttling. Something hot stung the corner of my eye.

~ *Eili*, I said, but not aloud.

'Oh, you'll get a taste of it.' Eili was so close I could feel her breath on my neck. 'Seth will die long before you do. Even if he survives me. Even if he survives the war, and Laszlo, and Kate, he'll die, and if you don't die with him you'll have centuries without him. And I put you on warning, Finn.' She dropped her voice to a light whisper. 'I don't intend him to survive me.'

I spun to face her. 'Oh, leave him alone, Eili. Conal was his brother. He made a mistake but he loved him. When did you last pay so dearly for one mistake?'

'I'll tell you when,' hissed Eili. 'The day I trusted Murlainn with the life of my lover. The day I had to cut Cù Chaorach's throat to release him. *That* day.'

'You haven't released him,' I said.

Eili ignored that. 'Do you think I feel it any less now?'

'Of course you don't feel it less,' I snapped. 'You're hanging onto your pain with your fingernails, just so you can kill Seth with it. What would Conal say?'

Eili bared white teeth. 'You never liked me, did you, Finn? Not from the day we met.'

'I grew out of that. What's your excuse?'

'I don't need one. I haven't cared for anyone but Sionnach since the day I left Conal's corpse on Brokentor. You're nothing to me, Finn. I only grudge you happiness because yours is all bound up in Murlainn's.' Eili spat on the floor. 'And his death is the deal I made with myself the day I healed him. I'll keep Seth to it. Unless he can kill me first.'

'He'll never do that and you know it.'

'More fool him. In the meantime he owes it to his brother to suffer.'

The aria was programmed on repeat. And repeat. The first sad bars swelled again. I couldn't take my eyes off Eili.

I'd never looked at madness before and there was something hypnotic about it.

'Seth doesn't owe Conal a thing. Neither do you or I. We couldn't, even if we wanted to. There's nothing we can give him. He's *dead*.'

Eili's eyes blazed like ice. 'I can give him the life of the man who killed him.'

I shoved my hands into my hair and hauled it behind my ears. 'Even if he wanted it − which he can't because he's *dead* − it's Jed who's hunting down his killer, and God knows what it's doing to him. Seth didn't kill Conal, *Laszlo did*.' I stared into Eili's glittering eyes. 'There's only one thing you can give Conal. His freedom.'

Eili's smile died, the bones of her face set hard.

'I know you won't, but I'll ask you anyway.' I swallowed. 'Let him go.'

'Don't beg twice in your life. This time I can't give you what you want. I don't have him here.' Eili's teeth clenched hard. 'As you are so keen to remind me, he is *dead*.'

I shut my eyes, feeling him beyond all doubt, there locked in the massive grief, and I felt the terrible sadness snaking into my heart in a black tide. Shoving past Eili I made for the exit, forcing myself not to run, and when I flung open the door I breathed clean air as if it was the first oxygen I'd tasted since entering Eili's mausoleum.

'One more thing, Finn.' Eili's voice stopped me in my tracks. 'I'll tell you this much. After you've had Seth, after you've had this kind of love, you'll never find anyone who matters as much. Never, not in all your unbearably long life. And I want you to know that.'

RORY

The tide was far out, leaving a vast plain of pleated sand patched with shallow lakes of silver. There were fishers' boats dragged up beside the flat rocks at the end of the bay, and the pungent tang of smouldering oak drifted from barrels. We'd traded good gutting knives for a sizeable quantity of smoked herring and sea trout, delivery promised within two days, but the barter hadn't exactly been urgent at this time of year. My father had wanted the excuse to talk to the fishers, that was all.

Seth always insisted that the noncommittal wavering of some of the communities beyond the dun lands didn't bother him, but I knew otherwise. The longer Kate's reach grew, the less secure he felt. He thought she was up to something. He thought her strategy had taken a subtle but crucial turning. He'd dearly have liked to know where it led.

He said he was sorry, but there were times he had to parade me.

'You're the Bloodstone. Bad luck, sunshine.'

'You've spent my life telling me that's all bollocks.'

He gave a shrug. 'I've spent your life telling you it doesn't matter what I think. They have to believe you exist and that you matter. If they don't see me flaunting you, they'll think I'm on the run, or that I'm scared, or that I've already lost you. Sorry,' he muttered again.

I knew it was what he hated most of all. 'It's okay,' I told him with a rueful grin. 'Flaunt away.'

His mind brushed mine affectionately, as if he'd tousled

my hair with an invisible hand. 'You're all that stops half of them actively fighting me. They'll sit on that fence till their fat arses fall in half.'

I laughed. The moments when we were in tune with one another grew rarer by the day, and I treasured them. Which never stopped me falling violently out with him at a later time.

And sometimes sooner than I expected. 'Nuall MacInnes at Dunster wants to broker talks,' I ventured.

'Nuall MacInnes can kiss my rear end.'

'Would it kill you to try a little diplomacy?'

'Probably,' he snapped. 'And you and all.'

'Only I've been reading about the Clann Ranald siege and—'

'Why in the name of the gods did I give you an education if you're only going to pick the bits you like? How do you think any diplomat fares without a snarling army at his back? That's what saved Sorcha NicRanald, not getting pissed in her great hall with three enemy captains.'

'Fine,' I growled. 'Fine. But if you're so worried about the full-mortals, why are you spending every ounce of clann blood fighting Sithe?'

He uttered a curse he'd slapped me for before now. 'One chapter of your Sun Tzu and one page of Clausewitz. Off by heart, and I'll want you to recite by the end of the week. Jesus and all the *saints*.' And he gave the roan a kick that made it snap its jaws in anger, and rode ahead.

'Ah, cheer up, Rory.' Iolaire nudged his horse to my side. 'Your father's theology's as confused as he is.'

'Confused?' I growled. 'He's too damn sure of himself.'

'You think?' Iolaire raised an eyebrow at me, and I shrugged and changed the subject.

'I'm worried about Jed,' I said in a low voice.

'Aren't we all.' Iolaire sighed.

'He's obsessed.'

~ *Driven,* came my father's instant correction.

My heart contracted with anger. Sometimes I understood my brother's revulsion for silent communication. ~ *I wasn't talking to you.*

Ahead, his back still turned to me, Seth shrugged. He must have been slightly ashamed, though, because he let Jed ride up beside him and said, 'You shouldn't hunt alone any more.'

'What brought that on?' Jed laughed.

'You know fine. She's up to something. The situation's changed and I don't know how.' Pointedly he added, 'It's not as if you catch much.'

'Yet,' growled Jed, and Seth slapped him consolingly on the back.

It was hard to believe they'd once loathed one another. They fought often enough, verbally and sometimes physically, but you only had to watch them play shinty or football on the same team, or see their slightly drink-fuddled eyes meet in the great hall at night as Seth tuned his guitar for the key of Jed's whistle, to know that they were soulmates of a sort.

They joined their blood when I was eight. I was sent to bed early, but I didn't go. I crouched in the shadows outside the great hall, holding my breath when I heard Carraig draw his dirk. I was scared, because I knew it wasn't easy. I'd heard the toughest men shout with pain when the savage cut was made, I'd seen stains from the blood that was spilt, and the healers always stayed out of it. I knew my father had tolerated worse things in the great hall without crying out, but I worried for him, and even more for Jed.

But there had been only a long silence, then fierce pride racing through me when I realised it was over, that neither my father nor my brother had made a sound. I'd curled up outside the door, letting the music and the raucous laughter wash over me till I fell asleep there. But I woke up in my own bed, and nobody ever gave me hell for disobeying my father. Indeed I had a vague half-formed memory that it was my father who carried me to bed. There was even a cloudy image in my mind: blood soaking through a bandage on Seth's left hand, staining my t-shirt. I knew it wasn't a dream because I still had the outgrown t-shirt, and the t-shirt still had the bloodstain.

Now, as they cut across the wide expanse of beach towards the pinewood, it would be easy to think Seth was pulling rank, throwing his weight around as Captain of all the captains and the only surviving son of Griogair. Watching his scarred left hand clench and unclench, I knew my father was only afraid for Jed. Really afraid, behind the cool sarcasm and the laughter.

'Besides,' Jed shrugged, 'I don't hunt alone.'

'Yeah, yeah.' Seth jerked his thumb back at Iolaire. 'I know he's a superhero, but there's still only two of you.'

'And Liath.'

'And Liath. Where is she?'

'Hunting.' Jed's brow furrowed. 'What you'd call proper hunting. She's been gone all day.'

'Must be a good hunt.' Seth raised an eyebrow.

'She's been gone for longer before now.'

'Fine. Anyway, this Turlach. Where are they getting the nerve to come so close? Right into the dun lands.'

'That bothers me,' said Iolaire. 'Turlach wasn't the type to be taken unawares.'

Jed made a face. 'A kelpie that size wouldn't have to take him unawares. It didn't take Seth by surprise and it nearly killed even him.'

'Seth was, ah…'

'Incapable,' grimaced Seth.

'Disarmed,' said Iolaire with a kindness that I knew would set my father's teeth on edge. 'And Turlach would not have been alone if he was spying. Why wasn't he saved? His corpse, at least?'

'I see what you're saying,' said Seth.

'Well, I don't,' I snapped. I was sick of cryptic remarks.

Glancing back at me, Seth sighed through his teeth. 'All right. Iolaire is saying Turlach was given to the kelpie.'

'He – what?' The blood drained from my face. 'Why?'

'Don't know,' said Iolaire, sucking his teeth. 'Even Kate's a little too evolved for blood sacrifices, so why would she do such a thing?'

'I wonder if he was dead before the kelpie got him?' said my father. 'The state he was in, it's not like we'd see a disabling wound. His throat could have been slit and we wouldn't have known it.'

'I hope it was,' I muttered.

'There's another possibility,' said Iolaire. 'Turlach could have been trying to get to us.'

'Yes, but why? And they didn't come after you when you defected, not straight away.'

'I had a head start. And I didn't know anything important. If I had, it might have been different.'

'It's the most likely explanation.' My father sounded glum. 'I wonder what the hell he wanted.'

'Maybe nothing,' said Jed. 'Kate would do anything, and Laszlo would do it for her. Maybe she didn't like him. Maybe she did it for fun. Or to taunt us.'

'You think Laszlo's capable of that?' asked Iolaire. 'Giving a man to a kelpie for a laugh?'

'Course he is,' said Jed.

Iolaire nipped his lower lip in his teeth but he said nothing.

Seth spoke to the blue roan and it broke into a trot through the pine trunks, Jed moving in an echoing flanking movement to the right. They melted into the trees like mist to hunt for signs of spies or danger. I knew they were there close by, but I couldn't have pinpointed where. I knew how to do it but I wasn't as good at it as they were, because I didn't concentrate long enough. I didn't even care enough. Anything was more rewarding than learning the tricks of war.

Jed was good at it, but he would be. Jed should have been the half-breed Sithe. He had the instincts, the ruthlessness, the courage. He had that necessary, unflinching loyalty to his Captain, even when he disagreed furiously and vocally with him. Jed was much better at the Sithe life than I was. Which wasn't really fair, because one day Jed was going to die and leave me. I would be without Jed for years, for centuries, and that wasn't fair either.

I didn't like Iolaire's silence, but finally he looked at me and grinned. 'Don't let it put a damper on your day, Laochan. We'll celebrate tonight and you'll see your father and brother in a better mood.'

'You don't think Laszlo would do it.' I stared at my brother-by-love. 'Do you?'

'He'd do almost anything. I know that as well as anyone.'

Iolaire sighed. 'Just... not that. I don't think he'd do that. Not to one of his own men.' He chewed his cheek. 'Nils is a cold-blooded murderer. But as a captain he gets loyalty and trust, and he's a popular leader. Strikes me as odd, that's all.'

'What will you think when Jed kills him?'

Iolaire smiled at my confidence. 'I'll be glad, of course.'

'But you wouldn't do it, would you?'

'No.' Iolaire's face lost all expression. 'I don't kill for vengeance. Besides, Jed claimed him. He claimed Laszlo's life from me in the great hall, in front of witnesses.'

'I know. I was there. Didn't you resent that?'

Iolaire shrugged. 'Jed did it to spare me. Ach, Rory. He knew it wasn't in me, to turn my love for my child into killing-hate. It would have warped me, so your brother claimed Laszlo from me. It's one of the reasons I love him. *One*.' He twisted a strand of his horse's mane. 'I'm not morally against revenge killing. There's a place for it, and it's not for me to judge. It's just that it's not in *me*. I will have to kill Cluaran, but that isn't vengeance on either side.'

I hesitated. 'Then why do you have to?'

'I don't want to.' Distractedly Iolaire rubbed the little thistle tattoo on his collarbone. 'But I'll have to, unless he kills me first. He was my captain; it's his duty to kill his renegades. He won't like it any more than I do. But one of us has to kill the other, just to survive.'

'Iolaire.' I hesitated. 'I'm sorry. All this killing. Because of me.'

'We're at war, Rory.' Iolaire gave me a gentle smile. 'And we were killing each other centuries before you came along. It's the human condition.'

'I don't even know how to fix the damn Veil. It's like

I'm meant to be creating some brilliant tapestry and I can't even do cross-stitch.'

'Ah, Rory. You can only live and do your best, like the rest of us.' Iolaire sighed and slapped my horse's rump, making it start and buck. 'Now. I want to know if a boy with a name rides faster than one without. You've never beaten me yet.'

'You'll be sorry you said that.'

There was a mile to the dun, and the air was sweet, and for once I was free. I wrestled my horse's head back and then I drove it to a gallop. Iolaire never had a chance, not this time. I rode fast enough to drive my own thoughts, and everyone else's, from my mind.

FINN

I tugged on a t-shirt against the cool of the night. Yawning as I sat on the bed cross-legged, trying to make myself comfortable but not too comfortable, I touched Seth's back with my fingertips. He slept on his front, unsurprisingly. I traced the distorted pattern of the knotwork tattoo and then, avoiding the ugly raw punctures between his shoulder blades, I stroked the furrowed scars of his punishment. Those didn't hurt any more, and there was no chance of him waking up. I'd made sure of that.

Seth's mind was still tangled up in mine after lovemaking, and I could feel his innocuous unfrightening dream: that made sense, since all his nightmares were waking ones. I eased my mind apart from his, but he didn't even stir as the connection broke. That was better. I'd been this close to sending myself to sleep along with him, and I still felt leadenly drowsy.

Distantly I could hear music from the hall. Even Rory had long ago torn himself away and gone to bed, but plenty in the dun liked an excuse for a party and they'd probably go on till dawn, celebrating his nameday. I was still reeling a little, not so much from whisky as from the sudden realisation that I'd fallen in love with my clann at last, and they seemed to be fairly taken with me. Now that was what I called a party.

By the time Seth and I had left, Jed was seriously drunk but he was still going strong, and now, distantly, Iolaire was singing. I smiled. They were onto the maudlin stuff

and he was singing *Carrickfergus*. Half the battle-scarred
Sithe would be on the verge of tears by now, the other
half openly weeping. They sustained a lot of damage over
centuries, but no-one was more sentimental than one-eyed,
scar-faced faeries with missing ears and fingers and arrow-
holes in their flesh.

That reminded me. I blinked and forced my eyes back
open. On the headboard Faramach's talons scrabbled and
he eyed me, head tilted. I gave an exasperated sigh.

'Is she waiting for me to fall asleep or what?'

Faramach gave a soft croak.

'Come on, Eili,' I murmured. 'If you're hard enough.'

'Eili,' rasped Faramach. 'Ha!'

In his place by the fire, Branndair lifted his great black
head and stared first at me and then at the raven.

'No, no.' I gasped. 'Don't you dare. Don't you—'

The wolf took a running leap, landing on the mattress
with all the grace of an Airbus, but it wasn't enough to
wake Seth. I breathed again and glared at Branndair resentfully. 'What, just because Faramach's here?'

Branndair opened his jaws, grinning, then made himself
comfortable, head on his paws, yellow eyes intent on Seth.
Shifting a little, he licked my hand idly.

'Ach.' I rubbed his muzzle. 'Will you keep me awake,
then?'

Gently he nipped one of my fingers between his teeth,
then locked his eyes on my throat.

I swallowed. 'You still make me nervous,' I growled,
scratching his ear, 'but I see what you're getting at.'

At my throat I felt the empty claw that had once held
Rory's shield stone. There was tarnish in the angles and
corners but the coarsely-made talon hadn't got blunter with

age. I clutched it in my scarred palm. No need to draw blood this time. Drowsily my head nodded forward.

The sting of the claw and a nip from Branndair alerted me. Wide awake again, I laid my palm across Seth's crossbow scars. He didn't stir. The sleep I'd laid on him was so deep he'd have a stinking headache in the morning, but I could live with any foul mood of his. Hell, I was used to it.

My hand tingled at the knuckle and wrist and I forgot everything else, making myself think only of Eili, forcing my mind between her and Seth. A needle of pain shot up one of my finger bones and I fenced it away, feeling the recoil of another mind as the pain rebounded. I laughed softly.

'There you are, you mad witch. Well, here I am too.'

I had no idea how this was done but I was finding out, learning fast as Eili's hate dissipated, easing past my guard. I felt it like trickling shadows at the edge of my brain, and I backed my mind protectively closer to Seth. As Eili came up against the barrier, the hatred coalesced. It slammed into my mind like a fist, but there was no subtlety in that. It hurt, but it hurt Eili worse when it was flung back at her. Wincing, I waited.

The pause was too long, and I felt the stirrings of panic. Where was Eili?

Gone. *Oh, God.*

I swore aloud, almost crying with despair that I'd made it so easy for her—

In a split instant, there was another mind inside mine. Not Eili's and not Seth's: a black jagged intelligence, hard and ruthless. The alien mind guided me and then was gone, but so was my confusion.

There at the edge of my consciousness Eili was sliding past, her venomous hate snaking into Seth, on target and almost there. No time. Purely by instinct I separated my mind from my body and flung myself into the scars.

Blood and blackness: it was a vile place. My mind was on its own but still I felt the shudder go through my detached body. Feeling that detachment I was afraid, panic squeezing my distant heart, because I'd never done this and it was dangerous, there was a chance I wouldn't get back. I felt the itch of Eili's pleasure at my fear; then the panic faded before the awfulness of the place I was in. It was all dark pain and rage, guilt and grief, and the poisonous lick of hate as Eili closed in.

I barred her way, feeling my teeth clench hard somewhere far beyond me. The tentacles of pain were slick and sneaking and everywhere, and I broadened my block. Behind and around me was the black dull pulse of Seth's blood, the slow crash of his heart, and the razor thrill of nerves rising to a familiar attack. He stirred very slightly.

~ *You're not going to wake him*, I thought furiously.

I felt Eili's laughter. ~ *Who's going to stop me? Amateur.*

The hate slid against my disembodied mind like a sword blade, testing, forcing. I parried it. The sheer violence of the woman's loathing was her biggest handicap, I realised. Turn it back and it hurt her as it should have hurt Seth: the trick was to intercept her first. It hurt and throbbed in my mind, too, but I was wrestling the blade of hate aside. Eili withdrew, recoiling in shock, then flung it back in a massive hammer blow. I met it head on, heard my detached self gasp, felt my teeth clench and my distant fingers grip my distant scalp.

Seth's blood pulsed again. I thought: that's his life running in his veins, that's his life the witch is poisoning. This time, when the hate came at him, my mind touched a new plane of anger. I no longer cared that the hate was buffeting my own mind, no longer even felt it, only deflected it and fired it furiously back. The bolt I sent into Eili's mind was my rage, and my love, and Eili's own frantic hate. It hit Eili like a cannonball.

~ *Get back from him, Udhar!*

With a single furious shriek, Eili was gone.

I blinked. This time my eyes were where they ought to be; I was out of Seth's body and back in my own. Flexing my fingers, I sighed out soundlessly. Being back was more of a relief than I wanted to admit. My breath hissed unsteadily between my teeth and my hand was trembling; I clenched it into stillness with an angry conscious effort, then realised my whole body was shaking anyway. If I could string two coherent thoughts together I might cope, but for now I'd sit quiet and motionless, give my brain a chance to catch up. The scary truth was that my mind was fraying at the edges and I couldn't think how to stop it unravelling. Unravelling…

Oh, my God. Seth. I'm unravelling. Seth!

At my side Branndair sat up, stretched, and licked my face, nibbling at my ear, his massive paws planted one on either side of me. Laughing unsteadily, I put my arms round his thick-maned neck, burying my face in his fur. He felt ridiculously real and warm. He grunted as I clutched him, my eyelids leaden.

He lay down, letting me hug his huge body like a pillow. The beat of his wolf-heart was a soporific sound against my ear, and he stretched lazily, one paw across my body so that I lay like a cub against its mother's belly. My brain felt calm and it didn't hurt any more, and my mind was in one piece.

I fell asleep before another thought had time to cross it.

KATE

Why did it irritate her so much, the sight of Laszlo and Gealach together? She'd orchestrated the match herself, and lost a good fighter over it, but for her purposes at the time it had been worth it. She'd been sick of Laszlo's suffocating attentions and he'd fancied the woman; he was happier with a second and more devoted lover, and that made him more efficient. Everything she did had a purpose. *Play the long game, Kate.*

And the fact that Murlainn had finally bound himself to a lover was all to the good in the end. His temporary happiness was a vile itch that one day she'd enjoy scratching. *Put up with it, Kate.*

Of course, Laszlo's evident pleasure reminded her of Murlainn's; that was all it was. And when she wanted the full-mortal again, he always came back to her. There was no reason to be angry with him, but the softness and the physical longing in his eyes when he looked at Gealach. It wasn't jealousy on Kate's part. More... impatience. The man's emotional fulfilment had never exactly been part of her gameplan. Such a man was wasted on love. Perhaps she should never have indulged him. Perhaps she should have kept his edges sharp.

With a languid sigh she pushed aside her wine glass. At the far side of the hall, where the silver candlelight was faint and the shadows clustered, she knew her captains were muttering. That was a pity, but she'd never expected it to be easy. Setting Laszlo in command over Alasdair Kilrevin had only been the first and most cosmetic of her concessions to her people's resentful mood. There would be more. Alasdair was not a popular man, but after all she'd had her own doubts. It was amazing how swiftly the mind of a people could sway and bend when someone brought them successes and hope and victory.

Take it to the endgame, Kate.

She was their queen, and they loved her. More than that, she was their queen *because* they loved her. It counted for so very much. She bore it in mind when she saw Cluaran detach himself from the small group of mutterers and approach her raised chair.

Kate tightened her fist to stop herself tapping her long nails. 'Cluaran. You're worried.'

Bull-necked and shaven-headed, he looked every inch a hard man, but the loss of Iolaire had wounded him deeply; what kind of a queen would she be if she took no notice of these things? Besides, Cù Chaorach's lover had killed Cluaran's. She knew fierce loyalty when she saw it, and it was there in his eyes, glinting as bright as the golden torque round his throat. He took her proffered hand, kissed it and touched it to his forehead, then stepped back a pace.

'A few of us are concerned, Kate. There was a raid last night. Kinlaggan.'

She frowned and put a finger to her temple. 'Remind me.'

'The settlement thirty miles inland and north from Murlainn's dun. Loyal to him and his rebels, but outwith his claimed lands. Two dozen fighters attacked it at dusk and killed every man, woman and child.'

Kate shut her eyes as an expression of pain pinched her face. Then she opened them once more, gazed at him, folded her hands in her lap.

'This raid was nothing to do with me, Cluaran. But can I help it if my followers feel passionately?'

'Kate, they love you. But some need a firm rein.' Cluaran's gaze was steady on hers. *He's loyal to me,* she thought, *but that doesn't mean he believes me.*

'A crime like this: it wounds me in my heart, Cluaran. I would never condone it. *Never.* Do you know who did this thing?'

'The rumour is that Cuthag led the raid.'

Kate sighed as she rose to her feet and strode to the wall and back. 'Cuthag is impetuous. He tries to please me. I can no more punish him with exile than I could you, Cluaran.'

'I wouldn't suggest such a thing.' Cluaran kept pace at her side, urgency spilling out of him. 'But a word from you—'

She spun on her heel and stared at him. 'And is there proof of Cuthag's responsibility?'

'No, but—'

She raised a hand. Laszlo had listened to every word from his place in the shadow of the pillar, and she beckoned him with a quick sharp motion.

He was already protesting as he approached to kiss her hand. 'Kinlaggan was nothing to do with me, Kate. Cluaran knows it.'

The two men exchanged a glance, one that was not without hostility. Interesting.

Laszlo nodded at Gealach, who was busy comparing longbows with another fighter. He raised his voice. 'Gealach was with me last night, and we were not on the road to Kinlaggan. Isn't that true, Gealach?'

She nodded, raising bemused eyebrows, then returned to her discussion.

Irritation made Kate snap, 'I never accused you, Nils. I

want to ask you both. Is there proof the massacre wasn't Murlainn's doing?'

Both of them gaped at her. Gods, but these men were idiots sometimes. '*Murlainn?*' repeated Cluaran, incredulous. 'Murlainn wouldn't do it. I hate the man, but he wouldn't.'

'Once again, that wasn't my question.' Her voice dripped acid. 'I said, is there *proof* he did not kill those children?'

This time the pair of them shook their heads, slowly. The two men's eyes did not meet. They were not close. Would never be conspirators. Were both her loyal servants, in their way. And even a pair as obtuse as these two could catch her meaning if she laboured it.

'I know you both have doubts about Kilrevin,' she told them silkily. 'I understand your hesitation, but I ask you to trust that I have knowledge you do not have, and that I will use it wisely and against our common enemy. Yes?'

'Yes, Kate,' growled Cluaran.

'Though I wish you'd trust us with a little of that knowledge,' muttered Laszlo.

She gave him a sharp glance. 'As for Cuthag, my lands are extensive and my people scattered. He is loyal to me, he keeps order and enforces my law, and if my command of him has a certain informality, it is because I trust him and I trust his fighters. That doesn't mean I encourage brutality.'

'Perhaps you should discourage it more,' grunted Laszlo.

Her temper flared. 'Look to our real enemies, gentlemen. Murlainn's fortress is the one that harbours unlawful killers.'

'I understand, Kate.' There was something in Laszlo's tone, an underlying sarcasm she did not like. And she was impatient with his hypocrisy. She understood perfectly why he had no wish to meet the full-mortal Cuilean in the field

– that stupid prophecy that said he'd meet his death only at the hands of another full-mortal – but his strategic retreats were starting to look unpleasantly like cowardice, and that set a poor example. Perhaps it was time at last for the scales to fall from the besotted Gealach's eyes. That might teach the man a lesson.

She swept back her skirts and turned away from Laszlo as he returned to Gealach's side. Cluaran she beckoned with an imperious gesture.

Truly, she hadn't realised how angry she was until she returned to her seat, and found her fingers were trembling. This time, she let her nails tap the carved and gilded wooden arm. The click and rhythm of them soothed her.

She thought of Cuthag, and of Alasdair, and of Laszlo; of all her loyal, living weapons. There were other kinds of weapon, of course, and love could be the finest and the deadliest. And there were men who did not deserve happiness, however brief.

She raised her head. Cluaran waited, stoic and patient. Gods, how she admired him.

'I shall deal with Murlainn's boy soon,' she said, 'and I'll want you there.'

He nodded, and kissed her hand, and made to turn.

'Wait,' she said.

He hesitated. 'My queen?'

'There is a sacrifice I have always known I'd have to make,' she said. 'Do you know what that is?'

His eyes were cautious, but very steady on hers. 'Yes, Kate. We all know it.'

'Then, Cluaran?' There was the merest hint of regret in her smile. 'Finish it now.'

HANNAH

'What have you done to your hair?' Rory stared at me as I shut the heavy oak door.

I glanced around at the traces and imprints Rory had left on his room. Books and DVDs all over the place: action thrillers and science fiction. Old film posters and unframed photos were stuck carelessly on the wall around his bed and on the iron bedstead itself. Most were of Jed and Seth, Sionnach and Orach, but there were some dog-eared faded ones of his uncle, the dun's last Captain: Conal MacGregor.

Dad. Swallowing, I looked swiftly back at Rory. He hadn't seen my expression because he was still staring at my scalp.

I rubbed my hand across it. My hair was cut back to about an inch all over, not very expertly. I should have been wary of Eili's skills just from looking at the state of her own haircut, but I actually quite liked the amateurish result. I'd wanted it shorter, I'd wanted it shaved, but Eili had refused. It would give us away, she said.

'Don't you like it?'

Rory made a doubtful face. 'It's okay. But everybody's going to wonder who died.'

'Oh, are they?' Turning my back on the rough photo gallery, I smiled at him.

'Yeah, because – oh, it doesn't matter. I kind of liked it before.'

'Too bad.' I gave him another smile, a more belligerent one, and raked my fingers through my hair, making it stick up in spikes.

Rory frowned and squinted at me as if reaching for a lost memory, then shook his head and shrugged. 'Okay, okay. What's up?'

I wandered round his room, picking up DVDs and old toys, setting them down, flipping through books. 'Rory. Why wouldn't your dad let you go after the baby horse? After Sionnach shot its mother?'

Rory flopped back on his bed. 'Wasn't exactly a good time, was it?'

I nodded thoughtfully. 'She's still there, though. Foal without a mother. And us with a free morning tomorrow.'

'Don't start.' He rolled onto his side, watching me. 'I can't go to the mere on my own.'

I let that one hang in the air. I let my lips twitch, though.

'Your point is?' There was an edge of anger to his voice now.

Judging I'd got the timing about right, I flopped onto the bed beside him. 'Weird, isn't it? I've seen you with everybody else's kelpies. You can ride them all.'

'I'm not supposed—' This time, his mouth closed on the objection. I wanted to applaud but I knew I'd better not; instead I left him a moment to rejig his answer and recover his masculine pride. 'I mean, it's very unusual. They only answer to one person. Usually. That's all I meant.' His cheekbones coloured.

I nodded. 'So the rogue one, the white one, that was an exception for you. Only because it had a foal at foot. And its foal isn't going to be like that, is it? Especially if you get it young, 'specially if it hasn't got a mother now.'

'Ahhhh... Dad didn't think that was a good...'

'He never took his own horse, did he? When you went out before.'

'No. Thought it'd end up in a fight.'

'Even if that was true, it doesn't apply to the foal. A foal wouldn't fight an adult horse. Another kelpie would reassure it. Probably.'

'Not Dad's.' He laughed dismissively. 'It's a stallion. She'd run a mile.'

'I'm not thinking of your father's.' I gave him a withering look. *Careful, Hannah. Careful.* 'Eili's is a mare.'

'Eili's kelpie?'

Rory was visibly startled. After a moment, he shut his eyes and rubbed the bridge of his nose with finger and thumb.

I felt the curious brush of his mind, repelled smoothly by my perfect total block. I didn't need to See inside his head, after all. I knew he needed his father's respect; he needed it like he needed a heartbeat. And without any kind of telepathy I knew exactly what temptation was running through his head now, what thoughts of sweet bloodless revenge on Eili. Oh, to use her precious warhorse to get him his own...

'*Eili's is a mare,*' he repeated slowly. 'Dad would have thought of that, if it—'

'I sometimes wonder if your father wants you to have that much independence.'

For a moment I thought I'd timed it wrong, gone too far and too fast. Rory's face hardened and his eyes narrowed. I was just beginning to curse myself in the foulest inward terms when he sat up straight, fists clenched in the bedclothes.

'I sometimes wonder that too.'

And that was when I knew I had him.

FINN

I woke with a sneeze, wolf-hair in my nostrils. The smell that clung to them was Branndair's fur and his strong carnivorous breath, but it wasn't unpleasant and I didn't want to pull away from him. My arms tightened around his neck as his warm tongue lashed my cheek.

'I thought you didn't like him,' I heard Seth say. 'And now I'm all jealous.'

Reluctantly I pushed Branndair off and sat up, yawning. Seth was dressed and sitting on the edge of the bed, fighting the slight smile that tugged at his mouth.

'So.' I jiggled my eyebrows. 'Which one of us are you jealous of?'

'Ha, ha.'

'It's morning,' I said blearily as Faramach clambered onto my forearm and gave Branndair a raucous piece of his mind. 'Was that you in my head last night, Faramach?' I tickled the spiky feathers at his throat. 'Thanks, pal.' I looked him not quite in the eye, a little shy after sharing his eerie raven-mind in the night.

'I have the feeling I've been ganged up on,' said Seth, rubbing his temple hard with a forefinger. 'I didn't drink that much.'

'Have you got a headache?' I asked guiltily. 'I'm sorry.'

'Well. That's nothing, is it?' He stared at me. Branndair lifted his massive bulk and stalked up the bed, flopping down proprietorially next to him, and Seth scratched his neck.

I gave the wolf a rueful look. 'He'll never let me forget this.'

Seth laughed one of his low villainous laughs. 'No more hearth rug, my pet,' he told Branndair. He glanced at me. 'Thanks, lover. But don't do it again.'

'Oh, sure.' I looked skywards. What was it with him? Testosterone?

He snorted. 'Well. You're very talented.' Standing up, he took my hand and pulled me off the bed. 'But it's dangerous, what you did.'

'Yep,' I agreed. 'And riding around the woods with a sword on your back picking fights with kelpies is ever so safe.'

He had the grace to look sheepish. 'I've been at this game longer than you have.'

'As you never tire of telling me. Just stick at 'Thanks'.'

'Thanks. I love you, you know.' He held my wrist and kissed my temple. 'Only don't get mad at me if I don't say it again for a while. Ah, Finn, you must be hungry.'

'Starving, pal.'

'There'll be some kind of breakfast downstairs. Sulaire doesn't get hangovers.' Seth stretched and yawned. 'Oh, Finn. Seven hours' sleep feels so good.' He wrapped his arms around me and bent his face into my neck. Then he pulled away abruptly. 'You need some sleep yourself, though.'

'I know. I just want her never to know if I'll be there or not. She felt it, you know,' I said with vicious satisfaction. 'She felt it.'

'Your ruthless streak is showing. Not before time. You think you could help my son find his?'

I gave him a Look. 'Give him time, you old despot.'

'I got him something. Here, see what you think.' He

opened the low trunk at the foot of the bed. It was one of Sionnach's, the fretwork over its lid as delicate as lace, but three centuries old already and still strong. Seth reached inside and with a nervous smile, handed me a rolled bundle of soft leather.

I unwrapped it. A yew-and-deerhorn bow with a quiver of blue-fletched arrows. I drew one of them out and stroked the arrow's tip with my thumb.

'Do you think he'll like it? He's not keen on swords. I thought, you know... a longbow... and it belonged to his grandfather...'

'It's gorgeous.' I eyed him askance. 'Seth, I don't think he's ever going to be a mighty barbarian warrior, know what I mean?'

He sighed, raked his hair. 'I know. I just wish... he needs to defend himself.'

'He'll get there. Let him work it out for himself. What's that?'

I was glad of a distraction, but I was genuinely curious. I knelt by the trunk and lifted out a little wooden carving. Its edges were smoothed by time, the surface glowing with the sheen of years. The shape of it was primitive but it was still identifiable. I turned it very gently in my fingers as Seth crouched beside me.

'It's a wolf,' I said.

'It's not a very good one.'

'It's beautiful.'

'Yes. It is.'

I tucked my hair behind my ear, the better to see his face. 'And she was too?'

He nodded. 'She made better ones later, but that was always my favourite.'

216

'It's very old.' I stroked the little bumps of its wooden ears. 'That's a long time to miss someone.'

He just nodded. I laid the carving carefully back in its nest of soft cotton. I was about to close the trunk lid when he caught it and reached inside again. He drew out a faded photograph and passed it to me.

Conal and Seth, playing the fool. They were sitting on Leonie's sofa at Tornashee, arms folded and leaning against each other, and they wore happy stupid grins. Between them was propped an incredibly startled week-old baby, its eyes round with confusion. I'd been staring at the picture for a while before I realised Seth was holding his breath.

I looked up at him. 'I'm so tiny. This is before my father died.'

'Yup.'

'Don't take this the wrong way,' I said. 'But this looks almost as if you like me.'

Embarrassed, he shrugged.

'So what did I do?' I winked solemnly at him as I stood up and examined it again. 'Was I that awful a toddler?'

He stood up too, looking over my shoulder and twisting a strand of my hair between his fingers. 'It all went wrong after Aonghas was killed. You know that.'

'Uh-huh. So why did you take it out on me?'

'Oh Finn. I dunno. I was in a permanent rage with your mother, and you were a piece of her. And I was jealous of you and Conal and how close you were. And I'd been over there too long and I hated it. Hated it, hated the full-mortals, and I was afraid of getting fond of you because I didn't want to get close to somebody who was going to be a kind of honorary full-mortal and never even know where she came from.' He was counting mockingly on his fingers now. 'Oh, loads of reasons, no excuses.'

'That's not all,' I said.

'Well...' He looked shamefaced. 'It's embarrassing. I don't even want to say it.'

'Tell me or the wolf gets it.' I pointed a finger-gun at Branndair's head, and he made puppy-eyes at Seth.

Hands over his face, Seth mumbled, 'So there was this prophecy.'

'Not *another* one!' I couldn't fight my huge grin. 'About you and me? Couldn't somebody have shot that soothsayer?'

'She did catch it in the end,' he reminded me darkly. He stared at the photograph in my fingers.

'It's bad, isn't it?' I flicked its corner.

'Depends on your point of view. Stella wanted to have me killed.' He gave me a wry shrug. 'Finn. You and me. She said it would happen.'

I almost roared with laughter. I had to bite my cheeks. 'Is that why you wouldn't come near me? Because you *didn't want to prove a soothsayer right?*'

His mouth opened in the beginning of a laugh, the start of a shared joke. It never quite got there. He moved away from me, ever so slightly.

'What?' My neck prickled. 'What else?'

He said it so fast I almost couldn't make it out. 'I'm going to be the death of you.'

I thought about it. I came close to him again, touched his face, made him look at me. There were tears in his eyes, but he coughed a laugh that was almost hysterical.

'*I told you I was selfish.*'

'Seth,' I said. 'Seth. The two weren't connected?'

'No.'

'Because I wouldn't care,' I hissed. 'Even if they were.'

He laid his hand over mine, turned his mouth into my palm and kissed it. His eyes were closed. 'Not-binding, staying away from you. For all I know, *that* could have been your death. I don't know. Oh gods, I don't know.'

'Seth,' I whispered in his ear. 'It's a crock of shit. Remember?'

'Course it is. Yes. Even Conal said so.'

I pressed my forehead against his, fiercely. 'I'm not interested in what Conal thought. Do you hear me? Not him, and not my mother, and not Leonie.'

Seth's fingers curled round mine, and he dragged my hand down from his face. But he did not let me go.

'Finn. I won't let you die.'

'I second that.' I kissed his fingers and shot him a grin.

He hesitated, then laughed unsteadily. 'I was livid. Every damn thing in my whole damn life, that witch wanted to control. But I wasn't half as livid as Leonie, or your mother. I told myself as often as they did that it would never happen.' His sudden smirk was wicked. 'And when you did turn up, you were such an ugly baby...'

I jabbed him in the stomach, making him wince. 'Well. Never mind, dear. I hated you too.'

'You hated me because I hated you. *That's* okay.'

'Seth, I hated you because you were a complete tit.'

'Oh, okay.' He laughed and made a face.

I looked back at the discoloured photograph and saw that Seth's little finger was surreptitiously clutched in the baby's curled fist.

'I'm really sorry, Finn. I'm sorry how it all turned out.'

I pulled his face to mine again, and kissed him. 'Me too. I'm glad you showed me this.'

'And now I'm stuck with loving you senseless again, for the rest of my life.'

'I'll hold you to that, you schmuck.'

'You already have. And I still don't know if I've done the right thing.'

'Don't worry, sweetie. I'll do the knowing for the both of us.'

I felt his mouth grin against mine. 'You are going to be *intolerable*.'

I'd have replied, but his head jerked up suddenly and he turned to face the door. '*What*?' he barked, before whoever it was had a chance to knock.

The door swung open and Braon leaned in. 'Half an hour ago.'

'And I don't suppose Nuall MacInnes is going to lift a finger to help.' He picked up his sword.

'He probably invited them in,' remarked Braon. 'That one's playing his own game.'

'No he isn't, he's just chickenshit.' Seth cursed. 'Finn, they're raiding Letterhaugh. East of Dunster.'

'I caught that much,' I said. I lifted my knife belt.

He seized my wrist. 'No way, Finn. I haven't got time to look out for you.'

Braon shot me a sympathetic look as my cheekbones burned. 'It won't take that long, Finn,' she said. 'We only need to show our faces. He'll be back for a late breakfast.'

'Save us a bacon roll.' He kissed me and was gone.

For a full minute I stared at the door that closed behind them, mortified and angry. After that I came to my senses and realised he was right. I made myself picture it: me getting in a scrap; somebody having to rescue me, and not necessarily Seth. That would be a lot more mortifying than being left behind.

'Practise more, you silly cow,' I muttered. 'Then he'll take you.'

I made myself not-picture the other thing: Seth getting in a scrap he couldn't handle, Seth with no-one to watch his back or the sword plunging into it. Shaking the vision loose from my brain I sloped downstairs for breakfast, still bereft.

I wasn't the first. Seth had taken only a small detachment, and there were maybe twenty fighters awake in the hall, forcing down breakfast, plus the eight men and three women of the night patrol, gloating at their hungover comrades and preparing to hit the sack.

And Hannah. She glanced up expressionless, her mouth full of toast.

I stopped short. Her hair was cropped nearly as short as Eili's. It suited her, I thought, wondering why a tremor had run the length of my spine.

'Nice, Hannah,' I said. 'What's your aunt going to say?'

Hannah swallowed a mouthful of toast. 'Like I give a flying fu...'

'Suits you,' I snapped, and turned to the coffee pot that simmered on the range. Iolaire was there already, yawning, helping himself.

He kissed my cheek, his jaw rough with stubble. 'Your lover gone out fighting with a headache?'

'Uh-huh.' The real reason for Seth's sore head was too complicated to explain at this hour, and anyway, he deserved one however he'd got it. I grinned, remembering Iolaire slumped on a sofa last night, hands over his eyes in mortification as Seth and Jed danced an elaborate tango. 'Yours too?'

'Yep. He woke up at five and drank the entire water jug and then he was fine, the bastard. I don't know where he puts it.'

'Jed drinks too much,' I said. 'He's fun, but he drinks too much.'

'I know he does.' Iolaire bent to murmur in my ear. 'I look after him. Honest.'

'I know you do.' I kissed his cheek, just while it was there.

'And how's Eili this morning?'

'How would I know?'

'It's all over the dun, the mood she's in,' said Iolaire dryly. 'We know you gave her hell. Look out, Finn.'

I felt a hand on my arm, then Sionnach was taking the coffee pot out of my hands. 'Right behind me, Finn,' he said apologetically. 'Be warned. And *please* be careful.'

'Fionnuala.' Eili's voice cut the atmosphere. Eyes like chips of mica, she pointed at me, then at the doorway.

The hall had fallen silent, and a couple of fighters stood up, uncertain. Sionnach took a step towards me and Eili, but I raised a hand.

I followed Eili out to the courtyard, and the door closed softly behind us.

SETH

The day was already hot, and soon they were going to start to smell. Up in the blue, a buzzard soared, its cry piercing his bones. Seth sat very still on the blue roan, watching Jed pick his way through the bodies, rolling one over with a foot, hauling another by the armpits to lie next to its mother.

'What was the point?' Braon was off her horse too, but she leaned against its shoulder, frowning.

'They're not ready for a full attack. Kate's taunting us again.'

'That's not what I meant. Doesn't surprise *me* that Cuthag scuttled back to her skirts before we got here.' She sniffed. 'But Nuall was a useful idiot. Why do it at all?'

Seth didn't reply. He knew why, and she'd work it out in the next five minutes. At least, he hoped that was all it was. The headache he'd got from Finn and whisky was muddling him, but there was an odd and new and different throb of absence, deep in his brain. He couldn't pinpoint it, couldn't deal with it; it was like the itching void of a missing limb. He certainly had no words to spare for Braon, not right now.

Seth rubbed his forehead hard. Jed trudged back towards him, his face dark with hatred. Behind him surviving villagers were moving like animated dead things, hitching litters to horses, lifting corpses.

'Do we stay and help lay them out?'

'Yes.' Every word was an effort. 'Their death ground's two miles east.'

'It'll take a while. What about him?' Jed jerked his head at the glowering man bound to a rowan trunk. Branndair stood over the captive, stiff-legged and snarling, but still the man wore that truculent adamant expression he'd worn when they rode him down.

For a few seconds, Seth didn't trust himself to get off the roan. He wasn't sure his legs would obey him; no two parts of his body seemed to be connected. At last, with a deep breath, he dismounted. When, to his dizzying relief, he didn't fall, he walked across to Nuall MacInnes and ran his hand across Branndair's bristling neck, coaxing the wolf to sit. Then he crouched to stare into the man's eyes.

'They left you to me,' he said. 'Are you happy now?'

'You did this.' MacInnes spat. 'You, Murlainn.'

Seth stood up again, turning a slow circle to take in the carnage all over again. It was hard, at this moment, to argue. *Don't fall. Don't fall.*

'What did she offer you to close your gates to them? I mean, you didn't just turn a blind eye, you herded the poor bastards. For her dogs. What price did you get for a whole settlement, Nuall?'

Nuall glared up at him through sweat-soaked strands of hair. 'No price but peace, Murlainn. Peace and protection.'

'You had mine!' he yelled.

'We didn't ask for yours. And your peace is no peace at all.'

Seth bit down on his lip. He had no need to spit back. It would be such a small insult, after all. 'Where's her protection now?'

'Gone.' Nuall licked his dry lips and smiled. 'Ah, but one settlement for the whole of Dunster. It would have been worth it.'

'Not now it isn't. Not now.' Seth turned his back and drew his sword. 'Get him up.'

'It won't look good for you, Murlainn,' said Nuall as Jed and Braon cut the ropes that bound him and dragged him to his feet, gripping his arms hard. 'I've tried to broker peace here.'

'That's the point, isn't it? That it won't look good for me.' Seth lifted his blade and pressed the tip against the man's heaving ribcage.

'Indeed. I do see that now. But I'll hold that thought in my heart anyway.'

'Hold it while you can, then.' Seth gripped his hair to hold him still, gazed steadily into his blue eyes, and drove the sword hard between his ribs.

The man was still smiling as blood bubbled in his mouth, even as the body on his blade shuddered and Seth smelt piss and worse. When the eyelight was dead and the body went limp, Seth yanked the sword free, and Jed and Braon let the lifeless corpse slump to the earth. The stillness was horrible, and for long fantastical moments Seth thought nothing would ever break it.

Then Branndair sprang to his feet, startling all of them, and let out a great barking howl. It rose and swelled, louder and higher, piercing and wild and stricken.

'*What?*' said Jed, staring at the black wolf.

'Jed.' Gooseflesh rose on Seth's arms. 'Jed, go and find Liath.'

Jed's breath caught; then he nodded. Gripping the dun stallion's withers, Jed flung himself onto its back and sent it into a gallop from a standing start. Seth and the rest of his patrol watched him until he was lost in hazy distance. Branndair's howls never faded, echoing across the valley and the burned settlement.

Funny that despite the noise of it, Seth could think straighter. The howling iced his blood and it iced his brain, and the murk was clearing.

Braon was close by his side, her hand on his arm. 'Murlainn. What is it?'

And he knew. Suddenly he knew what the missing part of him was. 'Rory's blocking me.'

Braon looked disbelieving. 'Even Rory wouldn't dare that.'

'But he is. He's shut me out.' Seth raked his hands into his hair. He shattered his battle-block with a thought, and still he couldn't feel his son.

'You're imagining it. You had a block up. Anyway, why would he do such a thing?'

'I don't know. Block's down now. *Branndair!*'

The wolf hesitated, caught in mid-howl, his mournful yellow eyes fixed on Seth. Then he started up again, the sound worse than ever, freezing the summer air.

I don't understand...

'Braon, we need to get back.'

'But the bodies...'

'Leave them!' His heart was pounding so hard he was dizzy. There was a bloody great leaking hole in his head, didn't she understand? *No. No, of course she doesn't. I don't bloody understand.* He clutched his temple.

'Seth...'

'Sorry. Braon. No. The villagers. No. The villagers will do it. *We need to go home.*'

She didn't argue any more, but turned to summon the rest of the detachment. *Good woman.* Seth snatched wildly at the roan's bridle, and missed. Furious at himself, he clutched it again. It felt like trying to mount thin air, but he got there. In the end, dizzy and sick, he dragged himself onto the creature's back.

He did not wait for Braon, did not wait for his fighters. They'd follow soon enough. Seth dug his heels hard into the roan's side and turned its head for home. He wouldn't fall. Now that he was astride and cantering, even the yawning reeling void in his mind would not make him fall before he reached the dun. He was only afraid that he might dissolve, and evaporate from his own body, and never reach it at all.

FINN

The courtyard was hot with sunlight of an intensity that hurt the eyes. Grey dun stone was bleached to white and I could smell stone-dust and dry earth and thirsty herbs. I turned on my heel, putting my back to the sun, but Eili backed off. She narrowed her eyes against the glare, looking warier than I'd expected.

'Eili,' I said. 'I hate all this. What you're doing to Seth and to yourself. Please don't. Conal loved you and I'm sorry I was a cow to you. I was sixteen years old.'

'That's an excuse for so much, isn't it?' said Eili contemptuously.

'I never said that.' My gut twisted.

'Aw, you're sweet. You believe in Seth, don't you? Let me tell you, he believes in nothing.' Eili's smile was back in place. 'Nothing. He has no religion, no faith. He doesn't believe in God, or Fate, or the Devil. He couldn't even believe in his own brother. You think he believes in love? In you? I'll tell you what he believes in: his own survival.'

I shrugged. 'Eili, you've had your way for a long time. Stop it now.'

'Thirteen years for a whole Sithe life? You seriously think that's justice? I've barely started! You can't stay awake every night.'

'No, but I'll do it often enough to make you sorry.'

'So. Suppose you protect his nights.' Eili tapped her jaw thoughtfully. 'There are other ways to do this. I hurt Seth all the time, you know, though he rarely lets on. I'll have more energy for that now. You can't live in his scars forever, Finn. You nearly didn't get back to yourself last night, and that was only the first time.' Eili laughed. 'This way I'll get some extra sleep myself.'

I bit so hard on my lip I tasted blood. 'You cold-brained witch, *Udhar.*'

'How dare you,' snarled Eili. 'That is not my name.'

'Don't blame me,' I said. 'It's your doing, you that's so careless with your name and your soul. You're not *Eilid* any more.'

'That is not for you to say!' cried Eili hoarsely. 'This is between me and your lover.'

'You're the one who involved others. You didn't just do this to Seth, you did it to Rory! *How could you?* He was three years old!' I took a step towards Eili. 'Stop hurting both of them, or so help me...'

Eili's lips were white and dry. 'Don't make promises you can't keep. You won't get a blade near me.'

'I'll rip your mind right out of your brain stem!'

In the thick silence, my face slackened in shock. Oh, I thought, recoiling from Eili's disbelieving stare. Oh, God. *What did I just say?*

What were we doing, Eili and I, when we'd both loved the same man and he'd loved us? I felt sick. Something was terribly wrong, our minds were twisted, and there seemed to be nothing we even wanted to do about it.

'Witch.' Breath hissed between Eili's teeth, her face calming dangerously. 'You loathsome harpy. I should kill you where you stand, *Caorann!*'

My eyes widened. I thought for a second that she'd punched me hard in the gut, and I couldn't take breath to speak. Then I began to laugh, hysterically, through clenched teeth. 'I don't believe it.'

Caorann. *Caorann*. Did I like it? Yes. No. Yes. Oh, God, I'd waited all this time, desperate, longing, impatient. But I'd been certain, so certain that Seth would find it for me. Instead of which...

'Believe it?' Eili's face had gone into a spasm of rage, making her beautiful mouth a twist of ugly flesh. 'Nor do I. Gods, neither do I.'

'It seems we're linked in more ways than one.' I smirked. It was the nearest I could get to a smile.

She'd got control of herself now. She was very still, except for a muscle that twitched below her left eye.

'Two traitors together, you are; and Seth can't even respect the son he claims to love. Rory doesn't want what you've done; he doesn't want to lose his father to you. Did Seth have to bind? *Really*? After all these centuries?' Her lip curled. 'But you and Seth, you live your lives by prophecies. Funny, isn't it, when he's spent his life trying to deny them? I'm going to make you another one, right now.'

'Eili, you don't give a damn what Rory wants.'

'That's where you're wrong. So here's my prediction: when you want to finish this, you'll come and find me. And you'll know where. All you have to do is remember what Rory wants. Remember what he wants more than anything, because I'm going to make sure he gets it.' Eili tilted her head. 'One way or the other.'

I shoved past her, feeling her mad eyes boring into my back as I made for the stables. It was the closest place I could reach that was out of her sight. I snatched up my bridle, and stood for a moment breathing hard.

And then I slung it over my shoulder and made for the

dun gates. I couldn't even bear to be within the walls; thoughts ricocheted uselessly around my head, too light and fast to hurt but enough to make me feel sick. My skin felt so hot I wanted to strip it right off.

I kept walking along the grassy edge of the dunes and north past the headland. By the time I'd gone another mile I was alone with the breeze and the crying gulls. The Atlantic was in a fine mood, spindrift feathering on the wave-tips, light splintering into shards on the surface. When I'd walked far enough I sat on a rock and watched it, mesmerised, trying to count the beats of my heart as it slowed, trying to separate the colliding angry voices in my head. I didn't even know which of them was mine.

I shut my eyes.

The gull-clamour seemed to recede; there was something behind the song of the waves, some plaintive call scratching at the inside of my skull. I frowned, blinked my eyes open again.

I wasn't wrong, I was sure of it. Getting to my feet, I stared down at the sand below, then gripped spurs of rock and clambered down. I jumped the last few feet and then held myself still, listening.

The call remained in my head, but that didn't make it less real. It was close now, and insistent. No, desperate. Like a whine, or a whimper.

No. I ran up the sand towards the next outcrop of rock, judging the direction more by instinct than by any certainty. My instincts were sound enough, more's the pity. I saw blood and scraps of white fur on the cliffs before I saw her.

She lay in a cleft between slabs of granite, her body twisted and bloody from the fall. I didn't think it was possible, I didn't think Liath could slip from the rocks twenty feet up, the rocks she'd known and prowled for centuries. And then I saw the knife.

The handle was chased silver, I thought, but it was hard to tell beneath the clotted blood. The blade was sunk deep in her ribs, but when I stumbled down beside her and reached for it she gave a yelp of fear and pain, and I clenched my fist. I stroked her shaggy mane, rubbed her ears and her muzzle, pressed my face to hers.

~ *Wait. Liath. Don't go. I'll find help. I'll find Jed. He's searching for you.* Surely he was. He must be.

Jed, I thought with angry panic, *why won't you let us call you?*

With an effort the wolf raised her head enough to lick my face, but then it fell back again to the rock, with a thump that made me wince. I sank my fingers in her mane again, feeling blood and life pulse weakly through her. Her ribcage rose and fell so very feebly, and her tongue lolled.

~ *Eili. Eili can help you. Wait, Liath!*

This time the wolf lifted her head long enough to gaze into my eyes, the amber light dull in hers. Her claws scrabbled on rock, and though I tried to shush her and hold her still, she struggled up onto her forepaws. I put my arms round her head, cradling it, and shut my eyes. My world reeled and I fell forward into her.

The human girl had her back to me. She lay in the grass, her fear a crackling energy on the air. She peered through low scrub. The figures were defined by the glittering water behind. She was afraid. She should be afraid. I heard her breath. It rasped high, in and out of her throat, but they could not hear that, those figures on the shore. Only I could hear it. Only I could smell her terror.

wouldn't have let him be killed
not now not yet
sometimes I wish
my last breath, the last of my blood
you're still making him pay
it's yourself you're destroying
No.

Liath's memories shattered and dissolved, and it was all I could do to hold her great head still, to keep it from slamming back onto the rock again. Her tongue hung from her jaws and her shallow breath was an agony, and I realised I was panting like a dog myself.

I licked my lips, swallowed over my constricted throat, gathered my mind back from hers. Eili's voice, Sionnach's voice: I couldn't hear myself think for the echo. I didn't want to think at all. 'Liath,' I whispered.

Her eyes closed. The rise and fall of her ribs seemed calmer. Or was that only weaker?

'LIATH.'

Jed's scream silenced the gulls, almost silenced the Atlantic. He pounded across the sand, leapt up onto the rocks. I let go of the wolf just in time as he plunged down into the hollow between the slabs, wrapped his arms around her body and lifted her to him. Who'd have thought he had the strength? Not even him.

'Finn. *Help me.*'

I opened my mouth to answer Jed, but nothing would come. I was still trying to speak, still trying to tell him it would be fine, that Liath would be fine, when her eyes glazed, and Jed crushed her desperately to his breast, and the long last breath sighed from her jaws.

★ ★ ★

'You take her back to the dun,' I said. 'Go on.'

I was surprised how little I felt. Even the sight of Jed, his face pressed to Liath's, didn't stir a single emotion inside me. She lay across the dun stallion's back, and he was rubbing her lifeless head, threading his fingers into her white mane. The cold rage and grief surrounded him like an aura, impenetrable, but I felt no rage and no grief, only a frightening emptiness. Or it would have been frightening, if I'd been capable of fear just then.

Later, maybe.

'Who, Finn?' Jed lifted his head.

'I don't know,' I lied.

The dun horse shook its mane and glanced back, curious, at the strange weight on its withers. Jed laid a hand on its nose and it went stock-still. I'd have obeyed him too. But only if I was the horse.

'You didn't see anything? Anyone?'

'Of course I didn't.' I put a hand against his cheek, and felt the skin damp with silent tears. 'I found her right here. Jed, I'm so sorry.'

'She was his. She was *his*.'

'I know,' I said. 'And then she was yours.'

'I'll kill them. Whoever it was.'

'I know.'

'Finn.' With my face so close to his, it was easy for him to catch and hold me, and search my face. His own was tormented. 'This is too close to the dun. There's only one person mad enough.'

'Conal's wolf?' I shook my head violently. 'Never. Eili would *never* do this. Go, Jed. Take her back.'

As he pulled away, his teeth grinding, his fists clenching and flexing, I put my hand behind my back once more. Jed might have noticed, if he'd been half-sane, but his look was wild and he was grief-addled, and he never would willingly share his mind. *Just as well*, I thought. *Just as well.*

Jed mounted the horse, one hand taking up the reins, the other desperately raking the white fur of Liath's flank. His eyes were red but dry. 'Call Seth,' he said.

'Yes,' I lied again.

'Follow me back.'

'Yes,' I said; and this time my intention was truthful.

Just not yet, is all.

As I watched him ride away, back towards the dun, I drew the knife from behind me and turned it in my blood-sticky hands: the knife he'd forgotten in his distress, the knife I'd pulled from Liath's side when it couldn't hurt her any more. It was well balanced and simply shaped, but the curve of the blade beneath the gore was elegant, and its creator had not been able to resist a delicately carved design that ran from the handle to halfway up the blade. I wasn't sure if the inlay was red enamel, or simply blood lodged in the engraving. It wasn't her usual weapon, but I knew Eili's work when I saw it.

What Rory wants. What he wants more than anything.

Which of those aching desires of his would it be, though? The kelpie; his father's respect; or me out of his life?

Some perfect combination?

~ *Why don't you ask him?*

A ripple of fear tracked down my spine. Oh, that familiar, snaking mind. ~ *Udhar.*

~ *Not Udhar. Not Udhar! Eilid!* Her rage was almost irrepressible, leaking and seeping from the black corners of her mind. ~ *Come and talk to Rory, Caorann. Before his father does.*

I bit hard on my lip. Seth was far away, fighting; there was no time. Besides, I tried to imagine the scene if Seth caught Rory at the mere. Almost immediately, I tried to unimagine it again. Their relationship was bad enough at the moment, and that was partly my fault.

I glanced once, a little reluctantly, in the direction of the dun; but this was between me and Eili. I knew where to go, and Eili knew that I knew. I had the advantage of her. To hell with swords and arrows: I knew the name that was sucking her old one out of her, I knew where it hurt. This, I would not let anyone else do for me. This fight I'd finish myself.

I tucked the bloody blade into my belt, climbed back up the bluff to retrieve the bridle I'd dropped, and then I started walking: fast enough and thoughtlessly enough that I wouldn't change my mind.

I'd gone perhaps two miles when the black kelpie answered my call. It trotted to my side, snorting in perplexity, nibbling and tugging at my hair. I halted to stroke its shoulder and take a deep breath, but stopping had let the horror and the grief catch up with me, and for long moments all I could do was press my face into its sleek muscled neck, and wind my cold fingers tightly into its mane.

~ *FINN.*

I jerked my head up. The black turned its head and snuffed the breeze. Not far behind the call in my head I heard the hoofbeats, and then I saw the roan, cantering towards me across a windswept shoulder of the moor.

I thought of running, thought of trying to lose him or hide among the stones. What was the point? I sighed, and gave in, and waited for him.

The blue roan came alongside us, whickering and whinnying to the black. Seth stared down at me, and for all that had just happened, all I could think was how white he looked, how dark the shadows were around his feverish eyes.

~ *Murlainn! What happened to you?*

'What?' His voice was harsh with pain but I don't think he even knew it. 'Nothing. I don't know. It doesn't matter, Finn; what about Liath? Jed brought her into the dun half an hour ago. What happened to her?'

'I'm not sure,' I said; and then, because he was not Jed, I pulled the knife from my belt and handed it up to him, silently.

He let the reins fall loose on the roan's neck and turned the blade in his fingers. I heard his breath, shaky and harsh, as he trailed a fingertip across the scarlet inlay. It came away smeared with half-dried blood.

'Where's Branndair?' I asked.

'Still at the dun. Howling and crying for Liath.' There was dull agony in every syllable. 'Eili made this blade.'

'Made it,' I said quietly. 'She doesn't use throwing knives.'

He glared. 'I know that. Who did she make them for?'

I didn't answer. I think he knew as well as I did.

'She's gone,' he said. 'Both of them have: Taghan and Eili, they left the dun hours ago, Eorna says. It's chaos; nobody understands what the hell's happening. And now Hannah's gone too, and – and Rory. With Eili's horse. Her *horse.*'

Taghan? The horse? I swallowed hard. Eili's game had rules I hadn't thought of, rules I would never have expected, and perhaps it was time to stop playing by them.

'Call him!' I said. 'Call him *now.*'

'I can't,' he said, his voice high. His fingers twitched around the knife. 'He's blocking me.'

I circled the black to a high outcrop of rock and mounted it. 'He's *blocking* you?'

All he could do was shake his head in disbelief.

'I know where he is,' I said, and reached across to link my fingers with his. They shook in mine. 'I know where they all are. We have to go.'

'Bloody hell, Finn! I can't even think straight. Yes, we have to go. We can't wait.'

'No. Is Sionnach in the dun? Call him.' This was not about my private vendettas any more. 'Get him to bring the others.'

'Yes.' Seth nudged the roan into a trot, following me, and rubbed a hand fiercely across his forehead.

I frowned back at him. 'Rory must be there,' I said. 'In your head. Somewhere. He's your son. Even if he's blocking, he—'

'Like black water. Like stone. There's nothing. Finn. There's nothing.' Seth swayed on the roan's back, and clutched its wither. Yet again, he reined it in.

I halted the black, staring at him. 'Seth. You've got to get it together.'

'But he's dead to me, Finn. He's dead to me.' And then, very suddenly, his eyes focused, as if his mind was re-asserting itself; and his face paled to the colour of a wight.

'Finn. He's *dead*.'

The blue roan's sudden spring caught me unawares. It leaped into an insane gallop, but as Seth passed me his mind lanced into mine, so hard and piercing I recoiled, stung. And then, his senses re-gathered, he was racing for the place I'd known I was going. The black tossed its head and plunged, taken as unawares as I was; then it bolted too, and we were galloping after Seth across the moor.

I'd never have thought the roan could outpace the black so easily, but by the time silver sunlight flashed on the line of the mere, Seth was ten lengths ahead of us. The sun almost blinded me, but I bent low to the black's neck, trusting him to keep his footing. He was wild with the thought of a fight again, muscles thrilling with glee, and he took the last rise of ground with his hooves barely touching the earth. When we crested the ridge I pulled him up, horror washing over me in a violent tide.

There were other horses ahead, riderless. On the shore of the mere there was bloody chaos, men and women fighting like wild animals.

At least two bodies were down. Eili was there, hacking at two fighters I didn't recognise and one I thought I did. Her dappled kelpie, tethered to a pine, reared and screamed wildly, but it was too far away for Eili to cut it loose.

And Rory. Through grim and hideous shock, I felt the surge of relief. *Not dead*. Not yet, at least, though a fighter had him in a headlock and more piled in onto him.

'*Hold the bastard!*'

'*Hold him!*'

'*Don't let him tear the bloody Veil, don't—*'

'*He can't, not here, she said—*'

'*HOLD HIM!*'

Hannah leaped for the man who held Rory down, but she was knocked flying by a backwards slam of his free arm. She thudded into the heather, rolled, and tried to scramble back towards Rory, shrieking. Kate's fighter slammed his fist into her belly, harder this time, and she tumbled down the steep bank onto the beach.

As Seth rode down on them all, he pulled his sword from the sheath on his back, then flipped and caught it, the blade raised as I'd seen it raised only once before. I knew what was coming. When Seth leaned out of the saddle and hacked savagely to the side, I jerked my head reflexively away, feeling the black's silky mane lash my eyelids.

The blue roan scrabbled to a halt and doubled back, and the blade cut the air a second time. There was no defensive ring of metal, only the sickening sound it made in flesh. The black screamed its bloodlust, and I had to haul on its neck till my triceps nearly snapped before it would turn from the fight. I snarled and forced it round, down to the lochan shore.

I saw flashes of the fight as I galloped the black towards Hannah. Seth slashed again. Rory stumbled to his knees, his arms clutched over his head; his captor hovered oddly, then fell forward, the stump of his neck squirting aortal blood over the boy's back. Somewhere in my skirling head I heard a fury of hoofbeats, and I realised others were bearing down on the battle.

A moment's panic turned to relief: Jed and Iolaire and Sionnach had ridden from the dun, and I reckoned they'd started out before they were even called. *Sionnach,* I realised: Sionnach must have known something was wrong. And Branndair had not lingered to mourn Liath; he raced alongside the riders, his eyes glowing with vengeful hate. The enemy detachment fell back, shouting and running, and Seth was leaping off his horse onto the nearest of them.

I could not help him. All I could do was jump off the black as it slowed to a canter, and run to Hannah. She struggled up, retching and gasping for air, and seized a fistful of my t-shirt.

'Taghan!' she screamed hoarsely.

For a fleeting instant I thought she hadn't recognised me;

then she shook me with her almost-exhausted strength, dragging me round to see the body bent back almost double over the rocks, its empty eyes staring skywards.

'She's *dead*!'

I wanted to drop the little baggage on her arse on the rocks, but something made me lower her quite gently. I had time to hope it wasn't maternal instinct kicking in, and then I was running to Taghan, staring down at her, sick with fear.

A long blade impaled her chest, and she hadn't had time to fight back; her own dagger, still caught between her fingers, was free of blood. It was a beautiful thing: balanced and elegant, with an engraved design that trailed from the handle halfway up the blade, inlaid with scarlet enamel.

Not quite a corpse yet, for all Hannah's hysteria: there was the faintest glimmer of silver light in Taghan's glazed eyes. Hesitantly I reached out, and touched her temple.

Her hand snatched my wrist, so fast I yelled. Her grip was so tight my blood throbbed.

'Didn't know,' she rasped.

'What?' My brain reeled.

'Kate's men. Ambush. Sorry.'

'Sod that,' I hissed, close to her ear. 'Why Liath? Why did you kill her?'

'She knew. Saw us. Poor bitch. Didn't understand, 'course. But the risk...'

I wanted to wrap my fingers round her white throat and squeeze. 'Does Eili know what you did?'

'Nah.' She coughed blood. 'Eili said, wolf's no risk. Jed might've seen something in her head, but he doesn't look, hm? Stupid f'llmortal. But Liath, she was stalking me. S'spicious animal.'

'Liath showed me. She might not've understood it all, but she knew it was why she was dying. She showed *me*.' Too late. My heart clenched, and I gritted, 'Did you do this for Kate?'

'Nah. Was for. Was for...' There was something like happiness in her eyes. 'Feorag.'

I couldn't think for the anger. Didn't understand. 'Who the hell's Feorag?'

Sharp nails dug into my wrist, and Taghan slewed a grin at me.

'This was meant to be you.'

We froze, only for an instant, our eyes locked. I couldn't breathe.

And then the world spun briefly, violently, as something jolted through my fingertips and rippled into my blood. I gasped, and the world steadied, and she died.

As I staggered to my feet I had to wrench Taghan's dead fingers off me. I took an unsteady pace back, rubbing my wrist, incapable of turning to watch the clash of fighters behind me. One more step back, and someone snatched at me.

I spun round, growling, but it was only Hannah again, trembling and panting for breath. Fear and rage made my heart trip and slam inside my chest. 'What have you *done*?'

'It was – this wasn't supposed to happen. It was meant – it was Taghan, only Taghan. She was meant to be here. Not those men. They were here. Hiding. They *knew we were coming*.'

I raked my hair behind my ears; it was something to do with my hands that would stop me striking her. 'You gave them Rory!'

'No! No, he was only bait!'

'*Bait*?' I didn't understand. 'For Seth? For Kate?'

Some kind of reason came to her terrified face. She licked her lips, wrapped her arms round herself to control the shaking, and when she looked up at me again she was almost calm. 'For you.'

I stood up and shoved her away, but the shriek and smash of weapons had already faded to silence. Eili stumbled to her horse and freed it with a slash of her blade; Seth's sword arm dropped to his side as the last enemy fighter scrambled into his saddle and made off. Out of the corner of my eye I saw Iolaire change course as fast as a fish to intercept him, heard the collision of horseflesh, but I didn't watch.

Nor did Seth. He was staring at me and at Hannah; he was sprayed with Sithe blood from his thigh to his ear. He dropped to a crouch and splayed his free hand across his face, but his right hand didn't let go of his sword.

'They had him. Oh, Finn, they had him.'

'I know.' If Hannah had been closer I'd have hit her.

'Why? Why now?' Seth raked his hand through his hair. He didn't know that he was smearing himself with trails of blood; he didn't know that Rory was watching the blood trails, grey eyes wide with horror. Eili stood exhausted, panting, her eyes still glinting diamond-hard. Branndair lay panting on the coarse sand, his loathing gaze riveted on the lifeless Taghan. Sionnach dismounted and began to examine the corpses, turning their faces to him, and in one case lifting a head by its hair. Jed only sat on his dun horse and stared emptily at Rory.

Seth seemed to focus on his son properly for the first time. He was breathing hard, but there was sick relief on his face as well as fury. 'What *happened*?'

'The kelpie. I wanted – I'm sorry I'm sorry I'm sorry–'

'The *kelpie*? Taghan's dead!'

'I didn't know, I didn't – want anyone to die.' Rory made an agonised sound. '*I don't want anyone to die over me*!'

A sound made us all turn, then. Iolaire was kneeling over a figure propped against the corpse of a horse, while his own horse limped oddly and badly behind him. Iolaire's sword was pressed to the throat of the man beneath him: a strongly built, shaven-headed man. There was a gold torque round his neck, visible at the open collar of his bloodstained khaki shirt. Staring up calmly at Iolaire, he waited for death.

Rory took a breath. 'No. Not another one.'

Iolaire's fingers trembled slightly. Jed growled and drew his own sword for backup.

'*Please*, Iolaire. He doesn't have to die. He's beaten.'

'Stay out of this, Rory.' There was an edge of fear to Seth's anger.

At last Iolaire spoke. 'I can't kill you, Cluaran. If I kill you I lose myself anyway.'

Cluaran gazed up with narrowed eyes. 'Careful, Iolaire. You're playing with your own life as well as mine.' His mouth twisted. 'If you show me mercy now, I will not do the same for you tomorrow. I'll kill you when I catch you. Listen, you are young and beautiful and in love.' His eyes slid briefly to Jed. 'Your lover is young too, and he won't live as long as you. He won't live long at all, so love him while you can. I am old and gnarled and my woman is already dead. Don't gamble with your life, Iolaire. You know what the rules are? They're changing faster than you know, so play the game quickly.'

Iolaire's eyes flickered to Rory and back. 'It's not a game.'

'Are you worried about the boy?' Cluaran laughed

humourlessly. 'We came to get him today, Iolaire. We'll come again. We'll keep trying until we get him, because that's what Kate wants and those are Laszlo's orders.' His tone gentled, so slightly as to be almost imperceptible. 'Remember what they did to you, Iolaire? Murlainn was right to kill us where he found us, and he'll have to go on doing it. Perhaps it'll go on and on, back and forth, till there's none of us left and that'll solve everyone's moral dilemmas.'

Iolaire held his hilt two-handed, the tip of the blade pressed to Cluaran's throat at the narrow gap in the torque. A bead of blood welled. The gleam of the sword was reflected in the gold torque, the torque in the silver blade, light bouncing between them. Iolaire's face contorted with pain as if it was his skin the steel pierced.

'Cluaran,' he said hoarsely. 'You brought me up from when I was a boy. I was younger than Rory when I was made your bondsman. You made me what I am, but I'm not you. I'm not even like you.' He lifted the blade. 'Go. *Go.*'

Cluaran hesitated for a second.

'You heard him. Go before I kill you instead.' Seth's voice was low and even. 'Tell her she can't have my son.'

Cluaran stumbled across the moor, and there was heavy silence till he was out of sight.

'Iolaire,' said Rory, 'thank y—'

'Rory,' said Iolaire. 'I'm dead. Don't talk to me. You've talked enough.'

Seth jabbed a finger at Hannah. 'You,' he said. 'You were a mistake. You're going back to your aunt. And you,' he snarled at Rory, 'are confined to the dun.'

'What's new?' snapped Hannah, grabbing Rory's arm protectively. Glaring at Seth, she jerked a thumb in my direction. 'This was between us and her. *You* weren't even supposed to show up.'

Seth's throat jerked and he had trouble speaking for a moment. 'What did you want with my lover?'

'Eili and Taghan were getting rid of her. Sending her away forever, they told me. I didn't know they were going to kill her. At least,' she murmured, 'I think I didn't.'

'You.' Seth came close to Rory, unable to keep the hurt off his face. 'You were *part of this*?'

'No, I–'

'Is that why you've started to block me? *Is it*?'

Rory exploded. 'I'm blocking *you*? That's rich!'

Seth's face was a mask of pain. 'Do you hate me that much?'

Rory put his face in his hands, then looked up, eyes glittering. 'I hate what you do in my name. I hate what we are. And her? Eili? I hate her most of all. For *what you've let her do to you*.'

The wind whispered across the heather, sent early fallen leaves bounding and rustling. Otherwise, the only sound was Branndair's low constant whimper of sorrow.

Seth said, 'How did you–'

Eili's lips twitched. She cocked her head at Hannah. 'So you told him? You told Rory about me? Though you swore you wouldn't?'

'Oh yes. I lied to you,' Hannah said, so coldly I shivered. 'The way you lied to me.'

There was a dry brief laugh from Eili, and the smile she gave Hannah was almost admiring. 'Clever girl.'

'Rory, I'm sorry I didn't tell you,' said Seth. The muscles of his face were taut. 'I'm sorry, all right? Now you know.

Does it make you feel better? Or do you want to hurt me worse than Eili ever could?'

'I'm not worth more than any other Sithe. Stop fighting over me!'

'Rory.' Seth rubbed his temples. 'You know I don't give a damn that you're the Bloodstone. It matters less to me than a flea on Branndair's neck.'

'Why did those guys have to die instead of me?'

'Because you're mine, rot your thick hide!' Seth shouted. 'Because I love you! Because I was stronger and faster than they were. Because I didn't start it, *they did!*'

'Sometimes you do start it, though, don't you?'

'Yes, when I have cause! You want me to say you're not worth more than them? All right, you're not.' Seth flung his sword to the ground. 'Does it make you happy? *Does it?* You're worth more *to me.* They tried to take you, Rory. You think I should have let them? They wouldn't be dead if you hadn't –'

~ *Don't say it!* I screamed in his head, and he shut his mouth in shock.

Breathing hard, Seth turned to Hannah and seized her jaw. She didn't even flinch.

'You know, I quite like you, Hannah. When did you get to hate me so much?' Smiling sourly, Seth tilted his head and looked hard into her eyes.

There was an angry intake of breath from Eili. 'Murlainn! You have no right.'

'Oh, Eili,' he murmured, 'I think I have every right, in the circumstances.' As his silver glare intensified, Hannah shivered once.

He dropped her jaw like a spent match and took a step back, his breath caught in his throat.

'Jesus,' he said. 'Jesus.'

I couldn't watch, and not know. I slipped my mind inside his, and my blood froze colder than nitrogen.

With a helpless shrug Seth turned back to Hannah. She was smiling.

~ *Gotcha.*

'Do you hate the girl, Eili?' Seth's voice had no inflection at all. He might have been asking if she hated butter, or hunting, or the colour green.

Eili's own smile was gone, making her look almost normal. 'I hate it that she exists and that my child doesn't. Can you understand that, Murlainn? But every time I look at her face I see *him*. That might well break my heart, but how can I hate it?'

'I didn't see it,' he whispered.

'I didn't let you see it.'

Iolaire stepped between them. 'If I could, ah... it's Laszlo.' Iolaire glanced at Jed. 'He's coming.'

That got our attention. And Jed opened his mouth for the first time. 'He's *coming*?'

Iolaire touched his temple. 'I can still feel Cluaran. I stayed with him a little.' He flushed. 'To make sure he was okay. And now he's with Laszlo.'

Jed paled. 'Cluaran didn't have a horse.'

'No. They're close.'

Jed touched the hilt of his sword almost unconsciously. His face was hungry and lean, and dark with hate.

'You.' Seth stabbed a finger almost in Eili's face. 'Take the girl back to the dun.'

'You're sending *Eili*?' I stared at him.

'She'll be safe with Eili. Oh, ever so safe, won't she? Udhar?'

Eili's mouth twisted.

'And Finn? You take Rory. Stay together, the four of you. A patrol will meet you; get them to escort you in and wait for us. Don't leave the dun and don't let Rory...' he paused only briefly '...don't let Rory or Hannah out of your sight.'

I opened my mouth to argue, then shut it again. Rory's mind was a torrent of white noise, but none of it penetrated his father's. Their gazes clashed like shields. Seth wasn't even Seeing his son, let alone hearing him.

'Finn,' said Seth. 'Now or sooner?'

There was nothing I could do but nod, and go to my horse, and slip the bridle over its head.

There was no fear in Hannah's face, only cool defiance. She looked contained, and terrifyingly self-reliant. I didn't even try to get past her slick new block. The only two people I cared about right now were Rory and Seth. Father and son, but I could feel nothing between them. Nothing.

I placed my mind gently between them, knew that each of them felt it, but in the direct line between Seth and Rory there was only a blank meaningless absence. It was as if they were blocking one another completely, uncompromisingly, for the first time in their lives. The father's eyes were lightless on his son, and Rory's were entirely blank.

SETH

It wasn't what he'd expected. Seth forced the blue roan to halt although the creature was sweating with the longing for a fight, its muscles jolting with tiny excited tremors. He murmured to it absently, staring out from the mossy green shadows of the wood.

Despite the roan's keenness he knew Laszlo hadn't seen them. But the rest of Laszlo's patrol had, five men and three women. Seth knew that fine. His eyes met Cluaran's across a hundred yards of open space and he knew, sickeningly, that anything Cluaran had given away to Iolaire had been deliberate. Perplexity made him hesitate even as Sionnach rode to his side.

'Where is Jed?' Seth asked curtly.

'Sharpening his blade.' Sionnach looked at the small patrol across the dip of the moor. 'They were behind a little. He shared his horse with Iolaire because we had to kill Iolaire's. What's going on?' He tensed. 'Lammyr?'

Seth shook his head. 'Kate's had trouble with the Lammyr, that's what I hear.'

'Well.' Sionnach gave him a droll glance. 'Skinshanks was promised prey, Murlainn, not his head in tiny pieces.'

'Yeah.' Seth scanned the faces of Laszlo's patrol. They all knew he was there. All but Laszlo, who was off his mount and had his back turned on Seth as he spoke to the young scarlet-haired Sithe woman with the longbow in her left hand.

'I don't like this,' said Sionnach quietly.

Seth saw Laszlo's shoulders tighten, saw his head come up a fraction.

'The last time I liked something as little as I like this, Murlainn,' said Sionnach, 'your brother didn't live till nightfall.'

Seth shook his head. There was nothing to say. Laszlo turned, very slowly, and those warm beautiful burnt-sugar eyes met his.

'Murlainn.' Laszlo's sword whispered out of its scabbard.

Seth bit gently on the inside of his lip, but left his sword on his back. Conal had taken Laszlo's bait. Conal had let himself be provoked. Conal was dead.

Laszlo laughed. 'You out of your hole, you rat? Where have you been all my life?'

'Look who's talking,' murmured Seth, raising an eyebrow at Sionnach. The blue roan was almost insanely desperate to be at Laszlo, but he kept his hand on its wither and his pressure in its mind. The roan was remembering the bite of a crossbow bolt, but then so was Seth, and he'd had double what the horse got. Lightly he reminded it, and it snorted with disgust.

A breeze moved through the summer-green branches above them. 'Come out, little faeries,' called Laszlo. 'Come and get flesh, Murlainn.'

Beside him, Sionnach shuddered with a memory.

Laszlo gestured his soldiers into a right flanking movement. Sionnach's hand went to his hilt, but Seth still didn't move. When Laszlo signalled more urgently, he cocked his head and stared at Laszlo's patrol. They moved now, but not in response to their captain's increasingly angry gestures. They pulled back into a semicircle around him, exposing him to Seth, effectively blocking any retreat. He saw the moment of dawning realisation on Laszlo's face as the scarlet-haired woman withdrew from him, her smile sharp and white as a cat's.

'Gealach?' Laszlo said, and his voice was beyond disbelief.

She just watched him, her smile contented. No moral conflict for Gealach, thought Seth with a kind of dreadful admiration.

Laszlo met the stares of each one of his patrol. 'Is this to do with Turlach? Because as God is my witness, that was not my doing.'

'Supposing your God gets hold of Turlach's loyal soul, then may he preserve it,' murmured Gealach. 'But this has nothing to do with him.'

Laszlo took a breath. He had to take another, deep and shaking, before he could cough out a laugh. 'All this time and I still don't understand your twisted Sithe minds. But come to me, Murlainn. First you, then the others. I'm protected by the strongest of you.' He turned on his own patrol. 'Would you go against her?' he yelled. 'Would you dare?'

Gealach chuckled, and Laszlo touched his trembling fingers to his temple. His eyes widened and he swore violently. 'Kate! What's your game, bitch-queen?'

The silence was heavier than before. Breaching it, Laszlo's laughter was a little crazier. 'Faeries! God's sake! I should have known better, but this is not how I die, understand? That's beyond even Kate. You Sithe can't harm me, none of you.' Laszlo yanked a dagger out of a sheath on his belt and gripped it in his left hand, then darted a look at Seth, who shook his head slightly.

Laszlo's face was distorted with contempt. His chest rose and fell swiftly with his rage, there was a glint of sweat on his skin, and Seth found it in him to pity the man, just a little. Only a very little, though, and nothing compared to the savage glee that was born in his genes and thrilled into his blood as he watched. He couldn't take his hungry eyes off Laszlo's face.

And then, what he'd waited for: what they all had. Laszlo's expression froze as Jed walked calmly out of the trees, a dirk in his left hand and his honed sword in his right.

Jed didn't speak or break stride, only saluted casually with his sword as he walked on. Laszlo's face was so hideous with shock that he barely parried Jed's first brutal slash, and the Sithe semicircle feinted back to give him space. But the line did not break.

Laszlo barely held off Jed's first relentless attack, and when Jed paused with his blade sliding contemplatively against Laszlo's, he had not even broken a sweat.

'Cù Chaorach showed some courtesy, wolf-whelp,' hissed Laszlo.

Jed gave a small laugh. 'Cù Chaorach's dead.'

'And I should have killed you when I had the chance.'

'Yeah, you bottled it. Too bad.' Jed lifted one shoulder idly and contemplated the edge of Laszlo's blade as it scraped against his. When Laszlo pulled back and lunged he met it easily. Laszlo stepped back. Around him there was calm silence.

Laszlo raised his sword. 'Where's my renegade? Is he with you? Iolaire! Are you watching? You'll get no replacement brats out of this lover, Iolaire!'

Up among the trees Seth glanced sideways at Iolaire. He was expressionless, but his skin was stretched taut across his prominent cheekbones.

'Only, you could wait till he's dead, couldn't you, Iolaire? You could still breed, if you're capable! You've plenty time to change your *proclivities* again.' Laszlo's grin was suicidally vicious. 'He'll die young, your full-mortal faggot! Temporary aberration, is he?'

Iolaire did not move at all, not a muscle of his face, but Seth slipped his mind swiftly inside Iolaire's anyway. A twist of pain writhed up through his ribcage and he clenched his teeth against it. Iolaire gave him a look of gratitude.

Jed leaned on his sword. He did not turn to Iolaire or to Seth, but he met Gealach's cold eyes, then looked back at Laszlo. 'You talk a lot,' he said.

'It's the odds that are giving me pause, you see.'

Jed sighed and turned his back on Laszlo to walk ten paces back towards Seth. 'If I don't kill him,' he yelled, 'nobody does.'

Seth hesitated before nodding.

'Stay out of his mind. You all know fine to stay out of mine.' Jed turned back. 'Happy?'

'And the wolf?'

Jed rolled his eyes and gave an exaggerated sigh. 'Seth?'

Seth clicked his fingers. Branndair's muzzle curled back from his sharp teeth, but he lay down and lowered his head to his forepaws, growling softly.

Laszlo's morale was visibly restored. 'Now. Where were we, Cuilean? Any last words?'

'Um. Please shut up?' Jed hacked his blade hard at Laszlo's neck, and the man dodged and parried, flinging Jed's blade away. Jed staggered slightly, recovered his footing, and edged round Laszlo. When they came together the noise was explosive, steel against steel.

Their struggle seemed interminable. Each was as nimble

as the other; each knew tricks they hadn't been born with. Even Seth grew dizzy watching them dodge, duck and lash out, feet flying when swords and dirks didn't, bodies turning catlike in the air. Seth thought Laszlo had Jed's head off at one point, till Jed doubled backwards, his body arching impossibly, and sprang back to lash out with his own blade.

Seth shut his eyes, breathing again. The deep scar on his left palm ached but he could ignore that. Better to hurt there, when Jed's life was in the balance, than to feel the pain in his heart and lungs.

There was a time he'd have spat in contempt if anyone had told him he'd be blood brother to any full-mortal, let alone one who used to hate him with his whole being. Love was a funny old thing, especially such an improbable and unexpected love. That brought his thoughts back to Finn, and he felt a fleeting terror for her, but shook it off. She was riding to safety right now, and Rory with her. Seth focused on Jed once more. The sharp ache in his hand felt blunter and he looked sideways at Iolaire, who grinned, his left hand curling with pain. Returning the favour, Seth realised.

Even two fighters so expert had to draw breath some time. When they locked against each other, breathing hard, Jed's left hand twisted, forcing Laszlo's blade up and away with his dirk, but Laszlo parried his thrust and sprang back. They stared coolly at each other.

When did Jed get so damn good, Seth wondered, and so capably pitiless? He'd been good enough when Seth was training him, but he was infinitely better now. *What did I miss and when did I miss it?* It was too easy to pay less attention when you trusted someone completely. It was too easy to leave them on their own to get on with life and death, because the love and the trust were absolute. It was too easy to focus on the eddies and currents on the surface, not dive down to see what lay beneath.

I'll talk to him, Seth promised himself. *Back at the dun. Soon. Tonight.*

Why did I leave it so late?

I should have listened to Rory.

With an abrupt yell, Laszlo spun, leaped and crashed down on Jed, who rolled nimbly and slapped the man's blade away with his own. Scrambling to his feet, he lunged again.

Seth leaned forward, gripping the roan's neck. Laszlo was older, but he hadn't lost his touch. If anything he was wilier, and Seth wouldn't have liked to place a bet. Realising his teeth were clenched hard, he forced his jaw to relax.

Jed, Jed. Don't die.

And then Seth thought he had, because Jed had closed too tightly to dodge away, dropping his dirk to clutch Laszlo's sword hand, keeping him anchored to the earth. As Laszlo struggled to get control of his sword back his dirk hacked down at Jed's neck, but it caught only the side of his skull as Jed dropped to his knees right at Laszlo's feet and thrust his sword up hard through his navel and into his ribcage.

Oh, thought Seth. *I see.*

Jed stood up, his bloody hand lodged under Laszlo's breastbone, his other supporting the man in a kind of embrace, and jerked the hilt of his sword once more. Dropping both his weapons Laszlo gave him a wavering smile, a gout of blood choking from his mouth.

And Laszlo's lips moved. And Jed's eyes widened at the whispered words.

JED

'Cuilean,' said Iolaire, snapping the bewitched stillness. '*Cuilean*. Come back now.'

Where had he come from? Jed did not remember Iolaire running to him. He stood with his eyes locked on Laszlo's, their noses almost touching.

Still, the sound of his name brought him back from what seemed a long distance. Laszlo was close enough for Jed to feel his breath, his last breath as it rattled out, and the weight of him dragging on the sword was an awful thing.

Jed did not move. The grin of triumph wouldn't form on his rigid face. He would have kicked the body, except that his legs trembled and he didn't trust himself not to stumble. All there was in his throat was bile and pity and disgust, for the man impaled on his sword. For the man gripping its hilt. Intertwined, interchangeable. For a fraction of a second his brain spun, and he didn't know which he was.

Then, wrenching his sword out, he stepped back. Laszlo thudded forward, face hitting the earth, the last dead breath thumped out of his lungs.

'I thought–' His tongue dried.

'I know,' said Iolaire gently, and Jed thought he probably did.

He touched Laszlo's shoulder with the tip of his sword. The man did not stir.

'The guilt wasn't yours, Jed. You can't undo what you didn't do.' Iolaire shrugged. 'Conal's not sulking in his tent, waiting for your apology. He's dead.'

'So's Laszlo.' He was all desolation. 'So what?'

Iolaire stepped closer and put a hand to Jed's bloody face, turning it so that he could look at his eyes. 'You don't need to worry about what the Lammyr said. You really don't.'

'He was me, Iolaire.' Jed looked straight through his lover. 'And I'll be him.'

A voice cut across them. 'Iolaire!'

Gritting his teeth at the ill-timed interruption, Iolaire looked up at Gealach.

'See you, Iolaire. We won't fight today.' She nodded to Jed. 'Thank you, Cuilean.'

None of the patrol even looked at Laszlo's lifeless body as they turned, and Gealach didn't look at Iolaire again, just urged her horse into a canter. It was Cluaran, bringing up the rear on Laszlo's horse, who hesitated. He didn't look at Iolaire or Jed. He turned to Seth.

'I'm sorry, Murlainn,' he said, then hauled the horse around and spurred it to a gallop.

Seth stared after him for only a moment. Then he swore obscenely, spun the blue roan and rode hard in the opposite direction, Branndair at his heels and Sionnach only a length behind him.

RORY

I felt sick as I rode at Finn's back, and it was nothing to do with the speed of the black horse as it raced across the bleak miles of moor. I'd meant every word I told my father, or I had at the time, but now there was a knot of horrible shame in my stomach, as if they were words I'd regret but never have a chance to take back. Wrapped up in remorse, I almost didn't notice when the black horse broke stride and Finn stared off to the side. Then she reined to an abrupt halt.

'Stella?' she said.

I blinked. 'Finn? What?'

Finn was staring up at the rough heathery slope, doubt and confused hope in her face.

'My mother.' Her voice died, then she rubbed her forehead uncertainly. She yelled up at the empty slope. '*Eili?*'

I wanted to shake her. Instead I gestured ahead. 'Eili is *there*. With Hannah.'

'No, she's...' Finn's voice trailed off, and all she could do was stare at the hillside.

For a moment I wondered if Finn's mind had broken unexpectedly loose. The light was dull, heavy clouds massing at the horizon, but the sky above was clear and blue and hot. Still she gazed transfixed at that deserted slope, and I had the shivering sense that she did see someone on the rise of heathery ground. But hard as I peered, I could see no-one.

'But I saw them,' Finn whispered.

'Finn,' I told her urgently. 'Your mother is dead. *Ride.*'

'Oh. God.'

'What?'

'God. No,' Finn said. '*No.* Not again!'

Snapping out of it, she kicked her heels against the black's flanks, and he snorted and put on speed. 'Eili!' she yelled as she raced after the grey horse.

'Finn? What is it?' I pressed my ear against her back. Her heartbeat was very light and fast.

'It's too late,' she said emptily. 'That's what it is.'

A rise of low hills enclosed the shallow valley, concealing the further horizon. The way to the dun followed a narrow defile and a rocky riverbed, dried to a peaty trickle in the heat. Cutting off our way through it was a line of riders. Not the four riders of my father's patrol, since they lay dead with their horses among the scattered stones. A force of twenty watched our approach in complete and contented silence.

Eili came to a halt facing the hostile fighters, her swords off her back, her reins knotted on the grey's neck. Hannah's chestnut, made uneasy by the grey's growling snorts, began to back away from it, partly from its own nerves and partly from the pressure of Hannah's legs and her hands on the bit. Finn rode up the black beside her.

Turning, Hannah met my eyes, mouthing something I couldn't make out.

'Hannah wants you both to get out of here,' said Finn. 'She's right.'

My breath was stuck in my windpipe. 'They'll know before we even turn. They'll cut us off.'

'Block,' said Finn, 'both of you block now. Rory. Can you get through the Veil here?'

'I dunno.' I crushed down the stirrings of panic. 'We're so close... I don't know.'

'Rory, *try.*'

I snatched and tugged at the air. 'Can't.'

'Got to,' hissed Finn.

I clenched my teeth. 'She *knows.*'

'Knows what?'

'My limits. Never mind. I'll do it. Bitch,' I added under my breath.

'Do it. Then run. They'll follow but we'll try to delay them.' Finn leaned forward and pressed her cheek against the sleek hard neck of the horse. 'He'll go with you.'

I stared at her as she swung a leg over the black's neck and jumped down. 'You too?'

'Don't be silly. Eili's on her own and I'm not going to leave her.'

'Why not?' Hate shivered through me.

'Look,' said Finn, closing her eyes so I could no longer see the fear in them. 'The longer they're kept away from the hole, the harder it'll be for them to find it. Just run as fast and as far as you can. Your father will come for you; you just have to wait for him and not get caught.' She made it sound so straightforward. 'Hannah! Go!'

'Come after us, Finn.' My whisper was desperate. 'The tear will stay open.'

Finn said nothing, just turned away, but I could see her trembling. As Hannah scrambled across from the chestnut onto the black's back, it turned its head to look at her intently, a piercing green light in its eye, nostrils flaring.

I found and gripped the membrane. The skin of my fingers distorted, whitened, but I forced my hand down through the air. The thing was as unyielding as oilcloth. I gritted my teeth so hard I thought they'd shatter, but the Veil began to rip, jerkily, awkwardly.

The sense of triumph was bitter. I turned briefly to see Finn draw a knife and walk away towards Eili.

Then the membrane shimmered and the scene blurred. In less than a second the moor was empty, but for the long scar of a deer fence and a pair of ramblers on the path beyond it, staring at us loose-jawed and bug-eyed.

FINN

Had to stay, had to. Couldn't leave; she couldn't leave Eili.

For a savage moment Finn wondered why not. Then she remembered. Because Eili was the love of Conal's life. Because once she and Finn had been friends, or very nearly. Most of all, because she'd saved Seth's life. Whatever her twisted motives, she'd let Seth live when she could have let him die.

Taking a breath to steady her hand, Finn lifted her knife. Two figures walked forward from the line of riders, and stepped delicately across the corpses of Seth's fighters.

The face of one of the dead was turned towards her: Eorna. Last night he'd played his fiddle in the great hall; he'd heckled Seth and Jed. He'd told her a bad-taste joke that had made her hoot, and given her a dram of his whisky. And *I taught your lover to fight,* he'd told her, *when he was barely more than a suckling brat. And what a useless, pointless, fusionless shortarse he was!* The pride and fondness in his voice were irrepressible.

Eorna's lover Caolas would have been on patrol with him, but she was pregnant. Finn shut her eyes.

She opened them again, to get the brief satisfaction of seeing Kate's eyes widen in anger as Rory and Hannah disappeared beyond the Veil. They were gone, then, and with them Conal's horse. She felt a pang of regret about the loss of him, fierce and strong and a killer in a fight, but he'd be more use to Rory, and he'd stay with the boy. Finn knew the kelpie's strange mind and he did not have the demonic fickleness of Seth's roan.

Besides, there were so many of them, she thought as she cast her nervous gaze along the line, and she didn't want Conal's horse to die. She hoped Seth could retrieve his bridle later somehow, and return it to the sea. Not her problem anyway. Not any more.

Eili had dismounted to face her enemies, and she walked a pace forward. Finn strode to her side and stood with her, their backs half-turned to each other.

'Is this anything to do with you?' Finn hoped Eili was covering her. She hoped the woman wasn't about to slide a knife between her ribs.

'How can you ask me that?'

'Oh, come on,' said Finn witheringly.

A long and painful pause. 'All right, then. No, it's nothing to do with me.'

Kate stopped twenty feet away, the anger smoothed off her features. 'It's everything to do with you, Eili. You've been so distracted, you and your little friend Hannah! She arrived at such an opportune time! Not that *that* was much of a coincidence. Herding her and the Bloodstone together took all of twelve hours. They were – what is it the full-mortals say? – they were gagging for each other!'

'Eili,' whispered Finn, 'don't listen. Don't listen.'

'Do, Eili,' called Kate. 'I want you to know what you've done for me. After all, I was afraid you were close to retrieving your sanity till Hannah turned up. But I needn't have worried. Thanks to the girl, you lost all your perspective along with your reason. You stopped even guarding yourself!'

Eili breathed hard through her nose.

Kate smiled a little cat-smile. 'How funny that Rory turned into such a rebel, and how apt! How *inevitable*. A bad little rebel like his father!' She looked intently at Finn, twisting her copper hair idly between elegant fingers. 'You know, Fionnuala, if I'd had him from a baby I'd have let him live. The boy could have lived a long happy life with me. But his father chose to defy me, chose to bring Rory up himself. Now Rory's loyalties are fixed, so when I'm finished with the boy he'll have to die. And Seth does love that boy, doesn't he, Fionnuala? More than life itself, I think! No wonder Rory started running off like that! Is Seth's love so very oppressive, Finn? So suffocating?'

'You wouldn't know.' Finn licked her dry lips. 'You wouldn't know love if it poked you in the eye.'

Kate sighed. 'Now Seth will pay for his filthy heresy. He'll pay for what he did all those years ago when he dared put a knife to my throat. He'll pay with your life, and Rory's, and the life of every man, woman and child in his dun. And after quite a long time, he'll pay with his own. By that time he'll be begging me to put him out of his misery, and I'll be delighted to take my time obliging him.'

Shudders ran down Finn's spine. She tried to suppress them but she couldn't. 'Jed will kill your Laszlo.'

'Fionnuala, he already has!' Kate closed her eyes dreamily. 'Poor tiresome Laszlo: couldn't take a hint. I've a better champion now, a more ruthless one, and to cap it all he's one of us.' She wore a distant smile. 'Jed has done me a favour. And now I'll have plenty of time to deal with Jed! Seth's blood brother! Oh, *bliss*. Goodness, they're wasting time they haven't got, admiring Laszlo's corpse.' Her eyes snapped open. 'By the way, Udhar, I'm curious. Why didn't you try to kill Laszlo yourself? A fine killer like you! Leaving all your vengeance to Jed!'

'Not all of it.' Eili spoke through her teeth.

'Of course; how silly of me. The torment of Murlainn. Oh! Such remorseless hate! I love an obsessive! And I'm grateful to you, I truly am. I couldn't have done it without you. I'd make you my Captain of captains, if I wasn't going to kill you.'

'Goodness.' Eili's voice was smooth but there was an undercurrent of something awful that made Finn's chest clench for her. 'I feel a little…'

Kate tilted her head sweetly at Eili.

'Used,' finished Eili on a breath.

'Quite. Well, it's nice to chat but a little pointless,' said Kate. 'I'm impressed with Rory's talent, by the way. He's better than I thought and I've made a minor misjudgement, but nothing we can't fix. You know, Fionnuala, I always have a contingency plan.' She beckoned the dark bearded man who stood a sword's length behind her. 'Off you go, Alasdair. He's torn the Veil, the little vandal. Behind them, thirty feet or so that way. He can't have gone far. Bring him back, please.'

'And the girlfriend?' The bearded man smiled, but his voice was as cold as stone.

'Oh, kill her.' Kate shrugged. 'Or not. Whatever. Do as you like with her.'

'You'll leave that girl alone.' With a snarl Eili stepped in front of him. He sighed, drew a sword and swung lightly at her. Her twin swords caught his and she forced it up and away, and he laughed and lunged harder. She swerved, parried, and he met her head on.

The grey kelpie reared behind her, but it didn't get time to join the fight. A single yellow-fletched arrow buried itself in its throat, and then four, five, six more. It bellowed, neck bristling with yellow feathers and welling with blood, and as the first archer stepped back into line, lowering her longbow, the creature sank to its knees, teeth bared and eyes rolling. The archer lifted a hand, staying her detachment's fire. With a bubbling of pink froth the kelpie blew out its last breath and pitched sideways.

Finn ripped a dagger from her belt, breathing hard. As soon as the hilt nestled in her palm, as soon as her thumb found the edge of the blade, she knew she could do this thing without thinking. Confused, she glanced down at the weapon, but her hand was already going through the motions: the adjustment of angle, the flexing of muscle and tendon.

Forget that Kate lived and moved and breathed. That was all.

Your ruthless streak is showing, Finn.

Oh God. Her damp palm was one with the hilt.

Don't let him down. Not now.

The smooth motion of her arm, the iron control of each muscle, the delicate flick of fingers: it was all instinctive. *Taghan. Thank you.* Her dagger flew straight and true towards Kate's throat.

Kate's head snapped round, and she flung up her hand as if to deflect the blade. Instead, the blade never reached her. It juddered to a halt in mid-air, quivering as it hung for a moment before clattering to the ground.

No. An accidental bad spin, a freak gust of breeze.

Finn drew another knife, sent it flying at Kate's throat. Almost before it left her fingers, she followed it with a third.

One braked in mid-air, clattered to the rocky earth. The third Kate allowed within a finger's breadth of her jugular, where it hovered for a tantalising instant. Then it too smashed to the ground.

Kate lowered her hand and walked closer, smiling up through her long lashes at Finn.

'Now, you see?' The queen shook her head sadly. 'That's the kind of aggressive behaviour that's got your lover in so much trouble. Think yourself lucky I want you to die today, Fionnuala, because you really deserve a more prolonged punishment.'

What was that, telekinesis? What Conal called witchcraft? Whatever it was, it was nothing she could fight. Not a soldier in Kate's line moved. Finn looked at Eili's grey kelpie. Its black eye was dead, the green light gone, and Finn was glad she had sent the black away.

As if the volume had suddenly been turned up in her head, she heard the explosive noise of a fight not ten feet away. Eili and the bearded man Alasdair were fighting it out on the flat smooth rocks of the riverbed, water trickling languid between their feet as they hacked lethally at each other, striking, parrying, turning.

So, Finn thought, she could throw a knife – a little late in the day – but she still couldn't wield the sword sheathed uselessly on her back. Eili wouldn't thank her for a distraction, and Finn would probably only manage to hurt Eili. She was an amateur, for God's sake. Maybe she should just have gone with Rory: she might have been more use, might even have lived into the bargain. *The tear will stay open,* Rory had said.

Yes, but even if Finn lunged for it and found it right away, even if by some miracle she turned and ran and made it to the tear in the Veil without an arrow between her shoulder blades, that would only help Kate pinpoint it. She couldn't, wouldn't try. She'd made her choice, and like all her other choices, she had to live with it. Die with it.

More bitterly than ever she mourned the loss of the years, as she raised her eyes to Kate's and gripped her sword hilt.

'Seth will be right behind you,' she said.

Kate smiled wolfishly. 'As he so often was.'

'You're a guinea a minute. What's the plan, Kate, when the Veil's gone?' Finn gave Kate a reckless grin. 'I'm not sure you'll cope with full-mortal politics.'

Kate's smile froze. Ignoring the frenzied clash of swords and Eili's gasping breaths, she took a step towards Finn.

Finn slid her sword carefully from its scabbard, desperate for it not to catch and stick. She raised it, hoping she looked even vaguely professional. 'You can't harm me.'

'No, but *he* will, when he's finished with that whore of Conal's. He'll take his time, too.' Kate sighed in sorrow. 'Oh, Fionnuala. You're such a disappointment to me.'

'I promise you.' Finn swung the blade lightly in front of her. She could feel her jaw trembling and she wanted Kate to look at anything but that. 'Seth won't be in time for us but he'll be in time for Rory.'

'Alasdair will have all the time he needs. Ah, Finn: have you forgotten how easy it was for me to do away with Rory's mother? I know how the time warps, I feel it in my marrow.' Kate tilted an eyebrow sweetly. 'Besides, when Seth gets here his heart will break. The mind and the body don't take so long after that.'

Finn set her teeth. 'It doesn't matter what happens to me. He'll get his son back.'

Kate laughed gently. 'Oh, you're such a child still. No emotional intelligence, that's your trouble. That's what comes of being such an incorrigible loner. Of course it matters, you silly girl, it matters enormously. It'll affect everything: his morale, his judgment, his *soul*.'

'And what would you know about souls?'

Finn risked a glance at Eili, breathing raggedly now. Her deep red hair was darkest claret, slick with blood, and a gash had been opened across her beautiful face. As she dodged another blow, she lurched, and blood spilled from a deep cut on her thigh. Her arms were cross-hatched with sword slashes, her grip slippery on her sword-hilt.

The man Alasdair was as fresh as if he'd just begun to fight, his superior smile unshaken.

'You're bound, you and Murlainn, aren't you?' Kate smirked at Finn. 'But dear me! That means he swore to protect your life, Finn. Where is he?' She glanced innocently around at the empty moor.

'I'm glad he's not here,' said Finn.

'Are you? I don't think so.'

Finn tried to swallow but couldn't. She knew her turn was coming, but she hadn't thought for a moment that Eili would be bested by the first of them. And nor had Seth. Seth had sent her because he'd known Laszlo was occupied, because he had thought they were safe with Eili, that Kate had no-one else who could compete with her. But the man Alasdair was better than Laszlo. Experienced, wily, he was the best swordsman Finn had ever seen.

Finn would barely delay him; what a waste of her life. It all seemed so horribly imminent now. Hell, and she'd thought she had all the time in the world. Over on the other side, homesick and miserable, she'd consoled herself with the knowledge that her Sithe life stretched out before her into an unseeable future. And now, just like that, it was over.

It hadn't been her mother, that blurred and indistinct

figure behind Eili's fetch. Of course it hadn't: Stella was dead and gone. Finn didn't see dead people. She saw people on the brink of death, doomed people, living ghosts.

She'd seen herself.

She was scared, terribly scared, but she was most afraid of losing her dignity. The only way she might preserve it was to go to Alasdair voluntarily before he turned his attention to her.

'Yes,' she told Kate, 'I am glad. I'm glad Seth's not here because he'll live to come after you. Seth will kill you now.'

'He won't have the heart for it, my dear.' Kate tossed her hair back over her shoulder. 'Not after he finds you.'

And that was what finally decided her, because after all she'd rather die fast, and not just for her own sake. Finn shot Kate a last look of hatred and then, as Alasdair drew back his arm for a killing blow to Eili's throat, she darted to the left, gripping her sword, and leaped for his back.

Eyes in the back of his head, he had. He dodged and his left fist swung back, catching her in the cheekbone so that she fell stunned like a shot bird. With his attention deflected, Eili ducked from his thrust and swung wildly, but he dodged with ridiculous ease. His blade missed Eili's gut, but his flying foot caught her in the throat. She dropped like a stone.

Eili's breath gurgled in her gullet as he straddled her prone body, and as she struggled to get air into her partially crushed windpipe Finn went for him again. This time he paid Finn a little more attention, enough to flip his sword in his hand and drive it backwards between her ribs. Her impetus took her right up to its hilt, and then he yanked it hard back out of her, turned back to Eili and skewered her to the ground.

He looked around, as if his interest was mildly piqued

by what he had done. One of Eili's swords lay inches from her twitching hand and he lifted it, examining the blade.

'A beauty,' he said, taking time to admire the light springing steel. 'That's quite a talent of yours. But it's gone now. And I'm so used to my own sword.'

He put a foot on Eili's chest and drew out his blade. As if he'd sucked it physically from her lungs, a high tremor of sound escaped her. Eili pressed her lips hard back together. She did not make another sound, not even when he took her own sword and thrust that into her instead, impaling her once again on the peat.

He looked from her to Finn, fingering his dirk.

Kate shook her head as she hurried forward to touch his arm. 'My sympathies are with you, Alasdair, but I was bluffing her. You haven't time for any of that nonsense. I didn't know Fionnuala had it in her, but it's quite convenient. You'd have held us up far too long otherwise.'

'All the same... just for Murlainn...'

Kate stooped to touch Finn's forehead with a cold fingertip, cocked her head in mild interest, then stood up and shook her fingers.

'Dear me, Alasdair, no. Your blow was too good; she's far beyond you. There's nothing in her worth taking. And I doubt she'd feel a thing you did; it wouldn't be worth the time you'd waste. These two aren't going anywhere, and we don't want to be here when Murlainn arrives, not in the first flush of his rage. Besides,' she added with coquettish severity, 'it's high time you were going after the boy.'

'You did what I showed you?'

'To the letter. It's a stroke of genius and I thank you from the bottom of my royal heart. There's nothing either of them can do about it. Go.'

Alasdair looked from Finn back to Eili, and shrugged. 'Healer, heal thyself,' he said with an ironic smile, and sauntered off towards the tear in the Veil.

Finn was vaguely aware they were all leaving, the killer and Kate and the riders too, but it was as if they existed beyond thick plate glass; she couldn't hear them any more, and nothing they did could affect her. For herself she could see only the sky. She was afraid to move, because there seemed a slim possibility that if she lay very still and did not allow the blood to flow, she might live. Then it occurred to her that they wouldn't have left her like this if that were true. A hot tear flowed out of her eye, tickling her cheekbone and ear and dissipating at her hairline.

It didn't hurt. At least, it hadn't hurt when it happened, and now it didn't hurt as much as she'd expected. Actually, though, it was beginning to hurt. Soon, she realised, it would hurt a lot.

Mostly, though, she just felt scared, and sad, because she didn't want to die. She'd had so little time here. She'd only just got her name, and now Seth would never know it, because Eili was the only other one who knew it and she was dying too.

Another tear welled up and flowed out into her hair. She could almost hear her mother's fond jeering: *I warned you, Fionnuala*. She could hear Hannah's chestnut moving uncertainly, then the rip of its teeth as it began to graze. Kate's troops hadn't bothered to kill or steal it, and it wasn't so nervous now that the grey kelpie lay dead, a blood-spattered unthreatening hulk. Finn was aware of Eili's hand twitching uselessly against the ground, and the horror of it twisted in her chest and gut. That made the sword hole hurt. Now, it hurt a lot.

Finn became aware of someone else, someone near her. With great reluctance, she lolled her head to the side.

Conal smiled at her and she smiled back, surprised that she wasn't surprised. She wasn't scared at all, but then there was no reason to be afraid of him. All she felt was an intense, quiet happiness. He was crouching close to her, and as she moved her head to see him better, a lance of awful pain went through her. He put a comforting hand against her face.

No. Nothing to be afraid of. Conal couldn't help her, of course, but it was nice to have him there, and it felt right. There was no wound in his throat, and though the faded blue shirt he wore was half-blackened and stiff with blood, when he leaned forward and the gash in it sagged open, there was no hideous hole beneath it, only his damp tanned skin and muscles all in one piece. Conal was free, then. Eili must be dead, or closer to it even than Finn, because he was free of her suffocating grief.

~ *I've missed you,* she told him happily.

~ *I missed you too.* He smiled. ~ *A lot.*

There was someone behind Conal, someone she could see only vaguely, a dark-haired man with intense green eyes. She didn't know him and yet she did, always had, because he was the man she could see in her own face. He stood back as if he was shy of coming closer. Conal glanced at him, then looked back at Finn, his smile softening.

His finger stroked her cheekbone the way it had the last time she'd seen him alive. This time, though, she was the one who couldn't move, she was the one with her lifeblood soaking into the peat. Panicking a little, she choked, coughing thick blood.

~ *Sh, sh*. He touched the corner of her mouth gently with his thumb, catching the blood. His fingers caressed her temple. ~ *Oh, Finn, love. What about Seth?*

Seth. Oh, Seth. But he was in a different dimension now, and receding. Soon she'd be far beyond him and this crippling sadness of separation would be permanent. Couldn't be helped. Finn's eyeballs slewed to the twitching half-corpse on the periphery of her vision.

~ *Well, what about Eili?*

~ *Eili and I have time enough, toots*. His fingertips brushed her forehead, raked gently through her hair, gripped the back of her skull. ~ *But you have to go to her.*

Then he paused just for a moment, and smiled. ~ *Tell him not to be so scared, okay?*

The air rushed into her lungs without any invitation, and she curled upright, gasping. For a moment she was shocked silent and then she cried out with the pain and the sadness. There was no-one there. No-one at all. Conal and her father had never existed: hallucinations, that was all. The vast moorland was deserted but for her and the chestnut horse and Eili, and the dead kelpie, and fifty yards away the scattered corpses of the slaughtered patrol.

The glassy screen was gone: everything was real and vile again. Finn sobbed once and clenched her teeth, then rolled over onto her hands and knees so that she could see Eili. The woman was whiter than bleached rock but her pale lips trembled with remnants of breath.

'Come here.' It was a vehement whisper.

'...what...'

'Don't waste your last breath.' Eili sucked in one of her own. 'Come here.'

Finn sagged down, sobbing at the sight of her own blood spilling onto the heather.

'*I cannot come to you!*' Eili snarled.

Finn pulled herself on her elbows. It hadn't seemed so terribly far before, when she'd been afraid of the near-corpse in the heather, but now it was the longest journey she'd ever made. Oh, it hurt now, all right, and terror bit hard in the wound with every pulse of blood.

'Come. *Here.*'

Finn crawled by her fingertips, inch by inch, because the elbow-crawl opened her veins too far and she was terribly scared now. Scared, but she had to get there. Had to. There was a message to deliver. Right now she couldn't remember it, not a word of it or even what it was about, but it was lodged in her brain like an axe-blade and it had to be delivered.

Her fingertips found more peat, more grass, more solid earth, and dragged the rest of her after. It felt like the last effort she would ever make when she slumped down at Eili's side and coiled against her splayed jerking hand.

Eili gave a long rattling sigh that Finn was mortally afraid was her last. Then another breath sucked into the skewered lungs and Eili's fingers were creeping across her flesh, finding the sword hole, thrusting into it.

Finn didn't have the strength to scream. If she'd had any energy left in her she might have recoiled from those creeping fingers, but she didn't. Maybe Eili only wanted to kill her, but it was all the same now. Finn laid her cheek against the bloodstained peat and stared at Eili's bone-pale face and the dark lashes that lay on her jutting cheekbone. She'd have thought Eili was dead now, if she hadn't felt the residual heat of that hand in her raw flesh.

And then it began to hurt a great deal and Finn began to cry, watching Eili's face until it was lost in blackness and she was no longer aware of anything at all.

HANNAH

As soon as we passed through the Veil I felt the change in Rory. I swear he hardened like soft shell fossilising. When my mind brushed experimentally against his, I felt nothing but steely resistance.

Rory looked back at the tear once, shimmering like a scratch in the air. I could practically hear him willing Finn to come through after us, but nothing stirred and broke through the gash, no running figure materialised, and at last he kicked the horse's flanks and galloped it down the length of the deer fence. I hung onto his waist, scared of him for the first time since the day I met him. The horse arched its neck and kept to its unhurried canter. Rory didn't seem worried, and that alarmed me as much as anything else. He was way too calm.

'Rory,' I said.

He didn't answer. He was counting the horse's strides under his breath, watching the ground, monitoring every dip and rise of the moorland. The horse huffed questioningly and he steered it with his heels. He looked to the rise of hills, hesitated, then pushed it on another hundred metres. The horse made a sound like a laugh, but cantered on obediently and came to a halt when he asked, beating the earth with a hoof.

'Rory, look...'

'Hannah, shut up. I'm concentrating.' He half-turned. 'All right. Hold tight. If I've got this wrong we're going to die now.' Reaching out once again to grab the Veil, he ripped it downwards, and ducked back through to the Sithe side. Breath hissed through my teeth.

'Jee-sus!'

Rory took no notice. He was concentrating entirely on the black horse and on the surrounding moorland. Very quietly he turned, and took a silent breath, but he was grinning. When I followed his gaze, I only just stopped myself screaming.

The line of horsemen and women was stretched out behind us, but they were riding away and none of them bothered to look back. I realised we'd come right past the riders on the other side, and were now behind them. Rory's grin died, and the thought struck me a moment after it must have struck him. There was no sound of a fight, no sign of anyone beyond the riders apart from the chestnut horse, grazing.

Rory urged the black horse up and over the rise of hills. We were out of the possible sightline of Kate's troops within fifty metres. Making a sound with his teeth Rory kicked the horse back to a canter, choosing his direction quite deliberately, and it responded to him as if he was its only master and always had been.

I looked over my shoulder. There was no-one in sight but there was an edge of menace to the air, and when I thought about the file of riders, my bones chilled. 'Rory?'

'What?' He was distracted. Slowing, he twitched the reins and the horse veered right.

'What's happened to Finn and Eili?' I asked in a small voice.

'Want to go back?' His coldness made me feel like a worm. I didn't even have to answer. He knew how terrified I was. He knew as well as I did that I'd get off the horse and run on alone on foot, rather than turn back to help the two women.

'Finn and Eili are dead,' he said. 'Their minds are gone, they don't exist any more. Maybe Jed's dead too. And I suppose my father's going to die now.' He gave a shrug of his shoulders, and suddenly he didn't seem so tough. He looked like a small boy who was trying too hard to be cool. 'This is how it all ends up. I always knew it would. I tried to tell them.'

I hardly dared to ask. 'So what are we doing back here?'

'Getting away. You don't think they just watched us go, do you? I should have closed the Veil but I couldn't do that to Finn, I thought she might have a chance to follow. *Bad* move. Kate'll have sent someone after us. She's timed this, timed it carefully. If there's a warp in the time she'll know it. But this way we call her double-bluff.'

'Yeah, but if your dad's...' I couldn't say it. 'If your dad has lost, this is the last place we should be. Please, Rory. Let's go back to the real world.'

'That's not the real world,' he sneered.

'All right, all right. I just want out of *this* world, okay? You heard what Finn said.'

'Finn has no say in it any more. Finn's dead. We have to work it out ourselves now, see? Follow our own instincts, not some dead woman's.'

I let go of his waist for a moment, not wanting him to feel the shiver that went through me. He was scary, as scary as his father. But if what he said was true, scariness wouldn't save us. Otherwise Eili would still be alive, and Finn. And Seth.

Seth was my uncle. He was my father's brother, and my father had loved him. Seth had been okay, actually, considering how I'd behaved, and I hoped violently that he wasn't dead. I wondered how he'd react when he found Finn's corpse. I wanted to be sick.

'Why can't we do what you just did?' It seemed obvious. 'We can travel on the other side, go to where the dun is, come back through and we're in the dun.'

'I can't get through at the dun, even within a few miles of it. The Veil's too tough there. And if I try the approaches, I could bring us out in the middle of one of Kate's patrols. She's been planning this, see? Dad and Jed and Iolaire and Sionnach will have to fight their way back to the dun, if they're still alive. We wouldn't have a chance.' He thought for a moment. 'Anyway, I don't think I should try for the dun. It won't be safe any more. Kate must be confident of overrunning it or she wouldn't have made her move. I have to keep away from her. Me and her together, that's what would be fatal. She can't have me.' He chewed his thumb. 'All we can do is run. And I hate to admit it, but you're right. We need to go to the other side.'

'For how long?'

'Long as it takes. Till Dad finds us, tells me it's safe to go back.'

If ever, I thought, but I didn't say it. 'So where are we going?'

Rory nodded ahead, and I peered over his shoulder. The ruined castle loomed at the edge of the loch, its eastern wall rising straight and forbidding from the black water.

'There,' said Rory, and as he cantered the horse out onto the promontory he was already reaching out his hand to grasp at something unseen.

SETH

He was off the blue roan before it stopped running and Sionnach was only a heartbeat behind, but he knew they were too late. The two women lay together, Finn curled against Eili, with the dappled grey ten feet beyond them, and further off what was left of the patrol. Seth sank to his knees beside Finn, then looked hopelessly up and around.

'Rory!' he howled, though he knew it was futile and the breeze whipped his voice into nothingness. *'Rory!'*

Sionnach stared down at his twin in the rain that was closing in like a mist. His face was entirely blank but as white as hers as his trembling fingers reached for the sword that impaled her. As they brushed the hilt her eyes opened wide, creasing with pain and the semblance of a smile. An answering smile shivered on Sionnach's lips, and he closed his eyes and slipped into her mind.

'Murlainn.' Eili's breath was shallow, her voice barely audible, but she was laughing, a horrible bubbling sound. Seth gave her a sharp look. It was eerie enough being watched by a near-corpse, let alone by her twin inside her. He'd been experiencing it for more than four hundred years, and it still made him shiver when they became one. What in the name of all the gods would become of Sionnach now?

Then he looked back at Finn's body, and felt grief begin to cut out his heart, and wondered what in the name of the gods would become of *him*.

'What d'you think, Murlainn?' Eili's laughter gurgled again. 'Think I'd let her die? Or let her live?'

His breath caught painfully. Eili's blood-boltered hand lay limp against Finn's ripped chest. Tentatively he lifted Finn, easing her backward into his arms, and a sound came from her throat. That didn't mean anything, as he knew from bitter battlefield experience, so he cradled her against his chest and put his cheek close to her lips. No breath that he could feel.

Eili: savage and remorseless to her end. It was one last stab at him, he knew: one last thrust that would be worse than anything else she'd done, because now he had to know for sure. Sick to his stomach, he tightened his arms round Finn. He didn't want to know but he had to.

Hesitantly he reached out his mind for Finn's, expecting nothing. There most likely wasn't a mind there any more, and he desperately did not want to touch the absence of it. Not after he'd felt her chaotic delight when they raced their horses across the machair, not after he'd heard her mocking laughter in his head, snapping him out of a dark misanthropic mood. Not when he'd so recently tangled his mind up in hers as they locked eyes and he moved inside her. He did not want to sink into a hideous vacuum where her whole life had been.

If Eili was lying to him, he'd finish her off himself, even if Sionnach killed him for it. With Finn and Rory gone it was all the same to him, so let Kate win. She probably had, anyway. It was just as it had been with Conal. He thought again what he'd thought then: *You're not meant to die. It's supposed to be me. ME.*

All right. One last try. Terror choking him, he reached further through the dark emptiness in search of her, his mind on a blade-edge and ready to recoil.

Then he felt it. Withdrawn far, far below the surface to

escape the pain and fear, he felt a tiny moth-wing flutter of awareness. And her name. He felt her *name*.

Seth blinked. She was as white as death, but there was light breath on his skin, and a pulse jerked faintly in her throat.

'Ye of little faith,' sneered Eili.

'Finn,' he croaked, but no sound came out.

'He told me to heal myself!' Blood bubbled from Eili's smile. '*Nobody* tells me what to do.'

A blowing horse came to an exhausted halt behind them. He heard the ring of the bit and the light thud of first Jed and then Iolaire dismounting. 'Is she dead?' Jed sounded seventeen again.

'No.' It was all Seth could say as he reached out his thoughts, coaxing her back, terrified of frightening her away beyond his reach. ~ *Don't be scared. They've gone. It's me. Please come back. I love you. Please. Caorann. Caorann.*

'Give her to Jed. I said she'll live.' Eili's voice was reduced to a breath but it cut through his consciousness. 'C'm'ere, Murlainn.'

Raindrops glimmered in Finn's black hair, condensed out of the wet mist, so Seth looked at those as he eased her into Jed's arms, and not at the edges of the messy wound that looked as if they'd been sealed with a staple gun.

'Best I could do,' whispered Eili. 'Arteries are a bit neater but you can't see those.'

Turning reluctantly away from Finn, he crouched over Eili. Sionnach stood motionless beside them, his whole self submerged in his twin.

Eili had saved Finn's life, then, as she'd once saved his, only there wouldn't be the vicious aftermath, because Eili herself was not going to live. She'd spent everything she had saving Finn instead of herself, and Seth wondered why. He forgot the helpless rage of thirteen years, forgot that a moment ago he'd been ready to kill her. He remembered then how much he'd loved and wanted her. Hands cupping her face, he brushed away the film of rain with his thumbs. 'Who was it? You know him?'

'You bet. Kilrevin.'

Seth drew a breath. 'He's dead. Long since.'

'Assure you he isn't.' Her smile was asymmetrical, as if the two of them shared a private joke her dark half didn't get. 'Rory got away, Murlainn.'

His eyes widened as the dull despair lifted. 'But I can't See him.'

'He's over the Veil. It'll be obstructing you. You know how hard it is to See across it. Shut up. Listen. Doesn't hurt but I haven't long. The tear: it's ten yards beyond the horse.' She could move no more than a finger but she gave him the direction with the tip of it. 'Kilrevin followed, only him. Kate's cocky, Murlainn. She's in no hurry.'

'If Sionnach can take the sword out...' He bit his lip.

'No. No. It's taken everything just to stay till you got here. *Almost* everything.' She gazed at him, ancient fondness warring with something else, and he felt pain snake into his scars and bite hard. He clenched his teeth and met her eyes without flinching, and after a moment the pain ebbed. She gave a long hissing sigh. 'And now there's nothing left at all.'

'Eili.' His voice cracked.

'Murlainn. That was for old time's sake.' She gave him an odd smile and her eyes slewed to her brother's still figure. 'Now out, Sionnach. Out. You are not coming with me. Not this time.' Opening his eyes, Sionnach made an animal sound as his mind was forced out of hers. 'Don't cry, Sionnach. I got to be myself again. She's gone, that Udhar.' She ran her tongue along her teeth. 'But hold my hand. Like before. Remember? Like before we were born.'

Sionnach knelt at her head as Seth stood up. The dirk hissed out of his sheath as Sionnach took her hand, winding his fingers into hers.

'No, Sionnach,' she murmured. 'Wouldn't make you do that. I'll do it myself.' Eili's eyes lost their focus as she turned her gaze inwards, and the pulse in her throat slowed as Sionnach lay down and wrapped his arms around her.

Her facial muscles contorted once in a last spasm. Strange and horrible, Seth thought, how much it looked like a smile of pure joy. The pulse fluttered twice more, and he watched for it again, but it had gone, and her brown eyes were lightless and empty.

Turning his back on her, he went to Jed, standing helpless with Finn in his arms. Seth pulled aside his lover's slashed shirt with one finger and looked at the ragged wound. There was blood everywhere but it was dry and darkening despite the misty rain, and he could see living blood pulsing through her veins. As a distant rumble of thunder intensified the rain, he pushed aside the tendrils of wet hair that clung to her face.

He trusted Jed more than any living soul, but it wasn't good enough. He wanted to take care of her himself; he wanted to find Rory. He couldn't do both. *I told you this would happen,* he wanted to yell at her. *Do you think I can cut myself in two?*

But there was no point. It wasn't her fault, it wasn't Rory's, and for once it wasn't even his own. It was just how things were when you went and exposed your heart to the cold air, like a fool. His innards twisted like a rope, tightening from his gullet to his gut. He wouldn't have believed binding could hurt so much; perhaps it might kill him if it went on long enough. But that was what Kate wanted, after all.

'I'm sorry, Finn,' he said quietly, and looked up at Jed. 'Take them to the dun. Be careful. Kate has patrols out and you might need to fight. Iolaire can take Hannah's horse.'

'Let me come with you,' pleaded Jed.

'*No*. Get Finn back to the dun. You do that for me, Jed, and I'll find Rory.'

The moment was a long one, but 'All right,' said Jed at last. His jaw was tight. 'Be careful.'

Seth shut his eyes briefly. 'Jed, send patrols to the outlying communities and bring our people into the dun. Get them to bring what supplies they can. You don't have long. And if you get the chance, send a party out for those men.' He nodded to the corpses strewn among the stones. 'Tell them to go well-armed and get the water horse too if they can, but not at risk to themselves. You might be able to nego-tiate a sortie; depends how civilised Kate's going to be. Branndair.' He made a sound through his teeth and rubbed the wolf's head. 'Stay with Finn. Don't leave her side. Not for *anything*.'

Jed looked from Branndair back to Seth. 'I'll take care of her too. I promise.'

'I know you will. Jed? Take care of Sionnach as well.' He couldn't look at his lieutenant for more than a moment. There was no sound from him. The sword had been wrenched out of Eili and thrown aside. Sionnach knelt over her, hacking so hard and wildly at his hair that his dirk was leaving deep gashes on his scalp. Blood trickled in thin streams down his face and neck but there was no expression on his face. Seth winced.

'Go on, Jed,' he said. 'You haven't long. Kate'll be coming. Do your best till I get back.'

'Seth.' Iolaire touched his arm. 'Kilrevin's a tracker, he was famous for it. He *will* get to Rory, and he can force him to take him through the Veil. He won't need a water-gate. You *have* to get to Rory first.'

'I know.' The desolation could have unmanned him right there. 'I know.'

'Please find him.' There were tears in Jed's voice. 'And please live. This time *live*, MacGregor.'

'Same to you, you jumped-up whelp.' They glowered at one another for a moment, then looked away simultaneously. Seth mounted the blue roan. 'Listen, Cuilean, Rory's in good company. The closest he'll ever get to Conal.'

'I don't... oh.' Jed blinked. 'Hannah? Oh!'

'Hannah.' Seth tried to smile.

Clutching Finn tighter, Jed stared at him as he rode past the dead kelpie, stopping a few yards beyond it. The roan snorted as he rode it back and forth over a five-metre stretch, fingertips brushing the air. *Come on. Come on.*

The horse stopped, a tremor running in its flank, and Seth leaned a little forward and out of the saddle, his hand seeking something.

'Hah,' he said softly. '*Sgath*. There you are again.'

The roan sidestepped elegantly, and they crossed to the otherworld together.

ALASDAIR KILREVIN

He was a patient man. You didn't live to be Alasdair's age without a bit of patience. But he resented being ordered around by Kate NicNiven, especially when she had got it so clearly and colossally *wrong*.

There was no sign of Murlainn's boy or the redheaded girl. A deer fence stretched from one side of the moor, curved round a small forestry plantation and disappeared, but there was no-one hiding among the young trees. The low hills rose towards the west and the land fell away to the south and east. You could see a long way, but the boy was not here. Not anywhere.

Alasdair didn't get to be this age without stopping to think.

The time balance was screwed up, Kate had known that before she made her risky move, and Alasdair didn't fancy ducking straight back through the tear in the Veil and coming face to face with Murlainn, a sword in his hand and his dead lover at his feet. That would not be a good scenario, not for him, though it might give a little brief satisfaction to Murlainn.

Alasdair, after all, was running quite an account with that boy, and payment had been overdue even before this latest development. It was more than four hundred years since he'd pulled his sword from Griogair Dubh's gurgling throat, but he would never forget his glimpse of the black-haired boy's reflection in the oily, bloody black water of the well. He would never forget the look on the child's white face. And it was a fair bet that Murlainn hadn't forgotten that day either.

He should have slaughtered the boy then and there, put an end to any vengeful notions in that young romantic head. But there had been a hell of a mess to clear up after the battle, and men to control in victory.

He had to be honest with himself about his motives. One did not grow old by feeling pity or showing mercy. But somewhere in his soul he'd liked leaving the child alive: a witness, a teller of the tale, a terrified survivor. He hadn't wanted to snuff out that delicious terror; not yet. And he'd made that most elementary mistake: not underestimating a twelve-year-old, exactly, but forgetting for a vital moment that twelve-year-olds grew up, if you let them.

After all, look what had happened to Nils Laszlo. Alasdair grinned. Laszlo's mistake had been even worse than his. It was a sixteen-year-old he'd let off the hook, and what had happened? The sixteen-year-old had grown into a thirty-year-old who hunted him down and gralloched him just as he'd gutted Cù Chaorach. Kate had giggled helplessly about that. The young full-mortal had been kinder than Laszlo deserved, putting the blade through his heart instead of leaving him for the birds the way Laszlo had left Cù Chaorach; but he hadn't shown Laszlo any mercy that mattered.

There was a lesson for everyone. Alasdair hoped Kate would bear it in mind, given that she wanted Murlainn's brat alive. When she had what she wanted from the boy, he really must remind her that you didn't leave little cauldrons of revenge simmering away over the years. They always boiled over eventually and burned your house down.

Which brought him back to his present dilemma.

There were two ramblers on the other side of the deer fence, hastening away from him, trying not to look panicky. Clearly his sudden appearance wasn't all that had spooked them. From a standing start he took a run at the deer fence and leaped, scrambling over and dropping lightly down. He overtook the ramblers easily, bringing them to a wary halt as he stood in their path and smiled.

'A boy and a girl,' he said without preamble. 'On a horse.'

'What?' Puzzlement, as if they could barely remember what they were hurrying away from.

'Focus,' he said brusquely. 'Focus and you'll remember. A. Boy. And. A. Girl.'

A light of memory dawned in the woman's eyes, and with it suspicion. 'Now, wait just a minute.'

Middle-aged, handsome, grey hair tinted to pale and unconvincing blonde. She was probably a mother and a grandmother, probably felt an instinctive protectiveness even towards two children she didn't know, and a moment ago had barely remembered. Alasdair knew he did not look reassuringly normal. Full-mortals judged so much by surface detail. She wasn't likely to believe he had the little dears' best interests at heart, not with his shabby leather coat (not that she'd recognise bloodstains) and his tangled black beard, and the two braids of unwashed hair at his temples. Not to mention the sword on his back, the bloody-hilted sword that even these two might notice.

He'd been over-occupied lately. There was vanity in him, but he was a busy man.

The woman wore tough walking boots and a backpack, well-used and expensive like her windproof jacket. An experienced walker, then. She'd be fit. Not fit enough, but fit. She'd give him sport if she felt she had to run. Alasdair beamed at her, toying with the idea, and saw a tremor run through her.

'Now look here.' The man was probably her husband. Examining him, Alasdair sighed. He didn't look much of a challenge, and after all he'd already made one widower today.

'We're on a role-playing holiday,' Alasdair said softly. 'The activity centre down the glen.'

'Oh, I see.' The man looked relieved, though the woman still looked uncertain.

'That nephew of mine. Any chance to run off with the girls!' Nephew, he decided, had more of a ring of truth than *son*. He couldn't have kept a straight face for that.

'Well, they rode off that way. Along the deer fence. I expect they went into the wood. We didn't see them go, they just disappeared.'

Just disappeared. He didn't realise what he was saying, thought Alasdair dryly. Still, the man was convinced of his innocent intentions. He *wanted* to be convinced. His wife still looked unsure, but the husband would talk her round, and the brats would slip out of her memory. If they featured on some reconstruction her memory might be jogged, she might turn to her husband, mouth open, and say *We saw them on the moor and we saw that man…*

But there wasn't going to be a reconstruction. There wouldn't even be bodies, not on this side of the Veil. There wouldn't be so much as a paragraph in the local paper, so they'd have nothing to feel guilty about.

'I see. Thank you!' Alasdair gave them a broad smile. The woman shuddered as they turned away, gave him a nervous glance. He felt a pang of regret. A hunt would have been fun…

But he was a busy man with a job to do.

He glanced at the deer fence. So they'd gone back through, had they? The boy was as cunning as his father. No way would Alasdair find the second tear in the Veil before nightfall. Even if he went after the ramblers, asked them in his own direct efficient way exactly where the brats had vanished, they wouldn't remember. They'd panic under pressure, if they'd even taken enough notice to begin with. Full-mortals saw only the surface. They were unobservant, and so forgetful.

Chewing his thumb, he stared thoughtfully at the moorland. Kate had planned well. Murlainn's lover and his best soldier were dead; his lieutenant Sionnach was incapacitated by grief, if he knew anything about those twins. The boy would know that his chances of reaching the dun were minuscule, and that anyway Kate was bent on the dun's destruction. He'd bank on his father coming after him. The tricksy little bastard might have hidden temporarily back on his own side, but he'd come back sooner rather than later to the full-mortal world, to what he naïvely thought was safety. All Alasdair had to do was wait for him.

The boy would head for a familiar place, preferably with crowds. Some playground of old where he'd feel safe, where he wouldn't know he'd ever been watched.

Well, Alasdair had playgrounds too. He'd always had his favourites. He turned to the east and began to run, in a steady economical lope like a wolf.

HANNAH

The black horse's hooves sounded horribly loud on the cobbles as Rory led it into the darkness. The old stables were closed, roped off for yet more renovations, but there was still a good chance we'd be seen. We'd be a lot less conspicuous without the kelpie, but Rory was reluctant to take off its bridle. Finn's horse was the only escape we'd have in a crisis.

'With luck we'll have screwed up Kate's plan.' Leading the black into the furthest stall, he crouched against the wall, and I slumped down beside him, eyeing the beast's legs with trepidation. 'She'll have waited for a time warp before she risked acting. She knew how the time was balanced when we came through, but then we went back, and came through a second time. So that's maybe ruined it for her. I hope, anyway.' He shrugged. ''Cause they should have caught up with us ages ago.'

I shivered, and hugged myself. 'Won't she have thought of us doing that?'

'You didn't see her face when we disappeared. She chose her spot and she'd no idea I could break the Veil there. She underestimated me.' Rory sounded a little too pleased with himself.

I gave him a thoughtful look. 'She won't do that again.'

'No.' He chewed the knuckle of his thumb. 'Listen, Hannah, you should go home. They're not after you. With me you're in danger. On your own you won't interest them.' He looked at me kindly. 'Just leave me. I won't mind, honest.'

'Of course I won't leave you! This is my fault.'

He didn't instantly contradict me to make me feel better or anything. I waited a few seconds, then blew out a breath. Inside I was wincing.

'Why did you tell me, Hannah? Why'd you tell me about Eili and my father, if you were in league with Eili?'

'I didn't trust her,' I muttered. 'I didn't trust her or Taghan any more than I trusted Finn. I was hedging my bets. I wanted you to know. I thought you *should* know. Just in case.'

He licked his lips, flicked his gaze away. 'Did she really want Kate to get hold of me?'

'No. No! God knows how those men knew we'd be there, but they did. Eili was as shocked as we were. And Taghan – Taghan was–'

'Dead. Like Finn. I guess they're quits.'

'I didn't want Finn to die.' I shut my eyes. 'I thought I maybe did but I didn't. Shit.'

'Well.' He shrugged. 'It's the way we live. You weren't to know. Besides, this would have happened somehow, somewhen. Kate's clever.'

I twisted my fingers tightly together. 'Listen, about Eili? There's a reason I – there's something else. I'm...'

'Uncle Conal's daughter, yeah.'

Stupefied, I stared. 'How'd you know?' I narrowed my eyes. 'Did you look?'

'Didn't have to; I worked it out. Besides, your blocking is *fantastic* now. You learn fast.'

I ignored the compliment. Eili had taught me for a reason, after all. 'How'd you work it out?'

'Dad was upset about something, wasn't he? And it explains Eili. In a lot of ways.' Rory's face grew sour. 'I'm sorry Finn's dead, but I'm not sorry about Eili.'

I decided I'd better say nothing to that. 'We're cousins, you know.'

'Uh-huh. Funny, isn't it?'

'Bloody hilarious,' I said dismally. 'I think that counts as consanguinity.'

'Consang*what?*'

'Never mind. Though I do. Hang on, sh!' I froze, then crawled forward on my hands and knees to the door of the stall and peered round. 'Uh-oh.'

I reversed quickly into the stall, baring warning teeth at Rory. Shrinking against the partition we both looked up at the massive horse. There really was no hiding that thing. The black stilled, tail flicking, ears pricked forward. I did not like the look in its eye.

The footfalls drew closer, hesitant, and fast shallow breathing echoed in the stable. We didn't have to read the intruder's fear: we could hear it.

Rory dropped his block; I heard him, fiercely insistent. ~ *You don't want to be here. We don't want you here. So go away. Turn round.*

The steps halted. Rory shut his eyes tight, cajoling the man, who obediently glanced back towards the square of bright sunlight at the door.

~ *You don't want to be in the dark. Go to the daylight, go on. It's dark in here.*

It was working. I blew out a silent breath. The intruder was hesitating, turning on his heel.

~ *Go back to the light.*

And then the black horse moved its hoof.

Rory seized its fetlock, uselessly. The sneaky brute.

The man had gone absolutely still; he was holding his

breath. Slowly, reluctantly, he turned once more. He walked trembling towards our hiding place.

I'd never seen anyone physically jump with fright, but the little tour guide did. In an instant his fear turned to rage, but when the horse lightly shook its neck, he took an involuntary step backwards. The horse nickered softly, top lip curling back from grinning teeth.

The guide stared at it. His hand was shaking uncontrollably but he was reaching out to the horse's muzzle, fingers splayed and straining to touch it. Trance-like he took a step forward, and the black arched its neck and reached for his hand.

'No. *Eachuisge,* don't.' Rory stood up, easing between tour guide and horse. The black's teeth shut with a disappointed snap, an inch from the little man's hand, and it blew through flared red nostrils. As its hot breath touched his skin, the man snatched back his hand, eyes wide.

'I do not believe it,' he hissed, recovering. 'You again! Why do I never remember to report you?'

'Hello,' said Rory. Awkwardly he kicked at the cobbles, glancing up at the guide from beneath long dark lashes. Strands of blonde hair fell endearingly forward into his huge grey eyes, and I chomped hard on my cheeks to stop myself laughing.

The guide looked more confused than convinced. 'I can't believe you've got the brass neck. I'm calling your parents. Tell me their name and address right now, or I'll call the police. This time I *really will.*'

'My mum's dead,' whispered Rory, his voice catching. 'My dad's dead too.'

I was awestruck, but uneasy. He was good, but it shocked me that he could even say that.

'Well, I'm – look, I'm sorry. I'm very sorry for your loss, but you can't loiter around this castle. This is private property and the stables are under renovation.' Glowering, he tugged at his collar. 'I cannot allow you to play in these stables, horse or no horse. They are a dangerous place to be.'

'That's an understatement,' said a new voice.

Rory froze. His block was back up in an instant; I felt it slam down and I followed suit. Meeting his eyes, I edged up the wall to a standing position. Rory nodded at me, his hand slipping into the mane of the horse.

The guide turned, exasperated. 'Now, look here, there are clearly marked barriers. These stables are out of bounds and the general public are not permitted–'

'I'm not the general public,' said the newcomer, smiling. 'I'm the owner.'

'Mr Stewart?' The guide squinted into the dimness, neck reddening. He gaped at the long scruffy leather coat, at the untidy black beard and woven braids. Glancing over the burly shoulder, he frowned. It was too dark for the sword hilt to be clearly visible, but something was worrying him. 'I don't...'

'That's me. Alasdair Farquhar-Stewart.' The bearded man gave him a thin-lipped smile, and his employee returned it uncertainly. 'You've met me before, remember? Oh, come to think of it: probably not.'

'I...'

Alasdair Farquhar-Stewart rolled his eyes wryly at me and Rory. 'Bloody Veil. Doesn't it drive you *mad*?' He turned back to the guide. 'These... children... are trespassing on my property. There is no need to involve the police, understand? I will deal with this myself.'

The guide glanced back at us in the shadows. For the first time a flicker of self-doubt crossed his angry features. 'Look, that's all very well, but...'

'I don't think you heard me. I said I'll deal with it.'

'Mr Stewart – Mr Farquhar-Stewart, I know it's your property, but there are procedures. I'm sure...'

'Yes. It's my property. It's mine twice over.' Pushing his hair out of his face, the man stepped into a better light and smiled at the guide. 'Do you see what I mean?'

'I...'. The little man stopped, swallowing. At least, he tried to swallow. There was a dry clicking sound in his throat where he couldn't quite manage. As he stared up at the grinning bearded face, I knew a shock of horrible recognition.

My mouth dried. I knew what the tour guide was feeling: the disbelief, the realisation, the crawling horror. Oh, I knew exactly what was in his head. It was in mine too.

The eyes of our minds were seeing the same thing, after all. The guide was seeing that portrait in the library, my own favourite and most special attraction: the Wolf of Kilrevin. And he was thinking how awfully like Alasdair Farquhar-Stewart it looked.

'I... well, my goodness, I didn't know you were a direct descendant. Because I mean, I quite see it now, and I must say the family resemblance is startling...'

The Wolf's hand went to the hilt on his back. 'I'm not a descendant.'

'You're not.' The tour guide licked his lips. 'No. You're not. Oh, my God.' His beady eyes widened as the bright blade slid out of its scabbard.

'Please stand aside, now. There won't be a problem.'

'But...'

The Wolf rolled his eyes. 'Please be assured. There *will not* be a problem. These brats do not exist, do you understand? They don't exist, any more than I do. There will be no ramifications, and no-one will blame you for anything, and you will forget this ever happened. Really. It'll be like a bad dream.' The casual voice took on a new edge as the guide went on staring at him in disbelief. 'Now kindly get your scrawny arse out of the way.'

Terror flowed cold in my veins. The guide was going to stand back and let this psycho get on with it. It wasn't as if he even liked us. And I'd gone right off the Wolf of Kilrevin.

'Listen.' The guide glanced back at me. His eyes were dilated, and there was a sheen of sweat on his skin. 'Mr Farquhar... Mr, uh, Wolf... I don't know what you're thinking of, but...'

'You do know.' The Wolf's voice had gone entirely cold. 'So stand aside.'

I felt Rory's fingers close on my wrist, and I realised he was already on the horse's back, leaning low over its neck as he reached for me. Frantically I scrambled, my feet kicking the horse's foreleg as I tried to climb up, and Rory grunted with the effort of dragging me. My foot flailed its black flank.

The tour guide's voice was high-pitched, a vein throbbing in his temple. 'They're children. They're just children. You can't—'

I wasn't properly astride the black as it sprang forward, so all I could do was cling to its side like a desperate spider. One of Rory's hands locked tight around my wrist as he bent low on the horse's neck, gripping its mane.

The Wolf of Kilrevin gave a shriek of anger and frustration, and his blade sighed as it cut the air. I didn't hear another word from the tour guide: only a small surprised gasp, abruptly cut off.

From the wrong side of the horse I saw almost nothing. I saw Rory turn his face and lock horror-struck eyes with me. I saw dim light catch a swinging blade. I saw a fountaining fan of blood. And that was all. I did not see the guide hit the ground, but I heard two separate thumps and knew with a lurch of nausea that he'd hit it in two halves.

Then the blade was swinging again, missing only because the black horse shouldered the Wolf aside and he stumbled against the wooden partition. By the time he'd righted himself the black was flying through the stable entrance and across the tarmac of the car park, its hoofbeats deafening. Screaming tourists flung themselves out of our path.

Rory leaned away from me, far out of the saddle like a yacht racer, grunting as he hauled my wrist. When desperation at last gave me the strength to drag myself on board and properly astride, Rory righted himself and urged the horse on.

I didn't think we merited so many screams of horror, until I looked down and saw that the horse's side was drenched with the tour guide's blood, and so was a great deal of Rory. Droplets of it sprayed the nearest people, flying off with the speed of the horse.

I couldn't see faces, and didn't want to. Clutching Rory's waist I shut my eyes tight as the black galloped across the car park. My stomach lurched as it leaped the wire fence on the boundary; then the clattering hoofbeats became soft thunder and the racket of screams died behind us.

ALASDAIR KILREVIN

He breathed hard, glaring down at the aggravating jobsworth who'd lost him his prey. He was too efficient, that was his curse. If only the little tosser was alive again, he could take out some of his frustration.

Alasdair was an easygoing man. He didn't usually lose his temper so comprehensively, but the fool just wouldn't get out of the *way*. Rolling his eyes, he wiped his blade fastidiously on a corner of the little man's jacket, then rose to his feet and looked down at him. Well, at both of him, in a sense.

That was droll. Alasdair chortled and shook his head. It was a gift, being able to see the humour in any situation.

But this was going to put the cat among the panicked pigeons.

It already had. He tried to walk casually across the car park, and in fact he wasn't drawing too many stares, since the tourists and guides were still stunned by the passage of the black horse and its bloodied riders. All the same, a few eyes turned towards him, and there was no hiding the sheathed sword now. There were gasps, and stifled squeaks, and as Alasdair passed by, the surreptitious bleep of mobile phones making follow-up calls to the police. Taking no notice he strode on, and when he reached the wire fence he leaped it easily and began to run again in his easy loping wolf-stride. It was a practised pace that let him run for hours.

Alasdair knew this country. He knew how to be inconspicuous, so long as people weren't forcing him to slice them in half, so long as reckless youngsters weren't spurring kelpies across crowded car parks. He sighed. There was going to be a reconstruction now, all right, and a distressing amount of newspaper coverage.

He needed a bath, transport, a change of clothing, but what he needed most was a safe house. And Alasdair knew exactly where to find one.

HANNAH

'I'm glad it's summer,' said Rory. The pool had a reddish tint to its clear brown water as he scrubbed at his blood-stiffened hair.

I sat on the bank and stared at him. I was still too shocked even to look decorously away from the naked boy who stood up to his waist in the water. I did like the wet green place he'd chosen, a cleft in rocks where a burn fell almost perpendicular through lush green foliage, then pooled in a deep and broad hollow. Around us the trees and ferns were almost tropically dense, and a hunter would have to be standing five feet away before he saw us.

Rory backed against the mossy black rocks to rinse his hair clean under the running burn. Above us, among the ferny rowans, the black horse grazed in a desultory way, turning now and again to stare out towards the sea.

Rory glanced at me. 'You ought to take a bath too,' he said critically. 'There's blood all over you. Who'd've thought that little prig had it in him?'

'That's like Macbeth.' I was barely able to focus. 'Who'd have thought he had so much blood in him? Or something. Lady Macbeth. I think.'

'Well, that's not quite what I meant.' Rory ducked his head underwater, and reappeared gasping. 'Anyway, thank the gods for the Wee Prig. We'd be dead if he hadn't got in the way.'

I felt as if I was going to faint, like there was no blood in my head at all. 'I suppose he had a name,' I whispered. 'He tried to protect us.'

'He'd no idea,' said Rory shortly. 'Just as well. He'd have run a mile if he did.'

'Maybe,' I said, 'but he had a bit of an idea, didn't he? And he was brave enough to try and stop him.'

'He did stop him. So you don't need to feel so terrible for him, do you? I don't suppose he ever imagined he'd die a hero.' Rory gave me a hard look. 'You're going to have to get a grip, y'know. Feeling bad about him isn't going to help us.'

I stared at him. 'You're different.'

'Found out I want to stay alive.' Rory shrugged, cupped water in his hands and threw it on his face. 'Hannah. Get washed.'

'Yes, sir.' Some healthy sarcasm brought me back to myself a bit, so I stood up and stripped off my t-shirt. Rory turned his back politely as I undressed and put a toe in the water. Fast, I had to do this fast. Gasping, I plunged in till the water was up to my armpits.

'Summer. Huh. You could call it that.' Teeth chattering, I wrung the blood out of my t-shirt, then flung it clumsily up onto a branch. I scrubbed more blood off my skin. 'What do we do now?'

Rory let himself float backwards in the water, toes breaking the surface, pale hair drifting around his head. He looked like some beautiful pre-Raphaelite youth in a painting, I thought with a pang of vague longing. Those were the kind of paintings I'd stick to in future, come to think of it.

As he floundered upright, I ducked my head underwater and shook it out. This pool was more effective than a cold shower. 'Where to, then?'

'Oh, 'scuse me.' Blushing scarlet, Rory turned away as I

clambered out of the water. 'We need to head across country. If my father's going to come across I'm pretty sure which watergate he'll use, and it comes out near his old house. All we need to do is get to him before the Wolf gets to us.'

'Oh. No pressure then.'

'We'll go cross-country. Try and avoid roads.' Rory hauled on his jeans and pulled his damp t-shirt over his head. 'Avoid people, too.'

'Yeah. For their good as much as ours.' I stepped back and slapped the black horse's neck.

That was probably a little over-familiar. It snapped its head round to glare at me, turning empty black eyes on mine.

Hypnotised, I stared back. I felt a dizzying vertigo, as if I was toppling into its alien mind. The wood blurred and I felt a presence rub against my consciousness, a memory inside the horse. And I saw

someone almost familiar, his features clear: grey eyes lit by a mercury spark, a near-smile on his lips. He crouched, glancing back over his shoulder at me, a naked sword across his knees, a white wolf alert at his side. His face was sharp and beautiful and a little like my own, his dark blond hair short and damp with sweat, sticking out in tousled spikes over his forehead. His clothes were like something from last century, the nineteen-twenties or thirties: brogues, rough brown trousers and braces, and a collarless white shirt. He crouched there as if waiting for an unseen attack, but he was smiling, looking at me with absolute trust. And I stood among the trees, silent and loyal, and waited on his word

I gave a short scream, and stumbled back. The horse turned away and nibbled nonchalantly at Rory's wet hair. I was no longer in its head. I was no longer the *horse*.

Rory pushed its head away and stared at me, alarmed. 'Hannah! What?'

I rubbed my temples. Call me devious, call me over-suspicious, but I had no intention of sharing what just happened.

'Nettles,' I lied.

The horse snorted as Rory pulled himself onto its back. I hated the way that always sounded like laughter.

'All right.' He sounded doubtful. 'Let's get going.'

Gripping Rory's wrist, I let him haul me up onto the horse behind him. 'So what if we don't, ah... find your dad?' It seemed the most tactful way to put the question.

His shoulders rose and slumped. 'We'll just have to keep running, then, because otherwise we're going to get killed. Still want to come?'

I slipped my arms round his waist and squeezed. It was the only excuse I'd had all day.

'Listen, I know how annoying it is,' I said. 'When I'm going to run out on you, I'll let you know.'

ALASDAIR KILREVIN

Tornashee, he thought with a sigh. He gazed up at the stone ravens on its flanking gateposts, at the sun-warmed walls and the weather-burnished slates. It was in perfect condition. Reultan and her daughter – that black-haired good-looking whore of Murlainn's – they must have looked after it well since Leonora's death, because its lack of deterioration was an amazing thing.

He always could appreciate talent; he stood for a long time admiring it. So this was where Leonora had hidden herself and her family. It was the finest house in the neighbourhood, but no-one would ever search it. Alasdair could sense the thickness of the Veil around it, a shimmering invisible presence that made his blood itch.

What would happen if the Veil survived to protect the house, he wondered idly? Murlainn would never return to live here now, and all the others were dead. Here it might sit till the end of time, a beautifully preserved mausoleum. Or in fifty years' time, when it finally became clear the owners were not just away on holiday, some property developer with a touch of Sithe blood might notice it and convert it into flats. Alasdair chuckled. It'd be hard to interest buyers, that was all.

Anyway, the Veil wasn't going to survive. In a few weeks this would be just another house, unprotected, deteriorating, *available*. He breathed in happiness. They were so close now, him and Kate: so close to winning. Perhaps he'd live here himself: a fitting prize for breaking the stalemate of the years and inspiring her malice anew. He loved that woman: funny, quick-witted and ruthless. They made a good team, he knew. Teamwork was everything.

He was yet to share her bed, of course, but that only fed his admiration for her manipulative brain. The fact that she'd shared it with the runt Murlainn already: she knew that was a goad to his ambitions.

And as he always liked to remind himself: he was a patient man.

The outbuildings were of no interest, except for the one that served as a garage. Pushing open the doors, peering into the dimness, his eyes lit first on the powerful black motorbike. He chuckled. Murlainn's mid-life crisis: it could be fun.

Perhaps not, though. He wasn't used to bikes and he didn't fancy his great schemes coming to a pile of twisted metal on a bad bend on a B road. His eyes flicked to the other vehicles. The battered Jeep had to be Cù Chaorach's: practical, but he might need something a little speedier. Cù Chaorach's Audi Quattro was more the thing: the four wheel drive might come in handy and besides, he liked its look. He reached up to the row of keys and found the Audi's. The car sprang to life and growled at him, and some adolescent Glaswegian wailed from the CD speakers.

There was more to this than that old Veil, he thought dryly as he snapped the ignition quickly off. He could almost smell witchcraft on the air, sharp and acrid like electricity before a storm. Leonora had done something more to protect this house. If her son or stepson ever had to come back unexpectedly, she clearly didn't want them to waste time charging batteries.

Contented, Alasdair left the garage, and as he climbed

the steps to the main house, victory thrilled in his bones. He could almost imagine applauding crowds. When you'd kept as low a profile as he had, for as long as he had, it felt sweet to know that it had taken him mere weeks – days – to rid himself of all that might threaten him. Except Murlainn, of course, but he could be easily dealt with now that he'd been stripped of everyone he loved. In the meantime, Alasdair would help himself to the house and its contents. The rebel fools owed him as much.

He touched the oak door, turned the brass handle. The door swung inwards without so much as a creak. Not even lockfast! Well, really, by eternal tradition that made it fair game. Carelessness and complacency: that was how rebels got swords in them, got their children taken away, died unnamed and unnoticed. That was how they died with their homes in ruins and – he devoutly hoped – their dun burning around them, its inhabitants' screams the last thing echoing in their ears. Because they were cocky. It was as if they'd never heard of security. Thick and ancient telepathic spells might prevent full-mortal interference, but they wouldn't keep out the Wolf of Kilrevin.

In the rooms there was a thin layer of dust, no more. No cobwebs, not so much as a mouse dropping. Alasdair spent a happy interlude just wandering, rifling through wardrobes, emptying drawers, examining the furnishings. They'd lived pretty well, that old witch and her family. He combed through Leonora's workshop, examining the unsold and half-finished pieces, choosing the best to keep for souvenirs and quick funds.

He was *such* a people person. It was extraordinary what individuals gave away about themselves, just through the things they chose to own. The reflection in the bathroom mirror gave him an approving smile, encouraging him to swing open the narrow cabinet. He sighed happily. Razors, soap, toothbrushes, the lot.

Then he heard it. He caught his breath and went absolutely still.

A door opening, closing. Footsteps, controlled but confident. Incautious. Alasdair barely wanted to believe his luck. Very quietly he backed out of the bathroom, that bearded reflection still beaming down on him.

There was only one person it could be. Oh, it was too good to be untrue. The gods loved Alasdair Kilrevin.

His fingers stroked the hilt of his bloody sword as he glanced around the landing, then crept across the bare wood floor to the closest room. Perfect. Closing his fingers round the hilt he drew his sword.

He had to wait what felt like an age, but he did pride himself on his forbearance. Why, he played almost as long a game as Kate. Blocking was easy; the intruder had a block up himself, but clearly he did not expect company. Would the man never learn? Alasdair could have laughed.

The intruder stepped through the door. Alasdair counted to two, then three, eyeing the back of his neck. It was just as well he was an expert on heads and necks, after a long life spent severing one from the other. Why didn't the fool get a haircut?

Alasdair let him walk right into the room, then lifted his sword and brought the pommel down hard. Murlainn didn't even have time to yell before he crumpled lifeless to the floor.

RORY

The timing wasn't going to get any more perfect. The moon was no more than a scribble of pale light behind scraps of cloud. The darkness was going to be all too brief at this time of year, but Hannah was out of it, snoring lightly on a bed of fir branches and moss under our hastily-erected lean-to. She was tucked snugly in the angle where the cut boughs were closest to the ground, leaving the opening free and easy for me.

I went barefoot like I'd been taught, my trainers slung round my neck by their laces, my toes finding and avoiding anything that might crackle or snap. A few splinters wouldn't kill me.

Other things might.

I didn't especially want to be alone, but she was an encumbrance, mostly on my conscience. I didn't want another corpse weighing that down. Besides, even a kelpie was going to move faster and quieter with only one person on its back.

More quietly, an exasperated inner voice corrected me. I wished the voice was real and not just a memory. I wondered if he was dead. I wondered if for some reason he was prevented from crossing the Veil, if he was a captive.

I wondered why else I wouldn't hear or See him.

I couldn't waste any more time wondering, so I ducked down once more to reassure myself that Hannah was asleep. That was all. Not to look at her or say a silent goodbye. She knew where the stream was, and surely she'd have the sense to follow it after she'd drunk from it. I'd left her just half a cooked rabbit; she hadn't thought much of it anyway. If she was clever and tough enough – and I was pretty sure she was both – she'd find the nearest village before long, and something edible to shoplift. She'd make her way home.

The horse was an indistinct black mass under the trees, the reins loose on its neck; I was still reluctant to take the bridle off. I laid my hand on its wither, wound my fingers into its mane, then led it away from the camp. Its hooves were quiet, its eyes soft and cooperative, and the stars were visible through the treetops. I let the creature guide me. Except for my cracking heart, and the fear that was suddenly more oppressive, it all went so very smoothly.

I'd been right about the darkness, though. Already, as we came to open moor and I hauled myself onto the horse's back, there was a smear of pale grey across the eastern horizon. The world was still all shades of grey, but its features were distinctly outlined. I paused, thinking about direction, as the horse swished its tail and flared its nostrils.

East was not where it should have been.

I frowned, then twitched the left rein. The horse tossed its head and obeyed, and we followed the edge of the wood as the world around us paled. It was my father's favourite time. He loved the hour when the world was nothing but monochrome, because the day hadn't had time to give it any colour. *And the wind off the sea, cold and grey as its mother sky. The beginning of morning, and the smell of it, with the breeze singing in off the distant sea, and there isn't a third dimension.*

I shivered and rubbed my eyes, because it wasn't him, it was only the memory of his mind again. I wondered if that was going to have to do from now on.

Stop it. Stop thinking that...

'SonofaBITCH!'

A tree-shadow had raced out into our path. I yelled again in fright and yanked the reins, clumsy in my shock, but the horse didn't back off or rear, and it didn't lunge for the shadow. It fought me, head high, hooves square on the earth, a snarl rumbling in its throat.

'Me? *You're* the sonofabitch, you little bastard!' Right in front of us the shadow grabbed the bridle's cheekpiece, fists clenched, teeth bared, eyes flashing cold and silver. Gods, her eyelight was developing fast.

'Hannah, let go!' Fear for her made me wrench the horse's mouth, and it squealed in fury.

'I don't have to! He's more mine than he is yours!'

Even as she said it the horse's rage subsided to quiet snorts, and it nudged her, almost making her stumble. But she recovered, put her arms round its great head and glared up at me.

'You go without me, you go without my father's horse.'

'You – that's no choice!'

'No indeed.' She brandished something in her fist. 'And I *hate* bloody rabbit.'

Silence. There was an air of smugness to her as she flourished the scrap of rabbit under the horse's nose; it took it delicately in its jaws, then lifted its head, snapped and swallowed.

Hannah stroked its glossy neck. 'You're a good horse. You're a very good horse.'

I was angry and resentful and relieved all at once. 'Did this bastard horse *call you*?'

Her teeth flashed in the lightening dawn.

So did the horse's.

314

SETH

The headache started in the back of his neck and went all the way to the top of his skull, but there were two separate points of pain behind his eyes. It was a beauty. Seth didn't think he'd ever had a headache like it, and that was saying something.

As awareness crept through his body, he began to feel all the other places where it hurt. There were a lot of them, some pretty sensitive. That wasn't just one whack on his head. The bastard had taken the opportunity to give him a good kicking while he lay there, and Seth knew it. He knew it intimately and painfully.

He was face down and prostrate on the floor – not the most dignified position – but at least it was his own floor. At least he felt at home. He'd always liked that polished oak planking. He didn't much want to think about anything but that, but of course he had to. Shifting slightly, he tried to sit up.

Complete failure. When he tried to move his hands, they wouldn't budge from behind his back, even when he tugged hard at his wrists. The slightest movement sent lances of pain through his head from one side to the other and back again, so he stopped trying. Instead he lowered his head gently back to the floor and turned it very, very slowly to face the other way. And there was the Wolf of Kilrevin, whistling soundlessly at the bathroom mirror as he trimmed his ragged facial hair to a chic little goatee.

'Okay, I'm alive,' Seth said, blinking. He smiled brightly

at the Wolf, which hurt a lot in all sorts of ways. 'Am I alive for a reason?'

Catching his eye in the mirror, the Wolf returned his smile. 'Yup.'

Seth closed an eye. 'Am I going to stay alive?'

'No.'

'Uh-huh.' He bit his lip thoughtfully. 'Tell me about it, then.'

'As if.' The Wolf took a pair of nail scissors and sliced carefully through each of his braids, close to his scalp, dropping the discarded hair in the basin. 'I've seen all the movies too, you know. Explaining your evil schemes to the hero is never a good idea.'

'*Hero* is a bit of a stretch,' said Seth drolly. 'But it's sweet that you know you're evil.'

'Oh, you'll make me blush. I'm a pragmatist, that's all.' The Wolf examined himself in the mirror. 'I might take you back to Kate eventually. She'd love to hang and draw you in sight of your own dun. On the other hand, that's never a good idea either, is it? Plotting an extravagant death that you might get out of. So I'll probably slit your throat right here.'

'Eventually,' Seth put in quickly.

'Yeah, yeah, eventually.' The Wolf laughed. 'Don't panic, Murlainn.'

As the adrenalin rush subsided, another bolt of pain went through his head and he winced. Ouch, he told himself. Take it easy. He pressed his forehead to the cool floor. 'People need to stop whacking me on the head,' he muttered. 'It's not good for me.'

The Wolf guffawed. 'Happens a lot, does it?'

'What? You and everybody else. My father, my brother, Torc.' He eyed the Wolf. 'Finn.'

'Oh, yes, Murlainn.' The Wolf half-turned. 'Sorry about your lover. Nothing personal.'

'Oh, really?'

'Well. All right, it was. But business is business, too.'

Seth was still smiling. 'If I hadn't thought you were dead, I'd have had you long ago.'

'Still hold that against me, do you?' said the Wolf. 'Your father?'

'Why would I hold it against you?' His father probably wouldn't have bothered with him however long he'd lived, but it would've been nice if Griogair had had the option. Bitterness, hatred, regret: Seth bit them all back, and shrugged as best he could with his hands locked behind him. 'Be as much use as Reultan's daughter having a grudge against cancer. It's what you are, isn't it? It's just what you do.'

The Wolf sighed and grinned. 'You're so *evolved*. You know, I like you, Murlainn. I always liked you. I always thought we had a lot in common.' Amiably he nudged Seth's bruised ribs with his foot. 'That was a convincing death I had, wasn't it? It's a local legend, now. My poor lads, they got a bit of a shock when the devil arrived. Heh! It was them he came for, and he looked a lot like me!' He laughed helplessly for a while. 'I'm surprised you bought it, though, Murlainn. You're not a sucker for a supernatural yarn.'

'I know,' said Seth. But he'd wanted it to be true, so he'd let himself believe it. Let that be a lesson for the future, if he lived to see one. 'I always said I wanted to see your corpse.'

'Ah, you won't be seeing that now. Missed your chance, and you won't be getting another.' He leaned down to chuck Seth annoyingly under the chin. 'Too bad for your lover you didn't finish it years ago.'

Seth clenched his teeth and kept smiling. 'Actually? She's alive.'

'Alive?' The Wolf's eyes widened in disappointment. 'How'd she manage that? Looks like I missed a chance too, but I'll make up for it.' He gave Seth a meaningful grin. 'And by that time Kate won't have to be sweating with nerves that you'll turn up. 'Cause you won't be turning up. Eh?' He laughed.

'Maybe.' Seth laughed too. 'Maybe not.'

'I really do like you, Murlainn. You are so civilised.'

'Well. My brother had a temper, and look where it got him. By the way, if these are my old police handcuffs, I'll be mortified.'

'Found them in a drawer.' The Wolf laid down the scissors, his ragged hair cropped shorter and drawn into a little ponytail at the back. 'Theft of Her Full-Mortal Majesty's property, Murlainn! I'll bet you regret it now.'

'Yeah.' It was indeed galling. Seth rested his cheek on the floor as the Wolf took in his new look: the smooth-shaven throat, the well-shaped beard, the absence of the greasy braids. 'That's better.' Seth closed one eye. 'In fact, that's a good look. Only, uh… lose the ponytail.'

'You think?' Shrugging, the Wolf took a razor to the ponytail. 'Better?'

'Uh-huh.' Seth's arms were starting to ache almost as badly as his head.

The Wolf flicked a switch on Conal's electric razor and began to shave his head even closer. Seth wished he'd make his mind up. He wondered what Leonie would have said about the mess in the sink; even the Wolf might have backed off in the face of that old trout's slow-burning temper, and if she was here he'd never be stuffing one of her chamois jewellery rolls into his pocket. As for what Conal would have made of the Wolf nicking his leather jacket... and one of Seth's favourite t-shirts. It was tight on the Wolf's big frame, and he was going to end up ripping it.

'Why aren't you looting your own house? I take it you've got one.'

'Yeah, yeah.' The Wolf turned this way and that, admiring himself. 'Jings, even Cù Chaorach was a bit on the rangy side.' Tugging at the jacket, he finally left it unfastened. 'Ah, your brother was a bigger man than you in every way. Very much the runt of Griogair's litter, weren't you, Murlainn?'

Seth bit his cheek, but said nothing.

The Wolf grinned, knowing he'd touched a nerve. 'And my house is in Edinburgh, way too far away. Georgian New Town. I liked those as soon as they put them up.'

'Oh. Nice.' Seth was impressed despite himself. 'But your castle's full of tartan tat, Rory tells me.'

'Oh, yeah, I know. But it's lucrative.' The Wolf grinned as he put the final touches to his goatee. 'No entrepreneurial spirit, you MacGregors. This side of the Veil my castle looks a lot better than your dun, let me tell you. Have you seen your dun on this side, Murlainn?'

'Yes,' he said in a bored voice.

'It's nothing but a heap of overgrown rocks! The sheep graze it! The tourists climb it to photograph the bay, and they don't even know what they're standing on!' The Wolf laughed. 'Maybe I can turn it into a Heritage Destination. Would you like me to do that in your memory?' The Wolf grabbed a handful of his hair and yanked his head up. 'I'd give you a mention in the guidebook. You and your father and your sainted brother. Only a footnote, mind you! Will you like that, Murlainn? Being a footnote?'

Seth spat as hard as he could, managing to get a drop of spittle on the Wolf's nice new beard. His eyes darkening with rage, the Wolf dropped his head sharply so that his jaw banged hard on the floorboards. His conversational voice took on a sinister edge. 'That's a wily little rat you've sired, Murlainn.'

'I know.' Seth spat blood onto the polished oak. Sorry, Leonie, he thought. 'Great, isn't he?'

'Not so great he'll avoid me for long. But it'll be fun.' The Wolf winked. The bastard knew how much Seth's arms and head and the rest of him hurt, and he was having the time of his misspent life. Now the Wolf decided to twist the knife.

'You can't See Rory, can you?'

No, he couldn't, and he'd done a bit of weeping and banging his head against the barn wall when his confident calls to his son had turned to disbelief and then panic and finally to despair. It was unlikely he'd See Rory on the wrong side of the Veil, but once they were both on the same side, nothing but death or sorcery should keep their minds apart. And since he'd never heard of a sorcery like it, for a dark and hideous half-hour he had let himself believe the worst.

Now he turned his bloodied head away and stared at the wall, silent. It was long minutes before he stopped the pointless sulking and said: 'How is Kate doing that?'

The Wolf chuckled with delight. 'Oh, Murlainn, I've been dying to see how you'd react. I've got to tell you this bit. I'm a well-travelled man, you know?'

'Go on, then. I know you're going to show me your snaps.'

'Uzbekistan, Syria, Equatorial Guinea, all over the place. Busman's holidays, really.'

'I'm surprised we never bumped into each other.'

'Oh, we wouldn't have been drinking in the same mess, Murlainn. I did keep occasional tabs on your career. Careers. Anyway, there's more Sithe blood over here than you'd think, isn't there? I met a lot of it. In some bad places. Bad for them, not for me.'

Seth stayed silent, thinking. Nothing constructive.

'If they survived me and all I could do, I let them go. I'm merciful, Murlainn, and besides, they served me better that way. Do you know what they'd do then? To my enemies, their friends? It's not that they liked me better than they had. They were me, that's all. They didn't care any more.'

'I don't know what happens to your soul when you rip out someone else's,' murmured Seth. 'Go on. What does happen?'

'Cheeky. What do I want with a soul anyway? I had something far, far better, and that was time. A glut of it, and a glut of captives. They don't do early release in those places, Murlainn. I had time to learn new tricks, and if a person doesn't know he's half-Sithe, he doesn't know how to block, right?'

'Right,' said Seth, thinking of Hannah, and missing her a surprising amount.

'I developed some ideas I'd had. The mind's a fragile thing when it's unguarded. It's barely even witchcraft, really. You can practically snip a link with blunt nail scissors, if you know what you're doing. Even a strong link. A family one, or a bonding link.'

'No,' said Seth, pointlessly. An exclamation of rage, not a denial.

321

'Kate always accused me of a lack of subtlety, which is funny. D'you know that thing witches can do? Sucking out a dying man's strength and taking it? If she can't get a person to give up their soul, that's what she'll do. Gods, that's made her powerful, but on the whole she gets the soul too.'

'I know.'

'She's been taking souls out of people for centuries, but it took me to refine her methods. Me and my experiments! It's like pulling off a plaster, Murlainn. Hurts more if you do it slowly.'

'She needs your consent if she's going to take your soul. Even I know that.'

'Sure, but she's not actually taking them, is she? Not these ones. That's the beauty of my new trick! You cut a link and they just leak out, a little at a time, till they're gone. A tiny little pinprick in the artery of the soul, Murlainn. Ew! It makes me shiver.'

Seth too. The first searing pain of the cut, when he hadn't know what was happening, had faded now, but the emptiness was the unbearable thing.

'I'm curious. Is there any witchcraft she won't bloody her hands on?'

'Don't be silly. So, d'you want to know how it's done? All you need is a piece of the people involved. Blood, hair, body fluids... well, Kate had some of yours. And you don't need to ask how she got it, eh?' He nudged Seth's ribs and winked. 'And you know how Kate likes a long game. So she always saves playing pieces. She's had a lock of Rory's hair since he was a baby. Since *you* handed him over to her.'

Seth wanted to be sick. It was never going to stop coming back to haunt him. 'You can't See him either, Kilrevin.'

'No, that's true.' The Wolf eyed himself in the mirror and straightened a sleeve. 'He blocks very well, doesn't he? Wily little rat, like I said. But we'll find him, Murlainn, don't you worry. Rory has to ask for help some time.'

'You talk a lot of mince,' said Seth. 'And when I have my way, you're going to *be* mince.'

The Wolf's foot lashed out viciously, catching the side of his head. Through the intense shock of pain, Seth cursed his own stupidity. 'You're not going to have your way, Murlainn. Those days are *so* gone. Now. Get your block down.'

'No.'

'Get it down.' The sole of the Wolf's boot pressed lightly on the back of his neck.

Seth swore at him.

'I can make you do it.'

'I've kept my block up through worse than you can do.'

'Oh, don't bet on it.' The Wolf smirked and gave him a casual kick between the legs. 'Ach, don't worry. I can't be bothered. It's not like you have a hope in hell. Keep your worthless thoughts to yourself.'

When he got his breath back, Seth said: 'You thought you'd beaten my father, Kilrevin, four hundred years ago. But you hadn't.'

'It took a little longer than I expected,' hissed the Wolf, his foot hovering alarmingly close to Seth's temple, 'because I left a little bit of him behind. Thank you for reminding me. I won't be leaving any little living remnants of you, not once Kate's got what she needs from him.' The Wolf wrinkled his nose. 'Poor little rat.'

Seth smiled up at him levelly, and thought: That's it, pal. You're going to die.

The Wolf did not hear it, of course. 'Now, let's get down to business.' Sighing, he grabbed the handcuffs and hauled Seth to his feet, then gripped him by the shoulder and swung him round. Seth felt the sharp point of a sword tip in the small of his back.

'Call your son, Murlainn.'

'*What?* Did that last conversation not happen?' Seth took an involuntary breath as the blade point dug into his flesh.

'Don't go thinking we're stupid, Murlainn, or crude. You're to call him via me. I'll be very much in the background, so don't fret; he won't even know I'm there.' The Wolf's voice grew colder. 'Call your son.'

Seth glanced back over his shoulder, managing to curl his lip in a half-decent sneer. 'Oh, piss off.'

The sword pressed deeper, and he felt the warm trickle of blood on his skin. It didn't hurt much yet, but he knew it was going to. Closing his eyes, he breathed hard through his nose.

'You are wasting your time,' he said expressionlessly. 'I'm not going to call him. Under any circumstances. *Any*.'

The sword-tip twisted in his flesh, and he winced. 'You're scared, Murlainn,' said the Wolf softly. 'You're very scared of me.'

'Of course I'm scared.' Seth spat on the ground and snarled the foulest insult he could think of. 'But I'm not going to call my son. So think of something else.'

The Wolf paused, uncertain for the first time. Seth's block was total. He hated being unable to See, hated it, but the Wolf must not get in, must not, and so the block had to stay. The silence stretched till he thought his beating heart might explode.

'You know I can hurt you, Murlainn,' the Wolf said at

last. 'You know how much I can damage you, and I don't have to kill you. I've a very fine touch. Your spinal cord...'

'I'm sure. I said, think of something else. That is, if you can get your imagination round the fact that I'm not going to help you kill my *son*.' Seth spat again, partly out of contempt and partly because the terror tasted sour in his mouth.

The Wolf watched him. Block or no block, Seth could feel his cold black eyes between his shoulder blades. And then he felt the point of cold steel slide out of his flesh.

'Very well, Murlainn,' said the Wolf silkily. 'We'll do this together. Let's take a little road trip.'

HANNAH

'Are you still sulking about the horse?'

In front of me Rory snorted a laugh. 'Nah. That was clever. Also sneaky.'

I smirked to myself and snuggled closer against him. That was mostly for warmth, of course. We were high up now, high enough to have left the thickest of the trees behind, and wind funnelled through the pass straight into our faces. Above us icy patches of snow still lay in the gullies, waiting out the summer, and I could feel exactly why it hadn't melted. For all the singing birds, for all the golden light, it felt like spring had never arrived up here.

Our route was hardly what you'd call direct. We'd given houses and farms a wide bodyswerve, we'd followed half-dried-up riverbeds and belts of larches and pines where we could. As for the clotted patches of yellow whin, some of them were so dense and gnarled even the horse wouldn't try to get through. When I got off the beast once, growling with frustration and insisting I could find a path, I was forced to retreat almost in tears, my arms pincushioned with spikes and brambles.

I certainly wanted this journey to be as short as possible. 'Couldn't I try to contact your dad?'

'No, I told you. Don't let your block down. He'll track us if you do.'

I reckoned he wasn't talking about Seth. 'So all we can do is go to that house?'

'Tornashee. Yeah. My father's *bound* to go there.'

'Doesn't everybody else know that too, then?'

He didn't answer. I should really stop asking awkward questions, since they never made me feel any better.

'So anyway, why would I sulk about the horse? I've got my own.' Rory was back on the more comfortable subject of his kelpie obsession. 'I'll be back to get that filly one day. Properly this time.'

'Right,' I said. 'Sorry about that. Again.'

'You didn't know. Anyway, taking the kelpie mare was a good idea, I think.'

'It wasn't my idea, it was Eili's.'

'Oh. Well, I'm still going to try it.'

I liked it when he talked positive. I liked it when his every word didn't seem to assume we were going to die horribly and quite soon. Unfortunately, those moments never lasted long.

'Sh.' He halted the horse. It stood there with its ears pricked forward and its lip curled back from its teeth.

'Oh God,' I muttered.

He reached back and pinched my thigh quite hard. '*Sh*.'

Now I could hear it too: the throaty rumble of a diesel engine. Hard to tell which direction it was coming from; the air was so thin and clear up here, and there were plenty of scree slopes and granite escarpments to make sounds bounce and echo. 'Bugger,' I said.

'Would you shut *up*?'

'No.' I pointed to a narrow defile where a trickle of water was funnelled into something resembling an actual river. 'Down there. Hide.'

At least he didn't argue with that. The horse could be amazingly quiet when it felt like it, and it sidled into the feeble cover, placing its hooves delicately on moss patches and soft tussocks of mountain grass. Still pressed close to Rory, I could feel his heart hammering. Or maybe that was mine.

In mid-stream, the horse stood dead still. All I could hear was the wind, and the whisper of water round the creature's fetlocks, and smooth stones rattling like phlegm in the gullet of the burn.

Then it was on us out of nowhere, the roar of its engines sudden and loud. Rory sucked in a breath and the horse spun on its hindquarters and I might have let out a smallish squeal.

God, the way the mountain could distort sounds and make them vanish. The quad bike was right there, and the man riding it was squinting at us with a sharp callous interest.

'You want to hide from a Watcher,' he said, pushing hair out of his silver-pricked eyes, 'you don't do it in water.'

* * *

'Well, you don't smell like Lammyr to me,' said Suil, plugging a kettle into the wall, 'so I suppose you'll want a cup of tea instead of a quick death.'

A very good-looking osprey, that was what he reminded me of. The irises of his eyes were amber-yellow and his nose was aquiline and his tawny hair was flicked back above his ears, but it wasn't so much any of that as his hungry predatory look, as if he was dying to dive for a nice bit of fish.

Sure enough, as he swung open the fridge, illuminating his doubtful face, he said, 'Smoked trout? On toast? It's all I've got in.'

'Oh yes,' I said. 'Oh please. Thank God Almighty you haven't got any rabbit.'

Suil made a dry noise that might have been a laugh and shoved two slices of bread into the toaster. I liked his cottage, small and slightly messy but definitely this side of civilisation. I especially liked the loud hum of the generator out the back. Home comforts.

The only thing that unsettled me was the faint odour of decay and death. I glanced nervously over my shoulder again at the curtained box-bed along the back wall.

'My lover,' he'd said when we arrived, and the curiosity was killing me.

'How long has she been...' *sick,* I was going to say, but he shook his head.

'Like this? A month or so.'

'What's her n–'

'Teallach,' he said. 'It was Teallach.'

He rose and pulled back the curtain, sat down on the edge of the bed. Gently he stroked her hair out of her eyes. It was half-blonde half-grey, a messy filthy wild shock of it, and I can't explain it but she looked ninety and nineteen all at once.

I got up and sat beside him on the edge of the bed. The woman stared at me and then she stared at Suil. Her expression didn't change. She didn't recognise either of us. I took her hand; it was withered skin over bone but it wasn't twisted like an old person's hand. Same with her face: it was a young person's face, except that the skin was yellow and shrivelled tight across her skull and her eyes had sunk into the sockets. Her teeth were loose and she smelt of death.

'Is she dying?' I whispered.

'She didn't want to go to the Selkyr,' he said, kissing her forehead. 'Fair enough. Her choice.'

I didn't say anything because I had no idea what he was on about, and anyway I thought I might cry. The dying woman gave an incoherent cry of petulant anger.

'I think I will, though,' he murmured, distantly. 'When it's my turn. I think I'll take the Selkyr.'

Rory had come over to stand and look down at her. There was a superstitious look of fright on his face. 'She was all right till a month ago?'

'It's taking so much longer than I thought,' said Suil. 'I think it's taking far longer than she thought, too.' Almost absently, he massaged her bony fingers and kissed each knuckle. She watched him do it, uncomprehending.

He stood, abruptly. 'Toast's ready.'

* * *

'Hannah.' The whisper was insistent, and I knew fuzzily that it had been said more than once. 'You awake?'

I pulled the lumpy pillow off my head and sighed loudly. 'I am now. What?'

The night wasn't black at all. I doubted it ever had been. Sometimes I thought there would never be a proper night again, the kind you could hide in. Through the thin curtains the light was pearl grey; it could have been dusk or dawn. I had no idea what time it was. I felt as if I'd been asleep for all of three minutes.

Rory, having yanked me out of sleep, had suddenly gone silent. To make sure of that, I held my breath, but there wasn't so much as a grunt from him now. I got the sense he was having trouble speaking. I wondered if my block had slipped while I was asleep, because something hung in the air like the dissolving tatters of a dream: blaeberry scrub and oily black smoke and blood: an awful lot of blood. I blinked it all away.

'I don't know what consangwhatever is,' hissed Rory at last, 'and I don't care. I'm cold and I just wondered if...'

I sat up on my mattress and looked thoughtfully at him. 'It's a hot night.'

'Well, I'm cold.'

My fingers curled tightly into the musty bedclothes. I shouldn't get up. I knew that Suil wasn't here; I knew he was watching the still deep pool below the escarpment, a sword on his back, like he said he did every night. But his lover was here in the room next door, whether or not she had a mind left.

It was remembering the dying woman that made me sit up and swing my legs off the bed. I thought about that long decay, and the look in Suil's yellow eyes when he stroked her hair and spooned mashed trout into her slack mouth, and the sound of the spoon rattling on loose teeth.

I stood up quickly. Rory's bed was against the opposite wall; I sat down beside him and took his hand.

'Did you have a bad dream?'

'Yes.' His voice was muffled by the pillow.

The bed was saggy and narrow but I managed to wriggle under the sheets between him and the wall. The bad springs tipped me towards him, so I put my arms round his body. His back was to me and I could see the angular jut of his shoulder blades and the line of his spine. His arms found mine and clutched them more tightly round him.

I pressed my cheek to his shoulder. I was not going to let on that I could feel the dampness of the pillow beneath his face.

'I wouldn't even know if he was dead,' he said. His throat sounded as if it was full of ground glass.

'I think you would,' I said into his neck. 'I think you would anyway. And he isn't. Anyway.'

His fingertip stroked the back of my hand. An owl called, somewhere out in the night, and I heard the kelpie stir outside the window, stamping and snorting. Rory's body was so tense I thought every muscle in it might snap under the strain. I mustn't clutch him too tightly, I thought. I mustn't.

He rolled round to face me and said, 'Thanks.'

I stroked his cheekbone, feeling my innards clench. 'It'll be okay,' I said. 'He'll be okay.'

'Of course.'

He's my cousin. He's my cousin.

My fingers drifted into Rory's hair all by themselves, combing it back from his ear. 'No, it really will. It'll be fine.'

'Okay. Thanks,' he said again, and kissed me.

And who was I to shove him away at such a moment? His mouth lingered on mine, and it was like a puzzle fitting together. After a bit I stopped being surprised, and kissed him back. He tasted familiar. My arm round his waist, his hand on my neck, his leg hooked over mine: it was all exactly the right fit, like we'd been sculpted as one by some very talented artist.

Outside, beside a dark pool, a man sat hunched in the half-light and watched for monsters; and beyond the wall at my back a woman lay dreaming of a life she'd forgotten. Death seeped in everywhere, through the cracks in the loose window frames, down the sooty chimney, in the breath of breeze that stirred the cheap curtains. It touched the nape of my neck and crept across my skin on spider-feet.

We'd neither of us lived very long, Rory and me. The night was brief and it wasn't any kind of a hiding-place, but it was all we were getting, and we took it.

SETH

'Clunk click,' said the Wolf as he plugged in Seth's seatbelt.

'Gosh, that dates you,' said Seth. 'But thanks for your concern.'

'Well.' The Wolf patted his knee. 'I wouldn't want you hurting yourself. That's my job.'

Seth gave him a twisted smile.

The Wolf ejected the disc and threw it onto the back seat, then flicked through the ones he'd stolen from the house. 'The Stranglers! Murlainn, you old punk.'

'Are you more of a boy-band man?'

'Hold that.' The Wolf gave him a dark look and thrust a disc at his mouth while he examined the next in the stack. Seth held The Stranglers carefully between his teeth till the Wolf took it back, stuffed the others into the rack, and slotted it into the player.

'If you scratch my favourite CDs I'll kill you,' said Seth.

The Wolf sighed. 'Look, Murlainn, I know it's only a figure of speech, but that is not an option for you any more. Okay?' He gunned the car out through the raven gateposts.

The journey was a blur for a long time, partly because Seth's head still throbbed distractingly and partly because he didn't want to speculate on what came next. They drove for a long time in mutually hostile silence, Seth fidgeting and tapping his fingernails against his palms to keep the blood circulating, and half-singing along under his breath to annoy the driver.

When he thought they'd driven far enough, he squinted sideways at the Wolf.

'I need to go.'

The Wolf rolled his eyes and swore.

'Well, I do.' Seth moved his shoulders in an approximation of a shrug.

Swerving the Audi abruptly into a layby and stepping hard on the brakes, the Wolf turned and glared at him as a huge articulated lorry blared its horn. He'd only overtaken it thirty seconds before, after a long frustrating time staring at its tailgate. 'No tricks.'

'I mean, would I.' Seth gave him a sweet smile. 'I like to breathe.'

'Good. You're getting the message.' The Wolf unplugged the seatbelt and leaned across to swing the door open, then looked at him expectantly.

Seth rattled the handcuffs. 'Um. What am I supposed to do here?'

With an exaggerated sigh the Wolf grabbed his hair and yanked him forward. Seth felt the key click and the handcuffs give, and he stretched his arms. His muscles and joints protested at the sudden release, a combination of agony and sheer relief.

'Make the most of it.' The Wolf gave him a dark look. 'They're going back on. And by the way, I'll be right behind you. If you try anything I'll take out your kidneys, one at a time.' He returned Seth's innocent smile. 'That'll solve the problem, won't it?'

'Okay. Nice.' Seth flexed his aching arms again and got out of the car, then turned to the verge as the Wolf opened the driver's door. Where were those giant lorries, Seth wondered, when you really needed one to knock someone flying? He heard a footstep behind him, then the sibilant hiss of a knife coming out of its sheath.

'I believe you, okay?' he said over his shoulder.

'Just making sure.' There was a smile in the voice. 'You're a bundle of nerves, Murlainn.'

Seth shut his eyes. *If you only knew,* he thought dryly, the fingers of his right hand tugging surreptitiously at his carved belt buckle. He hoped fervently that he had enough in his bladder to keep him going. His muscles were clumsy, his fingers slippery with sweat, but at last he managed to get his thumb and fingernail round the slightly hooked tip of the bronze merlin's pinion feather.

'Come on.' The Wolf's voice was a threatening growl.

'Give us a chance. Haven't been for ages.' Frantically he jerked his fingertips and the pinion feather slipped loose, a needle of bronze alloy about two inches long. Suddenly he regretted his penchant for t-shirts; he could have used a sleeve right now.

'Now.' The point of a knife jabbed the small of his back as the Wolf's patience ran out.

'Okay, okay.' Seth pressed the pin between his third and fourth fingers, then zipped himself up and put his hands helpfully behind his back. They still weren't functioning too well and he could only pray desperately that he wouldn't drop the pin. He doubted the Wolf needed him alive so much that he'd forgive any skulduggery. Besides, the pin was probably his only chance. Not that he had a clue what to do with it, but it was two sharp inches of feverish hope.

The handcuffs clicked on, and the Wolf pushed him back into his seat. Seth let himself feel a brief shudder of despair, then let it go. As the Wolf slammed the passenger door he leaned forward, just enough to relieve the pressure on his hands and slide the pin into a tiny gap in the stitching of his belt. By the time the Wolf was in the driving seat, Seth was leaning back again. Smiling.

His arm muscles protested at being restrained again, and they punished him for it, but inwardly he was happier than he'd been in hours. He was used to lost causes. And a small rebellion always made him feel a hundred times better.

RORY

'Wake up.' The hand that gripped my shoulder was like steel.

For a dragging moment I dreamed it was Finn leaning over me, and I was swamped with relief. It had *all* been a dream. Everything was fine, Finn was waking me because my father wanted me... but there was something wrong, and I realised with embarrassed panic that there was a girl in my arms. My *cousin*.

I felt a sharp ache in my wrist, and I clutched the green stone on the silver bangle. Icy coldness cleared my brain, letting in a deadening knowledge that made my stomach turn over: the yellow eyes weren't Finn's. Suil was staring down at me with urgency and more than a little fear.

Hannah's palm tensed on my chest, and reflexively my arm tightened round her. My stone had been nagging me painfully for a while, only I'd been too fast asleep, too exhausted and content to feel it. Fear lifted the hairs on my scalp.

'Suil?'

'Get up. Go.'

I went cold. I couldn't bear the thought of moving on, leaving warmth and safety for the gods knew what. 'Suil, if we could just stay till morning, *please,* just till morning, I promise I...'

'Laochan, shut up. Listen.' Suil touched his thumb to my forehead. 'I know I can't talk to you properly, I know you

337

can't let me in, but I'm telling you the truth. You have to go, *now.*'

I sat up, so abruptly I felt a lurch of nausea. 'What, is...'

'The Wolf is coming, Laochan. You haven't long.'

I dragged my grubby t-shirt over my head. Hannah was already sitting on the edge of the bed, wriggling into her jeans, her eyes sharp and scared. Suil took a couple of paces to the window, pulling the curtain open a slit and peering out.

'I don't understand,' I said.

'The man's a tracker. Always was.'

'But my block's up. Hannah—'

'The horse.' Suil jerked a thumb at the window. 'He's tracking the horse.'

I shut my eyes and swore. How could a kelpie control its mind, after all? Why would it bother?

'Lose the horse,' he said. 'But go. He'll still track you, but he won't find it half so quick or easy.'

My heart was thrashing as we crept through the main room, past the little box bed where the woman who had been Teallach followed us with blank eyes.

'What about you?'

'We'll be fine. Can you get rid of the horse now?'

'I don't know.' I honestly didn't know, because the last thing I wanted to do was get rid of the horse; that was why I'd left its bridle on. I wondered if it would feel my reluctance. It seemed to have an unusual sense of personal loyalty, for a kelpie.

'You need to go where the horse can't. Come with me.'

The night was cold and the sky was pale, without a star to be seen. Suil closed the door very quietly behind us and drew in a breath of night, then set off in a crouching run towards the watergate.

'I can't go back through,' I whispered as loudly as I dared as I stumbled after him. Hannah was at my heels and behind her I could see the kelpie like a shape of proper night, pitch black against the scoured grey stone of the mountain. Its gigantic hooves resounded horribly loudly, ringing like a warning bell.

Suil didn't answer me, but he didn't stop at the watergate either. Its surface was still and steely in the half-light, undisturbed, and he barely gave it a glance. Beyond it, the stony slope fell away precipitously. At my back I heard Hannah draw in a frightened breath.

Suil stopped and looked past me at the horse. 'He can't come. Tell him.'

Now that the moment had come to leave it behind, I felt sick with fear and loneliness. I clambered a little way back up the stones and reached for its bridle.

'*Eachuisge*,' I said.

The horse gave me a doubtful look. Its eye swivelled, showing the white, as I unbuckled the throatlash, and its throat rumbled quizzically.

'I need to hide, *eachuisge*,' I told it, putting my arms round its muscular neck and pressing my face to its skin. It felt so solid and safe, so warm and full of life and fire.

Before I could think any harder, I tugged the bridle over its ears; putting its muzzle to my palm, it let the silver bit fall from its mouth. Clumsily, because my hands were shaking, I tugged off the bridle altogether and stepped back. The horse nuzzled my neck, and I hugged its head. 'Come back when I call you. *Please*.'

It tossed its head free of my hold and took a haughty

step back, hooves scrabbling loudly on scree. One last long look at Hannah, and it turned swiftly and sprang into a gallop. We watched till it vanished around the shoulder of the hill, and the drumming of its hooves had finally died away into the clear air.

I felt Hannah's hesitation when I took her hand, but Suil was already halfway down the rocky slope, leaping from slab to slab, and we couldn't afford to wait. I tugged her on, and she had no choice but to follow, but her whole body shuddered with relief when the ground levelled out no more than eight or ten metres down.

The cliff at Suil's back was in shadow, and the shadow was blacker than it should have been on such a light summer night. Resting his hand on the rock, he pointed, and I saw the slit in the face of the hill.

'There are watergates even the NicNiven doesn't know,' he said, low voice echoing. 'Inside the hill; watch your feet. You'll come on it very suddenly.'

'Suil,' I said, 'I can't go back. I mean it.'

'You have to, briefly. The tunnel in the hill is in the same position on the other side. There are two gates. When you come out through the first, take the left hand opening of three. Two hundred yards, and there's the second watergate. Come back to this side through that one. It'll take you out far away, but you'll be far from the Wolf too. For a while. Now go.'

Hannah grabbed his hand. 'Will you come?'

Suil and I both looked at her. It was impossible to tell if she was desperate for his protection, or if she was trying to save him.

'Teallach,' he said simply, a hint of a smile on the slash of his lips.

He drew his sword and saluted us briefly. Its silver blade glowed, the edge so sharp in the pale half-light it seemed to quiver with its own life. He kept it in his hand as he climbed back up the cliff faster than a spider, and vanished over the lip.

★ ★ ★

There was a faint whimpering at my side and it took me a moment to lock onto the source. 'Hannah?' I whispered.

'I can't see. I can't see.'

'Yes, you can. Open your eyes, there's light. Honestly.'

'No. I can't see and I can't do this.'

'Hannah, if there wasn't any light, how would I know you've got your hands over your eyes?' Taking her hands in mine, I drew them down, then stroked her cheekbones. 'Please. It's not completely dark, I wouldn't lie. Try.'

She blinked furiously, rapidly, and at last managed to keep her eyes open. She was still shaking, though.

'Is it the dark?' I whispered. 'Or the tunnel?'

'Both. No, the tunnel. The tunnel. Oh, God.'

'Hannah, you're half-Sithe. You can't be scared of being underground!'

Even in the near darkness, I caught the filthy look she gave me. 'Well I *am*.'

I sighed and nodded at the blackness: the left-hand opening of three. Behind us the last ripples we'd made lapped feebly at the edges of the watergate pool, and as we listened it calmed into utter stillness again. 'Come *on*. Unless you want to go back and explain yourself to the Wolf.'

Her fingers found mine. I squeezed them, and pulled so

hard she had no choice. She stumbled after me into the tunnel.

Inside it, the faint phosphorescence of the cave was lost. Here it truly was black, and I hoped vindictively that Hannah recognised the difference. I'd never felt so frantic and afraid about being on my own side of the Veil, and I did not want to be here for long. The beat of my own pulse in my eardrums was so loud, I almost missed the soft hiss in the darkness.

I halted, frozen.

And now we really were dead.

★ ★ ★

The glimmer of eyelight, tinged with sickly yellow. The slither of feet, the rattle of a muted laugh. Hannah, behind me, doubling over to retch up smoked trout and toast, the sound of it shattering the silence.

I stepped back, back towards the first watergate. What use would it be? Suil was not watching now, he was back at the cottage with Teallach and the Wolf, talking himself out of trouble. I hoped.

'What a funny place to find a couple of runts.' The voice was dry and cracked, but I heard a thin tongue flick out to lick thin lips. 'I think the little girl doesn't like the dark.'

''M not little.' Hannah spat frantically, gagged and retched again.

'Big enough to die.' It giggled. 'They're all big enough to die.'

I put out an arm to touch the damp icy wall of the cavern. My brain felt as if it was dissolving in panic and I was afraid I might fall. 'Don't kill her,' I said.

'Oh, don't be silly.'

No. Don't be silly. I scratched hard at the side of my head, trying to think straight. Fleetingly I thought of all the times I'd skipped weapons practice. Rather less fleetingly, I thought of the sword my father had tried to give me six months ago.

Would it kill you to try a little diplomacy?

'Let her go back to the watergate and I'll last as long as you want me to.' *And let her take her chances with the Wolf.*

'Let me think.' I heard its fingernail scratch the side of its papery scalp in a mocking echo of me. 'No.'

I swallowed. 'If you take me back to Kate,' I said, 'you won't get near me, you know that? You'll get no fun at all.'

'I'm *well* aware of that. That's why I'm not taking you back.'

A funny relief surged through my bones. At least Kate wouldn't get me, then. At least we'd have beaten her. *Oh please make it quick, then. At least make it quick.*

'I want you to know something.' A chuckle rattled. 'What I'm about to do, I'm doing for your brother. We like him, you know.'

I didn't get to ask him what that meant. There was a strangled screech of fury and terror off to my right. Hannah must have lunged for the creature, but she couldn't see and she had no idea what the thing was anyway. I saw its eyes swivel, felt the air stir, and she was flung back against the tunnel wall. I heard the cough of breath knocked out of her body. *She's okay. Stunned, is all. Maybe it'll forget her now, maybe...*

The glinting eyes vanished, and the air went still and silent.

Then a skeletal arm draped across my shoulders, making

me jump. I wondered how much the bite of the blade would hurt. More, if I struggled, but I couldn't not fight it. I shut my eyes and clenched my fists and waited for my moment. *Its face. Go for its face, get its eyes out—*

'You know what upsets me most about you people? It's the *condescension*. It's the *prejudice*.'

I couldn't breathe for the thrashing of my heartbeat in my throat.

'You think we're so straightforward, don't you? You think we have a one-track mind.'

'You're a Lammyr, for gods' sake!'

It went on as if I hadn't spoken. 'You think you're the only ones with a little sophistication.' It sighed dramatically, and I could practically hear its eyes rolling in its head.

Bone-dry lips brushed my earlobe. 'We can think for ourselves, little boy. We can play the game as well as you or Kate can. And wouldn't life and death be boring if we were all' – its thin tongue flicked into my ear – '*predictable?*'

There was such strength in the wiry things. I'd had no idea. It shoved me to the ground with one hand, and my legs went out from under me like twigs. Gasping, I rolled over, goggling up into the darkness, trying to find its eyes. I wanted to see it coming. I wanted a chance. Just a tiny chance, *oh please you gods—*

A soft frightened moan from Hannah, the scrape of her shoe on rock. I tensed, turned, swung back. No other sound but my own high-pitched breathing.

I scrambled up to crouch on all fours. I held my breath, hard as it was.

Nothing.

'Hannah?' I rasped.

The shuffling sound of her crawling across the rocky

ground, and then her body was in my arms and she was almost strangling the life out of me. I managed to dislodge her arm from my throat, but I didn't let her pull away; I hugged her head against me, tightly.

'I think it's gone.' Her voice was barely more than a squeak. 'It's gone, Rory. It let us go.'

SETH

'Now see what you made me do?' The Wolf shook his head sorrowfully as he quietly closed the cottage door and walked back towards the rowan, rattling the handcuff keys.

Seth stared at the sky beyond the branches as the Wolf released him, then locked his wrists behind his back again. 'Was that necessary?'

'Not necessary,' said the Wolf, 'but fun. Getting sentimental in your old age, Murlainn? You're not quite the man I thought you were.'

'Glad to hear it.'

Seth shut his eyes for a moment. He was more shaken than he wanted the Wolf to know. The Watcher's death reverberated in his head, grating against his brain. It hurt in all the places he hadn't been kicked already.

Suil had only reached his mind out at the last moment, unwilling to die alone, but Seth had barely even given him that much. Only a touch, for a fraction of an instant, while the Wolf was distracted with the killings. Quick as a dragonfly, and then his block was back up, but he'd felt the Watcher's dying moment ripple up his spine and into the nape of his neck, and he'd been unable to repress a violent shudder.

The Wolf had seen that shudder, but by then Seth's block was back up. It was too late for Kilrevin to get into his mind, but the man knew he'd missed a chance. Seth thought he'd probably pay for that later.

'I see you're on your own.' He grinned at the Wolf. 'Missed Rory, did you?'

'If I was in your position, Murlainn? I'd keep my fatuous observations to myself.' Wiping his bloody fingers on the lining of Conal's jacket, the Wolf yanked him to his feet. 'What now, Murlainn? I don't know where your son's gone, but he's on his own now. And he's lost the horse.'

'That was a smart move. And he'll find help somewhere else.'

'Without dropping his block?' The Wolf smirked. 'And even if he does, is Rory that ruthless? He knows by now that anyone who helps him is a dead man walking.'

'Like you.' Seth's hatred momentarily got the better of his common sense. 'Like you, Kilrevin.'

The Wolf gazed at him for long penetrating seconds. 'Maybe I can persuade you to call that son of yours.' His eyes glittered with visible evil. 'Or have a lot of fun trying. It'd cheer me up, Murlainn, so stop pushing your luck.'

Seth looked away, in case the fear that crawled across his scalp, lifting his hair at the roots, was somehow visible in his eyes. 'Don't waste your time.'

'Don't you waste your life, what's left of it.' The Wolf pinched his earlobe playfully. 'Good. We understand each other.'

Oh, Rory, *run*, Seth thought dully. *Just run.*

HANNAH

I would sell my soul for one more hour in the dun. One more hour in that warm solid bed with the goosedown quilt. They could tar and feather me if they liked, they could tear my skin off in strips. Just one hour's sleep afterwards, that was all I asked.

The other side of the mountains, that's where Rory said we were. He seemed happy. I didn't care where we were any more, I was just glad to be far from that second watergate in the depths of the earth. I never wanted to be anywhere but the open air again. Fragments of cloud were caught on the hills and when I looked back over my shoulder, the highest tops were swathed in it. As we made our stumbling way down into the valley, sun slanted between the dark layers of cloud and the forest tops, painting everything gold. Very pretty. I only knew that night was coming on again, and that I wanted to be far away from the hills when it arrived.

'Where are we?' I mumbled.

'Not far from Tornashee. The Wolf's gonnae be spitting rivets. He was chasing us west and we've gone east. We've come out behind him.' Rory actually giggled.

'No. I mean, are we on the right side of the Veil? I lost count.'

He gave me a dark look. 'We're on the wrong side of the Veil. Which is the right side for now.'

I rubbed my eyes. 'Fine. Whatever.'

Not far was clearly a relative concept. There wasn't any sign of civilisation; all I knew was that the air was warmer and the midge-clouds were thickening along with the trees and the twilight.

And then the road was there in front of us, looming out of nowhere, and Rory shoved me back as cars roared past in both directions. When the engine sounds faded he raised his finger to his lips and checked the road; then he seized my hand and pelted across the tarmac. He yanked me after him into the trees beyond the verge, grabbing and shoving me up and over a wire fence so that I could do nothing but climb and drop over. I felt my feet sink in soft squelching grasses, and when I blinked at the half-dark sky, it was almost blotted out by black fir-tops.

A branch caught my cheek painfully; I shoved it aside with a choice curse.

'Sorry,' muttered Rory. Somehow he was back in front of me.

I dodged the next branch just in time, and grabbed it. That made me stagger forward, and suddenly I was up to my knees in freezing water. 'Yikes.'

'I'd get back from that. You'll be pulled through. It's a watergate.'

Hurriedly I stumbled back, weeds catching at my legs. Right enough, the water felt draggingly heavy even at this depth. I found a flaking stump of rotten wood and sat down, my feet well clear of the water. High up behind me, I heard intermittent traffic on the road.

Even under the canopy of the trees, there was a sheen of half-light on the little loch's surface. I could make out rocks, a broken signpost, a wrecked rowing boat half-submerged at the far shore.

'Don't go near the water,' Rory told me. 'I bet Kate's got guards on all the opposite watergates.'

'She has,' said a raspy voice.

I squealed: embarrassing but true. I hadn't even seen the hut behind us. Now there was a man standing there with his hands in his pockets: a gruesome old tramp wearing a battered hat, a long leather coat and glasses stuck together with sellotape.

'Hi, Gocaman,' said Rory. 'I thought she might have.'

'So the last thing you want is to get pulled through. I'll get it.'

'Get what?' said Rory suspiciously.

'The gun. Do you think I was born yesterday?'

Rory's teeth flashed in the darkness. 'Hardly.'

'Gun?' I squeaked.

'Nils Laszlo's. Jed ended up with it.' Rory shrugged. 'Long story. No use to Jed on the other side, so he put it back here.'

'You are a dark horse,' I muttered. 'I'd no idea you had a plan.'

'I've *always* got a plan.'

'Liar.'

The deadbeat tramp was wading forward into the reedy fringes of the water, the ripples spreading till they lapped as little waves on the far shore. There was a thin cord wrapped round one of his wrists, and when I followed it back with my eyes I saw the other silky end of it bound round a pine trunk.

'Are you sure you won't–' began Rory.

'Not sure, but I've a better chance than you,' growled Gocaman. He tugged on the cord as if making sure of it, then turned and crouched to his waist in the water.

'This bank,' he muttered. 'I showed your brother the best place.'

He was rummaging in the murky water under a small overhang, his face creased with concentration. Suddenly he brightened, and tugged out a plastic parcel smothered in weed and mud.

He brandished it as he waded ashore, then drew a knife from his belt. Rory tore at the plastic wrapping as the old tramp cut and sawed.

'Didn't mess about with the wrapping, did he?' grumbled Gocaman, peeling off yet another layer of bubble wrap and disconsolately popping a few blisters before tossing it aside. 'The boy had foresight, I'll give him that.'

With a flourish Rory ripped off the last layer of plastic bag, and something dark and gleaming tumbled to the ground.

We all stared at it. Rory lifted it with trembling fingers.

'You think you can use that, Peacemaker?' Gocaman sounded sceptical.

Rory shrugged. 'Better than ending up a rib roast.'

'Your father might come here.'

Rory sat back on his haunches. 'Have you heard anything of him?' There was only the slightest crack in his voice.

'Nothing. He'll be blocking, of course, or he'd be dead. But he'll find you. Eventually he'll find you. Just hold out, and keep away from the Wolf and watergates.' The tramp made a face. 'Suil's dead, did you know? His lover too.'

I put a hand over my mouth to stop myself letting out a sob of shocked fright. Rory stiffened.

'He killed a *Watcher*?'

'He's Alasdair Kilrevin. He'll kill anything.' Gocaman shrugged. 'Best thing for Teallach, in the end. And Watchers don't bind, but I think Suil would have followed anyway.' He stared aside, at the still surface of the lochan. 'You could stay here with me, of course.'

I wasn't averse to that idea, but Rory shook his head violently.

'Can't. The Wolf'd come first, and he'd just kill you. He does it to everyone else.'

The tramp sounded exasperated as he adjusted his glasses. 'I would like to be with you. You know I can't leave here.'

'Exactly. So thanks, but we've got to go.'

'Not to Tornashee, you don't. It's the first place the Wolf looked for you, and it's the first place he will come when he doubles back.'

Rory's shoulders slumped a little. I'm pretty sure mine did too. I'd envisaged a roof, and beds. 'Where, then?'

'Where else will your father know to look for you? Where can you keep the Wolf at bay till he finds you?' Gocaman tightened his lips in something like a smile. 'Riddle me that, Laochan.'

Rory smiled. 'I know,' he said. 'I know where.'

'Then go there.'

Rory had begun to reach for his hand when Gocaman seized hold of his. He put his dry lips to it, then pressed Rory's hand to his forehead.

'Good luck to you, Laochan. You'll need it. And run now, boy. Run very fast.'

SETH

Is this not as much fun as you thought it would be?

He would have loved to say it out loud but he had to stay alive and it was getting harder now. The Wolf's mood was volatile, changing constantly, and never for the better.

Hunting my son was going to be fun, wasn't it? But he's beating you, you psychotic piece of bat-shit. He's beating you.

Seth pressed himself against the cottage wall, trying to melt into the shadows, staring hard at an industrious little spider as it ran up and down the spokes of its web. Anything to take his mind off his arms, and his burning throat, and his empty stomach. And the desiccated corpse in the cot bed, and Suil who slumped in the opposite corner, blood congealing on his throat, dead eyes locked on Seth.

Rory had been here. And Kate's witchcraft was immaterial: Seth could smell him. He could feel the empty space where he'd been, he could sense his fear and determination and his wild hope. Rory had curled up in the bed there and slept in Hannah's arms, and for that Seth forgave her everything.

Gods, he thought, what wouldn't he give to curl up safe against Finn? They didn't get long in the end. *Gods, let her be alive.* And Jed, and Sionnach. Let everybody be alive. Rory was. Rory was alive and free and he'd been here.

And now he was far away. Rory had eluded the Wolf by the skin of his hide, slipped past him like a rat in the night, doubled back and wasted every mile and every minute the Wolf had pursued him. That tiny smile frozen in death on

Suil's face: Seth knew why it was there, and so did the Wolf. That was why the man was raging, storming, hacking furniture apart in his fury, kicking the walls, stamping glass and crockery into shards.

Seth cringed into the shadows and waited his turn. The secret of Rory's escape had died with Suil, and the Wolf might be ragingly angry at his own lack of foresight, but he was hardly going to take it out on himself, or on a corpse.

Seth didn't mind making himself obsequious and puppyish. He didn't mind taking the punishment, but he had to survive it. Rory could not evade Kilrevin forever; in the end he'd be caught. Seth couldn't die before that happened. Afterwards, fine, he'd die. That would be okay. He wished he could be with Finn one more time but it would be okay.

No, don't think about Finn.

To take his mind off her he glanced up. Mistake. The Wolf, pausing in his manic rampage, caught his gaze.

'Look at me again, Murlainn, you lose an eye. You won't be needing them, after all.' The Wolf kicked a last chair aside and strode towards him.

It was the irony that was so galling. Not so long ago he'd been Captain of his own dun and father to his clann: all those things the unwanted boy in him had yearned and hungered for. Now he was a grovelling cur and all he wanted of the useless gods was to live till he knew his son wouldn't die.

So was that so much to ask?

'There's something I've always wondered about you, Murlainn.' The Wolf leaned over him. 'When I kill you, will you be screaming for your mother, or your big brother?'

The hell with this. The hell with it. He smiled an open sexy smile. 'Neither. I'll be screaming for *your* mother.'

Not my soul, you bastard, he told himself as the Wolf grabbed his hair and slammed his face against the wall, making blood explode out of his nose.

I'm damn sure you'll make me scream. But it'll still be my own voice.

HANNAH

'I always think this hill-climbing lark must be easier,' I said, breathing hard, 'if you're not scared of heights.'

I gripped a rock in my right hand, afraid to move my feet, which were jammed against the heathery slope. I'd glanced down once and had vowed to myself never to do it again, though not looking was almost worse. The imagined void was even huger. There seemed so little surface to the hillside, and such an awful lot of empty air beyond it. Most of my body mass was in the air part of the equation. And the rocks beneath were very large and jaggy and *hard*.

Seagulls whinged above me. Gull-sniggers, I thought, and my annoyance gave me another few seconds' courage. All the same, my hands were trembling so much as I hauled myself after Rory that my fingers began to cramp. It had looked so easy from the beach as we gazed up at the dark mouth of the cave in the hillside. It hadn't seemed steep or even particularly high. It had looked like a child's scramble. Clinging immobile to the flank of the hill, I thought that now, from halfway up, it was very, very high and steep.

'I can't,' I said, barely audible even to myself.

'You've got to.' Rory turned to stare down at me.

'There's no way up.'

'My father says there's always a way up,' said Rory, 'and there's always a way down.'

'Oh. Does he?'

'Yeah. Course, he also says the way up might be slower than you want. And the way down might be a hell of a lot faster.' He giggled.

'Ha feckin' ha.' I shut my eyes.

Rory's fingers clamped on my wrist and he hauled on me so that I had no choice but to scrabble with my feet. He pulled me on up and up, so that I didn't have the option of stopping. Then I was tumbling forward after him onto level ground, a grassy sheep track some twenty metres below the cave, and the slope was briefly at a reasonable, tame angle. All the same, I gripped tufts of grass in both fists. I knew I was theoretically safe but there was a chance the hill might throw me off in a last spiteful convulsion.

Gradually my breathing slowed. The earth stopped moving beneath me; the heaving hill had gone back to sleep.

'Look,' said Rory.

Staggering to my feet, I looked, and for a moment I understood his happy grin. I could see the entire world, blue and summery. The hills were far away, and the clouds were wisps of mare's tail, not solid looming banks of stratus. The sun shone warm on my bare arms and for a few seconds I forgot about imminent death.

The last twenty metres didn't seem so bad, with the safety net of that broad sheep track beneath us. When we stumbled into the cave mouth, I lay and gasped till my chest stopped heaving, while Rory crawled to the entrance on his belly and gazed out at the sheet-metal gleam of the sea and the shimmering molten horizon.

'I don't want to die,' he said, half to himself.

'Good-oh. 'Cause you're not going to.' I shuffled over to him and snuck my arms tight around his waist.

'You know he'll catch up now.'

'Yeah. But this is a great vantage point. He won't get near us. You'll get a clear shot if he tries.'

'Uh-huh. Exactly.' Rory scratched his neck. 'I hid out here once before. When Sionnach finally talked me down, he thrashed me within an inch of my life.' He stared emptily at the gun. 'The only place I could think of, but it is perfect. Don't know if I'll be able to shoot him, that's all.'

'Just you think of Suil and Teallach,' I reminded him dryly. 'And that poor little tour guide. And Finn. You'll be able.'

'You still don't have to stay.' Nervously he poked at the trigger; I wanted to slap his hand. 'Maybe you want to change your mind now? You'll have enough time. I reckon a full day before he gets to us.'

I grabbed a handful of his hair, shoving my face close to his. Then I called him something rude. And then I pulled his face right against me and kissed him.

'Go back to Sheena and Groper Marty? And never know if you're alive or dead? I don't *think* so.' I kissed him again. 'I'm not leaving, so get used to it.'

'Okay,' he said, blushing as he grinned. 'We're in it together.'

'Hey-ho. We've got time to kill.' I made myself comfortable against the rock wall, and yawned, then smiled my sleepiest and most seductive smile. 'And teamwork means it's high time you took the initiative.'

* * *

Later Rory fell asleep quickly, curled against me, his blond head in my lap. I didn't fall asleep myself till I'd stared down at his sleeping face for quite a long time, tracing my fingertip lightly along his ear and chin and cheekbone. We weren't safe, yet he slept more soundly than he had since we'd left the dun. Perhaps, now he'd made his decision, there was nothing more for him to fret about. Leaning back against the rock I felt sleep creeping up my spine, numbing my neck like warm chocolate.

I wasn't about to fight it.

★ ★ ★

I woke in that very sudden way: you think you're fully alert and then your brain spins when it realises it isn't ready to see or hear. Letting my head fall back on my arm, I lay on the gritty cave floor, the weight of Rory's head no longer in my lap. I let reality dawn properly, then, blinking, I sat up and wriggled round to peer at the cave mouth. Fear needled the back of my neck. Rory sat silhouetted against blue morning light, twisting the silver bangle violently against his wrist.

'He's coming,' he said, and ripped off a thumbnail in his teeth.

My heart tripped and thumped, and my head swam. Well, this was it, and better now than waiting endless days, getting cold and hungry and weak. But there was something awful in Rory's voice. I didn't understand that, because this had been his big idea. He should be excited now, or relieved, or plain terrified, but his voice held only dull despair. Scrabbling forward to the cave mouth, I leaned out as far as I dared.

Rory watched blankly over my head. 'You see,' he said, defeated. 'He's coming.'

He pointed at someone climbing the precipitous hillside. I squinted down, frowning.

The man did not look like the Wolf: too small, too lightly-built, and why would the Wolf be climbing this insane slope hands-free? Unbelievable, I thought, as my stomach contracted with terror. He was struggling up the hill with his hands behind his back. And then, below and to the right, the Wolf himself appeared over the curve of the slope, an instantly recognisable bruiser, climbing strongly with the use of both hands and grinning up at Rory.

'He's coming,' said Rory in that dead voice, 'and he's won.'

As I watched, the leaner man with the black hair lost his footing and began to slide. He flung himself forward, practically gripping the hillside with his teeth to stop himself falling. His foot caught a rock and he saved himself, his leg trembling as it took the weight of his body. When he had a secure foothold he lifted his face and looked straight at Rory.

Seth. Not immediately recognisable, with a week's black beard growth and his face bruised and swollen and streaked with blood, but it was my uncle. I knew his grey eyes, and his high cheekbones, and the familiar strands of hair falling across his eyes, limp and dirty now. I sucked in a horrified breath. Rory was absolutely silent but I slithered across and propped myself beside him, gripping his shuddering arm very hard.

'He's okay,' I muttered. 'He's okay. He's not going to fall.'

Seth's eyes slewed to me and he smiled, a big white grin in his dirty and mutilated face. No, I thought, he's not going to fall, because I'm not going to let him. No point in my block now. Tentatively I reached out, flailing with my mind, but his own block was absolute. He looked away. Doggedly he jammed his foot into the hillside and went on climbing.

He was a metre or so from the sheep track when the Wolf put on a burst of speed and overtook him easily. Rory's hands shook as he raised the gun but the Wolf was leaning down now, grabbing Seth by the hair and dragging him up to temporary safety. Each plummeting grip of sickness in my belly was overtaken by another, in horribly rapid succession. I could see Seth's hands now, and I knew why he was climbing without them. They were handcuffed behind his back.

The Wolf swung Seth to his feet, and Seth smiled up at Rory. He looked altogether brighter at the sight of the gun. I felt the panic race through Rory like an electric current as he aimed it downwards, jerking at the trigger.

'Thank God that didn't work,' I muttered, leaning across and carefully releasing the safety catch. 'You have to breathe, Rory. And squeeze it really gently.'

He gave me a quick glance and then looked back towards the two men. Shutting an eye he fired. The gun barked, earth and grass spat up from the edge of the cliff, and Rory was flung back by the recoil.

'Hah!' Jumping nimbly aside, the Wolf laughed in delight. 'They taught you to use a sword, Laochan, but not how to shoot. You haven't a clue, have you?'

'I could get lucky,' shouted Rory. I was amazed at how firm and level his voice was. Aiming the pistol once more, gripping it harder, he set his teeth and narrowed his eyes.

'Or you could get very unlucky!' The Wolf yanked Seth in front of him.

Rory blinked, lowering the gun a little, and we all watched each other in silence.

'So who's the redhead, you young rogue?' The Wolf jiggled his eyebrows.

I gritted my teeth, took a breath and screamed: 'It's. *Strawberry.* BLONDE.'

Seth laughed so hard he winced, and the Wolf grinned. 'Okay, Laochan, forget it. I'm glad you've had a little fun on the run. Now.' He patted Seth affectionately on the shoulder. 'Call your boy down.'

Seth tilted his head at the Wolf, loathing in his eyes. Then he looked up at me and Rory.

'Hello again. Little bastard of mine.'

Rory narrowed his eyes. 'Hello, Dad.'

'I'm your father, am I? Is that why you listened to feck all from me?'

Rory stared down at him, but said nothing.

'Here's the last thing I'm ever going to try and teach you.' Seth blew lank hair out of his eye. 'Did I ever explain to you about binding?'

Rory shook his head slowly. I felt my stomach turn over.

'It matters more than anything, did you know that? *Anything.*'

I swallowed. Rory still didn't speak.

'Indeed, a bound lover matters more than anyone. Certainly more than a half-breed spawn who couldn't even be arsed to defend himself.' Seth's cold stare slewed to me. 'And your little girlfriend conspired to kill my bound lover. Why's she still here?'

'She wouldn't leave me—'

'You're pathetic.' Seth shook his head. 'Can't defend yourself or her. Well, she can die for all I care.'

Rory's brow creased in a perplexed frown. The Wolf drew his sword over his shoulder and pressed the tip of it to Seth's neck, edging him closer to the lip of the slope. Seth glanced down and tensed a little, and his eyes brightened. Rory's fists clenched hard enough to draw blood.

'Dad, don't! Stop!'

Alarmed, the Wolf shoved Seth away from the lip of the cliff. Seth opened his mouth to say something, but the Wolf jabbed the sword against his neck and he stumbled sideways, gritting his teeth.

The Wolf grabbed Seth's handcuffs, keeping him carefully between himself and the muzzle of Rory's pistol. 'You speak sense to this fool, Laochan! So come on down and speak some more!'

Clenching his teeth Seth glared up at us both. 'Get it through your worthless head, bastard.' I thought for a moment there were tears on his cheeks, but it was impossible to tell, really, among all the blood and the sweat. 'I'm only here to tell you to bugger off out of my life. Out of my death, if it comes to that: you and her both. She as good as killed my lover with her own filthy hands.'

I shut my eyes, unable to bear the look in his. 'I didn't mean–'

'Shut it, you killer little bitch. The good news is, I don't give a flying fuck about either of you any more. That's what binding is, do you get it yet? It's a pity this batshit gob of spittle got hold of me, but that doesn't change how I feel. So you can kill him and you can kill me too, if you've got the guts. And you can do it with a clear conscience.'

My hand tightened on Rory's arm as the Wolf flicked his sword tip across Seth's cheekbone, drawing another bloody line in the network of cuts.

'Shut up, Murlainn,' he murmured. In the silence a look of puzzled anger had dawned on his face, but Seth only smiled a mirthless, hating smile.

Then Rory's laughter drifted on the clear air. 'Nice one, Dad. I love you too.'

Seth snarled. 'That makes one of us, you little water rat. You're *nothing to me*. Not any more.'

'Ah, shut up. Give it a rest, Dad.'

Seth glared, breathing hard through his nose. Turning his face away, he uttered his first believable obscenity in five minutes, and my heart skittered and thudded with unbelievable relief.

'Aw, sweet!' The Wolf grinned, his equilibrium restored. 'That was great, Murlainn! Now,' he turned and looked up to the cave mouth again. 'Back to business. Come here, Laochan!'

Seth smiled up at Rory, the light back in his eyes. 'Don't you dare. Love you or not, lad, I'll skelp your backside.'

The Wolf sheathed his sword. 'Don't you worry, Laochan. Remember your rights! Your father won't be skelping you again. Think of me as your social worker!' He punched Seth hard on the side of his head. Seth reeled, but kept his feet, and the Wolf moved sleekly behind him.

Rory swore, high and furious. '*Dad.*'

Seth shook his head. 'Don't you move, Ro–'

The Wolf struck him viciously in the face and when Seth looked up, blood running from his nose and mouth, his eyes blazed silver with impotent rage.

'I can make this very slow, Laochan!' yelled the Wolf. 'Don't think I won't enjoy it!'

'Don't listen to him, Rory. Listen to me. Stay where you...'

364

The Wolf lashed out with his forearm and this time Seth stumbled to the side and fell. 'Laochan, you've been the bane of my life, leading me this dance. I haven't been amused. Don't make it worse for your father now.'

Blinking blood and grit out of his eyes, Seth spat and tried to get up. 'Do. Not. Move.' Again he spat blood, and a tooth, and the Wolf kicked him hard in the ribs. He collapsed again.

The gun shook in Rory's hand as he swore; he clearly didn't dare fire the gun again. Seth's eyelight was so bright it almost crackled. He lay on his side, alarmingly close to the edge again, and the Wolf's foot was on his manacled arm, pressing it down hard against his ribcage.

'Fine, save your rounds, 'cause when I'm dead you *must kill him.*' Seth grunted as the Wolf's foot lashed hard into his kidneys, and for a moment he was speechless. He sucked in another breath. 'Wait till he's close and *SHOOT HIM.*'

'You know, the first thing I ought to cut off is your tongue.' Furiously the Wolf unsheathed his dirk. 'The *first*, mind you.'

Seth craned his neck to catch his son's eyes again. 'Rory.' The Wolf snatched a handful of his hair and jerked his head viciously back, tugging him away from the edge the better to get at him. 'Rory! Don't give him what he—'

He gasped as the Wolf kicked him savagely in the belly and rolled him over with his foot. Kneeling on Seth's chest, the Wolf started to lever his jaw open.

'Last chance, Laochan!' screamed the Wolf as he scored the dirk blade down Seth's face from temple to jaw. The flesh split like a ripe tomato skin and I looked away, pressing my face into Rory's arm but keeping my hard grip on him. I had no idea how I would stand this. I couldn't watch.

Couldn't. I wondered if Seth would scream and if I could bear to hear it. The Wolf forced open Seth's jaw and poised his blade.

And smiled up at Rory.

THE CLIFF

Seth's eyes locked on the Wolf, his rigid jaw aching. A disabling panic was turning his guts to jelly, and he tried to press his tongue against the roof of his mouth, but that was futile. The Wolf fumbled for a good strong grip and his fingertips caught Seth's tongue as tight as forceps.

Seth gagged as the Wolf dragged his tongue clear of his mouth. Christ, he couldn't afford to be sick, couldn't afford to choke. His terror might have frozen him, except that he was more scared of Rory. Rory wasn't going to take this and do nothing; he knew the boy better than that. Rory was already screaming his hate and Seth knew he was going to come out of the cave.

No. No.

'Watch this, Laochan!' The Wolf was still grinning upwards. 'Are you sick of your father giving you a tongue-lashing? I can help!'

Seth's swollen tongue slipped from his grasp and the Wolf fumbled for it once more, slapping the knife impatiently to the ground. His fingers were right inside Seth's mouth now and his thumb was in the corner of his jaw. Seth danced his tongue frantically out of his way, nearly swallowing the bloody thing.

He tried to breathe, tried to twist his head away. The Wolf was loving this. He was spinning out the performance, playing to his audience; now how was that professional?

And Seth's tongue was still in his mouth. And so were the Wolf's fingers. It was a lousy gamble and he knew

367

it, but it wasn't as if he was going to get another chance. Not ever.

Everything Seth had left, he put in his jaw muscles. His mouth snapped shut like a trap; sheer surprise broke the Wolf's hold and Seth crushed his teeth into the Wolf's hand, cutting and gripping. He bit hard. He went on biting.

Seth's teeth sawed through skin and flesh, severed nerves and ground into bone. He tasted blood and the gods knew what else – the man's black soul, maybe – and held on, biting, chewing, grinding. Someone was screaming horribly, but Seth didn't care. Whoever that was screaming, he knew in a dreamy way that it was that one's turn to scream. It was *his turn*. Let him scream.

Bite. A knife flailed at his face, but it only hacked his cheekbone and the bridge of his nose; then the Wolf dropped it again in panic and pain. *Bite. Keep biting.* He sawed savagely till the man at last stopped his animal screaming and recovered himself. The Wolf ripped his hand free of Seth's teeth, leaving long ribbons of flesh behind, and flung him off.

Seth lunged up, easing the pressure on his own hands and spitting out his enemy's. That was funny. He staggered, barely keeping his feet. There was blood all over his face, he could feel it and taste it, but it was cheering to know it wasn't all his own.

The Wolf looked down in disbelief at his blood-drenched hand. The skin of his thumb and his first two fingers hung in ragged tatters, inches of white bone showing, and his forefinger was sawed almost through, the bone dangling by a flap of skin. Blood dribbled to the earth. As if impervious to the pain, he lifted his dirk defiantly in his mauled hand and ran his good thumb over its edge. He lifted his head to gaze at Seth with ice-bright eyes.

'Are you. The one.' The Wolf was breathing hard, his voice high-pitched. 'Who was worried. About me. *Scratching your CDs?*'

Seth shrugged and grinned, and the Wolf gave a wild snarl of fury. For the first time, he realised, the Wolf had lost control: he'd flung Seth away with his mind.

Seth risked dropping his own block, just for a moment, and lashed his hate at the Wolf, who stumbled two more steps back with it, teetering on the brink. Not hard enough; but Seth blocked again before the man could retaliate.

The Wolf's shield was back up, too, but it had been long enough. The bronze alloy pin was out of Seth's belt stitching and between his fingers. For a hideous moment he thought it had slipped from his blood-slick grasp, but then he felt it cool and hard between his fingertips once more.

Seth twisted his wrists as the Wolf stalked towards him, slow murder in his eyes. The pin's point found the lock and he worked it frantically. Bend. Back. Bend, twist. A few metres away the Wolf casually moved the dirk from his wounded hand to his good right one, and drew it back for a killing blow.

The lock gave abruptly and Seth lashed out. The racking cramp in his muscles made him scream but the handcuffs cracked into the Wolf's cheek. Oh, it felt good to draw that blood; and the shock on the Wolf's face was better even than split flesh.

The Wolf shifted his dirk to his left hand again, and put his good hand to his cheekbone. When he drew it away it too was wet with blood, and he stared up at Seth, who drew the still-handcuffed wrist back for another strike.

'How did you do that?' The Wolf fumbled in his pocket and drew out the key. He frowned in bewilderment, shook his head. Then his face set hard again, and he smiled.

'And now,' he said, 'I'm just going to have to gut you.'

* * *

In the cave Hannah stared at Rory, at the pistol trembling in his hands.

'Give me that. What are you waiting for?' He couldn't be having moral scruples now. Not *now*. *'Give it to me!'*

Rory turned, terror and helplessness in his face. 'Can you clear a jam?'

Swearing, she grabbed the pistol, aimed and squeezed the trigger. Nothing, not even a click. 'No! I've *no idea.'*

She snatched at Rory, panic-stricken, but he'd snaked out of her grip. He was already sliding down the slope towards Seth, who was edging warily round the Wolf. Raising her eyes to the sky with a curse, Hannah bolted after Rory.

Seth put up his free hand in an unmistakeable gesture. Rory stopped, but his teeth were bared.

There was caution in the Wolf's expression as he drew his sword, but he was smiling. 'I could beat you if you had a sword, Murlainn, let alone a poxy pair of handcuffs.'

'Poxy indeed!' Seth snorted. 'I think they've served you very well.'

'But they've stopped being useful, now. Like you.' The Wolf chuckled. 'Tell me, Murlainn, how stupid did you feel when I caught you in your own house?'

Seth drew his lips back from his teeth, but it wasn't what Hannah would call a smile.

'I knew where you were. You think I didn't feel you there at Tornashee? It's my *house*, you big gobshite. You think I didn't feel you barge in without an invitation?'

The Wolf growled softly.

'I wanted to be with you,' said Seth coldly. 'How could I find Rory before you, when you wouldn't let me See him? *How else could I find him?*' His yell was rank with fury. 'I knew you would get to my son, Kilrevin. You were always going to find him, so I had to be with you when you did. *Didn't I?*'

Rory had gone entirely white. His eyes caught Hannah's.

~ *On purpose. He did this on purpose. Everything.*

But, 'You're lying.' The Wolf breathed hard.

'Nah. You're so predictable. Where would the fun be in killing me? When I could still watch my son die, and you could take a bit longer over me?'

The Wolf's eyes were wide with rage. 'I could have killed you on the spot!'

'Could have.' Seth shrugged. 'But you didn't.'

'Silly me!' said the Wolf after a long moment. 'Let's put that right.'

'Not just now.' Seth swung the handcuffs warningly.

'Of course just now.' The Wolf chuckled. 'I wouldn't have killed your son, you twat, not right away. Kate needs him! And you forgot about the handcuffs!'

'Okay, that's true. Silly me, this time. And I know you wouldn't have killed Rory,' said Seth, 'not right away. But you'd have killed Conal's girl on the spot. And I wasn't having that.'

Hannah's turn to pale, Hannah's turn to whimper softly.

He hadn't delivered himself into the Wolf's hands for Rory, she realised. He'd done it for her. She wanted to cry, or jump off the cliff.

'Kilrevin, man, you taste the way you are.' Seth wiped his mouth and spat. 'Foul.'

Drawing his sword, the Wolf leaped for Seth. Ducking, Seth charged forward, but it was a hopeless contest, and Seth had never really had a cat's chance. Reacting fast, the Wolf checked and dodged and thrust again, and the sword plunged deep into Seth's side.

* * *

Rory yelled in horror as his father sucked in a stunned breath. The Wolf withdrew the sword for another strike, Seth making a high sound in his throat as the blade came out of him.

Rory flung himself down the last few feet of slope, then sprang into the air, twisting and kicking. His foot caught the Wolf's shoulder and spun him aside so that the second lunge, aimed at Seth's heart, missed him altogether. Rory was in the air a moment longer, turning, but the Wolf was fast, and out of his reach. He dropped to the earth in a cat-crouch.

Roaring, the Wolf drew his sword back for a lethal swing. Rory eyed him, nerves screaming, waiting to sense which way to jump. He'd find out too late and he knew it. Fifty-fifty.

Somewhere inside the Wolf's rage, his orders from Kate must have lodged deep in his brain. Instead of slicing Rory's head from his shoulders, the sword stayed drawn back in the air for a fraction of an instant, and that was all Seth needed. He leaped onto the Wolf's back, wrapped his legs round the man's barrel chest and locked his left arm round his neck, handcuffs swinging. His free hand snatched the raised sword arm and hung on desperately.

Purple-faced, struggling for air, the Wolf clutched wildly at Seth with his mangled hand, somehow finding a handful of hair and dragging him inexorably down. Seth slid sideways but he clung on with his legs, and he didn't let go of the Wolf's sword arm.

Rory rolled out of reach and sprang up, but he hesitated. There was still no mental connection with his father, and without it he didn't know where to aim an attack. The wrong move would be a fatal move, and yet he could see Seth weakening, could see blood throbbing out of his side.

Seth was hanging almost upside down by now. All that was holding him on was one ankle hooked round the Wolf's neck, together with his loosening left arm. In seconds he was going to slip, and his grip would fail, and then the sword would arc down and cut him in half.

'Dad!' barked Rory.

Seth twisted his dangling head, making fleeting eye contact. His teeth were clenched but he was almost laughing at the ridiculousness of his position. *Sod this for a game of soldiers*, thought Rory. *He isn't going to die.*

Seth held his gaze for a second more; then he closed his eyes with an aching sigh and let go his grip on the Wolf's sword arm. The Wolf flung him off with a yell and the sword lashed down, but Rory leaped to intercept it. The Wolf hadn't expected him, didn't see him till he was locked on his arm like a yowling cat.

The Wolf gave a snarl that was all exasperation as his maimed left hand went round Rory's throat. There was raw flesh, slippery blood and exposed bone in that grip;

Rory could feel the loose forefinger flapping against his skin. His vision darkened as he struggled for breath but he held grimly onto the Wolf's arm.

'Give me a moment,' snarled the Wolf, 'while I throttle your son.'

'No.' Staggering to his feet, Seth slammed his fist into Kilrevin's face.

The man dropped Rory like a hot coal. As Seth collapsed to his knees, his gasp of pain was drowned by the Wolf's scream of agony.

Seth grabbed his wounded side, blood pumping out over his splayed fingers. The Wolf dropped his sword and reeled back, both hands clutched over his left eye.

Rory scrambled to his feet as the Wolf stumbled blindly, tottering on the edge. *Suil*, he thought. *Teallach*. The poor priggish guide whose name he'd never known. Finn MacAngus, whose violent death must have broken his father's heart. But the Wolf was screaming, helpless with pain, his centre of gravity lost, and the faces of the dead would not form in Rory's mind.

So Hannah walked calmly past him, and punched the Wolf hard in the nose.

As he reeled back, silenced by shock, the Wolf's hands came away from his face, flailing and windmilling in the air. Blood and vitreous fluid streamed from his left eye around the stump of a bronze pin. The Wolf careered backwards over the cliff edge, vanishing from sight. Distantly, there was a muffled thump; then a splash that was lost in a crash of waves.

Seth staggered to his feet, his t-shirt soaked with blood, and clutched his son into his arms. He moaned with pain but he wouldn't let Rory go.

'Dad! *Dad!*' Rory hugged him hard, tugging him back from the edge. 'Sit *down!*'

Seth slumped down, shocked. Hannah ran to him, pulling his t-shirt gingerly away from his side.

'Give me your shirt!' she yelled.

Rory stripped off his t-shirt and Hannah thrust it hard against Seth's side. She sobbed, shoving it hard into the wound and ignoring his yell of agonised protest.

'*Leave it!*' screamed Seth.

'*No!*' she screamed back.

'*LEAVE IT!*' he howled, trying to writhe away from her.

'But you're bleeding!'

Seth seized her arm. 'I'm bleeding to death, Hannah,' he hissed furiously. 'I can feel it. Get a grip, and get my son out of here.'

'He won't leave you!' she yelled at him. She took a gulp of air. '*I won't leave you!*'

Swearing violently, Seth yanked her hand and the t-shirt away, and blood jetted thickly out of the hole. 'Rory, call Finn's horse and *go!*' Again he cursed. '*And take Florence bloody Nightingale with you!*'

Hannah snarled, and hollered an insult at him. As his lip curled and he took a deep breath, entirely up for a profane screaming match, she lunged forward madly and shoved her bare hand into the wound.

Seth screamed, really screamed.

Rory snatched at Hannah's wrist, trying to drag her hand out of the hole, but her skin was slippery with blood and her strength was amazing. He cursed her, tore at her arm, but as they struggled, as she forced her hand inside his father's wound with vicious determination, he became gradually aware that Seth had stopped fighting.

He was still cursing wildly, but he wasn't fighting any more and his hand was tight round Hannah's bloody wrist, holding it steady inside his torso. Then, only a little more gently, she pushed in the fingers of her other hand too. His face contorted, Seth fell silent.

She bit her lip hard and her hands tightened inside him. Seth opened his mouth and howled with pain one last time; then Hannah snarled in his face, and yanked her hands out of the wound.

His voice strained, Seth said: 'The usual thing now, Florence, is you seal the cut.'

She grinned at him and he grinned back, and her fingers closed none too gently around the lips of the wound and pressed them together.

Rory swore, expressively.

'Language, laddie,' said Seth absently, wincing as he touched the sealed wound.

'Yeah,' said Hannah as she drew her hand tentatively away and stared at the congealed blood. 'I'm pretty surprised myself.'

'You could knock me down with a feather,' said Seth, flinching as he sat up. 'But maybe that's not so surprising.'

Hannah put her hand to his face, frowning, and traced the gaping gash the Wolf had drawn down the side of it. Seth watched her, eyes silver and intent, and her fingers trembled as she pinched the edges of the cut together.

She seemed to have lost the knack. Cursing, she lost her concentration and had to begin again. When she drew back, the scar like messy amateur stitching, she was weak and weepy.

She spat a curse. 'Shut up. Stop looking at me. Shut up.'

Seth went on looking at her, with a lot of amusement,

but he put his hand to her face, wiping the tears with his thumb. 'You'll feel rubbish for a bit,' he said comfortingly. 'You've only just discovered it. It takes a lot out of you. You've had no practice.'

Blinking hard, she shoved herself up and away from him. Leaning on Rory's shoulder, Seth hauled himself up. He was white and shaking but he was on his feet. 'We have to go,' he said.

'You need some rest,' said Rory, staring at him.

'Rory, I need rest and I need a shave and I need to hear what's happened to you. I need *Finn*,' he said a little desperately, and half to himself. 'But you can't always get what you need.'

'Do you ever listen to a single word your son says?'

For a second, Rory thought she was going to punch his father right in the face. Then Hannah's fist unclenched, and she seized Seth's shoulder and shoved him back to the ground.

'He said. You need. A rest. Now shut your overworked gob. Nursey's orders.'

HANNAH

'Gods' sake,' grumbled Seth. 'We're working against time here.'

'And a fine lot of use you'd be to anyone in your state.' I tucked my lighter back into my jeans pocket and poked more chocolate wrappers into the pile of sticks. The fire roared up; I never knew I was such a girl scout. 'You start charging around like a maniac, your belly'll open right back up.'

'And how do you know?'

'Stupid question.' I rolled my eyes. 'How would I know how I know?'

'And *why* have you got a lighter?'

'Another stupid question. I've given up anyway. You're not well off for corner shops in fairyland. Oh for Christ's sake, get closer to the fire. You're *freezing*.'

'Rory, is she this bossy all the time?'

'Oh, yeah. Get used to it. And I'm on her side. I haven't forgiven you for nearly getting yourself killed. Deliberately.'

'Well,' said Seth huffily, 'I wasn't about to let him murder Hannah. If there was an afterlife, my brother wouldn't let me live to enjoy it.'

My guts twisted with guilt, so 'We can move on,' I said sweetly, 'when you start talking sense.'

'Oh, you're welcome. Don't mention it. *Ow.*'

'Well, sit still! I don't know how you expect me to fix you when you keep fidgeting.' I shut one eye and chewed my lip as I tried to re-fix his slashed face. I'd already had to open it up again twice.

'I'm *bored* and my clann need me and I want to *get going*.'

'Your clann would rather have you breathing. You big kid.'

Really, he was still on a high. The pair of them were. Rory hadn't stopped grinning since he'd heard Finn was still alive. Nothing to do with the fact that Eili wasn't, or so I tried to tell myself.

The big smirk was still on his face when he said, 'Something I've got to say to you, Dad.'

'Look, I'm sorry. Those things I said. I didn't—'

'Sod that. I didn't believe a word of it.'

'I wasn't sure. I mean, if we still had any kind of a connection—'

Rory crumpled another piece of paper and dropped it onto the fire, and when he looked up I realised for the first time that his smile was taut and hard and lethally cruel. *Smile of a soul that doesn't care any more*, I thought out of nowhere, and I clamped my hand over my mouth.

Rory cocked his head and smiled at me. Just for a moment, he reminded me of Eili, and I'd rather have seen him weep.

'Kate's cut us,' he told me. 'She's split us. I can't See him and he can't See me. Which brings me to what I was going to say.'

Seth lifted his head, shocked. 'Don't—'

'So I'm claiming her.' Rory folded his arms. 'I'll kill Kate for you, Murlainn.'

'Laochan, don't say—' Seth's voice dried.

'Too late. For what she's done to us, Murlainn? She's mine. Hannah's my witness.'

Seth's lips parted, but he couldn't speak for a long moment. Then he rubbed his hands across his face.

'Success at last, boy. We've made a killer of you.' There was acid regret in his voice. 'And nothing has made me sadder in my life.'

'I'll live, won't I?' Rory stood up. 'I'll go and get some more wood.'

'I'll be finished in a minute...' I began.

'I said I'll get more wood.' He set off at a jog across the slope.

I unpicked a bit of the sealed flesh on the arm-wound; no need really, but Seth was tough, and I was glad to have something to do in the silence.

'Tell me about Eili,' I blurted at last. Anything to take his mind off his son.

'What about her?' he snapped.

'Okay. Thing is, I know she didn't like me. I know it was all about my father. She was using me. But...' I took a breath. 'She loved my father, didn't she? I mean, to the point of lunacy. And I suppose he loved her.'

'More than his own life. She wasn't always like – like that. *Ow.*' He winced. 'Anyway, I think she did like you. You were a part of him, but that wasn't all of it. You're a healer. Maybe she sensed it. You're a lot like her.'

'God help me.'

He gave a low laugh. 'Eili would have shoved that big tosser over the cliff too.'

I blushed. 'I didn't know I was going to do that, I swear. But I'm still glad I did it.'

'Are you?'

I let myself meet his eyes. I licked my lips. 'Yes.'

'Girl, you're a Sithe to your marrow.' He sighed and slumped back as I let his arm go. 'I wish your father was around. He was better than most of us at staying human.'

'I bet birds would suddenly appear every time he was near.' I pinched his arm very lightly. 'Say something horrible about him.'

'Gladly.' He gave me a twisted grin. 'He'd a filthy temper. Used to beat the lights out of me when I was bad. Not just when I was ten, either. Make you feel better?'

'No. You probably deserved it.'

'Oh, sure. Always.'

I shuffled back and put my arms round my knees. 'And he was unfaithful, wasn't he? Why did he sleep with my mother if he loved Eili so much?'

'Oh, Hannah, I don't know. We're none of us very faithful. It's not like that for us; we live an awful lot of years.' He wrinkled his battered nose. 'Conal was away from Eili a decade at a time. He was the perfect gentle knight, so he was, but even a big boy scout like your father gets lonely. I did, and I don't even like people very much.'

I grinned at the tone of his voice. 'You loved Rory's mother, didn't you? Everybody says so, even Finn. Conal couldn't have loved my mother.' I added sourly, 'Believe me, he couldn't.'

'You must have, once. Even if you don't remember. Maybe you still do.'

'Huh. You were right the first time, I don't remember.'

Seth sighed and let it go. 'Yeah. Look, I'm sorry you didn't know Conal but it wasn't his decision. I'd stake my life on that. He'd never have left you if he'd known, he'd never have done what I did to Rory. He'd have stuck around and loved you, okay?'

I wiped the back of my hand violently across my face. 'I wish there was an afterlife so I could see him.'

'Me too. But there isn't. Hi Rory.'

'Dad. Sorry.'

He hadn't brought any wood. He slumped down beside Seth.

'I hope you don't regret what you said, because it's too late now. You're buggered.'

'No,' said Rory. 'I don't. We should go.'

Seth flicked his hair, just catching his scalp enough to make Rory wince. 'Glad you're back. Wouldn't put it past you to go through the Veil without us. You had that look on your face. Tell me something.' Seth batted my hand away. 'Hannah, that's just a bruise. Leave me, I'm fine. Rory, why isn't the world full of holes where you've torn it?'

Rory shrugged. 'I seal them up.'

'You do?' Seth looked startled.

'Course I do. And if I don't bother, which I usually don't, they heal by themselves.

I could almost see the cogs turning in Seth's head.

Rory made a face. 'Now if I knew what else to do with it, we'd be laughing.'

'Oh, snap out of that.' Seth stood up too sharply, and staggered. 'You're not the only one.'

'What's that supposed to mean?' Rory kicked earth violently over the dying fire.

'Listen, I ached to be dun Captain. Soon as I had it, I knew it was beyond me. I don't know where to start any more than you do, but I've had to. And I'll have to finish it, because I *haven't got a choice*. There's no-one else to do it. And it doesn't make a damn bit of difference that it's a lost cause.'

'Stop it!' I snapped. 'Feeling sorry for yourself won't help. Or you!' I aimed the last bit at Rory.

I expected Seth to bite my head off. Instead he hooted with laughter.

'Hear her, Laochan? She's right, but so am I. Hannah, it's been a lost cause since we lost your father. Doesn't mean I'm giving up.' Turning away, Seth limped towards the slope. 'Lost or not, it's a cause worth fighting for. And if there was nothing worth fighting for, there'd be nothing worth living for. Life wouldn't be worth living by bloody definition. So do what you can and stop agonising, right? And if you'll keep your girlfriend at bay, *we need to go home*.'

He took the slope at a limping run, the idiot. 'Slow down,' I yelled.

Hesitating, Seth glanced over his shoulder and jerked his thumb towards the sheerest part of the cliff. 'You think he's dead?'

'Well, I was kind of *assuming* he was.'

'Well, that's what I did, a lot of centuries ago. I'm not jumping to any conclusions now.'

Fine; that got me moving.

I took a lot longer getting back down the hill than Seth or Rory, though Seth was a wreck and Rory looked as if he expected to have to catch him any minute when he fell. They waited impatiently, watching me slide backwards on my stomach, eyes shut tight, hands clutching the grass white-knuckled. Ten metres above them I stopped. I could not move another inch.

'What's with you?' Seth called up crossly.

'I'm *fine*,' I snapped.

My eyes were shut, but I could hear Rory muttering to his father, then a brief argument, and then I heard Seth climb doggedly back up the slope. Sod him, I would *not* feel guilty. I hadn't *asked* him to come.

He slumped beside me, wincing, and untwisted my fingers from a clump of heather. 'This figures.'

'What figures?' I glared sidelong at him.

'Your father was scared of heights too.' There was a note of satisfaction in his voice.

'I'm not scared.'

'Lucky girl. I was scared the last few days.'

I scowled. There was a good chance he was taking the mickey and I wasn't going to let him get away with it. 'Well, I'm *not*.'

'That's good, very good.' He squeezed my fingers. 'You won't have any call to be brave.'

He didn't let go of my hand, though, sliding down alongside me till I was on completely flat ground. Then he yanked me to my feet.

'Don't let me rush you, Hannah. We've only got a world to save.'

RORY

The black horse came back first. I told my father I'd only call it if he rode it himself, but I might as well have told the mountains to squat down and let us walk over.

'I've got my own.'

'Oh, yeah? How are you going to get him back?'

'Just call Finn's.'

I shouldn't have been surprised that the black cantered into sight before we'd walked three miles. When it was called, it found a way, and fast. The kelpies knew the watergates better than we did, my father pointed out, even if they couldn't climb down a cliff to reach one underground.

The black hooked its head fondly over my shoulder and whickered right in my ear, pacing alongside us. 'I still wish you'd get on it,' I said. 'You need a ride more than I do.'

Seth pointed at a car ahead of us, slewed across the end of the pitted track. 'There's mine. Or it will be soon.' He swung open the driver's side door and released the boot lock. I stared as he hefted the spare tyre with a gasp of pain, then reached into the hollow where it had lain, and drew out his bridle.

'When did you put that there?' said Hannah. She looked pale and suspicious and a little bit sick.

My father didn't look at her. 'When I got shot of the horse. At Tornashee.'

'You needn't feel bad,' I muttered to her. 'It was his choice.'

'Bit of a gamble, choosing which car,' said Seth. 'But I thought he'd like this one. If he'd gone for the motorbike I'd have been in trouble. But that was unlikely with me in tow, and I planned to be in tow pretty fast. Oh, knock it off,' he growled at Hannah. 'I told you I wouldn't let you die. But it wasn't you I owed. So wipe that guilty look off your face.'

She rolled her eyes at me. 'He's got a lovely way with a sentiment.' There was a tiny catch there in her voice, though.

'So anyway, I hid the bridle before I went into the house. Had to leave my sword in a shed at Tornashee, but we'll cross that rickety bridge when… ah!'

The black horse lifted its head and gave a screaming whinny of excitement, and a second later we heard the thunder of hooves. The blue roan looked as happy as a week-old foal in a clover field. It scrabbled to a halt, canting sideways so that it nearly knocked Seth flying, whinnying with crazy delight as it hooked its head over his shoulder.

My father wrapped his arms round its neck and buried his face in its warm pearly skin. 'Hello, my love.' His voice was muffled. 'Did you really stay so close? You didn't even wait for me to call, you lovely big bastard.'

'See?' Hannah nudged me. 'Deeply emotional turn of phrase.'

My father's turns of phrase were getting a lot more emotional, not to mention obscene, by the time we'd put enough miles behind us. Any breaks he allowed us for food or rest seemed to be over before they began, and I didn't dare ask Hannah how much her backside hurt. She wasn't used to so much riding at all, let alone the bareback kind, and her only escape was in fitful dozes that never lasted long.

I couldn't blame Seth for his urgency. It was a day and a night before we saw the western islands above the blue line of the sea, and I knew that in his head he was measuring the damage that might be done to his clann in that time. Besides, the time could be longer than we knew; I'd heard the tales as often as any Sithe, the horror stories about what happened when the time warped and the years slipped lethally out of sync. My father had once had *a bad experience*.

That was all I knew, of course. He didn't ever talk about it, not even on that endless hard ride through the eternally shadowed hill passes and along rivers, down stony gullies where the horses almost had to slide on their haunches. He didn't ever go into the details and I didn't expect it now, not even when he let us stop, let us eat, let us snatch a twenty minutes' sleep in the very darkest hours on offer.

But I knew, all the same. I knew, despite Kate and her vicious severing spell. I knew he was thinking about time, and the capriciousness of it, and I knew the fear twisted in his belly like a spear.

HANNAH

My arse was never going to be the same. By the time we'd ridden as far westwards as we could, I was sure it had worn down to nothing more than a scrawny jut of stripped bone. Still, I couldn't possibly be as tired as I felt. I kept slapping myself awake because I was too vain to drool on the back of Rory's t-shirt.

At first, where the land ran out, the gouge in the coast-line was only a shadow, a line in the earth; but abruptly, as Seth reined in the roan, emptiness opened in front of us, and I thought it would swallow us all.

I leaned over Rory's shoulder, suspicious. 'This isn't where the dun is. It's nothing like it.'

'No. I can't get through at the dun,' he said. 'Told you. It's a fortress.'

Seth stroked the roan's neck. 'Must have seemed sensible to the witches who wove the Veil, but it was a bit stupid in retrospect. It's the same as anything: a curtain, a fishing net, a spider web. You weave it tighter in one place, it'll rip in another. It has to give somewhere, it's elementary physics. That's why the damn thing's falling apart.' Seth blew out a sigh. 'And Kate will have the dun surrounded. We haven't a hope in hell of getting through.'

'So, uh... you've brought us where?'

Fifty metres below us lay a sea loch, a bolt of wrinkled blue silk. And only a mile or more beyond that water did the land begin again. With some trepidation I slid off the black's back. I could barely walk, and I knew I was shaking, and Rory clasped his hand around my wrist. I managed a couple of nervous steps.

On the only visible strip of beach below us and a little way to the left, a single heron stood motionless on a brown expanse of sea wrack. I swallowed. The shoreline where it stood didn't run out; it just disappeared beneath us, because there was no angle to the cliff at all. It was a straight unbroken plunge to the loch below, and beyond the loch's mouth the dying light was luminous on a metallic sea. My head swam and I took a quick step back.

'Where are we going now, then?'

Seth swung his leg over the roan's neck and jumped down, then unbuckled the throatlash of its bridle. 'Down there.'

'Yeah, right, listen,' I began, with all the aggression I could muster. 'I don't know why you're taking that bridle off because we're going to have to find another way round and we *might as well ride*. There's nothing left of my poor arse to hurt, believe me.'

'Believe *me*, there isn't another way,' said Seth curtly. 'Horses don't climb.'

'There's a happy coincidence. Neither do I.'

'Yes, you do.'

I shook my head, but when I stepped back I bumped into Rory. He put his arms round me but he didn't open his mouth in my defence, the tosser.

The blue was fading from the sea loch and in the evening light its still opaque surface was sheened with eerie ultra-violet. It was all a very long way away, vertically speaking. I stared at Seth. 'I'm not going down there.'

'You've got to,' said Seth with a banal smirk. 'I'm not leaving you here with two hungry kelpies.'

I gulped hard again and glanced nervously at the roan.

It had an expectant look on its face. 'You've got a point there,' I said. 'The trouble is I've got as much chance with that cliff as I've got with the kelpie.'

Seth muttered a curse. 'We're going down there, Hannah. Look. Climb above me, and I mean *right* above me. Follow me and use the same handholds. Okay? Would that make you feel better?'

'Great. So if I fall I'll just kill the both of us.'

'You're not going to fall,' he said patiently. 'It's an easy climb. So many handholds the hardest part is choosing one, okay? And if you *do* fall I'll catch you. Right? Now.' He'd lowered himself a metre down the rockface before I could argue, and now he was grinning up at me. Smugly. 'Come here, then.'

It seemed like I didn't have a choice. At least I'd kill him while I was killing myself, I thought vindictively.

I started to climb, practically in his arms. Handholds were easier to find than footholds, given that I was unwilling to open my eyes and look down, but Seth was tugging my reluctant feet onto jutting bits of rock or jamming them into cracks. He growled at the extra effort, but he said nothing intelligible.

I had to rely on him, I couldn't help it. I was shaking with fear and it was all I could do to seize the handholds after he let them go. Every time I gripped a solid blade of protruding stone, felt my weight hang securely on it, I knew I'd never be able to let it go to reach for another one. But every time I did, only because Seth was lowering himself painfully slowly but steadily, and if I held on too long he would get too far away and my safety net would disappear. He'd made out it was easy, but I couldn't help noticing that his own knuckles were white and strained.

Rory was making light work of it off to my right, but his anxious glance strayed constantly to me and his father. I risked a sideways look, and gave him a lovely confident smile, not wanting him to think I was pathetic.

So that was when I slipped.

My feet went first, flailing into Seth's face, and then in my panic first one hand lost its grip, and then, as I swung by one arm, so did the other. I screamed once, briefly, and then I thudded into Seth.

His body jerked back and he yelled with pain, but his fingers were dug deep into cracks in the rock and though his feet scrabbled wildly, they quickly found their contact with the cliff.

His voice when it came was a strangled screech. *'Hannah!'*

I knew from the sound of it how close he was to falling, and I grabbed at the rock, finding holds more by accident than intent. When my fingers were clinging to the rock again, I dragged my weight up and off him, and pressed myself to the cliff face. Since every cell in my body had turned to ice, I couldn't even cry.

'How many times do you need to be told, Hannah?' He was breathing fast and his laugh was brief and pitched high with fright. 'Get a *grip*.'

'Yes.' I shut my eyes and sucked in deep breaths. 'Sorry.'

'I've been kicked in the face enough, right?' he added.

I saw Rory turn away, and I thought that maybe it was just as well he couldn't see in Seth's head right now.

At least it couldn't get any worse than that moment. When my feet touched solid ground and Seth's hands closed briefly on my arms, I had never felt so proud of myself in my life. At least it was over. We *couldn't* go lower than sea level. From here on it would be *easy*.

'Now,' Seth said as Rory jumped down the last few feet, 'let's not hang about.'

He picked his way along between the cliff and the sea as the heron took off with lazy wingbeats along the tangle-strewn shoreline, disappearing round the curve of the bay to roost for the night. No such luck for us. I watched Seth run his hands along the rock. I had a bad feeling about this.

'There,' he said at last.

Rory and I looked at each other, then back at the cliff face where Seth stood staring with such satisfaction at a shallow cave in the rock. Even from outside, even in the deepening summer dusk, we could see it led nowhere. It was perhaps six feet deep, the entrance only five feet high, and Seth had to duck to go inside.

Seth moved deeper into the cave and ran his fingers down a crack in the rock. It widened towards the sandy floor, until it was large enough for a crawl space, but there was nothing behind it but more rock.

'See, Rory?' Seth took his wrist and drew him forwards. 'Feel something there?'

Rory frowned, touching it delicately with his fingertips. 'The rock... no, hang on...'

'Go on into the gap.'

Rory ducked down. He hesitated for a moment, then laughed, and my eyes widened as I saw him scramble forward into what looked like a solid rockface. And then it wasn't rock. It was just empty space, and darkness.

'There, see? There's a tunnel. All the way to the dun. Leonora's little secret.' There was a note of boyish smugness in Seth's voice.

'Nice glamour she cast,' said Rory admiringly. 'But doesn't Kate know about this?'

'Rory, nobody in the dun knows about it, let alone Kate. Leonora thought she took the knowledge to the Selkyr, the old witch. Conal and Aonghas and I found it, and the two of them...' He shrugged. 'Rory, when you open the Veil, how long will it stay open? I mean, minutes, hours? Days?'

'Days, if it's a decent-sized rip,' said Rory with confidence. 'Two or three at the most, though.'

'And you can seal it yourself?'

'Yes.'

'Good.' Seth smiled. 'Let's go. Let me know when you feel the Veil thicken near the dun, okay? Then we'll go through. As soon as we do, you have to block, both of you. Okay?'

'Yes,' said Rory.

'No,' I moaned. I'd stood here long enough in silence, knowing what was coming, but now that they'd said it out loud I reckoned I'd just swim out to sea and drown myself. Or maybe it was worth begging? 'No, no, no. I hate tunnels. Rory, you know I do. I hate tunnels more than I hate cliffs.'

'Aw, you're doing great.' Seth grinned. 'You're *fabulous*.'

★ ★ ★

And I fell for that kind of buttering-up, I thought hours later, as I fumbled and stumbled through pitch darkness. It was so much later that I barely liked to think how deep we were inside the coastline, how much rock there was above our heads. If Seth wasn't in such an almighty hurry, I thought grumpily, he might have gone back to the nearest shop for a torch. But oh, no, we were expected to find our way underground with no light whatsoever.

'There's no forks. No other tunnels. A few turns, a few ups and downs where the rock must have been tougher, but it's one long passage,' he'd said, shrugging. 'What d'you need a torch for? It'd be nicer but it wouldn't really help, would it?'

That was a matter of opinion. I had never been in such total darkness in my life. It was worse than Suil's caverns, blacker by far. I knew now that I'd *liked* Suil's tunnels with their faint phosphorescence. Besides, I'd seen plenty of movies and in these situations there was always a nice backlit glow. Water gleaming on the walls. *Anything.*

And it was so cold. My whole body shuddered with it from my skin to my bones, and the silence grated against my chilled nerves. Occasionally Seth would speak Rory's name, and Rory would say something monosyllabic in return, but it was hardly conversation, and I did not see the point of it. I couldn't help noticing that Seth hardly ever spoke to me, and I was starting to be offended, given that I'd just saved his life.

'Does this…' I began, and hesitated. Maybe that was why nobody said much. My voice seemed very small, drowned in blackness. I cleared my throat and tried to sound braver. 'Does this not bother you?'

'What?' said Rory behind me.

'The fact we can't see a thing.' That wasn't strictly true. When Seth turned to me, or when I glanced over my shoulder to locate Rory, their eyelight was visible, though it was nothing like strong enough to make any impact on the dark. It glowed on its own, a faint gleam like a fish in the deep ocean, lighting nothing beyond itself, though at least it was a visible touchstone in the darkness.

'Doesn't bother me. Why? Not *scared*, are you, Hannah?'

There was a touch of mockery in Seth's disembodied voice.

'All right,' I snapped. 'All right, I'm scared of heights, I'm scared of the dark. Oh, yeah, and I'm scared of your horse. And that's *it*, okay?'

'Okay. Deal.' The mockery was gone, though my ears and my dignity were alert for it. 'Look, try and feel a little ahead with your mind.' He paused. 'Rory?'

'Yeah, Dad.'

That little exchange yet again, and as usual neither of them said anything else. I scowled into the darkness, feeling left out, until my eyes widened with a sickening realisation. They were only checking each other's position. Each checking the other was still there. And Seth wasn't speaking to me because he knew where I was anyway. He could still See me, after all. I gulped.

'That's okay.' Seth's voice was a soft murmur ahead of me. 'I knew you'd work it out.'

And it would have hurt too much to explain out loud, I realised guiltily. Making an effort not to think about that, I thought about the dun instead, pictured it in my head, imagined how it would be to get a decent meal and some sleep. I even imagined the tongue-lashing I'd get from Jed and Finn. What was it like, being tarred and feathered? I'd always thought it might be kind of fun, like a very wild hen party.

Anything rather than think about how long this tunnel must be, how ancient it was and what prehistoric things might lurk in the darkness. Anything rather than contemplate how far we'd come already and how much further we'd have to go in the pitch dark. We must have walked miles already, entirely blind.

There was way too much time to think, and nothing to do but put one foot cautiously in front of the other. In my whole life I'd never felt so vulnerable. If something large and slimy and sharp-toothed came at me, I might hear a last-moment slither but I wouldn't really know about it till fangs closed on my throat...

Oh, *bad* imagination. I tried to put on a burst of speed, stubbed my toe on a rough lump of rock and yelped as I stumbled. A hand touched my arm and I shrieked, then saw the double pinprick glow of Seth's eyelight as he turned.

'Okay, Hannah?'

'Uh-huh,' I squeaked.

'Rory?'

'Dad.'

Seth let go of my arm and I felt him move away, but almost immediately there was a small splashing sound and he cursed.

'What? What?'

A few more experimental splashes, the tone changing so that I could hear he was wading deeper. 'It takes a dip here. It's flooded.'

I rolled my eyeballs, a wasted gesture and a disorienting experience when nothing was visible.

'Oh, *how* did I just *know* that was going to happen?'

'You're not really helping, Hannah.' Seth sounded as if he was speaking through his teeth. 'It's not the first time it's been flooded. There used to be a rope.'

'"Used to be",' I echoed. Rory was silent behind me.

There was a dull sound of iron banging against rock. 'That's the ring it was tied to. The rope's rotted. Rory?'

'Dad.'

Seth sighed. 'Okay, it's not that far but it's quite narrow. You just have to pull yourself along against the wall.'

'Okay,' said Rory.

'Okay?' I screeched. 'You mean we're going on? I've seen this bit in the movies and *somebody always drowns*.'

'You watch too many films,' said Seth. 'Have you got another suggestion?'

'I've got several, pal.'

'All anatomical, though.' There was a grin in his voice. 'Nothing constructive?'

I made a hideous face and mouthed some choice swear words in the darkness, but 'No,' I admitted at last.

'I heard every word of that, Hannah Falconer,' said Seth, but this time his teeth were clenched against laughter, I could hear it. 'Really it isn't hard. Take lots of breaths before you go and keep moving. Just don't panic. Okay?'

He must have taken silence for agreement because the next thing I heard was him wading forward into water. I heard him breathing deeply, filling his lungs, and then there was one more subdued splash and silence. It was worse than the silence that had gone before. I could feel less human presence in it, and I shivered.

'Want to go first, then?' asked Rory quietly.

I hesitated, torn. I did not want to go into that water at all, and I very much wanted to put off the moment as long as possible. On the other hand, I didn't want to be left alone in the darkness, not even for a moment. If I was left alone, I might never get the courage to go into the water, and then what would I do? Sit in the blackness alone till Doomsday, or make my way back along the miles of tunnel alone, blind and freezing and terrified? Oh, no. I might as well drown now as die of fear later.

I looked over my shoulder, locating Rory by the tiny silver dots of his eyes. The sight of it was eerie but reassuring. 'Okay,' I said.

'Hannah,' he said.

'What?' I was snappy with nerves.

I felt his fingertips graze my arm, then his hand closed around it. Rory pulled me carefully against him in the darkness, and he took an involuntary breath.

'What?' I said again, a lot less snappily.

In the silence I found his tangled grubby hair with my fingers, then ran my hands down across his ears and found his cheekbones. His face felt thinner. I hadn't noticed that, just looking at him in the daylight, but I could feel the difference in the darkness. It felt like an older face. Less like a boy, more like a man.

His hand slipped behind my neck and he laced his fingers through my roughly chopped hair. I was glad Eili had cut it, since there was less of it to be a greasy mess: maybe pitch darkness had its advantages. We were both filthy and sweaty and pretty smelly but he tasted the same, I decided, finding his mouth first with my fingers and then with my own mouth. What would be nice now would be just to melt into him, climb inside his head and body altogether and be protected until Seth came back with the cavalry.

It wasn't going to happen. I could feel the solid thump of his heart against my ribcage and the echoing banging of my own.

No, *really*, we couldn't just stand here. Nice as it would be.

Sighing, I ran my hands down his chest and stomach and shoved him reluctantly away. The manoeuvre provoked a satisfying squeak.

'What?' I said it yet again, clearing my own throat. Heat rushed into my skin.

'Nothing. That's fine.' His lower lip grazed my upper lip

in the darkness, and our noses bumped briefly. 'Just, I feel better now.'

That's nice, I thought, because I think I'm going to have a frigging heart attack, but okay, so long as you feel better…

Rory gave a nervous laugh, and I realised he'd heard me. If I could have seen his shin I might have kicked it. Instead, tentatively, I felt my way forward, one hand on the damp stone wall to make sure I was going in the right direction. For a moment I thought I'd got it wrong anyway, that I'd turned a hundred and eighty degrees and had my hand on the wrong wall, but just as I felt the stirrings of panic, the ground dipped beneath my feet. Shortening my steps, I felt my feet touch water. I walked on till I was ankle deep, and took a shocked breath.

Oh. *Oh.* The cold clamped around my ankles as if it was trying to cut off my feet. I considered the imminent prospect of immersing my entire body in it, and I whimpered.

'What is it?' hissed Rory.

'Cold. I'll just warn you.' I started to breathe the way I'd heard Seth do it, only I couldn't. The stale air shuddered in and out of my lungs as I waded deeper, my fingertips dragging the wall and then the ceiling as it sloped down to meet me. My next step took me up to my thighs, the next to my waist, and I knew if the slope was constant the next would take me out of my depth.

I knew if I waited and thought about it any more I wasn't going to do this. I took a final scared gasp and submerged.

I nearly pushed myself straight back out. The icy water tightened around my chest like steel bands, already trying to force the air out of me. A couple of bubbles escaped from my lips and I doubled over and kicked down, forcing myself head first into the flooded tunnel. My scalp scraped the rock ceiling and I pushed myself pointlessly down and away from it. For a moment I flailed there, unable to move, then my frozen brain remembered what Seth had said. *Pull yourself along against the wall.* I reached out numb fingertips and began to lever myself along, forgetting about kicking.

I was aware that the passage was narrowing, aware that when I had first reached for the wall I could barely touch it with both hands. Now my elbows had to stay awkwardly bent; I couldn't stretch my arms at all.

A terrible idea struck me. I might bump into Seth's body, stuck like a cork in an impossibly narrow bottleneck. There might have been a rockfall. Something could have got stuck in the tunnel ages ago and died: an animal, a fish, a *monster*... Anything could have happened. I blinked hard, but the view didn't change.

Another couple of bubbles leaked out with my tiny cry of panic. I began to flail my limbs, kicking violently, but I only kicked solid rock, painfully hard.

Behind me I was vaguely aware of Rory in the tunnel, but I couldn't See him clearly for the panic in my head, my skull and brain tight and shrunken with cold. It occurred to me that if I stopped swimming Rory would die too, and that Seth would kill me, but that didn't make a lot of sense.

My lungs protested desperately, squeezed by a giant fist. They didn't want the air inside them that was about to make them explode. They wanted a fresh lungful, they wanted me to breathe out and then breathe in again. I blew out a longer stream of bubbles, felt them tickle my face, and they were coming out of my nose now too. In a way it was bliss. Any second now I'd breathe out and then I could suck in a whole lungful of...

Fingers closed hard around my wrist and I was tugged forward through the blackness. A last few agonising seconds, and then I was yanked clear of the water, dumped on dry land, and I hauled in a lungful of stale air with a high-pitched wheeze.

It tasted so good. Best air I'd ever breathed. Seth let go of me but before he had time to plunge back into the water the surface of it broke, and another body erupted and tumbled forward onto dry land.

'You two took your time,' said Seth, relief in his voice. 'What was the last thing I told you, Hannah?'

'D-d-don't panic,' I gritted through chattering teeth.

'Whoa, yes,' came Rory's voice. He was panting. 'Glad I gave you a head start, there, Hannah. I was nearly bumping into your heels at one point.'

'Thanks a million.' I was shivering violently and I didn't need my nose rubbed in my panic. I didn't need the humiliation, not when I was already freezing to death.

'No, you're not,' said Seth kindly, rubbing my arms.

'I am.' My teeth chattered. 'Stop looking in–'

I'd been about to say *Stop looking in my head*, but I realised in time it would be a pretty tactless thing to say when he couldn't look in Rory's. Glancing up, I saw the pinprick lights of his eyes, and instead I thought, ~ *Sorry*.

'It's okay,' he said.

'Dad,' said Rory. 'The Veil starts to thicken here. We're getting nearer the dun.'

'Okay.' Seth breathed hard. 'Tear it, Laochan. Blocks up.'

It was reassuring to know we were getting somewhere. The end was, if not in sight, then at least within reach, and being back on the dangerous side gave all of us a renewed sense of urgency. Anyway, it was better to be moving. Our clothes were soaking now and putting on speed kept away the worst of the biting cold.

I tried to walk too fast, almost breaking into a jog in an effort to get warm, and several times I stumbled and fell. It was happening to the others too, though, and at one point even Seth sprawled on his face with a grunt of pain. When I fumbled to grab him and help him stagger to his feet, I felt the shuddering tremors of cold going through his body. He'd lost a lot of blood, of course, and he couldn't run forever on adrenalin and bloody-mindedness.

'Are you okay?' It felt funny having to ask him out loud, and I realised I was growing used to having my mind read. I almost resented the effort of speaking, and I did not like the echo my voice made in the cavern.

'Finn's going to kill me when she sees the state of you,' I added as Seth paused to catch his breath and recover his balance.

'Don't worry.' Seth's voice shivered through gritted teeth. 'She won't be looking too great herself.' Shaking himself audibly, he walked on.

That's probably true, I thought, guilty at forgetting. I was still picturing what must have happened between Finn and Eili and the Wolf, my imagination going into skidding overdrive in the dark, when I collided with Seth. He'd come to an abrupt halt. Rory in turn banged into me. His hand fumbled for mine in the darkness, and squeezed it reassuringly.

'This is it,' came Seth's voice. 'Now just hang on.'

No, I thought, *I'm not hanging on any more.* Elbowing the obstruction that was Seth out of the way, I barged forward. Some instinct made me turn my face aside at the last instant, or I'd have broken my nose. It was my cheek that connected with solid stone, and my knuckles, and one knee. I knew I'd drawn blood in all those places but I no longer cared. All I cared about was finding the gap.

There wasn't one. My fingers scratched at the blank stone, feeling above my head and out to the side and down to where the wall met the floor, but there wasn't so much as a crack.

'IT'S BLOCKED!' I screamed.

'Shut up,' said Seth quietly. 'I said hang on.' His finger-tips knocked into my shoulder, then travelled down my arm till they found the hand Rory wasn't holding, and wound tightly into my fingers. 'Don't lose it, Hannah,' he said. 'Not now. Rory?'

'I'm here, Dad.'

It suddenly occurred to me why this blackness was nothing to them. It didn't panic them because it was all external darkness, and the darkness inside was a lot worse. This was what it was like in their minds. Blackness, blindness, where there should have been constant light and an unbreakable connection. It seemed such an unspeakably evil thing to have done to them. I felt an awful pity, and anger. I squeezed Seth's fingers with one hand and Rory's with the other.

'Is there a way through?' I asked more calmly.

'There was thirty years ago.' Seth released my hand.

'Oh.' I swore.

'Language,' said Seth absently, but he was concentrating too hard on something to say any more. 'Got it,' he whispered at last, just as I was beginning to think we would at least be united in our unpleasant deaths.

'Got what?' I asked sceptically.

His eyelight gleamed. 'Keep blocking. Both of you. Rory, you're sure the hole in the Veil will stay open?'

'Oh, yes.' Rory's eyes sparked in the darkness. 'Long enough, anyway.'

Seth began to laugh. 'You still know what I'm thinking, Laochan. Despite Kate. Now, Hannah.'

'What?'

'You want out of this tunnel? Just you walk with me.'

THE DUN

Sulaire MacTorc was getting lonely in his job. On a normal day there were at least three cooks working at any one time. He liked his work and he liked the company, but these were not normal times. Not only was there no-one spare to work with, they all had to take their turn on the ramparts, fighting back the unremitting assaults. One of the cooks was already dead with a dagger in his throat. It wasn't reassuring. It was bloody sad, since he'd been a good friend, but they'd all be joining him soon.

At least there was plenty of food. Bit unusual, that, for a siege, but the full-mortal Cuilean had taken the decision to let them eat well. That was nice, but everyone knew what it meant in reality. It meant they weren't going to last long enough to starve.

He was a good man, Cuilean, humane and brave, and at least he was trying to keep their spirits high. Dolefully Sulaire stared at the side of bacon he was to turn into breakfast for the next shift. Plenty eggs, too. On the whole he'd rather be using his ingenuity with starvation rations, if it meant they had a cat's chance in hell, but they didn't. Cuilean knew it, the other captains knew it, they all knew it. They were going to die, that much was obvious, and anyone left alive beyond the battle was going to die horribly when Kate broke through, but it was nice to eat well in the meantime. Breakfast was unlikely to make things brighter, but he'd get on with it anyway. It wasn't just his job, it was his calling.

Sulaire wondered what had happened to Murlainn and his gorgeous wee boy. Well, not wee any more; it was just that it seemed like yesterday when Rory Bhan had been hanging around the kitchens sweet-talking Sulaire into giving him chocolate. Sulaire hoped they were okay, though it seemed unlikely. They were well out of this, anyway. He hoped they hadn't come to the same end as Murlainn's brother, the man Sulaire had worshipped, the man he would have happily died for and over whose death he had wept for days. He hoped they hadn't come to the same end as his father Torc, who had died with Cù Chaorach, and whose death had quite simply broken his heart.

He had just reached for a boning knife when he heard a low grinding sound, and he froze.

This was it, was it? His time had finally come.

They were under strict orders from the full-mortal Cuilean to block fully all the time, no exceptions. Kate NicNiven's abilities had taken a quantum leap over the last decade, he'd told them, sucking the strength out of defeated fighters like the witch she was. And Eili MacNeil had had Kate in her head for months without knowing it; Kate's telepathy was powerful and extreme and the witch was more than willing to misuse it. They didn't know all she was capable of but *don't let her in your head.*

It terrified Sulaire, and he had obeyed Cuilean every minute of every day, but for the first time the young cook was seriously tempted to drop his block. He wanted to know what was behind him – probably an entire division of Kate's troops breaking in through a wall – and he'd rather know without having to look. All the same, he was too afraid of Cuilean's reaction to disobey siege orders.

Instead he clenched his teeth to stop them chattering, and reached for a second knife. And then, slowly, he turned.

Oh. My. Dear. Gods, thought Sulaire.

Clearly it was some trick of Kate's. How else would the larder shelving be grinding slowly out from the wall? For a moment Sulaire shut his eyes, wondering why his father had backed the wrong horse at such clearly impossible odds. Then he remembered how much Torc had hated Kate and her gratuitous cruelty, and he opened his eyes again and set his jaw. Since there was no question he was going to die, there was no point dying like a coward.

The black gap opened wider, and Sulaire felt a breath of cold dank air that made him shudder. He gripped his knives tighter, one in each hand. He had to leave himself enough time to drop his block and alert the dun. Maybe it was time to do it.

'*Don't drop your block.*'

The gasping man who shoved through the gap didn't seem to be armed, was Sulaire's first thought. His second was that the man was temporarily blinded, his arm over his eyes with the shock of the light, which gave him a moment's breathing space to think about this.

Sulaire swallowed hard and raised the knives threateningly. If they could cut pig they could cut person, and Sulaire was no slouch at cutting pig. The intruder seemed to know that, because as he lowered his arm, his watering eyes creased narrow, he stood very still. Blinking furiously, he extended his palms, placating.

Sulaire snarled. He could be up to nothing good, this bloody bearded man with the ripped t-shirt and jeans, half his face bruised purple, the other half hacked with slashes; his eye blackened and a hideous barely-healed scar running from his temple to his jaw. Patches of blood had dried on his face and matted his hair into dreadlocks, despite the fact that he and his clothes were soaking wet. Whatever had soaked his t-shirt certainly hadn't been enough to wash out the great stain of Sithe lifeblood on it. Sulaire's lip twisted in hatred and he drew back his knives to disembowel the assassin.

'Sulaire!' the assassin hissed, just catching his right hand as it slashed down. 'Don't you dare!' He blinked desperately, eyes streaming, his fingers locked round Sulaire's wrist, and the muscles of both their arms trembled with the strain. 'I bought you those knives in the otherworld and they cost me a *fortune.*'

Flummoxed, Sulaire stared at the bloody apparition. And then another figure pushed between the man and the black gaping hole.

'Rory Bhan? *Laochan?*' Sulaire stared at the boy, and then at the redhead who appeared behind him. Rory and the girl were blinking too but they'd had longer to get used to the light, and they looked more like human beings anyway. In disbelief Sulaire looked back at the assassin.

'*Murlainn!* Oh, my god!'

'"Oh, my Captain" will do fine,' said Seth.

The knives clattered to the stone floor and Sulaire flung himself forward to hug Seth. 'Oh, Murlainn, I'm sorry. I didn't recognise – I'm sorry. Where'd you – how did you–'

'Later. Oh, please, Sulaire, later. Just get me Jed. I need to see Cuilean right now.' An arm round his shoulder, Seth drew him to the door between the kitchens and the great hall and shoved the door open. 'But, laddie, *do not drop your block.*'

Sulaire turned to run, but he was too late, because Jed

was already coming into the hall with five of the other captains. He was talking intently to them and for a moment he didn't look up, but Rory gasped at the sight of him. He was hacked and bloody and thin, and he had days of beard growth, but Rory didn't care. He was alive, still alive, and Rory realised in that instant how afraid he had been that he wouldn't be.

At the sound of his gasp Jed's head jerked up, and then he was running straight for them, not bothering to swerve round tables and chairs. He simply leaped them, knocking plates and cups flying as he ran the length of the hall and grabbed Rory into his arms.

'Rory,' he mumbled into his filthy blond hair. Jed's t-shirt was as ripped as Seth's and Rory could see the ugly slash a sword had made across his ribcage, and the gouge of an arrow that had narrowly missed its aim. Neither had been healed, not even roughly, and black blood crusted them. There was pus in the arrow wound, Rory noticed with alarm, and Jed winced as Rory brushed it by mistake. Rory pulled away and looked up at his brother in alarm.

Jed turned to Seth before Rory could ask any awkward questions, and they clasped each other in a ferocious hug.

'Seth. Oh, brother. I thought you were dead.'

'In your dreams.' Seth's voice was choked.

'Seth. *Rory.*' Tears made pale thin channels through the blood and dirt on Jed's bearded face. He let go of Seth to hug Rory again, then pushed him away, holding him and staring at him. 'You've grown, bruv. In a fortnight.' He bit his lip. 'Happy birthday.'

'What?' Rory's eyes widened.

'You turned fifteen while you were gone.' Jed ruffled his hair. 'Bloody Sithe never remember, do they? But I do.'

Rory grinned. 'What day?'

Jed shut one eye and counted. 'Wednesday.'

Rory glanced at Hannah, flushing slightly. Grinning back, she mouthed *Happy Birthday*.

Jed watched them both, frowning. When he stepped back his face was thoughtful and a little sad. Shaking himself, he turned back to Seth. 'So how did you... where...'

'Later.' Seth gripped his arms and gazed at him, grinning. The other captains were around them now, hugging them and slapping their backs, yelling with delight, and Hannah found herself kissed by four burly men, and by the blonde woman with the long woven hair she'd first seen doing target practice from a horse in the arena. That had been just after she arrived. A lifetime ago.

The blonde woman buried her face in Seth's neck and wouldn't let go, partly because tears were leaking helplessly from her eyes and she was trying to hide it. He was hugging her so hard it looked as if they might fuse. When she finally pulled away she hit him, feebly, on the shoulder, and then again. And then, ignoring his wince, again.

'You bastard. I thought you were *dead*.'

'I love you too, Orach.' He twisted her golden braid round one hand and reeled her back in to kiss her forehead. 'Please stop hitting me.'

As they wriggled awkwardly apart, someone thrust a sheathed sword into Seth's hand. He sighed with delight as he drew it from its scabbard and examined the blade. Then he blinked back at Jed. 'Did you say a *fortnight*?'

'Aye, the warp couldn't have worked better for her. I reckon if she's held back, she's only been waiting for her pal Alasdair. Doesn't want him to miss the fun.' Jed's face darkened, and the jubilant mood was snuffed out. He looked away, as if it pained him to look into Seth's eyes. 'They'll be through in a few hours, Murlainn. Twelve at the most.'

'Alasdair won't be joining in the fun.' Seth spat. 'And now?'

'Right now, she's withdrawn. I reckon she's gathering her clann for a last assault. Probably doing her hair for the occasion.'

Seth muffled a snort. 'And our clann?'

'They've picked us off with arrows, they've made God knows how many assaults. Lost a lot of their own – we've made it expensive for them – but there's so many of them. So many, and they have plenty healers. Ours can't keep up.' Jed looked desolate. 'We miss Eili.'

'Sionnach?' asked Seth, rather as if he didn't want to know the answer.

'Orach, you saw him last,' said Jed.

'Sionnach's doing his best to get killed,' said Orach. 'But he's taking so many of them with him, he hasn't quite managed it yet.'

'I'll get to work, then,' muttered Hannah.

Rory put an arm round her and returned their disbelieving stares with a touch of aggression. 'She's a healer,' he said.

Seth kissed the top of her head, and pushed her towards the captains. 'Yes, she is, and a good one. Take her to Grian.'

'But this is better news!' Orach beamed and put a slender arm round Hannah's shoulder and pushed her hurriedly towards the door. 'Come on, strawberry-blondie.'

'I like you,' said Hannah, and they were gone.

'Was that all it would have taken?' Seth shook his head in bewilderment. 'I wish I'd never called her Ginger. Right, keep everybody blocking. Kate mustn't know I'm here. Get everybody to the hall as soon as you can. Leave as few as you can defending the walls, and get fires set round the whole place. Where's Iolaire?'

'On the wall above the gate, last time I saw him.' Jed's voice was empty and exhausted. 'Though that was six hours ago.'

'And, Jed?' Seth hesitated. 'Burn the dead.' As Jed and the captains stared at him in shock, he added quietly: 'Make pyres and burn them. Did you get the patrol back?'

'Only just. We concentrated on getting the living in first, so we only just had enough time to get Eorna's patrol.' Jed smiled without mirth. 'Just as well we did. Kate would not have let us retrieve the bodies. It isn't like that any more, Murlainn. No civilities.'

'Thought not. Right, pile them all in the lanes with the livestock. Slaughter any cattle that are left, and use the furniture for kindling. If there's any god and he's got a shred of humanity he might forgive me, but I won't let Kate desecrate their bodies. Sulaire? Check all the remaining supplies. Divide it up and destroy what we can't carry. Uiseag, get together all the ropes and torches you can find. I'll be with you to help soon but...'

'Understood,' murmured Jed. 'Go on, go to her.' He held out the key to Seth's rooms and lifted an eyebrow dryly. 'She won't speak well of me, Seth. She was unconscious for three days and wanted to fight an hour after she woke up. I had to lock her in.'

Seth shook his head, laughing, and took the key. Then he was gone, taking the stone stairs three at a time.

SETH

The key would barely turn, his hand shook so badly. When he swung open the door, Finn was sitting on a long low bench beneath the window, hugging her knees and staring down at the courtyard. She looked scarily thin. Her left hand hung down, scratching the throat of the black wolf that lay on the floor beside the bench. Branndair's closed eyelids twitched in a half-dream.

Seth tried to say something, but his voice stuck in his throat. Branndair lifted his head, sat up and made a tortured little growling sound, but he didn't move from Finn's side.

Finn's hand froze in his fur and she turned her head very slowly. Her eyes were remote, dull with the gleam of old pain, but as they fixed on Seth's face, they opened very wide.

She screamed.

He didn't know what he'd expected, but it wasn't this. Stunned, he reached out a hand, but Finn backed harder against the wall, trembling. She put her fists to her eyes and ground them into the sockets.

'*Get away from me!*' she yelled. 'I DON'T SEE YOU. *GET AWAY FROM ME!*'

He started towards her, got halfway across the room and came to a halt again. Gods, had she gone mad? She wrapped her arms over her face, blocking her vision and pulling her head tight to her chest. 'Not again, not again,' she sobbed. '*I don't see you.*'

And then he realised what was wrong. 'Finn,' he said softly. 'Finn, it's me.'

She wasn't listening, refused to hear. Branndair wasn't helping; he only lifted his black head and gazed at Seth with extreme reproach. That he didn't need. For the first time in his life Seth lost his temper with his own wolf.

'*You* know it's me!' he yelled. 'You might say hello, you hairy bad-tempered bastard!'

Branndair drew his lips scornfully back from his teeth as Finn's breath stopped and she glanced up between splayed fingers. The wolf backed closer to Finn and gave a small cross growl.

'All *right!*' Seth shouted. 'You can *LEAVE HER SIDE NOW!*'

The wolf bounded for him, leaping up and knocking him like a blade of grass to the floor. For long seconds Seth was incapable of coherent speech while Branndair kissed his face. Then somebody was shoving the wolf aside and doing the same as the wolf, only at least she didn't lick, and her breath was a lot nicer.

Finn drew away and knelt over him, grabbing his t-shirt. 'You just stood there!' she screamed. 'You didn't say anything! *I thought you were a fetch.*'

'I'm sorry, Finn, sorry. I forgot all about that.' Seth winced as she shook him, and she released him more gently, staring down in shock.

'And you look like hell,' she whispered. 'Did you get hit by a truck?'

He shut one eye. 'In a manner of speaking. Sort of a human truck. You should have seen me before the blood washed off in the tunnel.'

'Not all of it, I can tell you.' She looked him up and down. 'I just hate to think.'

'I'm fine. Really I am. Hey, you should see the other

guy!' At her scowl he sobered again. 'Honestly, Finn, I'm sorry. I suppose I do look a bit, um... half-dead. I just didn't think.'

'It's okay, it's okay. I panicked.' She kissed him fanatically. 'But don't you dare be rude to that wolf.'

'You've changed your tune.' He grinned up at her.

'Takes one to know one, anyway. Hairy bad-tempered bastards.' She stroked the rough black stubble of his beard.

'I'll go and shave right now,' he said.

'No, you won't. Don't move. Stay there.'

'Like I have an option?' He cocked an eyebrow. 'How long for?'

Finn buried her face in his neck. 'Three days ought to do it. A week. No, two.'

His face softened as his arms went round her. 'We don't have that kind of time, Finn. It's over, we've lost.'

'I knew it!' she yelled, jerking back. 'If that swine Jed had... Seth, you don't know what he's been like, he...'

'Jed has my eternal gratitude for locking you up, you heidbanger.' He eyed her crossly. 'And he carried you back to this dun. How many did he have to fight to do it?'

She averted her eyes, ashamed. 'All right. I know. I'm sorry.'

Seth wriggled up to a sitting position and faced her. ''Scuse me.' He opened her shirt gently and drew it aside to stare at the brutal scar just above her heart, then trailed a fingertip across it. 'That looks better.' Tugging her shirt carefully down her shoulder, he turned her with a very light touch. 'The exit wound too. Did Grian have a go at those?'

'Uh-huh.' Finn made a wry face. 'I didn't think there was a healer rougher than Eili, bless him.'

'Hurt, did it? Good.' Seth's voice cracked slightly. 'That'll teach you to be more careful.'

'Poor Grian. He hasn't slept more than a few minutes at a time for a week.' She lifted his t-shirt where the blood-stain was and gasped. 'What the *hell* happened to you?'

'I'll tell you later. Right now we're getting out of here. All of us.' He stood up and drew her to her feet, then glanced up and went to the window. Smoke was rising from the courtyard in a black column, fires were leaping up around the ramparts and in a great semicircle around the gate. For a moment, he shut his eyes.

'Look, Finn. Our dead are giving us some breathing space. Let's not waste it.'

RORY

I sat on one of the huge oak tables, counting the clann as they stumbled through the hole in the kitchen wall. I did not like the total I'd reached, and there were very few of them left waiting their turn in the hall with their hastily gathered belongings. Even accounting for the men and women left on the ramparts, there were an awful lot missing. The missing, I supposed, were the ones piled in the great pyres that burned in every alleyway but one. The remaining pyre in that alleyway would be torched by Seth and Jed and the last guards as they withdrew. Even then I knew my father had doubts about the time they would buy.

My father's dun was burning. I wondered what Kate would be thinking right now. Probably that Seth's people had despaired over the loss of their Captain and his son, that they had grown sick of the stench of smoke and death that hung over the place, that they had decided to kill themselves fast and cleanly rather than wait for Kate and her filthy imagination to do it.

Finn said Kate's greatest weakness was her vanity. All the same, how long would it take her to realise that mass suicide was not what the clann had in mind? Finn knew Kate, she'd been with her for a while, but I didn't want to press Finn for any more answers. She was sitting on the floor at the other side of the hall with her head in her hands, and she hadn't spoken since Seth had gone out into the dun. He hadn't let her follow; indeed he'd threatened to lock her up again if the notion so much as crossed her mind.

He'd gone himself, though, despite his own wounds, and despite all Finn's reasonable, logical, desperate begging. He didn't want Kate to know he was there, but so what? From even a short distance he was unrecognisable, and any enemy who got too close did not live long enough to get over their shock and tell Kate.

Hannah limped into the hall in an exhausted daze, Grian gripping her arm. She was bloodied up to the elbows.

'Here, Rory,' he called. 'Take your friend. She's earned the right to go now, and then some.'

'I want to stay a bit longer,' she said dully.

'You're not capable any more,' Grian said as I clasped her hand in mine. 'There's nothing more to do anyway. Go.'

She edged so close to me as we stared round the hall together, I put my arm around her shoulder. 'Was it awful?' I said.

'Yes,' she said shortly. She gulped hard. 'Rory? There's a few won't get through the flood in the tunnel. They just won't make it.' She hesitated, and slight hysteria crept into her voice. 'I think that's why Grian sent me away.'

I put my other arm round her too. 'They're not going to want to wait for Kate,' I mumbled. 'That's the thing.'

She didn't say any more, just stood and stared with me as the hall emptied. Distantly there were shouts, screams and the renewed crackle of flames. A deafening bang and short explosions signalled one of the wind turbines being dragged over.

The pulse of my blood was a racing, powerful drumbeat. Hannah looked at me; I felt hers beat the same rhythm through her skin. And then I realised it wasn't us; it was the sound of real drums, and a rising sinister howling.

'She's coming,' I said.

Finn's head jerked up and we followed her gaze as the last defenders raced into the hall. Seth was last in, fresh blood on his sword, and he stood at the door counting heads, barking questions at Jed and the bloody, almost unrecognisable Iolaire. When he was satisfied with their answers and with his own head count, his eyes closed. I knew he was scanning the whole dun, and when he was finished he looked up and said, 'Rory?'

'Dad.'

'Then we're all here.' He and Jed and Iolaire swung the doors shut and heaved the barricade into place. Half-blinded with blood, Iolaire staggered back, close to collapse, and Jed caught his arm. Jed flinched as Iolaire's elbow brushed his arrow wound, and I frowned, but before I could say a word, Jed had turned to give me a ferocious warning glare. I took a step back and shut my mouth.

Seth was still for a fleeting, tantalising moment more. Distantly, as someone Saw his mind, a monstrous screech of female rage rose above the turmoil, silencing even the drums and the war howls.

'We have a few minutes,' said my father with a note of satisfaction. 'Get going.'

'She'll know where we are.' There was panic in Hannah's voice. 'She'll know where we've gone and she'll come after us.'

'She'll work it out, but it'll take her a while to find the tunnel. And when Rory's sealed the Veil she can't follow. She needs a watergate, like everybody else. Like everyone but Rory.' Seth grinned at me.

One man pushed forward through the remaining clann. 'I'll stay, Murlainn. It'll give you a little extra time to get to the gap in the Veil.' As Seth opened his mouth to argue, the man lifted his hand to his long brown hair and pushed it back from his temples and forehead, and whatever Seth had been going to say remained in his throat. Instead he stepped forward and embraced him tightly.

'Righil.' He stepped back. 'Don't let her take you.'

'No way.' Righil laughed unsteadily and caressed the handle of his dirk.

'*I'm staying too.*'

Another figure shoved past me to stand by Righil, and my breath stopped in my throat. Cadaverous where the others were thin, his body was bloodied and bruised and his eyes were sunk in deep dark hollows in his skull. His once-immaculate goatee had grown into a ragged dirty beard, but the hair on his head had been hacked off, leaving grotesque half-healed wounds in his scalp.

Seth stared at him. 'I see no grey on you, Sionnach.'

Hannah gave a shocked cry, then tugged free of me and ran to Sionnach. 'YOU'RE NOT STAYING!' she yelled in his face.

Just for an instant, shock thawed the blank freezing pain in his face, and something sparked in his brown eyes. Hannah seized her moment. Grabbing him by one bloody hand, she hauled him into the tunnel mouth. He cast one stunned look back at Seth, and then he was gone.

Righil turned to face the barricaded door, unsheathing his sword as the screams of the frustrated attackers drew closer and something heavy crashed against the door. He glanced back over his shoulder as if unable to believe we were still standing there. '*Go!*' he yelled. 'Hurry!'

I darted into the tunnel as my father grabbed the snarling Branndair by the scruff of the neck and yanked him in too. Lifting the last flashlight Seth took Finn's hand, but Finn was looking up at him in shock as he pulled her after him. 'Righil... why...'

'Didn't you see?' Seth wasn't looking at her as he hauled on a lever and shoved on the door with his shoulder. Beside him Finn and I shoved too, and it began to grind into place. 'Grey hairs. Righil only has a few weeks left. He'd rather spend them now than run and rot in exile.'

'A few *weeks?*' Enough weak light still filtered in from the kitchens for me to see that Finn had gone pale.

My father looked hard at Finn as the door swung into place and they were shrouded in darkness. His voice quietened, but I heard the edge to his murmur. 'I warned you, Caorann.'

Seth switched on the flashlight, making our faces ghostly, and played the light across the blank stone, hesitating as if suddenly reluctant to leave. We could hear no sound beyond it, but I suspected that was because of the thickness of the stone, not because the noise had stopped. Then we turned and ran. It was easier with light.

It didn't seem so far this time, but neither Seth nor Finn were in good shape and they were gasping and panting in the cold stale air when they came to a halt. I was anxious about them both. Distantly there was a scraping of stone on stone, ferocious vengeful shouts, footsteps breaking into a run and swiftly joined by many more.

Then I was concentrating on the Veil again, feeling in my bones the moment when we stepped through the gaping hole. In Seth's torch beam still water glinted, a tiny tremor left on its surface from the last of our people to pass through the flood. I felt for the edge of the ripped Veil, but as my fingers closed on something we all hesitated, Branndair growling deep in his throat.

The shouts had stopped, but the voiceless pack sounded louder now, deadlier, the pelting footsteps magnified by the tunnel and far closer already. Finn took a scared breath and held it in the echoing chamber, and we waited for what seemed an age too long.

Seth said desperately, 'I can't drop my block again, Finn. Righil? I need to know.'

A brief pause, and 'He's dead,' she said. She was weeping but her voice was clear and steady. 'Let's go. Let's *go*.'

My father turned to me. 'Rory,' he said, stepping back. 'Close the Veil.'

EXILE

'Dad,' said Rory dangerously. 'Dad, where did you get the boat?'

Seth didn't answer, too busy frowning at the chart in front of him and biting his nails, looking from the chart to the sea and back with unnerving frequency.

Rory tried again. 'Dad, did you steal this boat?'

Seth affected a look of wounded shock. 'We do not *steal*, Rory. We borrow. *Rent*. The owner will get it back, and there'll be money in the cabin, and if he's the superstitious type his grandchildren will be bored sick hearing about the night his boat was borrowed by the Little People. We're doing him a favour.' He winked. One hand on the wheel, he risked a glance up at a fading moon streaked with cloud. 'It's almost morning.'

It had taken a good many trips across the sea loch and back to get everyone to the other side, and Rory was glad this was the last time. Must have been a while since Seth sailed a boat anywhere but into the ocean off the dun, and anywhere at all on this side of the Veil. Rory hadn't told Seth he was reading the sea chart upside down, in case it was too much of a blow to his father's pride, but it didn't seem to have made a disastrous difference. The kyle was deep and the tide was racing, but the engine was strong and they had hit no hidden shoals, and Seth was well used to the route by now.

Hannah knelt at the stern, leaning over to watch the seals. She had parked herself there to be next to Sionnach. His eyes were empty and dazed as he stared into the middle distance, but Hannah was keeping up a stream of inane chatter in his ear and he occasionally glanced at her in a kind of bewildered shock.

'Jed,' said Seth. 'Want to take over?'

Jed's skin had a sick greenish tinge, but he sounded cheerful enough. 'I've never driven a boat with an engine.'

'There's a coincidence.' Seth grinned, flexing his left hand. Wincing, he glanced down at it in surprise, and frowned.

'Now you tell me.' Jed raised his eyes skywards and took the wheel as Seth sat down beside Rory and stretched his arms. A woman close by was weeping over her sheathed sword as she wrapped it and her dead lover's weapon in the same cloth. On the starboard side, someone quietly played on a whistle. Otherwise there was silence as almost all the Sithe on board stared back in the direction of their lost home.

'Hey, Dad.' Rory reached for his hand. 'Are you okay?'

'I'm fine,' growled Seth, drawing his other hand down over his face. 'But tell Carraig if he doesn't quit playing *Farewell to Fiunary* I'll stab him with his own tin whistle.'

Seth rested his arm across his eyes as he leaned back. Rory glanced back at Hannah, still gazing at the bobbing heads of the seals and talking incessantly to Sionnach.

'Rory,' said Seth after a moment. 'You can't have her.'

Rory tugged his hand out of Seth's, stiffening. 'What d'you mean, *can't?*'

'I mean you mustn't. Rory. If all you wanted was each other, it'd be fine.' Seth took his arm away from his eyes, but he went on staring at the sky. 'But she'll get broody, a gràidh. She'll want kids, and so will you. All of us do, we're never indifferent. It's too difficult for us to have them.'

'So why can't we?' Rory's voice was sullen.

'Ach, Rory, there's so much I've never told you. I thought I had all the time in the world, and I didn't. Look, Hannah's your cousin. You have the same blood and you can't mix it. The gene pool's shallow enough, Laochan.'

'Oh. That's what she talked about.' Rory paused. 'And that's why we can't have kids?'

'Same as I told you. Not can't. Mustn't. Why d'you think we keep track of our families? Why do you learn your birth name to four generations, Rory MacSeth MacGregor MacLorcan MacLuthais?'

Rory didn't smile. 'You're related to Finn, Dad.'

'No, Rory. Conal was, but I'm not. He and I had different mothers. And Reultan wasn't Griogair's.'

'Right.' Rory stood up. 'Right, Dad. I'll bear all that in mind.' He walked back to the stern of the boat, knelt down next to Hannah and put his arm ostentatiously round her shoulders.

Seth watched him for a moment, then got up and went to Finn. She was propped against the cabin bulkhead, staring back at the grey dawn-lit headland they'd left for the last time. Branndair lay at her feet, still not speaking to Seth after the indignity of having a bag tied over his head and being dragged with a rope through the flooded section of tunnel. Seth propped himself beside Finn, their shoulders touching.

He reeked of blood and smoke and sweat and death, but then so did she.

'You stink,' she said fondly.

'You too. I love you.' As he turned and kissed her, he caught sight of his reflection in the cabin window. 'Gods,' he said softly. 'Sure you still fancy me?'

425

She took his face in her hands and kissed the hideous gash on it. 'I love you more than my life. I'm going to look after you. It'll be all right, you'll see.' She kissed the cut on his cheekbone, the one on the bridge of his nose, the ugly swelling on his jaw, his half-shut eye that drooped slightly because of the cut nerves. 'You're lovely. Always will be. Can't help yourself, gorgeous.' Her lips moved to the next wound, and the next bruise.

'I failed, Finn.'

She kissed the corner of his eye. 'You got Rory back. You came back to us and saved us. Sh! As many as you could, as many as anyone could. *Anyone,*' she repeated fiercely. 'How's that failing?'

'I'm so sorry, Finn. For what happened to you.'

'You weren't to know.' She hesitated. 'Conal wouldn't have done anything different. He'd be proud of you. Okay?'

Gratefully he pressed his face into her hair and shut his eyes.

'Seth, you saved Hannah. I know you don't want to hear this, but you paid for Conal.'

He went very still, but she slipped her fingers beneath his t-shirt, running her fingertips along the ridges and furrows of the gouged scars on his back. 'See all this?' she whispered. 'That's not what made up for it.' Her touch strayed to the old crossbow marks, finally healed and hard and insensitive, but his skin shivered anyway. 'These didn't either. None of that made up for Conal. Hannah did. You saved his child. That's *it*, understand? That's the end of it, Seth.'

Because, damn it, all the pain in the world couldn't pay for Conal, but Seth had put his life up as a forfeit. Not to satisfy his clann's honour, she thought bitterly, and not to feed Eili's vengeance, but just to save a girl he barely knew.

He'd made the sacrifice that mattered and it was about life and love, not pain and death.

Tentatively Seth opened his mind and for the first time since his return to the dun, slipped his consciousness inside hers. He had never been so relieved in his life when he felt the connection spark. His fingers found hers and held them fiercely.

'Oh. Kate has nothing of yours, Finn. She can't split us. Thank the gods.'

'She expected me to be dead by now.' She eyed him askance. 'And quit that. You don't believe in gods.'

'Oh, aye, that's right. Neither I do.' Eyes still shut, he breathed the scent of her hair, then turned to look back at the paling sea. 'Pity, really. 'Cause it'd be nice if Eili found Conal.'

Finn stared straight ahead. 'Yes. Well. I mean, she did. I think… I know she did.'

He pulled her round to face him. Her black hair was disordered, breezing across her face, and he pushed a strand of it out of her eye. He said nothing, only looked.

Finn put the pad of her forefinger against the hollow of his throat, feeling his pulse in her fingerbones running a little faster. She was afraid to raise her eyes to his because she was afraid of what she was thinking of saying. She was afraid he'd laugh, or be angry, or worse, be hurt.

'Why?' he said at last, and through the tip of her finger she felt him swallow.

'There's another Veil,' said Finn.

Seth went absolutely still for a long time. 'There's another Veil,' he repeated at last.

'Yes. I know you won't believe me, but I saw through it, while I was dying. You'll tell me I was hallucinating, but I swear, Seth, it's another Veil, another *Sgath*, and I saw right through it. I saw *him*.' She gulped. 'He was mad at me. Because I wasn't trying hard enough not to leave you. So he made me. He made me try.'

And *Tell him not to be so scared*, Conal had said. *Conal, what did you mean?* Seth had had a right to be scared, and he'd beaten it anyway, and Finn wasn't about to give him a postmortem scolding from the brother who'd overshadowed his entire life. *No, Conal,* she thought. *No.* And the words stayed unspoken in her throat.

Seth was far from her mind at that moment, thank God. He only rested his head against hers, silent for an age. 'Eili smiled,' he said eventually. 'Just as she died. I thought she was smiling at Sionnach.'

Finn moved her fingers into his hair, her thumbs resting on his cheekbones. 'Seth? I...'

'Here they are.' Rory was beside them, Hannah's hand in his. 'Alone and Palely Loitering.' He grinned.

'Palely Loitering with Intent, if you ask me,' said Hannah with a suggestive wink.

'Hey Dad, cheer up. Think about Kate's face when she broke into an empty dun.'

'Yep,' said Hannah. 'And did you hear her scream when Rory sealed the Veil? Like a cat with a firework up its—'

'Whoa! Right.' Seth went up to the bow as Jed brought the launch inexpertly round, and jumped out to tie up the rope to its bollard as the gunwale of the boat banged and shuddered against the old tyres strung along the jetty.

'Summer's over,' Hannah said in disbelief as she looked up at the morning.

It was true. The season had turned as if by a snap of celestial fingers. The intense magical light of the previous night was gone from the hills, and now that dawn had come the landscape was flat and dun under a leaden sky.

'Oh, no,' groaned Rory. 'The time's slipped again.'

'Autumn. School. I'm going to have to go back to Sheena and Marty,' said Hannah miserably. That was the part that seemed like a parallel world.

'You're not going back,' said Rory. 'I'm keeping you.'

'Not without supervision, you're not,' muttered Jed as he wiped Iolaire's blood-blinded eyes.

'Jaysus. First I was your Xbox; now I'm your hamster.' She gave him a very showy, lengthy smooch.

The clann were dispersing, making their way in pairs and small groups down the single-track road, exchanging fierce farewell hugs. Where the jetty met the road, two huge dark shapes waited, pawing the tarmac and snorting. Seth extracted himself from Braon's snuggling embrace and made his way through the thinning crowd to the paler horse. He put his arms round its neck and pressed his face to its gilled cheek.

'Did you come to say goodbye, my love?' He closed his eyes. 'I won't be seeing you for a long time. Try to be good. Don't eat anyone.'

The horse blew affectionately, then caught sight of Hannah over his shoulder. Flattening its ears, it snaked its head towards her and snapped its teeth.

Slapping aside its jaws, she grabbed the startled kelpie's muzzle.

'You ugly fleabag. How would you like it yourself?' She bared her own teeth, and bit its nose hard.

Not a breath could be heard, but the roan did not seem inclined to savage her to death. It tilted its head, then snorted hesitantly against her mouth.

Hannah hung an arm casually over its neck and scratched between its ears. 'Well, it asked for that.'

Seth said: 'Well I'll be f–'

'Ah-ah-ah,' interrupted Hannah sweetly. 'Language.'

Seth winked at Finn. 'Hannah,' he said, 'You're coming with us if I have to adopt you, gods help me.' He furrowed his brow curiously. 'Currac-sagairt.'

'Curracwhat?' Hannah stared at him open-mouthed.

'Currac-sagairt,' snorted Finn. 'You'd better practise.'

'Is that my *name?*'

'Jaysus. That was quick,' said Rory. 'What a mouthful. What's it mean?'

'It's a kind of flower,' taunted Seth.

'That's, uh... nice and uh... female,' said Rory.

'A pretty yellow flower.' Seth batted his lashes at Hannah. She glared at him. 'You're making this up.'

'And it's *poisonous!*'

'Murlainn, shut up.' Finn glowered at Seth. 'It's aconite, Hannah. You know, monkshood.' Her face split in a smile of realisation. 'Oh. Wolfsbane!'

Hannah flushed, and grinned.

Behind them lights began to glow in the cottages that lined the strip of road, and more of the clann slipped silently away from the jetty. Only Sionnach stood aside, alone, perfectly still. One of the passing Sithe put a donkey jacket round his shoulders, and a peaked cap on his wounded scalp, then hugged him, but he didn't react, did not even seem to notice. He didn't look indecisive, just motionless, as if he couldn't see the point of going anywhere. He looked as if he might stand there, staring dully at the sea, till the end of time.

Hannah clasped his hand firmly and dragged him over to their small group. 'Sionnach's coming with us,' she said.

'But of course he is,' said Finn.

Seth took one look back across the paling sea loch towards the headland that was clearing in a colourless dawn. The remains of the dun were invisible, too far along the coast to be seen, but he didn't much want to see that tumble of rocks anyway.

Putting an arm round Rory he turned away from the sea, slinging his pack across one shoulder.

'All right,' he said cheerfully. 'Let's go and find somewhere to live.'

EPILOGUE: SETH

'We can't go back to Tornashee,' I murmured.

He didn't reply. He never did, and that was what I liked about him. It was an argument I was still to face with Finn, but I knew Tornashee would not be safe any more: maybe not ever. Branndair was more likely to understand, and besides, I had to practise on him, to keep my voice and my resolve steady for my lover.

I rolled onto my side and scratched the wolf's neck fur; he licked my face. The carpet was comfortable enough and the window went all the way to the floor, so we could both gaze out at the blackness beyond while Finn slept through the small hours. I wasn't accustomed to sleeping through the night; maybe it would take me a while.

The gods knew what this tartaned-up country hotel had cost my lover's credit card: it was nearly deserted, starting to wind down for the winter, and not looking for last-minute guests, especially not the kind who looked the way we did. The receptionist might have kicked up more of a fuss, but she had quailed before Finn's scary face. I grinned at the memory, then sighed and listened to a moth beat against the window. Branndair pricked an ear and whined sleepily.

'It bleeds, Branndair.'

He wriggled up and gazed at me, his yellow eyes mournful. He still missed Liath. Gods knew, we all did, and Jed more than anyone. But who was left to rage against? Dead, they were all dead.

I curled up and put an arm round the wolf's neck. The tail lights of a plane blinked high across the clouds, and I thought of cities, and civilisation, and exile. Branndair must have thought of it too, and known that he'd have to leave me. And Branndair knew how, now of all times, I needed him not to.

'The unsealable wound,' I said into his neck fur. 'It bleeds. You know it.'

He licked my ear, then pressed his head against mine. I felt the life pulsing beneath his warm skin. I touched my mind lightly to his, for the warmth and for the comfort. Finn had warned me, but I couldn't be without him, not tonight. I'd brought him in silently through the basement fire escape, smuggled him up the back stairs. I needed him with me, and alarms were nothing, not when my brother and I had disabled so many and slipped through unseen. But that was in our past lives, our long-ago lives when Conal still lived, and we searched for a Bloodstone that was not a human boy.

A human boy. 'You feel it, Branndair. It's bleeding my soul.'

He whined softly.

Oh yes, the wolf would have to leave me. I knew this world of old.

'I'll stay with you,' I whispered. 'Sometimes. When you're running in the night. Will you let me in?'

He growled softly and nuzzled my hair.

'How long does a man last while his soul drains away?' I asked him. 'How long does a boy?'

~ *Till a man gives in.*

I grunted a laugh into his fur. It was my own mind talking to me. Or more than likely it was.

I lay back on the carpet and the wolf stretched and lay down beside me, warm heart beating through his black fur.

~ *Branndair. I can never go back.*

~ *Then go with me.*

I tipped my head back and watched Finn, stirring in her sleep, one hand reaching drowsily for me.

I had my life with her, I thought; an hour, perhaps, with him.

I took Branndair's head between my hands and let myself sink in his mind. I closed my eyes, and felt wildness and hunger and grief for a lost white wolf; and then, for what might have been an hour, there was nothing conscious. There was only a strong heart, and a powerful body, and dreams of prey; and the painful, mortal comfort of an intact soul.

THE END